You're staring at Jija, bu

Don't know why.

"One person's normal is another person's Shattering." Your face aches from smiling. There is an art to smiling in a way that others will believe, and you're terrible at it. "Would've been nice if we could've all had normal, of course, but not enough people wanted to share. So now we all burn."

The villager stares at you for a long, vaguely horrified moment. Then he mumbles something and finally goes away, skirting wide around Hoa. Good riddance.

You crouch beside Jija. He is beautiful like this, all jewels and colors. He is monstrous like this. Beneath the colors you perceive the crazed every-which-wayness of the magic threads in him. It's wholly different from what happened to your arm and your breast. He has been smashed apart and rearranged at random, on an infinitesimal level.

"What have I done?" you ask. "What have I made her?"

Hoa's toes have appeared in your peripheral vision. "Strong," he suggests.

You shake your head. Nassun was that on her own.

"*Alive.*"

You close your eyes again. It's the only thing that should matter, that you've brought three babies into the world and this one, this precious last one, is still breathing. And yet.

I made her me. Earth eat us both, I made her into **me**.

And maybe that's why Nassun is still alive. But it's also, you realize as you stare at what she's done to Jija, and as you realize you can't even get revenge on him for Uche because *your daughter has done that for you* . . . why you are terrified of her.

Praise for

THE INHERITANCE TRILOGY

"A complex, edge-of-your-seat story with plenty of funny, scary, and bittersweet twists."

—*Publishers Weekly* (starred review)

"An offbeat, engaging tale by a talented and original newcomer."

—*Kirkus*

"An astounding debut novel...the world-building is solid, the characterization superb, the plot complicated but clear."

—*RT Book Reviews* (Top Pick!)

"A delight for the fantasy reader."

—*Library Journal* (starred review)

"*The Hundred Thousand Kingdoms*...is an impressive debut, which revitalizes the trope of empires whose rulers have gods at their fingertips."

—*io9*

"N. K. Jemisin has written a fascinating epic fantasy where the stakes are not just the fate of kingdoms but of the world and the universe."

—*SFRevu*

"Many books are good, some are great, but few are truly important. Add to this last category *The Hundred Thousand Kingdoms*, N. K. Jemisin's debut novel...In this reviewer's opinion, this is the must-read fantasy of the year."

—*BookPage*

"A similar blend of inventiveness, irreverence, and sophistication—along with sensuality—brings vivid life to the setting and other characters: human and otherwise... *The Hundred Thousand Kingdoms* definitely leaves me wanting more of this delightful new writer."

—*Locus*

"A compelling page-turner."

—*The A.V. Club*

"An absorbing story, an intriguing setting and world mythology, and a likable narrator with a compelling voice. The next book cannot come out soon enough." —fantasybookcafe.com

"*The Broken Kingdoms*... expands the universe of the series geographically, historically, magically and in the range of characters, while keeping the same superb prose and gripping narrative that made the first one such a memorable debut."

—*Fantasy Book Critic*

"*The Kingdom of Gods* once again proves Jemisin's skill and consistency as a storyteller, but what sets her apart from the crowd is her ability to imagine and describe the mysteries of the universe in language that is at once elegant and profane, and thus, true."

—*Shelf Awareness*

Praise for

THE DREAMBLOOD DUOLOGY

By N. K. Jemisin

THE INHERITANCE TRILOGY
The Hundred Thousand Kingdoms
The Broken Kingdoms
The Kingdom of Gods
The Awakened Kingdom (novella)

The Inheritance Trilogy (omnibus)

DREAMBLOOD
The Killing Moon
The Shadowed Sun

THE BROKEN EARTH
The Fifth Season
The Obelisk Gate
The Stone Sky

THE
STONE SKY

THE BROKEN EARTH: BOOK THREE

N. K. JEMISIN

www.orbitbooks.net

Copyright © 2017 by N. K. Jemisin
Excerpt from *The Hundred Thousand Kingdoms* copyright © 2010 by N. K. Jemisin
Excerpt from *Wake of Vultures* © 2015 by Delores S. Dawson

Map © Tim Paul

Orbit
Hachette Book Group
1290 Avenue of the Americas
New York, NY 10104
orbitbooks.net

Simultaneously published in Great Britain and in the U.S. by Orbit in 2017

First Edition: August 2017

Orbit is an imprint of Hachette Book Group.
The Orbit name and logo are trademarks of Little, Brown Book Group Limited.

The publisher is not responsible for websites (or their content) that are not owned by the publisher.

The Hachette Speakers Bureau provides a wide range of authors for speaking events. To find out more, go to www.hachettespeakersbureau.com or call (866) 376-6591.

Library of Congress Cataloging-in-Publication Data

Names: Jemisin, N. K., author.
Title: The stone sky / N.K. Jemisin.
Description: First Edition. | New York : Orbit, 2017. | Series: The broken earth ; book 3
Identifiers: LCCN 2017017064| ISBN 9780316229241 (paperback) | ISBN 9781478916291 (audio book downloadable) | ISBN 9780316229258 (ebook open)
Subjects: | BISAC: FICTION / Fantasy / Epic. | FICTION / Action & Adventure. | GSAFD: Fantasy fiction.
Classification: LCC PS3610.E46 S76 2017 | DDC 813/.6—dc23
LC record available at https://lccn.loc.gov/2017017064

ISBNs: 978-0-316-22924-1 (trade paperback), 978-0-316-22925-8 (ebook)

Printed in the United States of America

LSC-C

3 5 7 9 10 8 6 4 2

To those who've survived: Breathe. That's it. Once more. Good.
You're good. Even if you're not, you're alive. That is a victory.

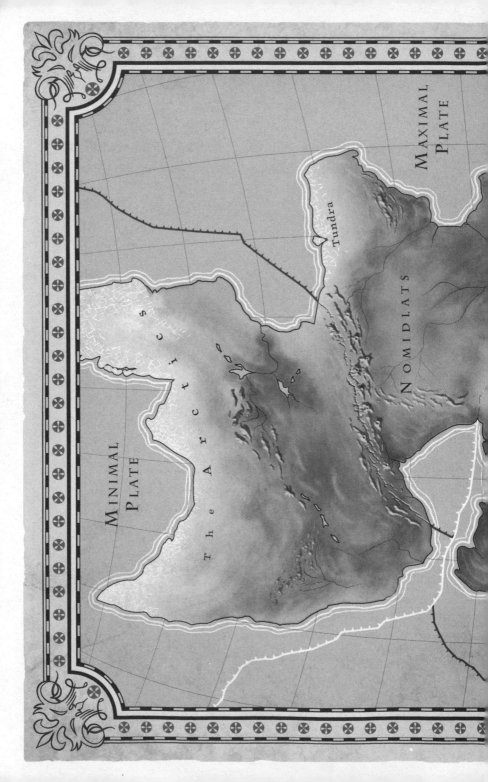

THE
STILLNESS

distance in miles

0   1000   2000

THE
STONE SKY

prologue

me, when I was I

TIME GROWS SHORT, MY LOVE. Let's end with the beginning of the world, shall we? Yes. We shall.

It's strange, though. My memories are like insects fossilized in amber. They are rarely intact, these frozen, long-lost lives. Usually there's just a leg, some wing-scales, a bit of lower thorax—a whole that can only be inferred from fragments, and everything blurred together through jagged, dirty cracks. When I narrow my gaze and squint into memory, I see faces and events that should hold meaning for me, and they do, but…they don't. The person who witnessed these things firsthand is me, and yet not.

In those memories I was someone else, just as the Stillness was someworld else. Then, and now. You, and you.

Then. This land, then, was *three* lands—though these are in virtually the same position as what will someday be called the Stillness. Repeated Seasons will eventually create more ice at the poles, sinking the sea and making your "Arctics" and "Antarctics" larger and colder. Then, though—

—*now*, it feels of now as I recall myself of then, this is what I mean when I say that it is strange—

Now, in this time before the Stillness, the far north and south are decent farmland. What you think of as the Western Coastals is mostly wetland and rainforest; those will die out in the next millennium. Some of the Nomidlats doesn't yet exist, and will be created by volcanic effusion over several thousand years of eruptive pulses. The land that becomes Palela, your hometown? Doesn't exist. Not so much change, all things considered, but then *now* is nothing ago, tectonically speaking. When we say that "the world has ended," remember—it is usually a lie. The planet is just fine.

What do we call this lost world, this *now*, if not the Stillness?

Let me tell you, first, of a city.

It is a city built wrong, by your standards. This city *sprawls* in a way that no modern comm would be permitted to do, since that would require too many miles of walls. And this city's outermost sprawls have branched off along rivers and other lifelines to spawn additional cities, much in the manner of mold forking and stretching along the rich veins of a growth medium. Too close together, you would think. Too much overlap of territory; they are too connected, these sprawling cities and their snaking spawn, each unable to survive should it be cut off from the rest.

Sometimes they have distinct local nicknames, these child-cities, especially where they are large or old enough to have spawned child-cities of their own, but this is superficial. Your perception of their connectedness is correct: They have the same infrastructure, the same culture, the same hungers and fears. Each city is like the other cities. All of the cities are, effectively, one city. This world, in this now, is the city's name: Syl Anagist.

Can you truly understand what a *nation* is capable of, child of the Stillness? The entirety of Old Sanze, once it finally stitches itself together from fragments of the hundred "civilizations" that live and die between now and then, will be nothing by comparison. Merely a collection of paranoid city-states and communes agreeing to share, sometimes, for survival's sake. Ah, the Seasons will reduce the world to such miserly dreams.

Here, *now*, dreams have no limit. The people of Syl Anagist have mastered the forces of matter and its composition; they have shaped life itself to fit their whims; they have so explored the mysteries of the sky that they've grown bored with it and turned their attention back toward the ground beneath their feet. And Syl Anagist lives, oh how it lives, in bustling streets and ceaseless commerce and buildings that your mind would struggle to define as such. The buildings have walls of patterned cellulose that can barely be seen beneath leaves, moss, grasses, and clusters of fruit or tubers. Some rooftops fly banners that are actually immense, unfurled fungus flowers. The streets teem with things you might not recognize as vehicles, except in that they travel and convey. Some crawl on legs like massive arthropods. Some are little more than open platforms that glide on a cushion of resonant potential—ah, but you would not understand this. Let me say only that these vehicles float a few inches off the ground. No animals draw them. No steam or chemical fuels them. Should something, a pet or child perhaps, pass underneath, it will temporarily cease to exist, then resume on the other side, with no interruption of velocity or awareness. No one thinks of this as death.

There is one thing you would recognize here, standing up from the core of the city. It is the tallest, brightest thing for miles, and every rail and path connects to it in some way or another. It's your old friend, the amethyst obelisk. It isn't floating, not yet. It sits, not quite quiescent, in its socket. Now and again it pulses in a way that will be familiar to you from Allia. This is a healthier pulse than that was; the amethyst is not the damaged, dying garnet. Still, if the similarity makes you shiver, that's not an unhealthy reaction.

All over the three lands, wherever there is a large-enough node of Syl Anagist, an obelisk sits at the center of each. They dot the face of the world, two hundred and fifty-six spiders in two hundred and fifty-six webs, feeding each city and being fed in turn.

Webs of life, if you want to think of them that way. Life, you see, is sacred in Syl Anagist.

Now imagine, surrounding the base of the amethyst, a hexagonal complex of buildings. Whatever you imagine will look nothing like the actuality, but just imagine something pretty and that will do. Look closer at this one here, along the southwestern rim of the obelisk—the one on a slanting hillock. There are no bars on the building's crystal windows, but visualize a faint darker lacing of tissue over the clear material. Nematocysts, a popular method of securing windows against unwanted contact—although these exist only on the outward-facing surface of the windows, to keep intruders out. They sting, but do not kill. (Life is sacred in Syl Anagist.) Inside, there are no guards on the doors. Guards are inefficient in any case. The Fulcrum is not the first institution to have learned an eternal truth of humankind: No need for guards when you can convince people to collaborate in their own internment.

Here is a cell within the pretty prison.

It doesn't look like one, I know. There's a beautifully sculpted piece of furniture that you might call a couch, though it has no back and consists of several pieces arranged in clusters. The rest of the furniture is common stuff you would recognize; every society needs tables and chairs. The view through the window is of a garden, on the roof of one of the other buildings. At this time of day, the garden catches sunlight slanting through the great crystal, and the flowers growing in the garden have been bred and planted with this effect in mind. Purple light paints the paths and beds, and the flowers seem to glow faintly in reaction to the color. Some of these tiny white flower-lights wink out now and again, which makes the whole flower bed seem to sparkle like the night sky.

Here is a boy, staring through the window at the winking flowers.

He's a young man, really. Superficially mature, in an ageless sort of way. Not so much stocky as *compact* in his design. His face is wide and cheeky, his mouth small. Everything about him is white: colorless skin, colorless hair, icewhite eyes, his elegantly draped clothing. Everything about the room is white: furniture, rugs, the floor under the rugs. The walls are bleached cellulose, and nothing grows on them. Only the window displays color. Within this sterile space, in the reflected purple light of the outside, only the boy is obviously alive.

Yes, the boy is me. I don't truly remember his name, but I do remember that it had too many rusting letters. Let us therefore call him Houwha—the same sound, just padded with all manner of silent letters and hidden meanings. That's close enough, and appropriately *symbolic* of—

Oh. I am angrier than I should be. Fascinating. Let's change tracks, then, to something less fraught. Let us return to the now that will be, and a far different here.

Now is the now of the Stillness, through which the reverberations of the Rifting still echo. The here is not the Stillness, precisely, but a cavern just above the main lava chamber of a vast, ancient shield volcano. The volcano's heart, if you prefer and have a sense of metaphor; if not, this is a deep, dark, barely stable vesicle amid rock that has not cooled much in the thousands of years since Father Earth first burped it up. Within this cavern I stand, partially fused with a hump of rock so that I may better watch for the minute perturbations or major deformations that presage a collapse. I don't need to do this. There are few processes more unstoppable than the one I have set in motion here. Still, I understand what it is to be alone when you are confused and afraid and unsure of what will happen next.

You are not alone. You will never be, unless you so choose. I know what matters, here at the world's end.

Ah, my love. An apocalypse is a relative thing, isn't it? When the earth shatters, it is a disaster to the life that depends on it—but nothing much to Father Earth. When a man dies, it should be devastating to a girl who once called him Father, but this becomes as nothing when she has been called *monster* so many times that she finally embraces the label. When a slave rebels, it is nothing much to the people who read about it later. Just thin words on thinner paper worn finer by the friction of history.

("So you were slaves, so what?" they whisper. Like it's nothing.) But to the people who live through a slave rebellion, both those who take their dominance for granted until it comes for them in the dark, and those who would see the world burn before enduring one moment longer in "their place"—

That is not a metaphor, Essun. Not hyperbole. I *did* watch the world burn. Say nothing to me of innocent bystanders, unearned suffering, heartless vengeance. When a comm builds atop a fault line, do you blame its walls when they inevitably crush the people inside? No; you blame whoever was stupid enough to think they could defy the laws of nature forever. Well, some worlds are built on a fault line of pain, held up by nightmares. Don't lament when those worlds fall. Rage that they were built doomed in the first place.

So now I will tell you the way that world, Syl Anagist, ended. I will tell you how I ended it, or at least enough of it that it had to start over and rebuild itself from scratch.

I will tell you how I opened the Gate, and flung away the Moon, and smiled as I did it.

And I will tell you everything of how, later, as the quiet of death descended, I whispered:

Right now.

Right now.

And the Earth whispered back:

Burn.

1

you, in waking and dreaming

Now. Let's review.

You are Essun, the sole surviving orogene in all the world who has opened the Obelisk Gate. No one expected this grand destiny of you. You were once of the Fulcrum, but not a rising star like Alabaster. You were a feral, found in the wild, unique only in that you had more innate ability than the average rogga born by random chance. Though you started well, you plateaued early—not for any clear reason. You simply lacked the urge to innovate or the desire to excel, or so the seniors lamented behind closed doors. Too quick to conform to the Fulcrum's system. It limited you.

Good thing, because otherwise they'd never have loosened your leash the way they did, sending you forth on that mission with Alabaster. *He* scared the rust out of them. You, though... they thought you were one of the safe ones, properly broken in and trained to obey, unlikely to wipe out a town by accident. Joke's on them; how many towns have you wiped out now? One semi-intentionally. The other three were accidents, but really, does that matter? Not to the dead.

Sometimes you dream of undoing it all. Not flailing for the garnet obelisk in Allia, and instead watching happy black children play in the surf of a black-sand beach while you bled out around a Guardian's black knife. Not being taken to Meov by Antimony; instead, you would've returned to the Fulcrum to give birth to Corundum. You'd have lost him after that birth, and you would never have had Innon, but both of them would probably still be alive. (Well. For values of "alive," if they'd put Coru in a node.) But then you would never have lived in Tirimo, never have borne Uche to die beneath his father's fists, never have raised Nassun to be stolen by her father, never have crushed your once-neighbors when they tried to kill you. So many lives saved, if only you had stayed in your cage. Or died on demand.

And here, now, long free from the ordered, staid strictures of the Fulcrum, you have become mighty. You saved the community of Castrima at the cost of Castrima itself; this was a small price to pay, compared to the cost in blood that the enemy army would have extracted if they'd won. You achieved victory by unleashing the concatenated power of an arcane mechanism older than (your) written history—and because you are who you are, while learning to master this power, you murdered Alabaster Tenring. You didn't mean to. You actually suspect he wanted you to do it. Either way, he's dead, and this sequence of events has left you the most powerful orogene on the planet.

It also means that your tenure as most powerful has just acquired an expiration date, because the same thing is happening to you that happened to Alabaster: You're turning to stone. Just your right arm, for now. Could be worse. *Will* be worse, the next time you open the Gate, or even the next time you wield enough of that strange silvery not-orogeny, which Alabaster called magic. You don't have a choice, though. You've got a job to do, courtesy of Alabaster and the nebulous faction of stone eaters who've been quietly trying to end the ancient war between life and Father Earth. The job you *have* to do is the easier of the two, you think. Just catch the Moon. Seal the Yumenes Rifting. Reduce the current Season's predicted impact from thousands or millions of years back down to something manageable—something the human race has a chance of surviving. End the Fifth Seasons for all time.

The job you *want* to do, though? Find Nassun, your daughter. Take her back from the man who murdered your son and dragged her halfway across the world in the middle of the apocalypse.

About that: I have good news, and bad news. But we'll get to Jija presently.

You're not really in a coma. You are a key component of a complex system, the whole of which has just experienced a massive, poorly controlled start-up flux and emergency shutoff with insufficient cooldown time, expressing itself as arcanochemical phase-state resistance and mutagenic feedback. You need time to...reboot.

This means you're not unconscious. It's more like periods of half-waking and half-sleeping, if that makes sense. You're aware of things, somewhat. The bobbing of movement, occasional jostling. Someone puts food and water into your mouth. Fortunately you have the presence of mind to chew and swallow, because the end of the world on the ash-strewn road is a bad time and place to need a feeding tube. Hands pull on your clothing and something girds your hips—a diaper. Bad time and place for that, too, but someone's willing to tend you this way, and you don't mind. You barely notice. You feel no hunger or thirst before they give you sustenance; your evacuations bring no particular relief. Life endures. It doesn't need to do so *enthusiastically*.

Eventually the periods of waking and sleep become more pronounced things. Then one day you open your eyes to see the clouded sky overhead. Swaying back and forth. Skeletal branches occasionally occlude it. Faint shadow of an obelisk through the clouds: That's the spinel, you suspect. Reverted to its usual shape and immensity, ah, and following you like a lonely puppy, now that Alabaster is dead.

Staring at the sky gets boring after a while, so you turn your head and try to understand what's going on. Figures move around you, dreamlike and swathed in gray-white...no. No, they're wearing ordinary clothing; it's just covered with pale ash. And they're wearing a lot of clothes because it's cold—not enough to freeze water, but close. It's nearly two years into the Season; two years without the sun. The Rifting's putting out a lot of heat up around the equator, but that's not nearly enough to make up for the lack of a giant fireball in the sky. Still, without the Rifting, the cold would be worse—well below freezing, instead of nearly freezing. Small favors.

In any case, one of the ash-swathed figures seems to notice that you're awake, or to feel the shift of your weight. A head wrapped in face mask and goggles swivels back to consider you, then faces ahead again. There are murmured words between the

12

two people in front of you, which you don't understand. They're not in another language. You're just half out of it and the words are partially absorbed by the ash falling around you.

Someone speaks behind you. You start and look back to see another goggled, masked face. Who are these people? (It does not occur to you to be afraid. Like hunger, such visceral things are more detached from you now.) Then something clicks and you understand. You're on a stretcher, just two poles with some stitched hide between them, being carried by four people. One of them calls out, and other calls respond from farther away. Lots of calls. Lots of people.

Another call from somewhere far away, and the people carrying you come to a halt. They glance at each other and set you down with the ease and uniformity of people who've practiced doing the same maneuver in unison many times. You feel the stretcher settle onto a soft, powdery layer of ash, over a thicker layer of ash, over what might be a road. Then your stretcher-bearers move away, opening packs and settling down in a ritual that is familiar from your own months on the road. Breaktime.

You know this ritual. You should get up. Eat something. Check your boots for holes or stones, your feet for unnoticed sores, make sure your mask—wait, are you wearing one? If everyone else is... You kept that in your runny-sack, didn't you? Where is your runny-sack?

Someone walks out of the gloom and ashfall. Tall, plateau-broad, identity stripped by the clothes and mask but restored by the familiar frizzy texture of the ashblow mane. She crouches near your head. "Hnh. Not dead, after all. Guess I lose that bet with Tonkee."

"Hjarka," you say. Your voice rasps worse than hers does.

You guess by the flexing of her mask that she grins. It feels odd to perceive her smile without the usual undercurrent of menace from her sharp-filed teeth. "And your brains are probably still intact. I win the bet with Ykka, at least." She glances around and bellows, "Lerna!"

You try to lift a hand to grab her pants leg. It feels like trying to move a mountain. You ought to be able to move mountains, so you concentrate and get it halfway up—and then forget why you wanted Hjarka's attention. She glances around then, fortunately, and eyes your upraised hand. It's shaking with the effort. After a moment's consideration, she sighs and takes your hand, then looks away as if embarrassed.

"Happening," you manage.

"Rust if I know. We didn't need another break this soon."

Not what you meant, but it takes too much of an effort to try to say the rest. So you lie there, with your hand being held by a woman who clearly would rather be doing anything else, but who's deigning to show you compassion because she thinks you need it. You don't, but you're glad she's trying.

Two more forms resolve out of the swirl, both recognizable by their familiar shapes. One is male and slight, the other female and pillowy. The narrow one displaces Hjarka at your head and leans in to pull off the goggles that you hadn't realized you were wearing. "Give me a rock," he says. It's Lerna, making no sense.

"What?" you say.

He ignores you. Tonkee, the other person, elbows Hjarka,

who sighs and rummages through her bag until she finds something small. She offers it to Lerna.

He lays a hand on your cheek while holding the object up. The thing starts to glow with a familiar tone of white light. You realize it's a piece of a Castrima-under crystal—lighting up because they do that in contact with orogenes, as Lerna is now in contact with you. Ingenious. Using this light, he leans in and peers closely at your eyes. "Pupils contracting normally," he murmurs to himself. His hand twitches on your cheek. "No fever."

"I feel heavy," you say.

"You're alive," he says, as if this is a completely reasonable response. No one is speaking a language you can understand today. "Motor skills sluggish. Cognition...?"

Tonkee leans in. "What did you dream?"

It makes as much sense as *Give me a rock*, but you try to answer because you're too out of it to realize you shouldn't. "There was a city," you murmur. A bit of ash falls onto your lashes and you twitch. Lerna puts your goggles back on. "It was alive. There was an obelisk above it." Above it? "In it, maybe. I think."

Tonkee nods. "Obelisks rarely linger directly over human habitations. I had a friend back at Seventh who had some theories about that. Want to hear them?"

Finally it sinks in that you're doing something stupid: encouraging Tonkee. You put a mighty effort into glaring at her. "*No.*"

Tonkee glances at Lerna. "Her faculties seem intact. Little sluggish, maybe, but then she always is."

"Yes, thank you for confirming that." Lerna finishes doing whatever he's doing, and sits back on his heels. "Want to try walking, Essun?"

"Isn't that kind of sudden?" asks Tonkee. She's frowning, which is visible even around her goggles. "What with the coma and all."

"You know as well as I do that Ykka's not going to give her much more recovery time. It might even be good for her."

Tonkee sighs. But she's the one to help when Lerna slides an arm under you, levering you up from prone to sitting. Even this takes an effort of ages. You get dizzy the instant you're upright, but it passes. Something's wrong, though. It's a testament to how much you've been through, maybe, that you seem to have developed a permanently crooked posture, your right shoulder sagging and arm dragging as if

as if it is made of

Oh. *Oh*.

The others stop bothering you as you realize what's happened. They watch you heft the shoulder, as much as you can, to try to drag your right arm more into view. It's heavy. Your shoulder hurts when you do this, even though most of the joint is still flesh, because the weight pulls against that flesh. Some of the tendons have transformed, but they're still attached to living bone. Gritty bits of something chafe within what should be a smooth ball-and-socket. It doesn't hurt as much as you thought it would, though, after watching Alabaster go through this. So that's something.

The rest of the arm, from which someone has stripped your shirt and jacket sleeves in order to bare it, has changed nearly past recognition. It's your arm, you're pretty sure. Beyond the fact that it's still attached to your body, it's got the shape you know like your own—well. Not as graceful and tapered as it used to be when you were young. You were heavyset for a while, and that still shows along the plush-looking forearm and slight sag under your upper arm. The bicep is more defined than it used to be; two years of surviving. The hand is clamped into a fist, the whole arm slightly cocked at the elbow. You always did tend to make fists while you were wrestling with a particularly difficult bit of orogeny.

But the mole, which once sat in the middle of your forearm like a tiny black target, is gone. You can't turn the arm over for a look at your elbow, so you touch it. The keloid scar from where you once fell is impossible to feel anymore, though it should be slightly raised compared to the skin around it. That level of fine definition has vanished into a texture that is gritty and dense, like unpolished sandstone. Perhaps self-destructively you rub it, but no particles break off beneath your fingertips; it's more solid than it looks. The color is an even, allover grayish tan that looks nothing like your skin.

"It was like this when Hoa brought you back." Lerna, who has been silent throughout your examination. His voice is neutral. "He says he needs your permission to, ah . . ."

You stop trying to rub your stone skin off. Maybe it's shock, maybe fear has robbed you of shock, maybe you're really not feeling anything.

"So tell me," you say to Lerna. The effort of sitting up, and seeing your arm, have restored your wits a little. "In your, uh, professional opinion, what should I do about this?"

"I think you should either let Hoa eat it off, or let one of us take a sledgehammer to it."

You wince. "That's a little dramatic, don't you think?"

"I don't think anything lighter would put a dent in it. You forget I had plenty of chances to examine Alabaster when this was happening to him."

Out of nowhere, you think of Alabaster having to be reminded to eat because he no longer felt hunger. It's not relevant, but the thought just pops in there. "He let you?"

"I didn't give him a choice. I needed to know if it was contagious, since it seemed to be spreading on him. I took a sample once, and he joked that Antimony—the stone eater—would want it back."

It wouldn't have been a joke. Alabaster always smiled when he spoke the rawest truths. "And did you give it back?"

"You better believe I did." Lerna runs a hand over his hair, displacing a small pile of ash. "Listen, we have to wrap the arm at night so that the chill of it doesn't depress your body temperature. You've got stretch marks on the shoulder where it pulls your skin. I suspect it's deforming the bones and straining the tendons; the joint isn't built to carry this kind of weight." He hesitates. "We can take it off now and give it to Hoa later, if you like. I don't see any reason why you have to . . . to do it his way."

You think Hoa is probably somewhere below your feet at this very moment, listening. But Lerna is being oddly squeamish about this. Why? You take a guess. "I don't mind if Hoa eats it," you say. You aren't saying it just for Hoa. You really mean it. "If it will do him good, and get the thing off me in the process, why not?"

Something flickers in Lerna's expression. His emotionless
mask slips, and you see all of a sudden that he's revolted by the
idea of Hoa chewing the arm off your body. Well, put like that,
the concept is inherently revolting. It's too utilitarian a way of
thinking about it, though. Too atavistic. You know intimately,
from hours spent delving between the cells and particles of Alabaster's transforming body, what's happening in your arm. Looking at it, you can all but see the silvery lines of magic realigning
infinitesimal particles and energies of your substance, moving
this bit so that it's oriented along the same path as that bit,
carefully tightening into a lattice that binds the whole together.
Whatever this process is, it's simply too precise, too powerful, to
be chance—or for Hoa's ingestion of it to be the grotesquerie
that Lerna plainly sees. But you don't know how to explain that
to him, and you wouldn't have the energy to try even if you did.

"Help me up," you say.

Tonkee gingerly takes hold of the stone arm, helping to support it so it doesn't shift or flop and wrench your shoulder. She
throws a glare at Lerna until he finally gets over himself and
slides an arm under you again. Between the two of them, you
manage to gain your feet, but it's hard going. You're panting
by the end, and your knees are distinctly wobbly. The blood in
your body is less committed to the cause, and momentarily you
sway, dizzy and light-headed. Lerna immediately says, "All right,
let's get her back down." Abruptly you're sitting down again, out
of breath this time, the arm awkwardly jacking up your shoulder
until Tonkee adjusts it. The thing really is heavy.

(Your *arm*. Not "the thing." It's your right arm. You've lost
your right arm. You're aware of that, and soon you'll mourn it,

but for now it's easier to think of it as a thing separate from yourself. An especially useless prosthesis. A benign tumor that needs to be removed. These things are all true. It's also your rusting arm.)

You're sitting there, panting and willing the world to stop spinning, when you hear someone else approach. This one's speaking loudly, calling for everyone to pack up, break's over, they need to do another five miles before dark. Ykka. You lift your head as she gets close enough, and it's in this moment that you realize you think of her as a friend. You realize it because it feels good to hear her voice, and to see her resolve out of the swirling ash. Last time you saw her, she was in serious danger of being murdered by hostile stone eaters attacking Castrima-under. That's one of the reasons you fought back, using the crystals of Castrima-under to ensnare the attackers; you wanted her, and all the other orogenes of Castrima, and by extension all the people of Castrima who depended on those orogenes, to live.

So you smile. It's weak. You're weak. Which is why it actually hurts when Ykka turns to you and her lips tighten in what is unmistakably disgust.

She's pulled the cloth wrapping off the lower half of her face. Beyond her gray-and-kohl eye makeup, which not even the end of the world will stop her from wearing, you can't make out her eyes behind her makeshift goggles—a pair of spectacles that she's wrapped rags around to keep ash out. "Shit," she says to Hjarka. "You're never going to let me hear the end of it, are you?"

Hjarka shrugs. "Not till you pay up, no."

You're staring at Ykka, the tentative little smile freezing off your face.

"She'll probably make a full recovery," Lerna says. His voice is neutral in a way that you immediately sense is careful. Walking-over-a-lava-tube careful. "It'll be a few days before she can keep up on foot, though."

Ykka sighs, putting a hand on her hip and very obviously rifling through a series of things to say. What she finally settles on is neutral, too. "Fine. I'll extend the rotation of people carrying the stretcher. Get her walking as soon as possible, though. Everyone carries their own weight in this comm, or gets left behind." She turns and heads off.

"Yeah, so," Tonkee says in a low voice, once Ykka's out of earshot. "She's a little pissed about you destroying the geode."

You flinch. "Destroying—" Oh, but. Locking all those stone eaters into the crystals. You meant to save everyone, but Castrima was a machine—a very old, very delicate machine that you didn't understand. And now you're topside, traipsing through the ashfall... "Oh, rusting Earth, I *did*."

"What, you didn't realize?" Hjarka laughs a little. It's got a bitter edge. "You actually thought we were all up here topside, the whole rusting comm traveling north in the ash and cold, for *fun*?" She strides away, shaking her head. Ykka's not the only one pissed about it.

"I didn't..." You start to say, *I didn't mean to*, and stop. Because you never mean it, and it never matters in the end.

Watching your face, Lerna lets out a small sigh. "Rennanis destroyed the comm, Essun. Not you." He's helping you shift back down into a prone position, but not meeting your eyes. "We lost it the minute we infested Castrima-over with boilbugs to save ourselves. It's not like they would've just gone away, or

21

left anything in the territory to eat. If we'd stayed in the geode, we'd have been doomed, one way or another."

It's true, and perfectly rational. Ykka's reaction, though, proves that some things aren't about rationality. You can't take away people's homes and sense of security in such an immediate, dramatic way, and expect them to consider extended chains of culpability before they get angry about it.

"They'll get over it." You blink to find Lerna looking at you now, his gaze clear and expression frank. "If I could, they can. It'll just take a while."

You hadn't realized he *had* gotten over Tirimo.

He ignores your staring, then gestures to the four people who have gathered nearby. You're lying down already, so he tucks your stone arm in beside you, making sure the blankets cover it. The stretcher-bearers take up their task again, and you have to clamp down on your orogeny, which—now that you're awake—insists upon reacting to every lurch as if it's a shake. Tonkee's head pokes into view as they start to carry you along. "Hey, it'll be all right. Lots of people hate me."

That is entirely unreassuring. It's also frustrating that you care, and that others can tell you care. You used to be such a steelheart.

But you know why you aren't, all of a sudden.

"Nassun," you say to Tonkee.

"What?"

"Nassun. I know where she is, Tonkee." You try to raise your right hand to catch hers, and there is a sensation that thrums through your shoulder like aching and floating. You hear a ringing sound. It doesn't hurt, but you privately curse yourself for forgetting. "I have to go find her."

Tonkee darts a look at your stretcher-bearers, and then in the direction Ykka went. "Speak softer."

"What?" Ykka knows full well you're going to want to go find your daughter. That was practically the first thing you ever said to her.

"If you want to be dumped on the side of the rusting road, keep talking."

That shuts you up, along with the continued effort of restraining your orogeny. Oh. So Ykka's *that* pissed.

The ash keeps falling, eventually obscuring your goggles because you don't have the energy to brush it away. In the gray dimness that results, your body's need to recover takes precedence; you fall asleep again. The next time you wake and brush the ash off your face, it's because you've been put down again, and there's a rock or branch or something poking you in the small of the back. You struggle to sit up on one elbow and it's easier, though you still can't manage much else.

Night has fallen. Several dozen people are settling onto some kind of rock outcropping amid a scraggly not-quite forest. The outcropping sesses familiar from your orogenic explorations of Castrima's surroundings, and it helps you place yourself: a bit of fresh tectonic uplift that's about a hundred and sixty miles north of the Castrima geode. That tells you that the journey from Castrima must have only just begun a few days before, since a large group can only walk so fast; and that there's only one place you could be going, if you're headed north. Rennanis.

Somehow everyone must know that it's empty and habitable. Or maybe they're just hoping that it is, and they've got nothing else to hope for. Well, at least on that point, you can reassure them ... if they'll listen to you.

The people around you are setting up campfire circles, cooking spits, latrines. In a few spots throughout the camp, little piles of broken, lumpy Castrima crystals provide additional illumination; good to know there must be enough orogenes left to keep them working. Some of the activity is inefficient where people are unused to it, but for the most part it's well-ordered. Castrima having more than its share of members who know how to live on the road is turning out to be a boon. Your stretcher-bearers have left you where they dumped you, though, and if anyone's going to build you a fire or bring you food, they haven't started yet. You spot Lerna crouching amid a small group of people who are also prone, but he's busy. Ah, yes; there must have been a lot of wounded after Rennanis's soldiers got into the geode.

Well, you don't need a fire, and you're not hungry, so the others' indifference doesn't trouble you for the moment, except emotionally. What does bother you is that your runny-sack is gone. You carried that thing halfway across the Stillness, stashed your old rank-rings in it, even saved it from getting scorched to powder when a stone eater transformed himself in your quarters. There wasn't much in it that still mattered to you, but the bag itself holds a certain sentimental value, at this point.

Well. Everyone's lost something.

A mountain suddenly weighs down your nearby perception. In spite of everything, you find yourself smiling. "I wondered when you would show up."

24

Hoa stands over you. It's still a shock to see him like this: a mid-sized adult rather than a small child, veined black marble instead of white flesh. Somehow, though, it's easy to perceive him as the same person—same face shape, same haunting ice-white eyes, same ineffable strangeness, same whiff of lurking whimsy—as the Hoa you've known for the past year. What's changed, that a stone eater no longer seems alien to you? Only superficial things about him. Everything about you.

"How do you feel?" he asks.

"Better." The arm pulls when you shift to look up at him, a constant reminder of the unwritten contract between you. "Were you the one who told them about Rennanis?"

"Yes. And I'm guiding them there."

"You?"

"To the degree that Ykka listens. I think she prefers her stone eaters as silent menaces rather than active allies."

This pulls a weary laugh out of you. But. "*Are* you an ally, Hoa?"

"Not to them. Ykka understands that, too, though."

Yes. This is probably why you're still alive. As long as Ykka keeps you safe and fed, Hoa will help. You're back on the road and everything's a rusting transaction again. The comm that was Castrima lives, but it isn't really a community anymore, just a group of like-minded travelers collaborating to survive. Maybe it can become a true comm again later, once it's got another home to defend, but for now, you get why Ykka's angry. Something beautiful and wholesome has been lost.

Well. You look down at yourself. You're not wholesome any-more, but what's left of you can be strengthened; you'll be able to go after Nassun soon. First things first, though. "We going to do this?"

Hoa does not speak for a moment. "Are you certain?"

"The arm's not doing me any *good*, as it is."

There is the faintest of sounds. Stone grinding on stone, slow and inexorable. A very heavy hand comes to rest on your half-transformed shoulder. You have the sense that, despite the weight, it is a delicate touch by stone eater standards. Hoa's being careful with you.

"Not here," he says, and pulls you down into the earth.

It's only for an instant. He always keeps these trips through the earth quick, probably because longer would make it hard to breathe...and stay sane. This time is little more than a blurring sensation of movement, a flicker of darkness, a whiff of loam richer than the acrid ash. Then you're lying on another rocky outcropping—probably the same one that the rest of Castrima is settling on, just away from the encampment. There are no campfires here; the only light is the ruddy reflection of the Rifting off the thick clouds overhead. Your eyes adjust quickly, though there's little to see but rocks and the shadows of nearby trees. And a human silhouette, which now crouches beside you.

Hoa holds your stone arm in his hands gently, almost reverently. In spite of yourself, you sense the solemnity of the moment. And why shouldn't it be solemn? This is the sacrifice demanded by the obelisks. This is the pound of flesh you must pay for the blood-debt of your daughter.

"This isn't what you think of it," Hoa says, and for an instant you worry that he can read your mind. More likely it's just the fact that he's as old as the literal hills, and he can read your face. "You see what was lost in us, but we gained, too. This is not the ugly thing it seems."

It seems like he's going to eat your arm. You're okay with it, but you want to understand. "What is it, then? Why..." You shake your head, unsure of even what question to ask. Maybe *why* doesn't matter. Maybe you can't understand. Maybe this isn't meant for you.

"This is not sustenance. We need only life, to live."

The latter half of that was nonsensical, so you latch onto the former half. "If it isn't sustenance, then...?"

Hoa moves slowly again. They don't do this often, stone eaters. Movement is the thing that emphasizes their uncanny nature, so like humanity and yet so wildly different. It would be easier if they were more alien. When they move like this, you can see what they once were, and the knowledge is a threat and warning to all that is human within you.

And yet. *You see what was lost in us, but we gained, too.*

He lifts your hand with both his own, one positioned under your elbow, his fingers lightly braced under your closed, cracked fist. Slowly, slowly. It doesn't hurt your shoulder this way. Halfway to his face he moves the hand that had been under your elbow, shifting it to cup the underside of your upper arm. His stone slides against yours with a faint grinding sound. It is surprisingly sensual, even though you can't feel a thing.

Then your fist rests against his lips. The lips don't move as he says, from within his chest, "Are you afraid?"

You consider this for a long moment. Shouldn't you be? But... "No."

"Good," he replies. "I do this for you, Essun. Everything is for you. Do you believe that?"

You don't know, at first. On impulse you lift your good hand, smooth fingers over his hard, cool, polished cheek. It's hard to see him, black against the dark, but your thumb finds his brows and traces out his nose, which is longer in its adult shape. He told you once that he thinks of himself as human in spite of his strange body. You belatedly realize that you've chosen to see him as human, too. That makes this something other than an act of predation. You're not sure what it is instead, but ... it feels like a gift.

"Yes," you say. "I believe you."

His mouth opens. Wide, wider, wider than any human mouth can open. Once you worried his mouth was too small; now it's wide enough to fit a fist. And such teeth he has, small and even and diamond-clear, glinting prettily in the red evening light. There is only darkness beyond those teeth.

You shut your eyes.

*   *   *

She was in a foul mood. Old age, one of her children told me. *She* said it was just the stress of trying to warn people who didn't want to hear that bad times were coming.
It wasn't a foul mood, it was the privilege that age had bought her, to dispense with the lie of politeness.

"There isn't a villain in this story," she said. We sat in the garden dome, which was only a dome because she'd insisted. The Syl Skeptics still claim there's no proof things will happen the way she said, but she's never been wrong in one of her predictions, and she's more Syl than they are, so. She was drinking sef, as if to mark a truth in chemicals.

"There isn't a single evil to point to, a single moment when everything changed," she went on. "Things were bad and then terrible and then better and then bad again, and then they happened again, and again, because no one stopped it. Things can be...adjusted. Lengthen the better, predict and shorten the terrible. Sometimes prevent the terrible by settling for the merely bad. I've given up on trying to stop you people. Just taught my children to remember and learn and survive...until someone finally breaks the cycle for good."

I was confused. "Are you talking about Burndown?" That was what I'd come to talk about, after all. One hundred years, she predicted, fifty years ago. What else mattered?

She only smiled.

—Transcribed interview, translated from Obelisk-Builder C, found in Tapita Plateau Ruin #723 by Shinash Innovator Dibars. Date unknown, transcriber unknown. Speculation: the first lorist? Personal: 'Baster, you should see this place. Treasures of history everywhere, most of them too degraded to decipher, but still...Wish you were here.

2

Nassun feels like busting loose

NASSUN STANDS OVER THE BODY of her father, if one can call a tumbled mass of broken jewels a body. She's swaying a little, light-headed because the wound in her shoulder—where her father has stabbed her—is bleeding profusely. The stabbing is the outcome of an impossible choice he demanded of her: to be either his daughter or an orogene. She refused to commit existential suicide. He refused to suffer an orogene to live. There was no malice in either of them in that final moment, only the grim violence of inevitability.

To one side of this tableau stands Schaffa, Nassun's Guardian, who stares down at what is left of Jija Resistant Jekity in a combination of wonder and cold satisfaction. At Nassun's other side is Steel, her stone eater. It is appropriate to call him that now, hers, because he has come in her hour of need—not to help, never that, but to provide her with something nevertheless. What he offers, and what she has finally realized she needs, is *purpose*. Not even Schaffa has given her this, but that's because Schaffa loves her unconditionally. She needs that love, too, oh how she needs it, but in this moment when her heart has been most thoroughly broken, when her thoughts are at their least focused, she craves something more...solid.

She will have the solidity that she wants. She will fight for it and kill for it, because she's had to do that again and again and it is habit now, and if she is successful she will die for it. After all, she is her mother's daughter—and only people who think they have a future fear death.

In Nassun's good hand thrums a three-foot-long, tapering shard of crystal, deep blue and finely faceted, though with some slight deformations near its base that have resulted in something like a hilt. Now and again this strange longknife flickers into a translucent, intangible, debatably real state. It's very real; only Nassun's attention keeps the thing in her hands from turning her to colored stone the way it did her father. She's afraid of what might happen if she passes out from blood loss, so she would really like to send the sapphire back up into the sky to resume its default shape and immense size—but she can't. Not yet.

There, by the dormitory, are the two reasons: Umber and Nida, the other two Guardians of Found Moon. They're watching her, and when her gaze lands on them, there is a flicker in the lacing tendrils of silver that drift between the pair. No exchanged words or looks, just that silent communion which would have been imperceptible, if Nassun were anyone but who she was. Beneath each Guardian, delicate silvery tethers wend up from the ground into their feet, connected by the nerve-and-vein glimmer of their bodies to tiny shards of iron embedded in their brains. These taproot-like tethers have always been there, but maybe it's the tension of the moment that makes Nassun finally notice how *thick* those lines of light are for each Guardian—much thicker than the one linking the ground to Schaffa. And at last she understands what that means: Umber and Nida are just puppets of a greater will. Nassun has tried to believe better of them, that they are their own people, but here, now, with the sapphire in her hands and her father dead at her feet... some maturations cannot wait for a more convenient season.

So Nassun roots a torus deep within the earth, because she knows that Umber and Nida will sense this. It's a feint; she doesn't need the power of the earth, and she suspects they know it. Still, they react, Umber unfolding his arms and Nida straightening from where she'd been leaning on the porch railing. Schaffa reacts, too, his eyes shifting sideways to meet hers. It's an unavoidable tell that Umber and Nida will notice, but it cannot be helped; Nassun has no piece of the Evil Earth lodged in her brain to facilitate communication. Where matter fails, care makes do. He says, "Nida," and that is all she needs.

Umber and Nida move. It's fast—so fast—because the silver lattice within each has strengthened their bones and tightened the cords of their muscles so that they can do what ordinary human flesh cannot. A pulse of negation moves before them with storm-surge inexorability, immediately striking the major lobes of Nassun's sessapinae numb, but Nassun is already on the offensive. Not physically; she cannot contest them in that sphere of battle, and besides she can barely stand. Will and the silver are all she's got left.

So Nassun—her body still, her mind violent—snatches at

the silver threads of the air around her, weaving them into a crude but efficient net. (She's never done this before, but no one has ever told her that it can't be done.) She wraps part of this around Nida, ignoring Umber because Schaffa told her to. And indeed, she understands in the next instant why he told her to concentrate on only one of the enemy Guardians. The silver she's woven around Nida should catch the woman up fast, like an insect slamming into a spiderweb. Instead, Nida stumbles to a halt, then laughs while threads of *something else* curl forth from within her and lash the air, shredding the net around her. She lunges for Nassun again, but Nassun—after boggling at the speed and efficacy of the Guardian's retaliation—snatches stone up from within the earth to spear Nida's feet. This impedes Nida only a little. She bulls forward, breaking the rock shards off and charging with them still jutting through her boots. One of her hands is held like a claw, the other a flat, finger-stiffened blade. Whichever of them reaches Nassun first will dictate how she begins tearing Nassun apart with her bare hands.

Here Nassun panics. Just a little, because she would lose control of the sapphire otherwise—but some. She can sense a raw, hungry, chaotic reverberation to the silver threads thrumming through Nida, like nothing she's ever perceived before, and it is somehow, suddenly, terrifying. She doesn't know what that strange reverberation will do to her, if any part of Nida should touch Nassun's bare skin. (Her mother knows, though.) She takes a step back, willing the sapphire longknife to move between her and Nida in a defensive position. Her good hand is still on the sapphire's hilt, so it looks as if she's brandishing a weapon with a shaking and far-too-slow hand. Nida laughs again, high and delighted, because they can both see that not even the sapphire will be enough to stop her. Nida's claw-hand flails out, fingers splaying and reaching for Nassun's cheek even as she weaves like a snake around Nassun's wild slash—

Nassun drops the sapphire and screams, her dulled sessapinae flexing desperately, helplessly—

But all of the Guardians have forgotten Nassun's other guardian.

Steel does not appear to move. In one instant he stands as he has for the past few minutes, with his back to the tumbled pile of Jija, expression serene, posture languid as he faces the northern horizon. In the next he is closer, right beside Nassun, having transported himself so quickly that Nassun hears a sharp clap of displaced air. And Nida's forward momentum abruptly stops as her throat is caught tight within the circle of Steel's upraised hand.

She shrieks. Nassun has heard Nida ramble for hours in her fluttery voice, and perhaps that's made her think of Nida as a songbird, chattery and chirruping and harmless. This shriek is the cry of a raptor, savagery turning to fury as she is thwarted from stooping on her prey. She tries to wrench herself back, risking skin and tendon to get loose, but Steel's grip is as firm as stone. She's caught.

A sound behind Nassun makes her jerk around. Ten feet from where she stands, Umber and Schaffa have blurred together in hand-to-hand combat. She can't see what's happening. They're both moving too fast, their strikes swift and vicious. By the time her ears process the sounds of a blow, they've already shifted to a different position. She can't even tell what they're doing—but she is afraid, so afraid, for Schaffa. The silver in Umber flows like rivers, power being steadily fed to him through that glimmering taproot. The thinner streams in Schaffa, however, are a wild chain of rapids and clogs, yanking at his nerves and muscles and flaring unpredictably in an attempt to distract him. Nassun can see by the concentration in Schaffa's face that *he* is still in control, and that this is what has saved him; his movements are unpredictable, strategic, considered. Still. That he can fight at all is astonishing.

How he ends the fight, by driving his hand up to the wrist through the underside of Umber's jaw, is horrifying.

Umber makes an awful sound, jerking to a halt—but an instant later, his hand lunges for Schaffa's throat again, blurring in its speed. Schaffa gasps—so quickly that it might be just a breath, but Nassun hears the alarm in it—and shunts away the strike, but Umber's still moving, even though his eyes have rolled back in his head and the movements are twitchy, clumsy. Nassun understands then: Umber's not home anymore. Something else is, working his limbs and reflexes for as long as crucial connections remain in place. And yes: In the next breath, Schaffa flings Umber to the ground, wrenches his hand free, and stomps on his opponent's head.

Nassun can't look. She hears the crunch; that's enough. She hears Umber actually continue twitching, his movements more feeble but persistent, and she hears the faint rustle of Schaffa's clothes as he bends. Then she hears something that her mother last heard in a little room in the Guardians' wing of the Fulcrum, some thirty years before: bone cracking and gristle tearing, as Schaffa works his fingers into the base of Umber's broken skull.

Nassun can't close her ears, so instead she focuses on Nida, who's still fighting to get free from Steel's unbreakable grip.

"I—I—" Nassun attempts. Her heart's slowed only a little. The sapphire shakes harder in her hands. Nida still wants to kill her. Steel, who has established himself as merely a possible ally and not a definite one, need only loosen his grip, and Nassun will die. But. "I d-don't want to kill you," she manages. It's even true.

Nida abruptly goes still and silent. The fury in her expression gradually fades to no expression at all. "It did what it had to do, last time," she says.

Nassun's skin prickles with the realization that something intangible has changed. She's not sure what, but she doesn't think this is quite Nida anymore. She swallows. "Did what? Who?"

Nida's gaze falls on Steel. There is a faint grinding sound as Steel's mouth curves into a wide, toothy smile. Then, before Nassun can think of another question to ask, Steel's grip shifts. Not loosening; turning, with that unnaturally slow motion which perhaps is meant to imitate human movement. (Or mock it.) He draws in his arm and pivots his wrist to turn Nida around, her back to his front. The nape of her neck to his mouth.

"It's angry," Nida continues calmly, though now she faces away from both Steel and Nassun. "Yet even now it may be willing to compromise, to forgive. It demands justice, but—"

"It has had its justice a thousand times over," says Steel. "I owe it no more." Then he opens his mouth wide.

Nassun turns away, again. On a morning when she has rent her father to pieces, some things remain too obscene for her child's eyes. At least Nida does not move again once Steel has dropped her body to the ground.

"We cannot remain here," Schaffa says. When Nassun swallows hard and focuses on him, she sees that he stands over Umber's corpse, holding something small and sharp in one gore-flecked hand. He gazes at this object with the same detached coldness that he turns upon those he means to kill. "Others will come."

Through the clarity of near-death adrenaline, Nassun knows that he means other contaminated Guardians—and not half-contaminated ones like Schaffa himself, who have somehow managed to retain some measure of free will. Nassun swallows and nods, feeling calmer now that no one is actively trying to kill her anymore. "Wh-what about the other kids?"

Some of the children in question are standing on the porch of the dormitory, awakened by the concussion of the sapphire when Nassun summoned it into longknife form. They have witnessed everything, Nassun sees. A couple are weeping at the sight of their Guardians dead, but most just stare at her and Schaffa in silent shock. One of the smaller children is vomiting off the side of the steps.

Schaffa gazes at them for a long moment, and then glances sidelong at her. Some of the coldness is still there, saying what his voice does not. "They'll need to leave Jekity, quickly. Without Guardians, the commfolk are unlikely to tolerate their presence." Or Schaffa can kill them. That's what he's done with every other orogene they've met who isn't under his control. They are either his, or they are a threat.

"No," Nassun blurts. Speaking to that silent coldness, not

to what he's said. The coldness increases fractionally. Schaffa never likes it when she says no. She takes a deep breath, marshaling a little more calm, and corrects herself. "Please, Schaffa. I just ... I can't take any more."

This is rank hypocrisy. The decision Nassun has recently made, a silent promise over her father's corpse, belies it. Schaffa cannot know what she has chosen, but at the corner of her vision, she is painfully aware of Steel's lingering, blood-painted smile.

She presses her lips together and means it anyway. It isn't a lie. She can't take the cruelty, the endless suffering; that's the whole point. What she means to do will be, if nothing else, quick and merciful.

Schaffa regards her for a moment. Then he twitch-winces a little, as she has seen him do often in the past few weeks. When the spasm passes, he puts on a smile and comes over to her, though first he closes his hand firmly around the metal bit he's taken from Umber. "How is your shoulder?"

She reaches up to touch it. The cloth of her sleep-shirt is wet with blood, but not sodden, and she can still use the arm. "It hurts."

"That will last for a time, I'm afraid." He looks around, then rises and goes to Umber's corpse. Ripping off one of Umber's shirtsleeves—one that isn't as splattered with blood as the other, Nassun notes with distant relief—he comes over and pushes up her sleeve, then helps her tie the strip of cloth around her shoulder. He ties it tight. Nassun knows this is good and will possibly prevent her from needing to have the wound sewn up, but for a moment the pain is worse and she leans against him briefly. He allows this, stroking her hair with his free hand. The gore-flecked other hand, Nassun notes, stays clenched tight around that metal shard.

"What will you do with it?" Nassun asks, staring at the clenched hand. She cannot help imagining something malevolent there, snaking its tendrils forth and looking for another person to infect with the Evil Earth's will.

"I don't know," Schaffa says in a heavy voice. "It's no danger to me, but I remember that in…" He frowns for a moment, visibly groping for a memory that is gone. "That once, elsewhere, we simply recycled them. Here, I suppose I'll have to find somewhere isolated to drop it, and hope no one stumbles across it anytime soon. What will you do with *that*?"

Nassun follows his gaze to where the sapphire longknife, untended, has floated around behind her and positioned itself in the air, hovering precisely a foot away from her back. It moves slightly with her movements, humming faintly. She doesn't understand why it's doing that, though she takes some comfort from its looming, quiescent strength. "I guess I should put it back."

"How did you…?"

"I just needed it. It knew what I needed and changed for me." Nassun shrugs a little. It's so hard to explain these things in words. Then she clutches at his shirt with her uninjured hand, because she knows that when Schaffa doesn't answer a question, it isn't a good thing. "The others, Schaffa."

He sighs finally. "I'll help them prepare packs. Can you walk?"

Nassun's so relieved that for the moment she feels like she can fly. "Yes. Thank you. Thank you, Schaffa!"

He shakes his head, clearly rueful, though he smiles again.

"Go to your father's house and take anything useful and portable, little one. I'll meet you there."

She hesitates. If Schaffa decides to kill the other children of Found Moon...He won't, will he? He's said he won't.

Schaffa pauses, raising an eyebrow above his smile, the picture of polite, calm inquiry. It's an illusion. The silver is still a lashing whip within Schaffa, trying to goad him into killing her. He must be in astonishing pain. He resists the goad, however, as he has for weeks. He does not kill her, because he loves her. And she can trust nothing, no one, if she does not trust him.

"Okay," Nassun says. "I'll see you at Daddy's."

As she pulls away from him, she glances at Steel, who has turned to face Schaffa as well. Somewhere in the past few breaths, Steel has gotten the blood off his lips. She doesn't know how. But he has held out one gray hand toward them—no. Toward Schaffa. Schaffa tilts his head at this for a moment, considering, and then after a moment he deposits the bloody iron shard into Steel's hand. Steel's hand flicks closed, then uncurls again, slowly, as if performing a sleight-of-hand trick. But the iron shard is gone. Schaffa inclines his head in polite thanks.

Her two monstrous protectors, who must cooperate on her care. Yet is Nassun not a monster, too? Because the thing that she sensed just before Jija came to kill her—that spike of immense power, concentrated and amplified by dozens of obelisks working in tandem? Steel has called this the Obelisk Gate: a vast and complex mechanism created by the deadciv that built the obelisks, for some unfathomable purpose. Steel has also mentioned a thing called the Moon. Nassun has heard the stories; once, long ago, Father Earth had a child. That child's loss is what angered him and brought about the Seasons.

The tales offer a message of impossible hope, and a mindless expression that lorists use to intrigue restless audiences. *One day, if the Earth's child ever returns . . .* The implication is that, someday, Father Earth might be appeased at last. Someday, the Seasons might end and all could become right with the world.

Except fathers will still try to murder their orogene children, won't they? Even if the Moon comes back. Nothing will ever stop that.

Bring home the Moon, Steel has said. End the world's pain.

Some choices aren't choices at all, really.

Nassun wills the sapphire to come hover before her again. She can sess nothing in the wake of Umber and Nida's negation, but there are other ways to perceive the world. And amid the flickering un-water of the sapphire, as it unmakes and remakes itself from the concentrated immensity of silver light stored within its crystal lattice, there is a subtle message written in equations of force and balance that Nassun solves instinctively, with something other than math.

Far away. Across the unknown sea. Her mother may hold the Obelisk Gate's key, but Nassun learned on the ash roads that there are other ways to open any gate—hinges to pop, ways to climb over or dig under. And far away, on the other side of the world, is a place where Essun's control over the Gate can be subverted.

"I know where we need to go, Schaffa," Nassun says.

He eyes her for a moment, his gaze flicking to Steel and back. "Do you, now?"

"Yes. It's a really long way, though." She bites her lip. "Will you go with me?"

He inclines his head, his smile wide and warm. "Anywhere, my little one."

Nassun lets out a long breath of relief, smiling up at him tentatively. Then she deliberately turns her back on Found Moon and its corpses, and walks down the hill without ever once looking back.

* * *

2729 Imperial: Witnesses in the comm of Amand (Dibba Quartent, western Nomidlats) report an unregistered rogga female opening up a gas pocket near the town. Unclear what gas was; killed in seconds, purpling of tongue, suffocation rather than toxicity? Both? Another rogga female reportedly stopped the first one's effort, somehow, and shunted the gas back into the vent before sealing it. Amand citizens shot both as soon as possible to prevent further incidents. Gas pocket assessed by Fulcrum as substantial—enough to have killed most people and livestock in western half of Nomidlats, with follow-up topsoil contamination. Initiating female age seventeen, reacting to reported molester of younger sister. Quelling female age seven, sister of first.

—*Project notes of Yaetr Innovator Dibars*

Syl Anagist: Five

H OUWHA," SAYS A VOICE BEHIND me.

(Me? Mc.)

I turn from the stinging window and the garden of winking flowers. A woman stands with Gaewha and one of the
conductors, and I do not know her. To the eyes, she is one of
them—skin a soft allover brown, eyes gray, hair black-brown
and curling in ropes, tall. There are hints of *other* in the breadth
of her face—or perhaps, viewing this memory now through the
lens of millennia, I see what I want to see. What she looks like
is irrelevant. To my sessapinae, her kinship to us is as obvious as
Gaewha's puffy white hair. She exerts a pressure upon the ambient that is a churning, impossibly heavy, irresistible force. This
makes her as much one of us as if she'd been decanted from the
same biomagestric mix.

(You look like her. No. I *want* you to look like her. That is
unfair, even if it's true; you are like her, but in other ways than
mere appearance. My apologies for reducing you in such a way.)

The conductor speaks as her kind do, in thin vibrations that only ripple the air and barely stir the ground. *Words*. I know this conductor's name-word, Pheylen, and I know too that she is one of the nicer ones, but this knowledge is still and indistinct, like so much about them. For a very long time I could not tell the difference between one of their kind and another. They all look different, but they have the same non-presence within the ambient. I still have to remind myself that hair textures and eye shapes and unique body odors each have as much meaning to them as the perturbations of tectonic plates have to me.

I must be respectful of their difference. We are the deficient ones, after all, stripped of much that would've made us human. This was necessary and I do not mind what I am. I like being useful. But many things would be easier if I could understand our creators better.

So I stare at the new woman, the us-woman, and try to pay attention while the conductor *introduces* her. Introduction is a ritual that consists of explaining the sounds of names and the relationships of the…families? Professions? Honestly, I don't know. I stand where I am supposed to and say the things I should. The conductor tells the new woman that I am Houwha and that Gaewha is Gaewha, which are the name-words they use for us. The new woman, the conductor says, is Kelenli. That's wrong, too. Her name is actually *deep stab, breach of clay sweetburst, soft silicate underlayer, reverberation*, but I will try to remember "Kelenli" when I use words to speak.

The conductor seems pleased that I say "How do you do" when I'm supposed to. I'm glad; *introduction* is very difficult, but I've worked hard to become good at it. After this she starts speaking to Kelenli. When it becomes clear that the conductor has nothing more to say to me, I move behind Gaewha and begin plaiting some of her thick, poufy mane of hair. The conductors seem to like it when we do this, though I don't really know why. One of them said that it was "cute" to see us taking care of one another, just like people. I'm not sure what cute means.

Meanwhile, I listen.

"Just doesn't make sense," Pheylen is saying, with a sigh. "I mean, the numbers don't lie, but..."

"If you'd like to register an objection," begins Kelenli. Her words fascinate me in a way that words never have before. Unlike the conductor, her voice has weight and texture, strata-deep and layered. She sends the words into the ground while she speaks, as a kind of subvocalization. It makes them feel more real. Pheylen, who doesn't seem to notice how much deeper Kelenli's words are—or maybe she just doesn't care—makes an uncomfortable face in reaction to what she's said. Kelenli repeats, "*If* you'd like to, I can ask Gallat to take me off the roster."

"And listen to his shouting? Evil Death, he'd never stop. Such a savage temper he has." Pheylen smiles. It's not an amused smile. "It must be hard for him, wanting the project to succeed, but also wanting you kept—well. *I'm* fine with you on standby-only, but then I haven't seen the simulation data."

"I have." Kelenli's tone is grave. "The delay-failure risk was small, but significant."

"Well, there you are. Even a small risk is too much, if we can do something about it. I think they must be more anxious than they're letting on, though, to involve you—" Abruptly, Pheylen looks embarrassed. "Ah...sorry. No offense meant."

Kelenli smiles. Both I and Gaewha can see that it is only a surface layering, not a real expression. "None taken."

Pheylen exhales in relief. "Well, then, I'll just withdraw to Observation and let you three get to know each other. Knock when you're done."

With that, Conductor Pheylen leaves the room. This is a good thing, because when conductors are not around, we can speak more easily. The door closes and I move to face Gaewha (who is actually *cracked geode taste of adularescent salts, fading echo*). She nods minutely because I have correctly guessed that she has something important to tell me. We are always watched. A certain amount of performance is essential.

Gaewha says with her mouth, "Coordinator Pheylen told me they're making a change to our configuration." With the rest of her she says, in atmospheric perturbations and anxious plucking of the silver threads, *Tetlewha has been moved to the briar patch*.

"A change at this late date?" I glance at the us-woman, Kelenli, to see if she is following the whole conversation. She looks so much like one of them, all that surface coloring and those long bones that make her a head taller than both of us. "Do you have something to do with the project?" I ask her, while also responding to Gaewha's news about Tetlewha. *No*.

My "no" is not denial, just a statement of fact. We can still detect Tetlewha's familiar *hot spot roil and strata uplift, grind of subsidence*, but...something is different. He's not nearby anymore, or at least he's not anywhere that is in range of our seismic questings. And the roil and grind of him have gone nearly still.

Decommissioned is the word the conductors prefer to use,

when one of us is removed from service. They have asked us, individually, to describe what we feel when the change happens, because it is a disruption of our network. By unspoken agreement each of us speaks of the sensation of loss—a pulling away, a draining, a thinning of signal strength. By unspoken agreement none of us mentions the rest, which in any case is indescribable using conductor words. What we experience is a searing sensation, and prickling all over, and the *tumbledown resistance tangle* of ancient pre-Sylanagistine wire such as we sometimes encounter in our explorations of the earth, gone rusted and sharp in its decay and wasted potential. Something like that.

Who gave the order? I want to know.

Gaewha has become a slow fault ripple of stark, frustrated, confused patterns. *Conductor Gallat. The other conductors are angry about it and someone reported it to the higher-ups and that's why they have sent Kelenli here. It took all of us together to hold the onyx and the moonstone. They are concerned about our stability.*

Annoyed, I return, *Perhaps they should have thought of that before*—

"I do have something to do with the project, yes," interrupts Kelenli, though there has been no break or disruption of the verbal conversation. Words are very slow compared to earthtalk. "I have some arcane awareness, you see, and similar abilities to yours." Then she adds, *I'm here to teach you.*

She switches as easily as we do between the words of the conductors and our language, the language of the earth. Her communicative presence is *radiant heavy metal, searing crystallized magnetic lines of meteoric iron,* and more complex layers underneath this, all so sharp-edged and powerful that Gaewha and I both inhale in wonder.

But what is she saying? Teach us? We don't need to be taught. We were decanted knowing nearly everything we needed to know already, and the rest we learned in the first few weeks of life with our fellow tuners. If we hadn't, we would be in the briar patch, too.

I make sure to frown. "How can you be a tuner like us?" This is a lie spoken for our observers, who see only the surface of things and think we do, too. She is not white like us, not short or strange, but we have known her for one of ours since we felt the cataclysm of her presence. I do not disbelieve that she is one of us. I can't disbelieve the incontrovertible.

Kelenli smiles, with a wryness that acknowledges the lie. "Not quite like you, but close enough. You're the finished artwork, I'm the model." Threads of magic in the earth heat and reverberate and add other meanings. *Prototype.* A control to our experiment, made earlier to see how we should be done. She has only one difference, instead of the many that we possess. She has our carefully designed sessapinae. Is that enough to help us accomplish the task? The certainty in her earth-presence says yes. She continues in words: "I'm not the first that was made. Just the first to survive."

We all push a hand at the air to ward off Evil Death. But I allow myself to look like I don't understand as I wonder if we dare trust her. I saw how the conductor relaxed around her. Pheylen is one of the nice ones, but even she never forgets what we are. She forgot with Kelenli, though. Perhaps all humans think she is one of them, until someone tells them otherwise.

What is that like, being treated as human when one is not? And then there's the fact that they've left her alone with us. We they treat like weapons that might misfire at any moment... but they trust her.

"How many fragments have you attuned to yourself?" I ask aloud, as if this is a thing that matters. It is also a challenge.

"Only one," Kelenli says. But she's still smiling. "The onyx."

Oh. Oh, that *does* matter. Gaewha and I exchange a look of wonder and concern before facing her again.

"And the reason I'm here," Kelenli continues, abruptly insistent upon delivering this important information with mere words, which somehow perversely serves to emphasize them, "is because the order has been issued. The fragments are at optimum storage capacity and are ready for the generative cycle. Corepoint and Zero Site go live in twenty-eight days. We're finally starting up the Plutonic Engine."

(In tens of thousands of years, after people have repeatedly forgotten what "engines" are and know the fragments as nothing but "obelisks," there will be a different name for the thing that rules our lives now. It will be called the *Obelisk Gate*, which is both more poetic and quaintly primitive. I like that name better.)

In the present, while Gaewha and I stand there staring, Kelenli drops one last shocker into the vibrations between our cells:

That means I have less than a month to show you who you really are.

Gaewha frowns. I manage not to react because the conductors watch our bodies as well as our faces, but it is a narrow thing. I'm very confused, and not a little unnerved. I have no idea, in the present of this conversation, that it is the beginning of the end.

Because we tuners are not orogenes, you see. Orogeny is what the difference of us will become over generations of adaptation to a changed world. You are the shallower, more specialized, more natural distillation of our so-unnatural strangeness. Only a few of you, like Alabaster, will ever come close to the power and versatility we hold, but that is because we were constructed as intentionally and artificially as the fragments you call obelisks. We are fragments of the great machine, too—just as much a triumph of genegineering and biomagestry and geomagestry and other disciplines for which the future will have no name. By our existence we glorify the world that made us, like any statue or scepter or other precious object.

We do not resent this, for our opinions and experiences have been carefully constructed, too. We do not understand that what Kelenli has come to give us is a sense of *peoplehood*. We do not understand why we have been forbidden this self-concept before now... but we will.

And then we will understand that *people* cannot be *possessions*. And because we are both and this should not be, a new concept will take shape within us, though we have never heard the word for it because the conductors are forbidden to even mention it in our presence. *Revolution*.

Well. We don't have much use for words, anyway. But that's what this is. The beginning. You, Essun, will see the end.

3

you, imbalanced

IT TAKES A FEW DAYS for you to recover enough to walk on your own. As soon as you can, Ykka reappropriates your stretcher-bearers to perform other tasks, which leaves you to hobble along, weak and made clumsy by the loss of your arm. The first few days you lag well behind the bulk of the group, catching up to camp with them only hours after they've settled for the night. There isn't much left of the communal food by the time you go to take your share. Good thing you don't feel hunger anymore. There aren't many spaces left to lay out your bedroll, either—though they did at least give you a basic pack and supplies to make up for your lost runny-sack. What spaces there are aren't good, located near the edges of the camp or off the road altogether, where the danger of attack by wildlife or commless is greater. You sleep there anyway because you're exhausted. You suppose that if there's any real danger, Hoa will carry you off again; he seems able to transport you for short distances through the earth with no trouble. Still, Ykka's anger is a hard thing to bear, in more ways than one.

Tonkee and Hoa lag behind with you. It's almost like the old days, except that now Hoa appears as you walk, gets left behind as you keep walking, then appears again somewhere ahead of you. Most times he adopts a neutral posture, but occasionally he's doing something ridiculous, like the time you find him in a running pose. Apparently stone eaters get bored, too. Hjarka stays with Tonkee, so that's four of you. Well, five: Lerna lingers to walk with you, too, angry at what he perceives as the mistreatment of one of his patients. He didn't think a recently comatose woman should be made to walk at all, let alone left to fall behind. You try to tell him not to stick with you, not to draw Castrima's wrath upon himself, but he snorts and says that if Castrima really wants to antagonize the only person in the comm who's formally trained to do surgery, they don't deserve to keep him. Which is...well, it's a very good point. You shut up.

You're managing better than Lerna expected, at least. That's mostly because it wasn't really a coma, and also because you hadn't lost all of your road conditioning during the seven or eight months that you lived in Castrima. The old habits come back easily, really: finding a steady, if slow, pace that nevertheless eats up the miles; wearing your pack low so that the bulk of its weight braces against your butt rather than pulling on your shoulders; keeping your head down as you walk so that the falling ash doesn't cover your goggles. The loss of the arm is more a nuisance than a real hardship, at least with so many willing helpers around. Aside from throwing off your balance and plaguing you with phantom itches or aches from fingers or an elbow that doesn't exist, the hardest part is getting dressed in the morning. It's surprising how quickly you master squatting to piss or defecate without falling over, but maybe you're just more motivated after days in a diaper.

So you're holding your own, just slowly at first, and you're getting faster as the days go by. But here's the problem with all of this: You're going the wrong way.

Tonkee comes over to sit by you one evening. "You can't leave until we're a lot further west," she says without preamble. "Almost to the Merz, I'm thinking. If you want to make it that far, you're going to have to patch things up with Ykka."

You glare at her, though for Tonkee, this is discreet. She's waited till Hjarka is snoring in her bedroll and Lerna's gone off to use the camp latrine. Hoa is still nearby, standing unsubtle guard over your small group within the comm encampment, the curves of his black marble face underlit by your fire. Tonkee knows he's loyal to you, though, to the degree that loyalty means anything to him.

"Ykka hates me," you finally say, after glaring fails to produce anything like chagrin or regret in Tonkee.

She rolls her eyes. "Trust me, I know hate. What Ykka's got is... scared, and a good bit of mad, but some of that you deserve. You've put her people in danger."

"I *saved* her people from danger."

Across the encampment, as if to illustrate your point, you notice someone moving about clunkily. It's one of the Rennanis soldiers, a few of whom were captured alive after the last battle. They've put a pranger on her—a hinged wooden collar round her neck, with holes in the planks holding her arms up and apart, linked by two chains to manacles on her ankles. Primitive but effective. Lerna's been tending the prisoners' chafing sores, and you understand they're allowed to put the prangers aside at night. It's better treatment than Castrimans would have gotten from Rennanis if the situations were reversed, but still, it makes everything awkward. It's not like the Rennies can leave, after all. Even without the prangers, if any one of them escapes now, with no supplies and lacking the protection of a large group, they'll be meat within days. The prangers are just insult on top of injury, and a disquieting reminder to all that things could be worse. You look away.

Tonkee sees you looking. "Yeah, you saved Castrima from one danger and then delivered them into something just as bad. Ykka only wanted the first half of that."

"I couldn't have avoided the second half. Should I have just let the stone eaters kill all the roggas? Kill *her*? If they'd succeeded, none of the geode's mechanisms would've worked anyway!"

"She knows that. That's why I said it wasn't hate. But…" Tonkee sighs as if you're being especially stupid. "Look. Castrima was—is—an experiment. Not the geode, the people. She's always known it was precarious, trying to make a comm out of strays and roggas, but it was working. She made the old-timers understand that we needed the newcommers. Got everybody to think of roggas as people. Got them to agree to live underground, in a deadciv ruin that could've killed us all at any moment. Even kept them from turning on each other when that gray stone eater gave them a reason—"

"*I* stopped that," you mutter. But you're listening.

"You helped," Tonkee concedes, "but if it had just been you? You know full well it wouldn't have worked. Castrima works because of *Ykka*. Because they know she'll die to keep this comm going. Help Castrima, and Ykka will be on your side again."

It will be weeks, maybe even months, before you reach the now-vacant Equatorial city of Rennanis. "I know where Nassun is *now*," you say, seething. "By the time Castrima gets to Rennanis, she might be somewhere else!"

Tonkee sighs. "It's been a few weeks already, Essun."

And Nassun was probably somewhere else before you even woke up. You're shaking. It's not rational and you know it, but you blurt, "But if I go now, maybe—maybe I can catch up, maybe Hoa can tune in on her again, maybe I can—" Then you falter silent because you hear the shaky, high-pitched note of your own voice and your mother instincts kick back in, rusty but unblunted, to chide you: *Stop whining.* Which you are. So you bite back more words, but you're still shaking, a little.

Tonkee shakes her head, an expression on her face that might be sympathy, or maybe it's just rueful acknowledgment of how pathetic you sound. "Well, at least you *know* it's a bad idea. But if you're that determined, then you'd better get started now." She turns away. Can't really blame her, can you? Venture into the almost certainly deadly unknown with a woman who's destroyed multiple communities, or stay with a comm that at least theoretically will soon have a home again? That's barely even a question.

But you should really know better than to try to predict what Tonkee will do. She sighs, after you subside and sit back on the rock you've been using for a chair. "I can probably wrangle some extra supplies out of the quartermaster, if I tell them I need to go scout something for the Innovators. They're used to me doing that. But I'm not sure I can convince them to give me enough for two."

It's a surprise to realize how grateful you are, for her—hmm. Loyalty isn't the word for it. Attachment? Maybe. Maybe it's just that you've been her research subject for all this time already, so of course she's not going to let you slip away when she's followed you across decades and half the Stillness.

But then you frown. "Two? Not three?" You thought things were working out with her and Hjarka.

Tonkee shrugs, then awkwardly bends to tuck into the little bowl of rice and beans she has from the communal pot. After she swallows, she says, "I prefer to make conservative estimates. You'd better, too."

She means Lerna, who seems to be in the process of attaching himself to you. You don't know why. You're not exactly a prize, dressed in ash and with no arm, and half the time he seems to be furious with you. You're still surprised it's not all the time. He always was a strange boy.

"Anyway, here's a thing I want you to think about," Tonkee continues. "What was Nassun doing when you found her?"

And you flinch. Because, damn it, Tonkee has once again said aloud a thing that you would have preferred to leave unsaid, and unconsidered.

And because you remember that moment, with the power of the Gate sluicing through you, when you reached and touched and felt a familiar resonance touch back. A resonance backed, and amplified, by something blue and deep and strangely resistant to the Gate's linkage. The Gate told you—somehow—that it was the sapphire.

What is your ten-year-old daughter doing playing with an obelisk?

How is your ten-year-old daughter *alive* after playing with an obelisk?

You think of how that momentary contact felt. Familiar vibration-taste of an orogeny which you've been quelling since before she was born and training since she was two—but so much sharper and more intense now. You weren't trying to take the sapphire from Nassun, but the Gate was, following instructions that long-dead builders somehow wrote into the layered lattices of the onyx. Nassun kept the sapphire, though. She actually fought off the Obelisk Gate.

What has your little girl been doing, this long dark year, to develop such skill?

"You don't know what her situation is," Tonkee continues, which makes you blink out of this terrible reverie and focus on her. "You don't know what kind of people she's living with. You said she's in the Antarctics, somewhere near the eastern coast? That part of the world shouldn't be feeling the Season much yet. So what are you going to do, then, snatch her out of a comm where she's safe and has enough to eat and can still see the sky, and drag her north to a comm sitting on the Rifting, where the shakes will be constant and the next gas vent might kill everyone?" She looks hard at you. "Do you want to help her? Or just have her with you again? Those two things aren't the same."

"Jija killed Uche," you snap. The words don't hurt, unless you think about them as you speak. Unless you remember your son's smell or his little laugh or the sight of his body under a blanket. Unless you think of Corundum—you use anger to press down the twin throbs of grief and guilt. "I have to get her *away* from him. He killed my son!"

"He hasn't killed your daughter yet. He's had, what, twenty months? Twenty-one? That means something." Tonkee spies Lerna coming back toward you through the crowd, and sighs. "There are just things you ought to think about, is all I'm saying. And I can't even believe I'm saying it. She's another obelisk-user, and I can't even go investigate it." Tonkee utters a frustrated grumbly sound. "I hate this damn Season. I have to be so rusting *practical* now."

You're surprised into a chuckle, but it's weak. The questions Tonkee's raised are good ones, of course, and some of them you can't answer. You think about them for a long time that night, and in the days thereafter.

Rennanis is nearly into the Western Coastals, just past the Merz Desert. Castrima is going to have to go through the desert to get there, because skirting around it would drastically increase the length of your journey—a difference of months versus years. But you're making good time through the central Somidlats, where the roads are decently passable and you haven't been bothered by many raiders or significant wildlife. The Hunters have been able to find a lot of forage to supplement the comm's stores, including a little more game than before. Unsurprising, since they're no longer competing against hordes of insects. It's not enough—small voles and birds just aren't going to hold a comm of a thousand-plus people for long. But it's better than nothing.

When you start noticing changes in the land that presage desert—thinning of the skeletal forest, flattening of the topography, a gradual drawing away of the water table amid the strata—you decide that it's time to finally try to talk to Ykka.

By now you've entered a stone forest: a place of tall, sharp-edged black spires that claw irregularly at the sky above and around you as the group edges through its depths. There aren't many of these in the world. Most get shattered by shakes, or—back when there was a Fulcrum—deliberately destroyed by Fulcrum blackjackets at local comms' commissioned request. No comm *lives* in a stone forest, see, and no well-run comm wants one nearby. Apart from stone forests' tendency to collapse and crush everything within, they tend to be riddled with wet caves and other water-hewn formations that make marvelous homes for dangerous flora and fauna. Or people.

The road runs straight through this stone forest, which is bullshit. That is to say, no one in their right mind would have built a road through a place like this. If a quartent governor had proposed using people's taxes on this dangerous bit of bandit-bait, that governor would've been replaced in the next election...or shanked in the night. So that's your first clue that something's off about the place. The second is that there's not much vegetation in the forest. Not much anywhere this far into the Season, but also no sign that there was ever any vegetation here in the first place. That means this stone forest is recent—so recent that there's been no time for wind or rain to erode the stone and permit plant growth. So recent that it didn't exist before the Season.

Clue number three is what your own sessapinae tell you. Most stone forests are limestone, made by water erosion over hundreds of millions of years. This one is obsidian—volcanic glass. Its jagged spikes aren't straight up and down, but more inwardly curved; there are even a few unbroken arcs stretching over the road. Impossible to see up close, but you can sess the overall pattern: The whole forest is a blossom of lava, solidified mid-blast. Not a line of the road has been knocked out of place by the tectonic explosion around it. Beautiful work, really.

Ykka's in the middle of an argument with another comm member when you find her. She's called for a halt about a hundred feet away from the forest, and people are milling about, looking confused about whether this is just a rest stop or whether they should be making camp since it's relatively late in the day. The comm member is one you finally recognize as Esni Strongback Castrima, the use-caste's spokesperson. She throws you an uneasy glance as you come to a halt beside them, but then you take off your goggles and mask, and her expression softens. She didn't recognize you before because you've stuffed rags into the sleeve of your missing arm to keep warm. Her reaction is a welcome reminder that not everybody in Castrima is angry with you. Esni is alive because the worst part of the attack—Rennanis soldiers trying to carve a bloody path through the Strongbacks holding Scenic Overlook—ended when you locked the enemy stone eaters into crystals.

Ykka, though, doesn't turn, although she should easily be able to sess your presence. She says, you think to Esni, though it works for you as well, "I really don't want to hear any more arguments right now."

"That's good," you say. "Because I understand exactly why you've stopped here, and I think it's a good idea." It's a bit louder than it needs to be. You eyeball Esni so she'll know you mean to have it out with Ykka right now, and maybe Esni doesn't want to be here for that. But a woman who leads the comm's defenders isn't going to scare easily, so you're not entirely surprised when Esni looks amused and folds her arms, ready to enjoy the show.

Ykka turns to you, slowly, a look of mingled annoyance and incredulity on her face. She says, "Nice to know you approve," in a tone that sounds anything but pleased. "Not that I actually *care* if you do."

You set your jaw. "You sess it, right? I'd call it the work of a four- or five-ringer, except I know now that ferals can have unusual skill." You mean her. It's an olive branch. Or maybe just flattery.

She doesn't fall for it. "We're going as far as we can before nightfall, and setting up camp in there." She nods toward the forest. "It's too big to get through in a day. Maybe we could go around, but there's something..." Her eyes unfocus, and then she frowns and turns away, grimacing at having revealed a weakness to you. She's sensitive enough to sess the *something*, but not to know exactly what she's sessing.

You're the one who spent years learning to read underground rocks with orogeny, so you fill in the detail. "There's a leaf-covered spike trap in that direction," you say, nodding toward the long-dead grass edging the stone forest on one side. "Beyond it is an area of snares; I can't tell how many, but I can sess a lot of kinetic tension from wire or rope. If we go around the other way, though, there are partially sheared-off stone columns and boulders positioned at points along the edge of the stone forest. Easy to start a rockslide. And I can sess holes positioned at strategic points along the outer columns. A crossbow, or even an ordinary bow and arrow, could do a lot of damage from there."

Ykka sighs. "Yeah. So *through* really is the best way." She eyes Esni, who must have been arguing for *around*. Esni sighs, too, and then shrugs, conceding the argument.

You face Ykka. "Whoever made this forest, if they're still alive, has the skill to precision-ice half the comm in seconds, with little warning. If you're determined to go through, we're going to have to set up a watch/chore rotation—the orogenes with better control, I mean, when I say 'we.' You need to keep us all awake tonight."

She narrows her eyes. "Why?"

"Because if any of us are asleep when the attack comes"—you're pretty sure there'll be an attack—"we'll react instinctively."

Ykka grimaces. She's not the average feral, but she's feral enough to know what will likely happen if something causes her to react orogenically in her sleep. Whoever the attacker doesn't kill, she very well might, completely by accident. "Shit." She looks away for a moment, and you wonder if she doesn't believe you, but apparently she's just thinking. "Fine. We'll split watches, then. Put the roggas not on watch to work, oh, shelling those wild peas we found a few days back. Or repairing the harnesses the Strongbacks use for hauling. Since we'll have to be carried on the wagons tomorrow, when we're too sleepy and useless to walk on our own."

"Right. And—" You hesitate. Not yet. You can't admit your weakness to these women, not yet. But. "Not me."

Ykka's eyes narrow immediately. Esni throws you a skeptical look, as if to say, *And you were doing so well.* Quickly you add, "I don't know what I'm capable of now. After what I did back in Castrima-under... I'm different."

It's not even a lie. Without really thinking about it, you reach for your missing arm, your hand fumbling against the sleeve of your jacket. No one can see the stump, but you're hyperaware of it all of a sudden. Hoa didn't think much of the way Antimony left visible tooth-marks on Alabaster's stumps, it turns out. Yours is smooth, rounded, nearly polished. Rusting perfectionist.

Ykka's gaze follows that self-conscious touch of yours; she winces. "Huh. Yeah, I guess you would be." Her jaw tenses. "Seems like you can sess all right, though."

"Yes. I can help keep watch. I just shouldn't... do anything."

Ykka shakes her head but says, "Fine. You'll take last watch of the night, then."

It's the least desirable watch—when it's coldest, now that the night temperatures have started to dip below freezing. Most people would rather be asleep in warm bedrolls. It's also the most dangerous time of the watch, when any attackers with sense will hit a large group like this in hopes of catching defenders sleepy and sluggish. You can't decide whether this is a sign of trust, or a punishment. Experimentally, you say, "Can I have a weapon, at least?" You haven't carried anything since a few months after

63

you left Tirimo, when you traded away your knife for dried rose hips to stave off scurvy.

"No."

For rust's sake. You start to fold your arms, remember you can't when your empty sleeve twitches, and grimace instead. (Ykka and Esni grimace, too.) "What am I supposed to do, then, yell really loud? Are you seriously going to put the comm at risk because of your grudge against me?"

Ykka rolls her eyes. "For rust's sake." It's so much an echo of your own thought that you frown. "Unbelievable. You think I'm pissed about the geode, don't you?"

You can't help looking at Esni. She stares at Ykka as if to say, *What, you aren't?* It's eloquent enough for both of you.

Ykka glares, then scrubs at her face and lets out a mortal sigh. "Esni, go...shit, go do something Strongbackish. Essie—here. Come *here*. Rusting walk with me." She beckons sharply, in frustration. You're too confused to be offended; she turns to go and you follow. Esni shrugs and walks away.

The two of you move through the camp in silence for a few moments. Everyone seems keenly aware of the danger that the stone forest presents, so this has become one of the busier rest stops you've seen. Some of the Strongbacks are transferring items between the wagons so as to put essentials onto those with sturdier wheels, which will be less heavily loaded. Easier to grab and run under pressure. The Hunters are whittling sharpened poles from some of the dead saplings and branches near the camp. These will be positioned around the perimeter when the comm finally sets up camp, so as to funnel attackers into kill zones. The rest of the Strongbacks are catching naps while they can, knowing they'll either be patrolling or made to sleep on the outer edges of camp when night falls. *Use strong backs to guard them all*, says stonelore. Strongbacks who don't like being human shields can either find a way to distinguish themselves and join another caste, or go join another comm.

Your nose wrinkles as you pass the hastily dug roadside ditch that is currently occupied by six or seven people, with a few of the younger Resistants standing around to do the unhappy duty of shoveling dirt over the results. Unusually, there's a brief line of people waiting for their turn to squat. Not surprising that so many people need to evacuate their bowels at once; here in the looming shadow of the stone forest, everyone's on edge. Nobody wants to get caught with their pants down after dark.

You're thinking you might need to take a turn in the ditch yourself when Ykka surprises you out of this scintillating rumination. "So do you like us yet?"

"What?"

She gestures over the camp. The people of the comm. "You've been with Castrima for the better part of a year now. Got any friends?"

You, you think, before you can stop yourself. "No," you say.

She eyes you for a moment, and guiltily you wonder if she was expecting you to name her. Then she sighs. "Started rolling Lerna yet? No accounting for taste, I guess, but the Breeders say the signs are all there. Me, when I want a man, I pick one who doesn't talk so much. Women are a surer bet. They know not to ruin the mood." She starts to stretch, grimacing as she works out a kink in her back. You use the time to get control of the horrified embarrassment on your face. The rusting Breeders obviously aren't busy enough.

"No," you say.

"Not yet?"

You sigh. "Not . . . yet."

"The rust are you waiting for? The road's not getting any safer."

You glare at her. "I thought you didn't care?"

"I don't. But giving you shit about it is helping me make a point." Ykka's leading you toward the wagons, or so you think at first. Then you move past the wagons, and stiffen in surprise.

Here, seated and eating, are the seven Rennanese prisoners. Even sitting they're different from the people of Castrima—all of the Rennanese being pure Sanzed or close enough not to matter, bigger than average even for that race, with fully grown ashblow manes or shorn-sided braids or short bottlebrushes to heighten the effect. Their prangers have been put aside for the moment—though the chains linking each prisoner to their set are still in place—and there are a few Strongbacks standing guard nearby.

You're surprised that they're eating, since you haven't made full camp for the night yet. The Strongbacks on guard are eating, too, but that only makes sense; they've got a long night ahead of them. The Rennies look up as you and Ykka approach, and that makes you stop in your tracks, because you recognize one of the prisoners. Danel, the *general* of the Rennanis army. She's healthy and whole, apart from red marks around her neck and wrists from the pranger. The last time you saw her up close, she was summoning a shirtless Guardian to kill you.

She recognizes you, too, and her mouth flattens into a resigned, ironic line. Then, very deliberately, she nods to you before turning back to her bowl.

Ykka hunkers down to a crouch beside Danel, to your surprise. "So, how's the food?"

Danel shrugs, still eating. "Better than starving."

"It's good," says another prisoner, across the ring. He shrugs when one of the others glares at him. "Well, it *is*."

"They just want us to be able to haul their wagons," says the man who glared.

"Yeah," Ykka interrupts. "That's precisely right. Strongbacks in Castrima get a comm share and a bed, when we have one to give, in exchange for their contribution. What'd you get from Rennanis?"

"Some rusting pride, maybe," says the glarer, glaring harder.

"Shut up, Phauld," says Danel.

"These mongrels think they—"

Danel sets her bowl of food down. The glarer immediately shuts up and tenses, his eyes going a little wide. After a moment, Danel picks up her bowl and resumes eating. Her expression hasn't changed the whole time. You find yourself suspecting that she's raised children.

Ykka, elbow propped on one knee, rests her chin on her fist and watches Phauld for a moment. To Danel, she says, "So what do you want me to do about that one?"

Phauld immediately frowns. "What?"

Danel shrugs. Her bowl's empty now, but she runs a finger around its curve to sweep up the last sauce. "Not for me to say anymore."

"Doesn't seem very bright." Ykka purses her lips, considering the man. "Not bad-looking, but harder to breed for brains than looks."

Danel says nothing for a moment, while Phauld looks from her to Ykka and back in growing incredulity. Then, with a heavy sigh, Danel looks up at Phauld, too. "What do you want me to say? I'm not his commander anymore. Never wanted to be in the first place; I got drafted. Now I don't rusting care."

"I can't believe you," Phauld says. His voice is too loud, rising in panic. "I *fought* for you."

"And lost." Danel shakes her head. "Now it's about surviving, adapting. Forget all that crap you heard back in Rennanis about Sanzeds and mongrels; that was just propaganda to unite the comm. Things are different now. 'Necessity is the only law.'"

"Don't you rusting quote stonelore at me!"

"She's quoting stonelore because you don't *get* it," snaps the other man—the one who liked the food. "They're feeding us. They're letting us be useful. It's a test, you stupid shit. To see if we're willing to earn a place in this comm!"

"*This comm?*" Phauld gestures around at the camp. His laugh echoes off the rock faces. People look around, trying to figure out if the yelling means there's some kind of problem. "Do you hear yourself? These people haven't got a chance. They should be finding somewhere to bunker down, maybe rebuild one of the comms we razed along the way. Instead—"

Ykka moves with a casualness that doesn't deceive you. Everyone could see this coming, including Phauld, but he's too stubborn to acknowledge reality. She stands up and unnecessarily brushes ash off her shoulders and steps across the circle and then puts a hand on the crown of Phauld's head. He tries to twitch back, swatting at her. "Don't rusting touch—"

But then he stops. His eyes glaze over. Ykka's done that thing to him—the thing she did to Cutter back in Castrima-under when people were working themselves into an orogene-lynching mob. Because you knew it was coming this time, you're able to get a better handle on how she does the strange pulse. It's definitely magic, some kind of manipulation of the thin, silvery filaments that dance and flicker between the motes of a person's substance. Ykka's pulse cuts through the knot of threads at the base of Phauld's brain, just above the sessapinae. Everything's still intact physically, but magically it's as if she's chopped his head off.

He sags backward, and Ykka steps aside to let him flop bonelessly to the ground.

One of the other Rennanis women gasps and scoots back, her chains jangling. The guards glance at each other, uncomfortably, but they're not surprised; word of what Ykka did to Cutter spread through the comm afterward. A Rennanese man who hasn't spoken before utters a swift oath in one of the Coaster creole languages; it's not Eturpic so you don't understand it, but his fear is clear enough. Danel only sighs.

Ykka sighs, too, looking at the dead man. Then she eyes Danel. "I'm sorry."

Danel smiles thinly. "We tried. And you said it yourself: He wasn't very bright."

Ykka nods. For some reason she glances up at you for a moment. You have no idea what lesson you're supposed to take from this. "Unlock the manacles," she says. You're confused for an instant before you realize it's an order for the guards. One of them moves over to speak to the other, and they start sorting through a ring of keys. Then Ykka looks disgusted with herself as she says heavily, "Who's on quartermaster duty today? Memsid? Tell him and some of the other Resistants to come handle this." She jerks her head toward Phauld.

Everyone goes still. No one protests, though. The Hunters have been finding more game and forage, but Castrima has a lot of people who need more protein than they've been getting, and the desert is coming. It was always going to come to this.

After a moment of silence, though, you step over to Ykka. "You sure about this?" you ask softly. One of the guards comes over to unlock Danel's ankle chains. Danel, who tried to kill every living member of Castrima. Danel, who tried to kill *you*.

"Why wouldn't I be?" Ykka shrugs. Her voice is loud enough that the prisoners can hear her. "We've been short on Strongbacks since Rennanis attacked. Now we've got six replacements."

"Replacements who'll stab us—or maybe just you—in the back first chance!"

"If I don't see them coming and kill them first, yeah. But that would be pretty stupid of them, and I killed the stupidest one for a reason." You get the sense that Ykka's not trying to scare the Rennanis people. She's just stating facts. "See, this is what I keep trying to tell you, Essie: The world isn't friends and enemies. It's people who might help you, and people who'll get in your way. Kill this lot and what do you get?"

"*Safety.*"

"Lots of ways to be safe. Yeah, there's now a bigger chance I'll get shanked in the night. More safety for the comm, though.

And the stronger the comm is, the better the chance we'll all get to Rennanis alive." She shrugs, then glances around at the stone forest. "Whoever built this is one of us, with real skill. We're going to need that."

"What, now you want to adopt..." You shake your head, incredulous. "Violent bandit ferals?"

But then you stop. Because once upon a time, you loved a violent pirate feral.

Ykka watches while you remember Innon and mourn him anew. Then, with remarkable gentleness, she says, "I play a longer game than just making it to the next day, Essie. Maybe you ought to try it for a change."

You look away, feeling oddly defensive. The luxury of thinking beyond the next day isn't something you've ever had much of a chance to try. "I'm not a headwoman. I'm just a *rogga*."

Ykka tilts her head in ironic acknowledgment. You don't use that word nearly as often as she does. When she says it, it's pride. When you use it, it's assault.

"Well, I'm both," Ykka says. "A headwoman, and a rogga. I *choose to be* both, and more." She steps past you, and throws her next words at you over her shoulder, as if they're meaningless. "You didn't think about any of us while you were using those obelisks, did you? You thought about destroying your enemies. You thought about surviving—but you couldn't get beyond that. That's why I've been so pissed at you, Essie. Months in my comm, and still *all you are* is 'just a rogga.'"

She walks off then, yelling to everyone in earshot that the rest break is over. You watch until she vanishes amid the stretching, grumbling crowd, then you glance over at Danel, who's since stood up and is rubbing the red mark on one of her wrists. There's a carefully neutral look on the woman's face as she watches you.

"She dies, you die," you say. If Ykka won't look after herself, you'll do what you can for her.

Danel lets out a brief, amused breath. "That's true whether you threaten me or not. Not like anybody else here would give me a chance." She throws you a skeptical look, all her Sanzed pride completely intact despite the change in circumstances. "You really *aren't* very good at this, are you?"

Earthfires and rustbuckets. You walk away, because if Ykka already thinks less of you for destroying all threats, she's really not going to like it if you start killing people who annoy you, for sheer pique.

* * *

2562: Niner shake in Western Coastals, epicenter somewhere in Baga Quartent. Lorist accounts from the time note that the shake "turned the ground to liquid." (Poetic?) One fishing village survived intact. From a villager's written account: "Bastard roggye killed lah shake then we killed hym." Report filed at the Fulcrum (shared with permission) by Imperial Orogene who later visited the area notes also that an underwater oil reservoir off the coast could have been breached by the shake, but the unregistered rogga in the village prevented this. Would have poisoned water and beaches for miles down the coast.

—*Project notes of Yaetr Innovator Dibars*

4

Nassun, wandering in the wilderness

SCHAFFA IS KIND ENOUGH TO guide the other eight children of Found Moon out of Jekity along with Nassun and himself. He tells the headwoman that they're all going on a training trip some miles away so that the comm won't be disturbed by additional seismics. Since Nassun has just returned the sapphire to the sky—loudly, thanks to the thunderclap of displaced air; dramatically, because suddenly there it was overhead, huge and deep blue and too close—the headwoman just about falls over herself to provide the children with runny-sacks containing travel food and supplies so they can hurry on their way. These aren't the kinds of top-notch supplies one needs for a long journey. No compasses, only moderately good boots, the kinds of rations that won't last more than a couple of weeks before going bad. Still, it's much better than leaving empty-handed.

None of the people of the comm know that Umber and Nida are dead. Schaffa carried their bodies into the Guardians' dorm and laid them out on their respective beds, arranged in dignified poses. This worked better for Nida, who looked more or less intact but for the nape of her neck, than Umber, whose head was a ruin. Schaffa then threw dirt over the bloodstains. Jekity will figure it out eventually, but by that time, Found Moon's children will be out of reach, if not safe.

Jija, Schaffa left piled where Nassun felled him. The corpse is nothing but a pile of pretty rocks, really, until one looks closely at some of the pieces.

The children are subdued as they leave the comm that has sheltered them, in some cases for years. They leave via the rogga steps, as they have come to be informally (and rudely) called—the series of basalt columns on the comm's north side that only orogenes can traverse. Wudeh's orogeny is steadier than Nassun has ever sessed it when he takes them down to ground level by pushing one of the pieces of columnar basalt back into the ancient volcano. Still, she can see the look of despair on his face, and it makes her ache inside.

They walk westward as a group, but before they've gone a mile, one or two of the children are quietly weeping. Nassun, whose eyes have remained dry even through stray thoughts like *I killed my father* and *Daddy, I miss you*, grieves with them. It's cruel that they must suffer this, being ashed out during a Season, because of what she has done. (Because of what Jija tried to do, she tries to tell herself, but she does not believe this.) Yet it would be crueler still to leave them in Jekity, where the commfolk will eventually realize what has happened and turn on the children.

Oegin and Ynegen, the twins, are the only ones who look at Nassun with anything resembling understanding. They were the first to come outside after Nassun snatched the sapphire out of the sky. While the others mostly saw Schaffa fight Umber, and Steel kill Nida, those two saw what Jija tried to do to Nassun. They understand that Nassun fought back as anyone would have. Everyone, though, remembers that she killed Eitz. Some have since forgiven her for that, as Schaffa predicted—especially shy, scarred Peek, who privately spoke to Nassun of what she did to the grandmother who stabbed her in the face so long ago. Orogene children learn early what it means to regret.

That doesn't mean they don't still fear Nassun, though, and fear lends a clarity that cuts right through childish rationalizations. They are not killers at heart, after all...and Nassun is.

(She does not want to be, any more than you do.)

Now the group stands at a literal crossroads, where a local trail running northeast to southeast meets the more westerly Jekity-Tevamis Imperial Road. Schaffa says the Imperial Road will eventually lead to a highroad, which is something Nassun has heard of but never seen in all her travels. The crossroads, however, is the place where Schaffa has chosen to inform the other children that they can follow him no longer.

Shirk is the only one who protests this. "We won't eat much," she says to Schaffa, a little desperately. "You...you don't have to feed us. You could just let us follow you. We'll find our own food. I know how!"

"Nassun and I will likely be pursued," Schaffa says. His voice is unfailingly gentle. Nassun knows that this delivery actually makes the words worse; his gentleness makes it easy to see that Schaffa truly cares. Farewells are easier when they are cruel.

"We will also be making a long journey that's very dangerous. You're safer on your own."

"Safer commless," Wudeh says, and laughs. It's the most bitter sound Nassun has ever heard him utter.

Shirk has started to cry. The tears leave streaks of startling cleanliness in the ash that's beginning to gray her face. "I don't understand. You took care of us. You *like* us, Schaffa, more than even Nida and Umber did! Why would you... if you were just going to—to..."

"Stop it," says Lashar. She's gotten taller in the past year, like a good well-bred Sanzed girl. While most of her my-grandfather-was-an-Equatorial arrogance has faded with time, she still defaults to hauteur when she's upset about something. She's folded her arms and is looking away from the trail, off at a group of bare foothills in the near distance. "Have some rusting pride. We've been ashed, but we're still alive and that's what matters. We can take shelter in those hills for the night."

Shirk glares at her. "There isn't any shelter! We're going to *starve to death*, or—"

"We won't." Deshati, who's been looking at the ground while she scuffs the still-thin ash with one foot, looks up suddenly. She's watching Schaffa as she speaks to Shirk and the others. "There are places we can live. We just have to get them to open the gates."

There's a tight, determined look on her face. Schaffa turns a sharp gaze on Deshati, and to her credit, she does not flinch. "You mean to force your way in?" he asks her.

"That's what you want us to do, isn't it? You wouldn't be

sending us away if you weren't okay with us...doing what we have to." She tries to shrug. She's too tense for such a casual gesture; it makes her look briefly twitchy, as if with a palsy. "We wouldn't still be alive if you weren't okay with that."

Nassun looks at the ground. It's her fault that the other children's choices have been whittled down to this. There was beauty in Found Moon; among her fellow children, Nassun has known the delight of reveling in what she is and what she can do, among people who understand and share that delight. Now something once wholesome and good is dead.

You'll kill everything you love, eventually, Steel has told her. She hates that he is right.

Schaffa regards the children for a long, thoughtful moment. His fingers twitch, perhaps remembering another life and another self who could not have endured the idea of unleashing eight young Misalems upon the world. That version of Schaffa, however, is dead. The twitch is only reflexive.

"Yes," he says. "That is what I want you to do, if you need to hear it said aloud. You have a better chance in a large, thriving comm than you do on your own. So allow me to make a suggestion." Schaffa steps forward and crouches to look Deshati in the eye, reaching out also to grip Shirk's thin shoulder. He says to all of them, with that same gentle intensity that he used before, "Kill only one, initially. Pick someone who tries to harm you— but only one, even if more than one tries. Disable the others, but take your time killing that one person. Make it painful. Make sure your target screams. That's important. If the first one that you kill remains silent...kill another."

They stare back at him. Even Lashar seems nonplussed. Nassun, however, has seen Schaffa kill. He has given up some of who he was, but what remains is still an artist of terror. If he has seen fit to share the secrets of his artistry with them, they're lucky. She hopes they appreciate it.

He goes on. "When the killing is done, make it clear to those present that you acted only in self-defense. Then offer to work in the dead person's place, or to protect the rest from danger—but they'll recognize the ultimatum. They *must* accept you into the comm." He pauses, then fixes his icewhite gaze on Deshati. "If they refuse, what do you do?"

She swallows. "K-kill them all."

He smiles again, for the first time since leaving Jekity, and cups the back of her head in fond approval.

Shirk gasps a little, shocked out of tears. Oegin and Ynegen hold each other, their expressions empty of anything but despair. Lashar's jaw has tightened, her nostrils flaring. She means to take Schaffa's words to heart. Deshati does, too, Nassun can tell...but it will kill something in Deshati to do so.

Schaffa knows this. When he stands to kiss Deshati's forehead, there is so much sorrow in the gesture that Nassun aches afresh. "'All things change during a Season,'" he says. "*Live. I want you to live.*"

A tear spills from one of Deshati's eyes before she can blink it away. She swallows audibly. But then she nods and steps away from him, and backs up to stand with the others. There's a gulf between them now: Schaffa and Nassun on one side, Found Moon's children on the other. The ways have parted. Schaffa does not show discomfort with this. He should; Nassun notices that the silver is alive and throbbing within him, protesting his choice to allow these children to go free. He does not show the pain, though. When he's doing what he feels is right, pain only strengthens him.

He stands. "And should the Season ever show real signs of abating...flee. Scatter and blend in elsewhere as best you can. The Guardians aren't dead, little ones. They will return. And once word spreads of what you've done, they'll come for you."

The regular Guardians, Nassun knows he means—the "uncontaminated" ones, like he used to be. Those Guardians have been missing since the start of the Season, or at least Nassun hasn't heard of any joining comms or being seen on the road. *Return* suggests they've all gone somewhere specific. Where? Somewhere that Schaffa and the other contaminated ones did not or could not go.

But what matters is that *this* Guardian, however contaminated, is helping them. Nassun feels a sudden surge of irrational hope. Surely Schaffa's advice will keep them safe, somehow. So she swallows and adds, "All of you are really good at orogeny. Maybe the comm you pick...maybe they'll..."

She trails off, unsure of what she wants to say. *Maybe they'll like you*, is what she's thinking, but that just seems foolish. Or *maybe you can be useful*, but that's not how it used to work. Comms used to hire Fulcrum orogenes only for brief periods, or so Schaffa has told her, to do needed work and then leave. Even comms near hot spots and fault lines hadn't wanted orogenes around permanently, no matter how much they'd needed them.

Before Nassun can think of a way to grope out the words, however, Wudeh glares at her. "Shut up."

Nassun blinks. "What?"

Peek hisses at Wudeh, trying to shush him, but he ignores her. "Shut up. I rusting hate you. Nida used to sing to me." Then, without warning, he bursts into sobs. Peek looks confused, but some of the others surround him, murmuring and patting comfort into him.

Lashar watches this, then throws a last reproachful look at Nassun before saying, to Schaffa, "We'll be on our way, then. Thank you, Guardian, for...for what it's worth."

She turns and begins herding them away. Deshati walks with her head down, not looking back. Ynegen lingers for a moment between the groups, then glances at Nassun and whispers, "Sorry." Then she, too, leaves, hurrying to catch up with the others.

As soon as the children are completely out of sight, Schaffa puts a hand on Nassun's shoulder to steer her away, westward along the Imperial Road.

After several miles of silence, she says, "Do you still think it would have been better to kill them?"

"Yes." He glances at her. "And you know that as well as I do."

Nassun sets her jaw. "I know." All the more reason to stop this. Stop everything.

"You have a destination in mind," Schaffa says. It's not a question.

"Yes. I...Schaffa, I have to go to the other side of the world." This feels rather like saying *I need to go to a star*, but since that's not too far off from what she actually needs to do, she decides not to feel self-conscious about this smaller absurdity.

To her surprise, however, he tilts his head instead of laughing. "To Corepoint?"

"What?"

"A city on the other side of the world. There?"

She swallows, bites her lip. "I don't know. I just know that what I need is—" She doesn't have the words for it, and instead makes a pantomime with her cupped hands and waggling fingers, sending imaginary wavelets to clash and mesh with each other. "The obelisks...pull on that place. It's what they're made to do. If I go there, I think I might be able to, uh, pull back? I can't do it anywhere else, because..." She can't explain it. Lines of force, lines of sight, mathematical configurations; all of the knowledge that she needs is in her mind, but cannot be reproduced by her tongue. Some of this is a gift from the sapphire, and some is application of theories her mother taught her, and some is simply from tying theory to observation and wrapping the whole thing in instinct. "I don't know which city over there is the right one. If I get closer, and travel around a little, maybe I can—"

"Corepoint is the only thing on that side of the world, little one."

"It's...what?"

Schaffa stops abruptly, tugging off his pack. Nassun does the same, reading this as a signal that it's time for a rest stop. They're just on the leeward side of a hill, which is really just a spar of old lava from the great volcano that lies beneath Jekity. There are natural terraces all around this area, weathered out of the obsidian by wind and rain, though the rock a few inches down is too hard for farming or even much in the way of forestation. Some determined, shallow-rooted trees wave over the empty, ash-frosted terraces, but most are now being killed by the ashfall. Nassun and Schaffa will be able to see potential threats coming from a good ways off.

While Nassun pulls out some food they can share, Schaffa draws something in a nearby patch of windblown ash with his finger. Nassun cranes her neck to see that he's made two circles on the ground. In one, he sketches a rough outline of the Stillness that is familiar to Nassun from geography lessons back in creche—except this time, he draws the Stillness in two pieces, with a line of separation near the equator. The Rifting, yes, which has become a boundary more impassable than even thousands of miles of ocean.

The other circle, however, which Nassun now understands to be a representation of the world, he leaves blank save for a single spot just above the equator and slightly to the east of the circle's middle longitude. He doesn't sketch an island or continent to put it on. Just that lone dot.

"Once, there were more cities on the empty face of the world," Schaffa explains. "A few civilizations have built upon or under the sea, over the millennia. None of those lasted long, though. All that remains is Corepoint."

It is literally a world away. "How could we get there?"

"If—" He pauses. Nassun's belly clenches when the blurry look crosses his face. This time he winces and shuts his eyes, too, as if even the attempt to access his old self has added to his pain.

"You don't remember?"

He sighs. "I remember that I used to."

Nassun realizes she should have expected this. She bites her lip. "Steel might know."

There is a slight flex of muscle along Schaffa's jaw, quick and there and then gone. "Indeed he might."

Steel, who vanished while Schaffa was putting away the other Guardians' bodies, might also be listening from within the stone somewhere nearby. Does it mean something that he hasn't popped up to tell them what to do yet? Maybe they don't need him. "And what about the Antarctic Fulcrum? Don't they have records and things?" She remembers seeing the Fulcrum's library before she and Schaffa and Umber sat down with its leaders, had a cup of safe, then killed them all. The library was a strange high room filled floor to ceiling with shelves of books. Nassun likes books—her mother used to splurge and buy one every few months, and sometimes Nassun got the hand-me-downs if Jija deemed them appropriate for children—and she remembers boggling in awe, for she'd never seen so many books in her life. Surely some of those contained information about... very old cities no one has ever heard of, that only Guardians know how to get to. Um. Hmm.

"Unlikely," Schaffa says, confirming Nassun's misgivings. "And by now, that Fulcrum has probably been annexed by another comm, or perhaps even taken over by commless rabble. Its fields were full of edible crops, after all, and its houses were livable. Returning there would be a mistake."

Nassun bites her lower lip. "Maybe... a boat?" She doesn't know anything about boats.

"No, little one. A boat won't do for such a long journey."

He pauses significantly, and with this as warning Nassun tries to brace herself. Here is where he will abandon her, she feels painfully, fearfully certain. Here is where he will want to know what she's up to—and then want no part of it. Why would he? Even she knows that what she wants is a terrible thing.

"I take it, then," Schaffa says, "that you mean to assume control of the Obelisk Gate."

Nassun gasps. Schaffa knows what the Obelisk Gate is? When Nassun herself only learned the term that morning from Steel? But then, the lore of the world, all its strange mechanisms and workings and aeons of secrets, is mostly still intact within Schaffa. It's only things connected to his old self that are permanently lost...which means that the route to Corepoint is something that Old Schaffa needed to know, particularly. What does that mean? "Uh, yes. That's why I want to go to Corepoint."

His mouth quirks at her surprise. "Finding an orogene who could activate the Gate was our original purpose, Nassun, in creating Found Moon."

"What? Why?"

Schaffa glances up at the sky. The sun's beginning to set. They could get maybe another hour of walking in before it gets too dark to continue. What he's looking at is the sapphire, though, which hasn't noticeably moved from its position over Jekity. Rubbing absently at the back of his head, Schaffa gazes at its faint outline through the thickening clouds and nods, as if to himself.

"I and Nida and Umber," he says. "Perhaps ten years ago, we

were all…instructed…to travel southward, and to find one another. We were bidden to seek and train any orogenes who had the potential to connect to obelisks. This is not a thing Guardians normally do, understand, because there can be only one reason to encourage an orogene along the obelisk path. But it's what the Earth wanted. Why, I don't know. During that time, I was…less questioning." His mouth curves in a brief, rueful smile. "Now I have guesses."

Nassun frowns. "What guesses?"

"That the Earth has its own plans for human—"

Abruptly Schaffa tenses all over, and he sways in his crouch. Quickly Nassun grabs him so he won't fall over, and reflexively he puts an arm around her shoulders. The arm is very tight, but she does not protest. That he needs the comfort of her presence is obvious. That the Earth is angrier than ever with him, perhaps because he's giving away its secrets, is as palpable as the raw, flensing pulse of the silver along every nerve and between every cell of his body.

"Don't talk," Nassun says, her throat tight. "Don't say anything else. If it's going to hurt you like this—"

"It does not rule me." Schaffa has to say this in quick blurts, between pants. "It did not take the core of me. I may have… nnh…put myself into its kennel, but it cannot *leash* me."

"I know." Nassun bites her lip. He's leaning on her heavily, and that's made her knee, where it braces against the ground, ache something awful. She doesn't care, though. "But you don't have to say everything *now*. I'm figuring it out on my own."

She has all the clues, she thinks. Nida once said, of Nassun's ability to connect to obelisks, *This is a thing that we culled for in the Fulcrum.* Nassun hadn't understood at the time, but after perceiving something of the Obelisk Gate's immensity, now she can guess why Father Earth wants her dead if she is no longer under Schaffa's—and through him, the Earth's—control.

Nassun chews her lip. Will Schaffa understand? She isn't sure she can take it if he decides to leave—or worse, if he turns on her. So she takes a deep breath. "Steel says the Moon is coming back."

For an instant there is silence from Schaffa's direction. It has the weight of surprise. "The Moon."

"It's real," she blurts. She has no idea if this is true, though, does she? There's only Steel's word to go on. She's not even sure what a moon is, beyond being Father Earth's long-lost child, like the tales say. And yet somehow she knows that this much of what Steel says is true. She doesn't quite sess it, and there are no telltale threads of silver forming in the sky, but she believes it the way she believes that there is another side of the world even though she's never seen it, and the way she knows how mountains form, and the way she's certain Father Earth is real and alive and an enemy. Some truths are simply too great to deny.

To her surprise, however, Schaffa says, "Oh, I know the Moon is real." Perhaps his pain has faded somewhat; now his expression has hardened as he gazes at the hazy, intermittent disc of the sun where it's managed to not quite pierce the clouds near the horizon. "That, I remember."

"You—really? Then you believe Steel?"

"I believe *you*, little one, because orogenes know the pull of the Moon when it draws near. Awareness of it is as natural to you as sessing shakes. But also, I have seen it." Then his gaze narrows sharply to focus on Nassun. "Why, then, did the stone eater tell you about the Moon?"

Nassun takes a deep breath and lets out a heavy sigh.

"I really just wanted to live somewhere nice," she says. "Live somewhere with…with you. I wouldn't have minded working and doing things to be a good comm member. I could have been a lorist, maybe." She feels her jaw tighten. "But I can't do that, not anywhere. Not without having to hide what I am. I *like* orogeny, Schaffa, when I don't have to hide it. I don't think having it, being a—a r-rogga—" She has to stop, and blush, and shake off the urge to feel ashamed for saying such a bad word, but the bad word is the right word for now. "I don't think being one makes me bad or strange or evil—"

She cuts herself off again, yanks her thoughts out of that track, because it leads right back to *But you have done such evil things*.

Unconsciously, Nassun bares her teeth and clenches her fists. "It isn't *right*, Schaffa. It isn't right that people want me to be bad or strange or evil, that they *make* me be bad…" She shakes her head, fumbling for words. "I just want to be ordinary! But I'm not and—and everybody, a lot of people, all *hate* me because I'm not ordinary. You're the only person who doesn't hate me for…for being what I am. And that's not right."

"No, it isn't." Schaffa shifts to sit back against his pack, looking weary. "But you speak as though it's an easy thing to ask people to overcome their fears, little one."

And he does not say it, but suddenly Nassun thinks: *Jija couldn't.*

Nassun's gorge rises suddenly, sharply enough that she must clap a fist to her mouth for a moment and think hard of ash and how cold her ears are. There's nothing in her stomach except the handful of dates she just ate, but the feeling is awful anyway.

Schaffa, uncharacteristically, does not move to comfort her. He only watches her, expression weary but otherwise unreadable.

"I know they can't do it." Yes. Speaking helps. Her stomach doesn't settle, but she no longer feels on the brink of dry heaves. "I know they—the stills—won't ever stop being afraid. If my father couldn't—" Queasiness. She jerks her thoughts away from the end of that sentence. "They'll just go on being scared forever, and we'll just go on living like this forever, and *it isn't right*. There should be a—a fix. It isn't right that there's no *end* to it."

"But do you mean to impose a fix, little one?" Schaffa asks. It's soft. He's guessed already, she realizes. He knows her so much better than she knows herself, and she loves him for it. "Or an end?"

She gets to her feet and starts pacing, tight little circles between his pack and hers. It helps the nausea and the jittery, rising tension beneath her skin that she cannot name. "I don't know how to fix it."

But that is not the whole truth, and Schaffa scents lies the way predators scent blood. His eyes narrow. "If you did know how, *would* you fix it?"

And then, in a sudden blaze of memory that Nassun has not

permitted herself to see or consider for more than a year, she remembers her last day in Tirimo.

Coming home. Seeing her father standing in the middle of the den breathing hard. Wondering what was wrong with him. Wondering why he did not quite look like her father, in that moment—his eyes too wide, his mouth too loose, his shoulders hunched in a way that seemed painful. And then Nassun remembers looking down.

Looking down and staring and staring and thinking *What is that?* and staring and thinking *Is it a ball?* like the ones that the kids at creche kick around during lunchtime, except those balls are made of leather while the thing at her father's feet is a different shade of brown, brown with purplish mottling all over its surface, lumpy and leathery and half-deflated but *No, it's not a ball, wait is that an eye?* Maybe but it's so swollen shut that it looks like a big fat coffee bean. *Not a ball at all* because it's wearing her brother's clothes including the pants Nassun put on him that morning while Jija was busy trying to get their lunch satchels together for creche. *Uche didn't want to wear those pants* because he was still a baby and liked to be silly so Nassun had done the butt dance for him and he'd laughed so hard, so hard! His laugh was her favorite thing ever, and when the butt dance was over he'd let her put his pants on as a thank-you, which means the unrecognizable deflated ball-thing on the floor is *Uche that is Uche he is Uche*—

"No," Nassun breathes. "I wouldn't fix it. Not even if I knew how."

She has stopped pacing. She has one arm wrapped around her middle. The other hand is a fist, crammed against her mouth. She spits out words around it now, she chokes on them as they gush up her throat, she clutches her belly, which is full of such terrible things that she must let them out somehow or be torn apart from within. These things have distorted her voice, made it a shaky growl that randomly spikes into a higher pitch and a louder volume, because it's everything she can do not to just start screaming. "I *wouldn't* fix it, Schaffa, I wouldn't, I'm sorry, I don't *want* to fix it I want to *kill everybody that hates me*—"

Her middle is so heavy that she can't stand. Nassun drops into a crouch, then to her knees. She wants to vomit but instead she spits words onto the ground between her splayed hands. "*G-g-gone! I want it all GONE, Schaffa! I want it to BURN, I want it burned up and dead and gone, gone, NOTHING l-l-left, no more hate and no more killing just nothing, r-rusting nothing, nothing FOREVER*—"

Schaffa's hands, hard and strong, pull her up. She flails against him, tries to hit him. It isn't malice or fear. She never *wants* to hurt him. She just has to let some of what's in her out somehow, or she will go mad. For the first time she understands her father, as she screams and kicks and punches and bites and yanks at her clothes and her hair and tries to slam her forehead against his. Quickly, Schaffa turns her about and wraps one of his big arms around her, pinning her arms to her sides so that she cannot hurt him or herself in the transport of her rage.

This is what Jija felt, observes a distant, detached, floating-obelisk part of herself. *This is what came up inside him when he realized Mama lied, and I lied, and Uche lied. This is what made him push me off the wagon. This is why he came up to Found Moon this morning with a glassknife in his hand.*

This. This is the Jija in her, making her thrash and shout and weep. She feels closer than ever to her father in this moment of utter broken rage.

Schaffa holds her until she is exhausted. Finally she slumps, shaking and panting and moaning a little, her face all over tears and snot.

When it's clear that Nassun will not lash out again, Schaffa shifts to sit down cross-legged, pulling Nassun into his lap. She curls against him the way another child curled against him once, many years before and many miles away, when he told her to pass a test for him so that she could live. Nassun's test has already been met, though; even the old Schaffa would agree with that assessment. In all her rage, Nassun's orogeny did not twitch once, and she did not reach for the silver at all.

"Shhh," Schaffa soothes. He's been doing this all the while, though now he rubs her back and thumbs away her occasional tears. "Shhh. Poor thing. How unfair of me. When only this morning—" He sighs. "Shhh, my little one. Just rest."

Nassun is wrung out and empty of everything but the grief and fury that run in her like fast lahars, grinding everything else away in a churning hot slurry. Grief and fury and one last precious, whole feeling.

"You're the only one I love, Schaffa." Her voice is raw and weary. "You're the only reason I w-wouldn't. But...but I..."

He kisses her forehead. "Make the end you need, my Nassun."

"I don't want." She has to swallow. "I want you to—to be alive!"

He laughs softly. "Still a child, despite all you've been through." This stings, but his meaning is clear. She cannot have both Schaffa alive and the world's hatred dead. She must choose one ending or the other.

But then, firmly, Schaffa says again: "Make the end you need."

Nassun pulls back so she can look at him. He's smiling again, clear-eyed. "What?"

He squeezes her, very gently. "You're my redemption, Nassun. You are all the children I should have loved and protected, even from myself. And if it will bring you peace..." He kisses her forehead. "Then I shall be your Guardian till the world burns, my little one."

It is a benediction, and a balm. The nausea finally releases its hold on Nassun. In Schaffa's arms, safe and accepted, she sleeps at last, amid dreams of a world glowing and molten and in its own way, at peace.

* * *

"Steel," she calls, the next morning.

Steel blurs into presence before them, standing in the middle of the road with his arms folded and an expression of faint amusement on his face.

"The nearest way to Corepoint is not far, relatively speaking," he says when she has asked him for the knowledge that Schaffa lacks. "A month's travel or so. Of course..." He lets this trail off, conspicuously. He has offered to take Nassun and Schaffa to the other side of the world himself, which is apparently a thing that stone eaters can do. It would save them a great deal of hardship and danger, but they would have to entrust themselves to Steel's care as he transports them in the strange, terrifying manner of his kind, through the earth.

"No, thank you," Nassun says again. She doesn't ask Schaffa for his opinion on this, though he leans against a boulder nearby. She doesn't need to ask him. That Steel's interest is wholly in Nassun is obvious. It would be nothing to him to simply forget to bring Schaffa—or lose him along the way to Corepoint. "But could you tell us about this place we have to go? Schaffa doesn't remember."

Steel's gray gaze shifts to Schaffa. Schaffa smiles back, deceptively serene. Even the silver inside him goes still, just for this moment. Maybe Father Earth doesn't like Steel, either.

"It's called a *station*," Steel explains, after a moment. "It's old. You would call it a deadciv ruin, although this one is still intact, nestled within another set of ruins that aren't. A long time ago, people used stations, or rather the vehicles kept within them, to travel long distances far more efficiently than walking. These days, however, only we stone eaters and the Guardians remember that the stations exist." His smile, which hasn't changed since he appeared, is still and wry. It seems meant for Schaffa somehow.

"We all pay a price for power," Schaffa says. His voice is cool and smooth in that way he gets when he's thinking about doing bad things.

"Yes." Steel pauses for just a beat too long. "A price must be paid to use this method of transportation, as well."

"We don't have any money or anything good to barter," Nassun says, troubled.

"Fortunately, there are other ways to pay." Steel abruptly stands at a different angle, his face tilted upward. Nassun follows this, turning, and sees—oh. The sapphire, which has gotten a little closer overnight. Now it's halfway between them and Jekity.

"The station," Steel continues, "is from a time before the Seasons. The time when the obelisks were built. All the lingering artifacts of that civilization recognize the same power source."

"You mean..." Nassun inhales. "The silver."

"Is that what you call it? How poetic."

Nassun shrugs uncomfortably. "I don't know what else to call it."

"Oh, how the world has changed." Nassun frowns, but Steel does not explain this cryptic statement. "Stay on this road until you reach the Old Man's Pucker. Do you know where that is?"

Nassun remembers seeing it on maps of the Antarctics a lifetime ago, and giggling at the name. She glances at Schaffa, who nods and says, "We can find it."

"Then I'll meet you there. The ruin is at the exact center of the grass forest, within the inner ring. Enter the Pucker just after dawn. Don't dawdle reaching the center; you won't want to still be in the forest after dusk." Then Steel pauses, shifting into a new position—one that is distinctly thoughtful. His face is turned off to the side, fingers touching his chin. "I thought it would be your mother."

Schaffa goes still. Nassun is surprised by the flash of heat, then cold, that moves through her. Slowly, while sifting through this strange complexity of emotion, she says, "What do you mean?"

"I expected her to be the one to do this, is all." Steel doesn't shrug, but something in his voice suggests nonchalance. "I threatened her comm. Her friends, the people she cares about now. I thought they would turn on her, and then this choice would seem more palatable to her."

The people she cares about now. "She's not in Tirimo anymore?"

"No. She has joined another comm."

"And they ... didn't turn on her?"

"No. Surprisingly." Steel's eyes slide over to meet Nassun's. "She knows where you are now. The Gate told her. But she isn't coming, or at least not yet. She wants to see her friends safely settled first."

Nassun sets her jaw. "I'm not in Jekity anymore, anyway. And soon she won't have the Gate, either, so she won't be able to find me again."

Steel turns fully to face her, this movement too slow and human-smooth to be human, though his astonishment seems genuine. She hates it when he moves slowly. It makes her get goose bumps.

"Nothing lasts forever, indeed," he says.

"What's that mean?"

"Only that I've underestimated you, little Nassun." Nassun instantly dislikes this term of address. He shifts again to the thoughtful pose, fast this time, to her relief. "I think I'd better not do so again."

With that, he vanishes. Nassun frowns at Schaffa, who shakes his head. They shoulder their packs and head west.

*   *   *

2400: Eastern Equatorials (check if node network was thin in this area, because . . .), unknown comm. Old local song about a nurse who stopped a sudden eruption and pyroclastic flow by turning it to ice. One of her patients threw himself in front of a crossbow bolt to protect her from the mob. Mob let her go; she vanished.

—*Project notes of Yaetr Innovator Dibars*

Syl Anagist: Four

ALL ENERGY IS THE SAME, through its different states and names. Movement creates heat which is also light that waves like sound which tightens or loosens the atomic bonds of crystal as they hum with strong and weak forces. In mirroring resonance with all of this is magic, the radiant emission of life and death.

This is our role: To weave together those disparate energies. To manipulate and mitigate and, through the prism of our awareness, produce a singular force that cannot be denied. To make of cacophony, symphony. The great machine called the Plutonic Engine is the instrument. We are its tuners.

And this is the goal: Geoarcanity. Geoarcanity seeks to establish an energetic cycle of infinite efficiency. If we are successful, the world will never know want or strife again...or so we are told. The conductors explain little beyond what we must know to fulfill our roles. It is enough to know that we—small, unimportant *we*—will help to set humanity on a new path toward an unimaginably bright future. We may be tools, but we are fine ones, put to a magnificent purpose. It is easy to find pride in that.

We are attuned enough to each other that the loss of Tetlewha causes trouble for a time. When we join to form our initializing network, it's imbalanced. Tetlewha was our countertenor, the half wavelengths of the spectrum; without him I am closest, but my natural resonance is a little high. The resulting network is weaker than it should be. Our feeder threads keep trying to reach for Tetlewha's empty middle range.

Gaewha is able to compensate for the loss, finally. She reaches deeper, resonates more powerfully, and this plugs the gap. We must spend several days reforging all the network's connections to create new harmony, but it isn't difficult to do this, just time-consuming. This isn't the first time we've had to do it.

Kelenli joins us in the network only occasionally. This is frustrating, because her voice—deep and powerful and foottingling in its sharpness—is perfect. Better than Tetlewha's, wider ranging than all of us together. But we are told by the conductors not to get used to her. "She'll serve during the actual start-up of the Engine," one of them says when I ask, "but only if she can't manage to teach you how to do what she does. Conductor Gallat wants her on standby only, come Launch Day."

This seems sensible, on the surface.

When Kelenli is part of us, she takes point. This is simply natural, because her presence is so much greater than ours. Why? Something in the way she is made? Something else. There is a...held note. A perpetual hollow burn at the midpoint of her balanced lines, at their fulcrum, which none of us understand. A similar burn rests in each of us, but ours is faint and intermittent, occasionally flaring only to quickly fade back to quiescence. Hers blazes steadily, its fuel apparently limitless.

Whatever this held-note burn is, the conductors have discovered, it meshes beautifully with the devouring chaos of the onyx. The onyx is the control cabochon of the whole Plutonic Engine, and while there are other ways to start up the Engine—cruder ways, workarounds involving subnetworks or the moonstone—on Launch Day we will absolutely need the onyx's precision and control. Without it, our chances of successfully initiating Geoarcanity diminish greatly...but none of us, thus far, has had the strength to hold the onyx for more than a few minutes. We observe in awe, however, as Kelenli rides it for a solid hour, then actually seems unfazed when she disengages from it. When we engage the onyx, it punishes us, stripping everything we can spare and leaving us in a shutdown sleep for hours or days—but not her. Its threads caress rather than rip at her. The onyx *likes her*. This explanation is irrational, but it occurs to all of us, so that's how we begin to think of it. Now she must teach us to be more likable to the onyx, in her stead.

When we are done rebalancing and they let us up from the wire chairs that maintain our bodies while our minds are engaged, and we stagger and must lean on the conductors to make it back to our individual quarters...when all of this is done, she comes to visit us. Individually, so the conductors won't suspect anything. In face-to-face meetings, speaking audible nonsense—and meanwhile, earthspeaking sense to all of us at once.

She feels sharper than the rest of us, she explains, because she is more experienced. Because she's lived outside of the complex of buildings that surround the local fragment, and which has comprised the entirety of our world since we were decanted. She has visited more nodes of Syl Anagist than just the one we live in; she has seen and touched more of the fragments than just our local amethyst. She has even been to Zero Site, where the moonstone rests. We are in awe of this.

"I have context," she says to us—to me, rather. She's sitting on my couch. I am sprawled facedown on the window seat, face turned away from her. "When you do, too, you'll be just as sharp."

(It is a kind of pidgin between us, using the earth to add meaning to audible words. Her words are simply, "I'm older," while a whitter of subsidence adds the nuancing deformation of time. She is *metamorphic*, having transformed to bear unbearable pressure. To make this telling simpler, I will translate it all as words, except where I cannot.)

"It would be good if we were as sharp as you *now*," I reply wearily. I am not whining. Rebalancing days are always hard. "Give us this context, then, so the onyx will listen and my head can stop hurting."

Kelenli sighs. "There's nothing within these walls on which you can sharpen yourself." (Crumble of resentment, ground up and quickly scattered. *They have kept you so safe and sheltered.*) "But I think there's a way I can help you and the others do that, if I can get you out of this place."

"Help me . . . sharpen myself?"

(She soothes me with a polishing stroke. *It is not a kindness that you are kept so dull.*) "You need to understand more about yourself. What you are."

I don't understand why she thinks I don't understand. "I'm a tool."

She says: "If you're a tool, shouldn't you be honed as fine as possible?"

Her voice is serene. And yet a pent, angry jitter of the entire ambient—air molecules shivering, strata beneath us compressing, a dissonant grinding whine at the limit of our ability to sess—tells me that Kelenli hates what I have just said. I turn my head to her and find myself fascinated by the way this dichotomy fails to show in her face. It's another way she's like us. We have long since learned not to show pain or fear or sorrow in any space aboveground or below the sky. The conductors tell us we are built to be like statues—cold, immovable, silent. We aren't certain why they believe we actually are this way; after all, we are as warm to the touch as they. We feel emotion, as they seem to, although we do seem less inclined to display it in face or body language. Perhaps this is because we have earthtalk? (Which they don't seem to notice. This is good. In the earth, we may be ourselves.) It has never been clear to us whether we were built wrong, or whether their understanding of us is wrong. Or whether either matters.

Kelenli is outwardly calm while she burns inside. I watch her for so long that abruptly she comes back to herself and catches me. She smiles. "I think you like me."

I consider the possible implications of this. "Not that way," I say, out of habit. I have had to explain this to junior conductors or other staff on occasion. We are made like statues in this way as well—a design implementation that worked in this case, leaving us capable of rutting but disinterested in the attempt, and infertile should we bother. Is Kelenli the same? No, the conductors said she was made different in only one way. She has our powerful, complex, flexible sessapinae, which no other people in the world possess. Otherwise she's like them.

"How fortunate that I wasn't talking about sex." There's a drawling hum of amusement from her; it both bothers and pleases me. I don't know why.

Oblivious to my sudden confusion, Kelenli gets to her feet. "I'll be back," she says, and leaves.

She doesn't return for several days. She remains a detached part of our last network, though, so she is present for our wakings, our meals, our defecations, our inchoate dreams when we sleep, our pride in ourselves and each other. It doesn't feel like watching when she does it, even if she is watching. I cannot speak for the others, but I like having her around.

Not all of the others do like Kelenli. Gaewha in particular is belligerent about it, and she sends this through our private discussion. "She appears just as we lose Tetlewha? Just as the project concludes? We've worked hard to become what we are. Will they praise her for our work, when it's done?"

"She's only a standby," I say, trying to be the voice of reason. "And what she wants is what we want. We need to cooperate."

"So she says." That is Remwha, who considers himself smarter than the rest of us. (We're all made to be equally intelligent. Remwha is just an ass.) "The conductors kept her away until now for a reason. She may be a troublemaker."

That is foolish, I believe, though I don't let myself say it even in earthtalk. We are part of the great machine. Anything that improves the machine's function matters; anything unrelated to this purpose does not. If Kelenli were a troublemaker, Gallat would have sent her to the briar patch with Tetlewha. This is a thing we all understand. Gaewha and Remwha are just being difficult.

"If she is some sort of troublemaker, that will show itself with time," I say firmly. That does not end, but at least postpones, the argument.

Kelenli returns the next day. The conductors bring us together to explain. "Kelenli has asked to take you on a tuning mission," says the man who comes to deliver the briefing. He's much taller than us, taller even than Kelenli, and slender. He likes to dress in perfectly matched colors and ornate buttons. His hair is long and black; his skin is white, though not so much as ours. His eyes are like ours, however—white within white. White as ice. We've never seen another one of *them* with eyes like ours. He is Conductor Gallat, head of the project. I think of Gallat as a plutonic fragment—a clear one, diamond-white. He is precisely angled and cleanly faceted and beautiful in a unique way, and he is also implacably deadly if not handled with precision. We don't let ourselves think about the fact that he's the one who killed Tetlewha.

(He isn't who you think he is. I want Gallat to look like him the way I want you to look like her. This is the hazard of a flawed memory.)

"A tuning…mission," Gaewha says slowly, to show that she doesn't understand.

Kelenli opens her mouth to speak and then stops, turning to Gallat. Gallat smiles genially at this. "Kelenli's performance is what we were hoping for with all of you, and yet you've consistently underperformed," he says. We tense, uncomfortable, hyperconscious of criticism, though he merely shrugs. "I've consulted with the chief biomagestre, and she's insistent that there's no significant difference in your relative abilities. You have the same *capability* that she has, but you don't demonstrate the same *skill*. There are any number of alterations we could make to try to resolve the discrepancy, fine-tuning so to speak, but that's a risk we'd rather not take so close to launch."

We reverberate in one accord for a moment, all of us very glad for this. "She said that she was here to teach us context," I venture, very carefully.

Gallat nods to me. "She believes the solution is outside experience. Increased exposure to stimuli, challenging your problem-solving cognition, things like that. It's a suggestion that has merit and the benefit of being minimally invasive—but for the sake of the project, we can't send you all out at once. What if something happened? Instead we will split you into two groups. Since there's only one of Kelenli, that means half of you will go with her now, and half in a week."

Outside. We're going outside. I'm desperate to be in the first group, but we know better than to show desire before the conductors. Tools should not want to escape their box so obviously.

I say, instead, "We've been more than sufficiently attuned to one another without this proposed mission." My voice is flat. A statue's. "The simulations show that we are reliably capable of controlling the Engine, as expected."

"And we might as well do six groups as two," adds Remwha. By this asinine suggestion do I know his eagerness. "Will each group not have different experiences? As I understand the...

outside...there's no way to control for consistency of exposure. If we must take time away from our preparations for this, surely it should be done in a way that minimizes risk?"

"I think six wouldn't be cost-effective or efficient," Kelenli says, while silently signaling approval and amusement for our playacting. She glances at Gallat and shrugs, not bothering to pretend that she is emotionless; she simply seems bored. "We might as well do *one* group as two or six. We can plan the route, position extra guards along the way, involve the nodal police for surveillance and support. Honestly, repeated trips would just increase the chance that disaffected citizens might anticipate the route and plan...unpleasantness."

We are all intrigued by the possibility of unpleasantness. Kelenli quells our excited tremors.

Conductor Gallat winces as she does this; that one struck home. "The potential for significant gains are why you will go," Conductor Gallat says to us. He's still smiling, but there's an edge to it now. Was the word *will* ever so slightly emphasized? So minute, the perturbations of audible speech. What I take from this is that not only will he let us go, but he has also changed his mind about sending us in multiple groups. Some of this is because Kelenli's suggestion was the most sensible, but the rest is because he's irritated with us for our apparent reluctance.

Ah, Remwha wields his annoying nature like a diamond chisel as usual. *Excellent work*, I pulse. He returns me a polite thank-you waveform.

We are to leave that very day. Clothing suitable for travel outdoors is brought to my quarters by junior conductors. I pull on the thicker cloth and shoes carefully, fascinated by the different textures, and then sit quietly while the junior conductor plaits my hair into a single white braid. "Is this necessary for outside?" I ask. I'm genuinely curious, since the conductors wear their hair in many styles. Some of them I can't emulate, because my hair is poufy and coarse and will not hold a curl or bear straightening. Only we have hair like this. Theirs comes in many textures.

"It might help," says the junior. "You lot are going to stand out no matter what, but the more normal we can make you seem, the better."

"People will know we're part of the Engine," I say, straightening just a little in pride.

His fingers slow for a moment. I don't think he notices. "That's not exactly... They're more likely to think you're something else. Don't worry, though; we'll send guards along to make sure there's no trouble. They'll be unobtrusive, but there. Kelenli insists that you can't be made to feel sheltered, even if you are."

"They're more likely to think we're something else," I repeat slowly, thoughtfully.

His fingers twitch, pulling a few strands harder than necessary. I don't wince or pull away. They're more comfortable thinking of us as statues, and statues aren't supposed to feel pain. "Well, it's a distant possibility, but they have to know you aren't—I mean, it's..." He sighs. "Oh, Evil Death. It's complicated. Don't worry about it."

Conductors say this when they've made a mistake. I don't ping the others with it right away, because we minimize communication outside of sanctioned meetings. People who are not tuners can perceive magic only in rudimentary ways; they use machines and instruments to do what is natural for us. Still, they're always monitoring us in some measure, so we cannot allow them to learn the extent to which we speak to each other, and hear them, when they think we cannot.

Soon I'm ready. After conferring with other conductors over the vine, mine decides to brush my face with paint and powder. It's supposed to make me look like them. It actually makes me like someone whose white skin has been painted brown. I must look skeptical when he shows me the mirror; my conductor sighs and complains that he's not an artist.

Then he brings me to a place that I've seen only a few times before, within the building that houses me: the downstairs foyer. Here the walls aren't white; the natural green and brown of self-repairing cellulose has been allowed to flourish unbleached. Someone has seeded the space with vining strawberries that are half in white flower, half in ripening red fruit; it's quite lovely. The six of us stand near the floor pool waiting for Kelenli, trying not to notice the other personnel of the building coming and going and staring at us: six smaller-than-average, stocky people with puffy white hair and painted faces, our lips arranged in defensively pleasant smiles. If there are guards, we do not know how to tell them from the gawkers.

When Kelenli comes toward us, though, I finally notice guards. Hers move with her, not bothering to be unobtrusive— a tall brown woman and man who might have been siblings. I realize I have seen them before, trailing her on other occasions that she's come to visit. They hang back as she reaches us.

"Good, you're ready," she says. Then she grimaces, reaching out to touch Dushwha's cheek. Her thumb comes away dusted with face powder. "Really?"

Dushwha looks away, uncomfortable. They have never liked being pushed into any emulation of our creators—not in clothing, not in gender, definitely not in this. "It's meant to help," they mutter unhappily, perhaps trying to convince themselves.

"It makes you *more* conspicuous. And they'll know what you are, anyway." She turns and looks at one of her guards, the woman. "I'm taking them to clean this dreck off. Want to help?" The woman just looks at her in silence. Kelenli laughs to herself. It sounds genuinely mirth filled.

She herds us into a personal-needs alcove. The guards station themselves outside while she splashes water on our faces from the clean side of the latrine pool, and scrubs the paint away with an absorbent cloth. She hums while she does it. Does that mean she's happy? When she takes my arm to wipe the gunk off my face, I search hers to try to understand. Her gaze sharpens when she notices.

"You're a thinker," she says. I'm not sure what that's supposed to mean.

"We all are," I say. I allow a brief rumble of nuance. *We have to be.*

"Exactly. You think more than you have to." Apparently a bit of brown near my hairline is especially stubborn. She wipes it off, grimaces, wipes it again, sighs, rinses the cloth and wipes at it again.

I continue searching her face. "Why do you laugh at their fear?"

108

It's a stupid question. Should've asked it through the earth, not out loud. She stops wiping my face. Remwha glances at me in bland reproach, then goes to the entrance of the alcove. I hear him asking the guard there to please ask a conductor whether we are in danger of sun damage without the protection of the paint. The guard laughs and calls over her companion to relay this question, as if it's ridiculous. During the moment of distraction purchased for us by this exchange, Kelenli then resumes scrubbing me.

"Why *not* laugh at it?" she says.

"They would like you better if you didn't laugh." I signal nuance: alignment, harmonic enmeshment, compliance, conciliation, mitigation. If she wants to be liked.

"Maybe I don't want to be liked." She shrugs, turning to rinse the cloth again.

"You could be. You're like them."

"Not enough."

"More than me." This is obvious. She is their kind of beautiful, their kind of normal. "If you tried—"

She laughs at me, too. It isn't cruel, I know instinctively. It's pitying. But underneath the laugh, her presence is suddenly as still and pent as pressurized stone in the instant before it becomes something else. Anger again. Not at me, but triggered by my words nevertheless. I always seem to make her angry.

They're afraid because we exist, she says. *There's nothing we did to provoke their fear, other than exist. There's nothing we can do to earn their approval, except stop existing—so we can either die like they want, or laugh at their cowardice and go on with our lives.*

I think at first that I don't understand everything she just told me. But I do, don't I? There were sixteen of us once; now we are but six. The others questioned and were decommissioned for it. Obeyed without question, and were decommissioned for it. Bargained. Gave up. Helped. Despaired. We have tried everything, done all they asked and more, and yet now there are only six of us left.

That means we're better than the others were, I tell myself, scowling. Smarter, more adaptable, more skilled. This matters, does it not? We are components of the great machine, the pinnacle of Sylanagistine biomagestry. If some of us had to be removed from the machine because of flaws—

Tetlewha was not flawed, Remwha snaps like a slipstrike fault.

I blink and glance at him. He's back in the alcove, waiting over near Bimniwha and Salewha; they've all used the fountain to strip off their own paint while Kelenli worked on me and Gaewha and Dushwha. The guards Remwha distracted are just outside, still chuckling to themselves over what he said to them. He's glaring at me. When I frown, he repeats: *Tetlewha was not flawed.*

I set my jaw. *If Tetlewha was not flawed, then that means he was decommissioned for no reason at all.*

Yes. Remwha, who rarely looks pleased on a good day, has now curled his lip in disgust. At me. I'm so shocked by this that I forget to pretend indifference. *That is precisely her point. It doesn't matter what we do. The problem is them.*

It doesn't matter what we do. The problem is them.

When I am clean, Kelenli cups my face in her hands. "Do you know the word 'legacy'?"

I've heard it and guessed its meaning from context. It's

difficult to pull my thoughts back on track after Remwha's angry rejoinder. He and I have never much liked one another, but... I shake my head and focus on what Kelenli has asked me. "A legacy is something obsolete, but which you cannot get rid of entirely. Something no longer wanted, but still needed."

She grimace-smiles, first at me and then at Remwha. She's heard everything he said to me. "That will do. Remember that word today."

Then she gets to her feet. The three of us stare at her. She's not only taller and browner, but she moves more, breathes more. *Is* more. We worship what she is. We fear what she will make of us.

"Come," she says, and we follow her out into the world.

* * *

2613: A massive underwater volcano erupted in the Tasr Straits between the Antarctic Polar Waste and the Stillness. Selis Leader Zenas, previously unknown to be an orogene, apparently quelled the volcano, although she was unable to escape the tsunami that it caused. Skies in the Antarctics darkened for five months, but cleared just before a Season could be officially declared. In the immediate aftermath of the tsunami, Selis Leader's husband—the comm head at the time of the eruption, deposed by emergency election—attempted to defend their one-year-old child from a mob of survivors and was killed. Cause disputed: Some witnesses say the mob stoned him, others say the former comm head was strangled by a Guardian. Guardian took the orphaned infant to Warrant.

—*Project notes of Yaetr Innovator Dibars*

5

you are remembered

THE ATTACK COMES, LIKE CLOCKWORK, near dawn.

Everyone's ready for it. The camp is about a third of the way into the stone forest, which is as far as Castrima was able to get before full darkness made further progress treacherous. The group should be able to get all the way through the forest before sunset the next day—assuming everyone lives through the night.

Restlessly you prowl the camp, and you are not the only one to do so. The Hunters are supposed to all be sleeping, since during the day they act as scouts as well as ranging afield to forage and catch game. You see quite a few of them awake, too. The Strongbacks are supposed to be sleeping in shifts, but all of them are up, as are a good number of the other castes. You spot Hjarka sitting atop a pile of baggage, her head down and eyes shut, but otherwise her legs are braced for a quick lunge and there's a glassknife in each hand. Her fingers haven't loosened with sleep.

It's a stupid time to attack, given all this, but there isn't a better one, so apparently your assailants decide to work with what they've got. You're the first to sess it, and you're pivoting on the ball of one foot and shouting a warning even as you narrow your perception and drop into that space of mind from which you can command volcanoes. A fulcrum, deep and strong, has been rooted in the earth nearby. You follow it to the midpoint of its potential torus, the center of the circle, like a hawk sighting prey. Right side of the road. Twenty feet into the stone forest, out of line of sight amid the wends and drooping greenery. "Ykka!"

She appears at once from wherever she was sitting amid the tents. "Yeah, felt it."

"Not active yet." By this you mean that the torus hasn't begun to draw heat or movement from the ambient. But that fulcrum is deep as a taproot. There's not much seismic potential gathered in this region—and indeed, much of the pressure on the lower-level strata has been absorbed by the creation of the stone forest. Still, there's always heat if you go deep enough, and this is deep. Solid. Fulcrum-precise.

"We don't have to fight," Ykka yells, suddenly, into the forest. You start, though you shouldn't. You're shocked that she was serious, though you really should know better by now. She stalks forward, body taut, knees bent as if she's about to sprint into the forest, hands held out before her and fingertips wiggling.

It's easier now to reach for magic, though you still focus on the stump of your own arm to begin, out of habit. It will never feel *natural* for you to use this instead of orogeny, but at least your perception shifts quickly. Ykka's way ahead of you. Wavelets and arcs of silver dance along the ground around her, mostly in front of her, spreading and flickering as she draws them up from the ground and makes them hers. What little vegetation you can sess in the stone forest makes it easier; the seedling vines and light-starved mosses act like wires, channeling and aligning the silver into patterns that make sense. Are predictable. Are *searching*...ah. You tense in the same moment that Ykka does. Yes. There.

Above that deep-rooted fulcrum, at the center of a torus that has not yet begun to spin, crouches a body etched out in silver. For the first time, in comparison, you notice that an orogene's silver is both brighter and less complex than that of the plants and insects around it. The same...er, *amount*, if that word applies, if not *capacity* or *potential* or *aliveness*, but not the same design. This orogene's silver is concentrated into a relative few bright lines that all align in similar directions. They don't flicker, and neither does his torus. He—you guess that, but it feels right—is listening.

Ykka, another outline of precise, concentrated silver, nods in satisfaction. She climbs up on top of some of the wagon cargo so her voice will carry better.

"I'm Ykka Rogga Castrima," she calls. You guess that she points at you. "She's a rogga, too. So's he." Temell. "So are those kids over there. We don't kill roggas here." She pauses. "You hungry? We've got a little to spare. You don't need to try to take it."

That fulcrum doesn't budge.

Something else does, though—from the other side of the stone forest, as thin, attenuated agglomerations of silver suddenly blur into chaotic movement and come charging toward you. Other raiders; Evil Earth, you were all so focused on the rogga that you didn't even notice the ones behind you. You hear them now, though, voices rising, cursing, feet pounding on ashy sand. The Strongbacks near the barrier of stakes on that side cry warning. "They're attacking," you call.

"No shit," Ykka snaps, drawing a glassknife.

You retreat to within the tent circle, acutely aware of your vulnerability in a way that's strange and deeply unpleasant. It's worse because you can still sess, and because your instincts prompt you to respond when you see where you *could* help. A cluster of attackers comes at a part of the perimeter that's light on stakes and defenders, and you open your eyes so you can actually see them trying to fight their way in. They're typical commless raiders—filthy, emaciated, dressed in an ash-faded combination of rags and newer, pilfered clothing. You could take out all six in half a breath, with a single precision torus.

But you can also feel how... what? How *aligned* you are. Ykka's silver is concentrated like that of the other roggas you've observed, but hers is still layered, jagged, a little jittery. It flows every-which-way within her as she jumps down from the cargo wagon and shouts for people to help the sparse Strongbacks near that cluster of raiders, running to help herself. Your magic flows with smooth clarity, every line matching perfectly in direction and flow to every other line. You don't know how to change it back to the way it was, if that's even possible. And you know instinctively that using the silver when you're like this will pack every particle of your body together as neatly as a mason lays a wall of bricks. You'll be stone the same way.

So you fight your instincts and *hide*, much as that rankles.

There are others here, crouching amid the central circle of tents—the comm's smaller children, its bare handful of elders, one woman so pregnant that she can't move with any real flexibility even though she's got a loaded crossbow in her hands, two knife-wielding Breeders who've obviously been charged with defending her and the children.

When you poke your head up to observe the fighting, you catch a glimpse of something stunning. *Danel*, having appropriated one of the spear-whittled sticks that form the fence, is using it to carve a bloody swath through the raiders. She's phenomenal, spinning and stabbing and blocking and stabbing again, twirling the stick in between attacks as if she's fought commless a million times. That's not just being an experienced Strongback; that's something else. She's just too good. But it follows, doesn't it? Not like Rennanis made her the general of their army for her charm.

It isn't much of a fight in the end. Twenty or thirty scrawny commless against trained, fed, prepared comm members? This is why comms survive Seasons, and why long-term commlessness is a death sentence. This lot was probably desperate; there can't have been much traffic along the road in the past few months. What were they thinking?

Their orogene, you realize. That's who they expected to win this fight for them. But he's still not moving, orogenically or physically.

You get up, walking past the lingering knots of fighting. Self-consciously adjusting your mask, you step off the road and slip through the perimeter stakes, moving into the deeper darkness of the stone forest. The firelight of the camp leaves you night-blind, so you stop a moment to allow your eyes to adjust. No telling what kinds of traps the commless have left here; you shouldn't be doing this alone. Again you're surprised, though, because between one blink and the next, you suddenly begin to see in silver. Insects, leaf litter, a spiderweb, even the rocks—all of it now flickers in wild, veined patterns, their cells and particulates etched out by the lattice that connects them.

And people. You stop as you make them out, well camouflaged against the silver bloom of the forest. The rogga is still where he's been, a brighter etching against more delicate lines. But there are also two small shapes crouched in a cavelet, about twenty feet further into the forest. Two other bodies, somehow high overhead atop the jagged, curving rocks of the forest. Lookouts, maybe? None of them move much. Can't tell if they've seen you, or if they're watching the battle somehow. You're frozen, startled by this sudden shift in your perception. Is this some by-product of learning to see silver in yourself and the obelisks? Maybe once you can do that, you see it everywhere. Or maybe you're hallucinating all of it now, like an afterimage against your eyelids. After all, Alabaster never mentioned being able to see like this—but then, when did Alabaster ever try to be a good teacher?

You grope forward for a bit, hand out in front of you in case it is some kind of illusion, but if so, it's at least an accurate one. While it's strange to put your foot down on a lattice of silver, after a while you get used to it.

The orogene's distinctive lattice and that still-held torus aren't far, but he's somewhere higher up than the ground. Maybe ten feet above where you stand. This is explained somewhat when the ground abruptly slopes upward and your hand touches stone. Your regular vision has adapted enough that you can see there's a pillar here, crooked and probably climbable, at least by someone who's got more than one arm. So you stop at the foot of it and say, "Hey."

No response. You become aware of breathing: quick, shallow, pent. Like someone who's trying not to be heard breathing.

"Hey." Squinting in the dark, you finally make out some kind of structure of stacked branches and old boards and debris. A blind, maybe. From up there in the blind, it must be possible to see the road. Sight doesn't matter for the average orogene; untrained ones can't direct their power at all. A Fulcrum-trained orogene, though, needs line of sight to be able to distinguish between freezing useful supplies, or just freezing the people defending same.

Something shifts in the blind above you. Has there been a catch in the breathing? You try to think of something to say, but all that's in your head is a question: What's a Fulcrum-trained orogene doing among the commless? Must have been out on an assignment when the Rifting occurred. Without a Guardian— or he'd be dead—so that means he's fifth ring or higher, or maybe a three- or four-ringer who's lost their higher-ranked partner. You envision yourself, if you'd been on the road to Allia when the Rifting struck. Knowing your Guardian might come for you, but gambling that he might instead write you off for dead...no. That ends the imagining right there. Schaffa would have come for you. Schaffa *did* come for you.

But that was between Seasons. Guardians supposedly do not join comms when Seasons come, which means they die—and, in fact, the only Guardian you've seen since the Rifting was that one with Danel and the Rennanis army. She died in the boilbug storm that you invoked, and you're glad of it, since she was one of the bare-skin killers and there's more than the usual wrong with that kind. Either way, here's another ex-blackjacket out here alone, and maybe afraid, and maybe hair-triggered to kill. You know what that's like, don't you? But this one hasn't attacked yet. You have to find some way to make a connection.

"I remember," you say. It's soft, a murmur. Like you don't want to hear even yourself. "I remember the crucibles. The instructors, killing us to save us. Did they m-make you have children, too?" Corundum. Your thoughts jerk away from memories. "Did they—shit." The hand that Schaffa once broke, your right hand, is somewhere in whatever passes for Hoa's belly. You still feel it, though. Phantom ache across phantom bones. "I know they broke you. Your hand. All of us. They broke us so they could— "

You hear, very clearly, a soft, horrified inhalation from within the blind.

The torus whips into a blurring, blistering spin, and explodes outward. You're so close that it almost catches you. That gasp was enough warning, though, and so you've braced yourself oro-genically, even if you couldn't do so physically. Physically you flinch and it's too much for your precarious, one-armed balance. You fall backward, landing hard on your ass—but you've been drilled since childhood in how to retain control on one level even as you lose it in another, so in the same instant you flex your sessapinae and simply slap his fulcrum out of the earth, inverting it. You're much stronger; it's easy. You react magically, too, grabbing those whipping tendrils of silver that the torus has stirred—and belatedly you realize orogeny *affects* magic, but *isn't* magic itself, in fact the magic flinches away from it; *that's* why you can't work high-level orogeny without negatively impacting your ability to deploy magic, how nice to finally understand! Regardless, you tamp the wild threads of magic back down, and quell everything at once, so that nothing worse than a rime of frost dusts your body. It's cold, but only on your skin. You'll live.

Then you let go—and all the orogeny and magic snaps away from you like stretched rubber. Everything in you seems to *twang* in response, in resonance, and—oh—oh no—you feel the amplitude of the resonance rise as your cells begin to align...and compress into stone.

You can't stop it. You can, however, direct it. In the instant that you have, you decide which body part you can afford to lose. Hair! No, too many strands, too much of it distant from the live follicles; you can do it but it'll take too long and half your scalp will be stone by the time you're done. Toes? You need to be able to walk. Fingers? You've only got one hand, need to keep it intact as long as you can.

Breasts. Well, you're not planning on having more children anyway.

It's enough to channel the resonance, the stoning, into just one. Have to take it through the glands under the armpit, but you manage to keep it above the muscle layer; that might keep the damage from impairing your movement and breathing. You pick the left breast, to offset your missing right arm. The right breast is the one you always liked better, anyway. Prettier. And then you lie there when it's done, still alive, hyperaware of the extra weight on your chest, too shocked to mourn. Yet.

Then you're pushing yourself up, awkwardly, grimacing, as the person in the blind utters a nervous little chuckle and says, "Oh, rust. Oh, Earth. Damaya? It really is you. Sorry about the torus, I was just— You don't know what it's been like. I can't believe it. Do you know what they did to Crack?"

Arkete, says your memory. "Maxixe," says your mouth.

It's Maxixe.

*   *   *

Maxixe is half the man he used to be. Physically, anyway.

He's got no legs below the thighs. One eye, or rather only one that works. The left one is clouded with damage, and it doesn't track quite with the other. The left side of his head— he's got almost nothing left of that lovely blond ashblow that you remember, just a knife-hacked bottlebrush—is a mess of pinkish scars, amid which you think the ear is healed shut. The scars have seamed his forehead and cheek, and pull his mouth a little out of true on that side.

Yet he wriggles down from the blind nimbly, walking on his hands and lifting his torso and stumpy legs with sheer muscle as he does so. He's too good at getting around without legs; must have been doing it for a while now. He makes it over to you before you're able to climb to your feet. "It really is you. I thought, I heard you were only fourth ring, did you really punch through my torus? I'm a sixer. Six! But that's how I knew, see, you still *sess* the same, still quiet on the outside and rusting *furious* on the inside, it really is you."

The other commless are starting to creep down from their spires and such. You tense as they appear—scarecrow figures, thin and ragged and stinking, watching you from stolen or homemade goggles and above wraparound masks that obviously used to be somebody's clothes. They do not attack, however. They gather and watch you with Maxixe.

You stare as he circles you, levering himself along rapidly. He's wearing commless rags, long-sleeved and layered, but you can see how big his shoulder and arm muscles are under the tattered cloth. The rest of him is scrawny. The gauntness of his face is painful to see, but it's clear what his body has prioritized during the long hungry months.

"Arkete," you say, because you remember that he always preferred the name he was born with.

He stops circling and peers at you for a moment, head tilted. Maybe this helps him see better with one functioning eye. The look on his face tells you off, though. He's not Arkete, any more than you are Damaya. Too much has changed. Maxixe it is, then.

"You remembered," he says, though. In that moment of stillness, this eye in his previous storm of words, you glimpse the thoughtful, charming boy you remember. Even though the coincidence of this is almost too much to digest. The only thing stranger would be running into . . . the brother you actually forgot you had, until just now. What was his name? Earthfires, you've forgotten that, too. But you probably wouldn't recognize him, if you saw him. The grits of the Fulcrum were your siblings, in pain if not in blood.

You shake your head to focus, and nod. You're on your feet

now, dusting leaf litter and ash off your butt, though awkwardly around the pulling weight on your chest. "I'm surprised I remembered, too. You must have made an impression."

He smiles. It's lopsided. Only half his face works the way it should. "I forgot. Tried hard to, anyway."

You set your jaw, steeling yourself. "I'm—sorry." It's pointless. He probably doesn't even remember what you're sorry about.

He shrugs. "Doesn't matter."

"It does."

"No." He looks away for a moment. "I should have talked to you, after. Shouldn't have hated you the way I did. Shouldn't have let her, them, change me. But I did, and now...none of that matters."

You know exactly which "her" he's referring to. After that whole incident with Crack, bullying that exposed a whole network of grits just trying to survive and a larger network of adults exploiting their desperation...You remember. Maxixe, returning to the grit barracks one day with both his hands broken.

"Better than what they did to Crack," you murmur, before it occurs to you not to say this.

Yet he nods, unsurprised. "Went to a node station once. It wasn't her. Rust knows what I was thinking...But I wanted to search them all. Before the Season." He utters a ragged, bitter chuckle. "I didn't even like her. Just needed to know."

You shake your head. Not that you don't understand the impulse; you'd be lying if you said you hadn't thought it, too, in the years since you learned the truth. Go to all the stations. Figure out some way to restore their damaged sessapinae and set them free. Or kill them as a kindness; ah, you'd have been such a good instructor, if the Fulcrum had ever given you a chance. But of course you did nothing. And of course Maxixe didn't do anything to save the node maintainers, either. Only Alabaster ever managed that.

You take a deep breath. "I'm with them," you say, jerking your head back toward the road. "You heard what the headwoman said. Orogenes welcome."

He sways a little, there on his stumps and arms. It's hard to see his face in the dark. "I can sess her. She's the *headwoman?*"

"Yeah. And everyone in the comm knows it. They're— This comm is—" And you take a deep breath. "*We*. Are a comm that's trying to do something different. Orogenes and stills. Not killing each other."

He laughs, which sets off a few moments of coughing. The other stick figures chuckle, too, but it's Maxixe's cough that worries you. It's dry, hacking, pebbly; not a good sound. He's been breathing too much ash without a mask. It's loud, too. If the Hunters aren't nearby, watching and perhaps ready to shoot him and his people, you'll eat your runny-sack.

At the end of the coughing fit, he tilts his head up at you again, with an amused look in his eye. "I'm doing the same thing," he drawls. With his chin, he points toward his gathered people. "These rusters stick with me because I'm not going to eat them. They don't fuck with me because I'll kill them. There: peaceful coexistence."

You look around at them and frown. Hard to see their expressions. "They didn't attack my people, though." Or they'd be dead.

"Nah. That was Olemshyn." Maxixe shrugs; it makes his

whole body move. "Half-Sanzed bastard. Got kicked out of two comms for 'anger management issues,' he said. He would've gotten us all killed raiding, so I told anybody who wanted to live and could stand me to come follow me, and we did our own thing. This side of the forest is ours, that side was theirs."

Two commless tribes, not one. Maxixe's hardly qualifies, though; only a handful of people besides himself? But he said it: Those who could endure living with a rogga went with him. That just didn't turn out to be a lot of people.

Maxixe turns and climbs halfway up to the blind again, so that he can sit down and also be on an eye level with you. He lets out another rattly cough from the effort of doing this. "I figure he was expecting me to hit you lot," he continues, once the cough subsides. "That's how we usually do it: I ice 'em, his group grabs what it can before I and mine can show up, we both get enough to go on a little longer. But I was all fucked up from what your headwoman said." He looks away, shaking his head. "Olemshyn should've broken off once he saw I wasn't going to ice you, but, well. I did say he was gonna get them killed."

"Yeah."

"Good riddance. What happened to your arm?" He's looking at you now. He can't see your left breast, even though you're slouching a little to the left. It hurts, weighing on your flesh.

You counter, "What happened to your legs?"

He smiles, lopsidedly, and doesn't answer. Neither do you.

"So, not killing each other." Maxixe shakes his head. "And that's actually working out?"

"So far. We're *trying*, anyway."

"Won't work." Maxixe shifts again and darts another look at you. "How much did it cost you, to join them?"

You don't say *nothing*, because that's not what he's asking, anyway. You can see the bargain he's made for survival here: his skills in exchange for the raiders' limited food and dubious shelter. This stone forest, this death trap, is his doing. How many people did he kill for his raiders?

How many have you killed, for Castrima?

Not the same.

How many people were in Rennanis's army? How many of them did you sentence to be steam-cooked alive by insects? How many ash-mounds dot Castrima-over now, each with a hand or booted foot poking out?

Not the rusting same. That was them or you.

Just like Maxixe, trying to survive. Him or them.

You set your jaw to silence this internal argument. There isn't time for this.

"We can't—" you attempt, then shift. "There are other ways besides killing. Other... We don't just have to be... this." Ykka's words, awkward and oily with hypocrisy from your mouth. And are those words even true anymore? Castrima no longer has the geode to force cooperation between orogene and still. Maybe it'll all fall apart tomorrow.

Maybe. But until then, you force yourself to finish. "We don't have to be what they made us, Maxixe."

He shakes his head, staring at the leaf litter. "You remember that name, too."

You lick your lips. "Yeah. I'm Essun."

He frowns a little at this, perhaps because it isn't a stone-themed name. That's why you picked it. He doesn't question it, though. At last he sighs. "Rusting look at me, Essun. *Listen to the rocks in my chest.* Even if your headwoman will take half a rogga, I'm not going to last much longer. Also—" Because he's sitting, he can use his hands; he gestures around at the other scarecrow figures.

"No comm will let us in," says one of the smaller figures. You think that's a woman's voice, but it's so hoarse and weary you can't tell. "Don't even play that game."

You shift, uncomfortable. The woman is right; Ykka might be willing to take in a commless rogga, but not the rest. Then again, you can never figure out quite what Ykka will do. "I can ask."

Chuckles all around, jaded and thin and tired. A few more rattly coughs in addition to Maxixe's. These people are starved nearly to death, and half of them are sick. This is pointless. Still. To Maxixe, you say, "If you don't come with us, you'll die here."

"Olemshyn's people had most of the supplies. We'll go take 'em." That sentence ends on a pause: the opening bid in a bargain. "And it's all of us, or none of us."

"Up to the headwoman," you say, refusing to commit. But you know haggling when you hear it. His Fulcrum-trained orogeny in exchange for comm membership for him and his handful, with the deal sweetened by the raiders' supplies. And he's fully prepared to walk away if Ykka can't meet his opening price. It bothers you. "I'll also put in a good word for your character, or at least your character thirty years ago."

He smiles a little. Hard not to see that smile as patronizing. *Look at you, trying to make this something more than it is.* You're probably projecting. "I also know a little about the area. Might be useful, since you're obviously going somewhere." He jerks his chin toward firelight reflecting off the crags closer to the road. "You *are* going somewhere?"

"Rennanis."

"Assholes."

Which means the Rennanis army must have come through the area on its way south. You let yourself smile. "Dead assholes."

"Huh." He squints his good eye. "They've been smashing comms all over the area. That's why we've had such a hard time; no trade caravans to raid once the Rennies were done. I *did* sess something weird in the direction they went, though."

He falls silent, watching you, because of course he knows. Any rogga with rings should have sessed the activity of the Obelisk Gate when you ended the Rennanis-Castrima war so decisively. They might not have known what they were sessing, and unless they knew magic, they wouldn't have perceived the totality of it even if they'd known, but they would have at least picked up the backwash.

"That...was me," you say. It's surprisingly hard to admit.

"Rusting Earth, Da—Essun. How?"

You take a deep breath. Extend a hand to him. So much of your past keeps coming back to haunt you. You can never forget where you came from, because it won't rusting *let* you. But maybe Ykka's got the right of it. You can reject these dregs of your old self and pretend that nothing and no one else matters...or you can embrace them. Reclaim them for what they're worth, and grow stronger as a whole.

"Let's go talk to Ykka," you say. "If she adopts you—and your people, I know—I'll tell you everything." And if he's not care-ful, you'll end up teaching him how to do it, too. He's a six-ringer, after all. If you fail, someone else will have to take up the mantle.

To your surprise, he regards your hand with something akin to wariness. "Not sure I want to know *everything.*"

It makes you smile. "You really don't."

He smiles lopsidedly. "You don't want to know everything that's happened to me, either."

You incline your head. "Deal, then. Only the good parts."

He grins. One of his teeth is missing. "That's too short to even make a good pop lorist tale. Nobody would buy a story like that."

But. Then he shifts his weight and lifts his right hand. The skin is thick as horn, beyond callused, and filthy. You wipe your hand on your pants without thinking, after. His people chuckle at this.

Then you lead him back toward Castrima, into the light.

*   *   *

2470: Antarctics. Massive sinkhole began to open beneath city of Bendine (comm died shortly after). Karst soils, not seismic, but the sinking of the city generated waves that Antarctic Fulcrum orogenes detected. From the Fulcrum, somehow shifted whole city to more stable position, saving most of population. Fulcrum records note that doing this killed three senior orogenes.

—*Project notes of Yaetr Innovator Dibars*

6

Nassun makes her fate

THE MONTHLONG JOURNEY TO STEEL'S deadciv ruin is uneventful by the standards of mid-Season travel. Nassun and Schaffa have or forage sufficient food to sustain themselves, though both of them begin to lose weight. Nassun's shoulder heals without trouble, though she is feverish and weak for a couple of days at one point, and on those days Schaffa calls a halt for rest sooner than she thinks he normally would have. On the third day the fever is gone, the wound is beginning to scab, and they resume.

They encounter almost no one else on the road, though that is unsurprising a year and a half into the Season. Anyone still commless at this point has joined a raider band, and there won't be many of those left—just the most vicious, or the ones with some kind of edge beyond savagery and cannibalism. Most of those will have gone north, into the Somidlats where there are more comms to prey upon. Not even raiders like the Antarctics.

In many ways the near-solitude suits Nassun fine. No other Guardians to tiptoe around. No commfolk whose irrational fears must always be planned for. Not even other orogene children; Nassun misses the others, misses their chatter and the comradeship that she enjoyed with them for so brief a time, but at the end of the day, she resented how much time and attention Schaffa had to give them. She's old enough to know that it's childish for her to be jealous of such a thing. (Her parents doted on Uche, too, but it is horrifyingly obvious now that getting more attention isn't necessarily favoritism.) Doesn't mean she isn't glad, and greedy, for the chance to have Schaffa all to herself.

Their time together is companionable, and largely silent, by day. At night they sleep, curled together against the deepening cold, secure because Nassun has reliably demonstrated that the slightest shift in the ambient, or footstep upon the nearby ground, is enough to wake her. Sometimes Schaffa does not sleep; he tries, but instead lies shuddering minutely, catching his breath now and again with half-suppressed muscle twitches, trying not to disturb her in his quiet agonies. When he does sleep, it is fitful and shallow. Sometimes Nassun does not sleep, either, aching in silent sympathy.

So she resolves to do something about it. It's the thing she learned to do back in Found Moon, though to a lesser degree: She sometimes lets the little corestone in his sessapinae have some of her silver. She doesn't know why it works, but she recalls seeing the Guardians in Found Moon all taking bits of silver from their charges and exhaling afterward, as if it eased something in them to give the corestone someone else to chew on.

Schaffa, however, has not taken silver from her or anyone else since the day she offered all of hers to him—the day she realized the true nature of the metal shard in his brain. She thinks maybe she understands why he stopped. Something changed between them that day, and he can no longer bring himself to feed on her like some sort of parasite. But that is why Nassun sneaks him magic now. Because something changed between them, and he's not a parasite if she needs him, too, and if she gives what he will not take.

(One day soon, she will learn the word *symbiosis* and nod, pleased to have a name for it at last. But long before that, she will have already decided that *family* will do.)

When Nassun gives Schaffa her silver, though he is asleep, his body swallows it so quickly that she must snatch her hand away to avoid losing too much. She can spare only dribbles. Any more and she will be the one tired and unable to travel the next day. Even that tiny amount is enough to let him sleep, however—and as the days pass, Nassun finds herself gradually making more silver, somehow. It's a welcome change; now she can ease his pain better without wearying herself. Every time she sees Schaffa settle into a deep, peaceful sleep, she feels proud and good, even though she knows she isn't. Doesn't matter. She is determined to be a better daughter to Schaffa than she was to Jija. Everything will be better, until the end.

Schaffa sometimes tells stories in the evenings, while dinner cooks. In them, the Yumenes of the past is a place both wondrous and strange, as alien as the bottom of the sea. (It is always the Yumenes of the past. Recent Yumenes is lost to him, along with his memories of the Schaffa he used to be.) Even the idea of Yumenes is hard for Nassun to comprehend: millions of people, none of them farmers or miners or anything that fits within the range of her experience, many of them obsessed with strange fads and politics and alignments far more complex than those of caste or race. Leaders, but also the elite Yumenescene Leadership families. Strongbacks of the union and those without, varying by their connections and financial security. Innovators from generations-old families who competed to be sent off to the Seventh University, and Innovators who merely built and repaired trinkets out of the city's shantytowns. It is strange to realize that much of Yumenes's strangeness was simply because it lasted so long. It *had* old families. Books in its libraries that were older than Tirimo. Organizations that remembered, and avenged, slights from three or four Seasons back.

Schaffa also tells her about the Fulcrum, although not much. There is another memory hole here, deep and fathomless as an obelisk—though Nassun finds herself unable to resist probing its edges. It is a space that her mother once inhabited, after all, and in spite of everything, this fascinates her. Schaffa remembers Essun poorly, however, even when Nassun works up the courage to ask direct questions about the matter. He tries to answer Nassun, but his speech is halting when he does, and the look that crosses his face is pained, troubled, paler than usual. She therefore forces herself to ask these questions slowly, hours or days apart, to give him time to recover in between. What she learns is little more than she has already guessed about her mother and the Fulcrum and life before the Season. It helps to hear it, nevertheless.

The miles pass like this, in memory and edged-around pain.

Conditions in the Antarctics grow worse by the day. The ashfall is no longer intermittent, and the landscape has begun to turn into a still life of hills and ridges and dying plants chiseled in gray-white. Nassun starts to miss the sight of the sun. One night they hear the squeals of what must be a large kirkhusa romp out hunting, though fortunately the sound is distant. One day they pass a pond whose surface is mirror-gray from floating ash; the water underneath is disturbingly still, given that the pond is fed by a rapid stream. Although their canteens are low, Nassun looks at Schaffa, and Schaffa nods in silent, wary agreement. There's nothing overtly wrong, but... well. Surviving a Season is as much a matter of having the right instincts as having the right tools. They avoid the still water, and live.

On the evening of the twenty-ninth day, they reach a place where the Imperial Road abruptly plateaus and veers southward. Nassun sesses that the road edges along something that feels a bit like a crater rim. They have crested the ridge that surrounds this circular, unusually flat region, and the road follows the ridge in an arc around the zone of old damage, resuming its westward track on the other side. In the middle, though, Nassun at last beholds a wonder.

The Old Man's Pucker is a sommian—a caldera inside a caldera. This one is unusual in being so perfectly formed; from what Nassun has read, usually the outer, older caldera is badly damaged by the eruption that creates the inner, newer caldera. In this case the outer one is an intact, nearly perfect circle, though heavily eroded by time and forested over; Nassun can't really see it under the greenery, though she can sess it clearly. The inner caldera is a little more oblong, and it gleams so brightly from a distance that Nassun can guess what happened without even sessing it. The eruption must have been so hot, at least at one point, that the whole geological formation nearly destroyed itself. What remains has gone to glass, naturally tempered enough that not even centuries of weathering has damaged it much. The volcano that created this sommian is extinct now, its ancient magma chamber long since emptied, not even a whiff of leftover heat lingering. Once upon a time, though, the Pucker was the site of a truly awesome—and horrific—puncturing of the world's crust.

As Steel instructed, they camp for the night a mile or two back from the Pucker. In the small hours before dawn, Nassun wakes, hearing a distant screech, but Schaffa soothes her. "I've heard that now and again," he says softly, over the crackling of the fire. He insisted on a watch this time, so Nassun took the earlier shift. "Something in the Pucker forest. It doesn't seem to be coming this way."

She believes him. But neither of them sleeps well that night.

In the morning, they rise before dawn and start up the road. In the early-morning light, Nassun stares at the deceptively still double crater before them. Up close, it's easier to see that there are breaks in the inner caldera's walls at regular intervals; someone meant for people to be able to get inside. The outer caldera's floor is completely overgrown, however, yellow-green and waving with a forest of treelike grass that has apparently choked out every other form of vegetation in the area. There's no sess of even game trails across it.

The real surprise, though, is underneath the Pucker.

"Steel's deadciv ruin," she says. "It's *underground*."

Schaffa glances at her in surprise, but he does not protest. "In the magma chamber?"

"Maybe?" Nassun can't believe it, either, at first, but the silver does not lie. She notices something else strange as she expands her sesunal awareness of the area. The silver mirrors the perturbations of topography and the forest here—the same way it does everywhere. Yet the silver here is brighter, somehow, and it seems to flow more readily from plant to plant and rock to rock. These blend to become larger, dazzling flows that all run together like streams, until the ruin sits within a pool of glimmering, churning light. She can't make out details, there's so much of it—just empty space, and an impression of buildings. It's huge, this ruin. A city, like no city Nassun has ever sessed.

But she has sessed this torrential churn of silver before. She cannot help turning to glance back toward the sapphire that is faintly visible some miles off. They've outpaced it, but it's still following.

"Yes," Schaffa says. He's been watching her, and missing nothing as she makes the connections. "I don't remember this city, but I know of others like it. The obelisks were made in such places."

She shakes her head, trying to fathom it all. "What happened to this city? There must have been a lot of people here once."

"The Shattering."

She inhales. She's heard of it, of course, and believed in it the way children believe most stories. She remembers seeing an artist's line rendering of the event in one of her creche books: lightning and rocks falling from the sky, fire erupting from the ground, tiny human figures running and doomed. "So that's what it was like? A big volcano?"

"The Shattering was like this *here*." Schaffa gazes out over the waving forest. "Elsewhere, it was different. The Shattering was a hundred different Seasons, Nassun, all over the world, all striking at once. It is a marvel that anything of humanity survived."

The way he's talking...It seems impossible, but Nassun bites her lip. "Were you...do you remember it?"

He glances at Nassun, surprised, and then smiles in a way that is equal parts weary and wry. "I don't. I think...I *suspect* that I was born sometime after, though I have no proof of that. Even if I could remember the Shattering, though, I feel fairly certain that I wouldn't want to." He sighs, then shakes his head. "The sun is up. Let's face the future, at least, and leave the past to itself." Nassun nods, and they step off the trail into the trees.

The trees are strange things, with long, thin leaves like elongated grass blades, and narrow, flexible trunks that grow no more than a couple of feet apart. In some places Schaffa has to stop and push apart two or three trees so that they can wriggle through. This makes for hard going, though, and before long Nassun is out of breath. She stops, dripping sweat, but Schaffa pushes on. "Schaffa," she says, about to ask for a break.

"No," he says, pushing over another tree with a grunt. "Remember the stone eater's warning, little one. We must reach the center of this forest by dusk. It's now clear we will need every moment of that time."

He's right. Nassun swallows, starts taking deeper breaths so she can work better, and then resumes pushing through the forest with him.

She develops a rhythm, working with him. She's good at finding the quickest paths that don't require pushing through, and when she does, he follows her. When these paths end, however, he shoves and kicks and breaks trees until the way is clear, while she follows. She can catch her breath during these brief lulls, but it's never quite enough. A stitch develops in her side. She starts having trouble seeing because the tree leaves keep pulling some of her hair loose from its twin buns, and sweat has made the curls lengthen and dangle into her eyes. She wants desperately to rest for an hour or so. Drink some water. Eat something. The clouds overhead get grayer as the hours pass, however, and it becomes increasingly hard to tell how much daylight is left.

"I can," Nassun tries at one point, while trying to think of how she can use orogeny, or the silver, or *something*, to clear the way.

"No," Schaffa says, somehow intuiting what she would have said. He's produced a black glass poniard from somewhere. It's not a useful knife for this situation, although somehow he has made it so by stabbing each of the grass-tree trunks before kicking them down. That helps them break more easily. "Freezing these plants would only make them more difficult to get through, and a shake could cause the magma chamber below us to collapse."

"The s-silver, then—"

"No." He stops for only a moment and turns to fix a hard gaze on her. He's not breathing harder, she notes with great chagrin, although a faint sheen of sweat does glisten on his forehead. His iron shard punishes him, but still grudgingly grants him greater strength. "Other Guardians may be near, Nassun. It's unlikely at this point, but still a possibility."

All Nassun can do is grope for another question, because this momentary pause is giving her time to catch her breath.

"Other Guardians?" Ah, but then he has said that they all go somewhere during a Season, and that this *station* that Steel told them about is the means by which they do it. "Do you remember something?"

"Nothing more, sadly." He smiles a little, knowingly, as if he can tell what she's doing. "Only that this is how we get there."

"Get where?"

His smile fades, expression settling into that familiar, disturbing blankness for the briefest of instants. "Warrant."

She remembers, belatedly, that his full name is *Schaffa Guardian Warrant*. It has never occurred to her to wonder where the comm of Warrant is. But what does it mean that the way to Warrant is through a buried dead city? "Wh-why—"

He shakes his head then, expression hardening. "Stop stalling. In this low light, not every nocturnal hunter will wait for night." He glances up at the sky with a look that is only mildly annoyed, as if it does not threaten their lives.

It's pointless to complain that she is ready to drop. It's a Season. If she drops, she dies. So she forces herself through the gap he has broken, and starts questing again for the best route.

In the end they make it, which is good because otherwise this would become the rather straightforward tale of you learning that your daughter is dead, and letting the world wither in your grief.

It isn't even a near thing. Abruptly the last patch of thick grass-trees thins out, revealing a smooth-cut pass through the inner caldera ring. The walls of the pass loom high overhead, though they did not look so tall from far away, and the pass itself is wide enough for two horse-drawn carriages to travel side by side without crowding. The walls of these passages are covered in tenacious mosses and some sort of woody vine, the latter of which is fortunately dead because otherwise it might entangle them and slow their progress more. Instead they hurry forward, cracking the dead branches aside, and then abruptly Nassun and Schaffa stumble out of the pass onto a wide, round slab of perfectly white material that is neither metal nor stone. Nassun's seen something like it before, near other deadciv ruins; sometimes the stuff glows faintly at night. This particular slab fills the entirety of the space within the inner caldera.

Steel has told them that the deadciv ruin is here, at the center—but all Nassun sees ahead of them is a dainty, rising curl of metal, seemingly set directly into the white material. She tenses, as wary of something new as any Seasoned survivor. Schaffa, however, walks over to it without hesitation. He stops beside it, and for an instant there is an odd expression on his face that Nassun suspects is caused by the momentary conflict between what his body has done out of habit and what his mind cannot remember—but then he puts a hand on the curlicue at the tip of the metal.

Flat shapes and lines of light suddenly appear out of nothingness on the stone around him. Nassun gasps, but they do nothing other than march and ignite others in turn, spreading and glowing until a roughly rectangular shape has been etched out on the stone at Schaffa's feet. There is a faint, barely audible hum that makes Nassun twitch and look around wildly, but a moment later the white material in front of Schaffa vanishes. It doesn't slide aside, or open like a door; it's just gone. But it *is* a doorway, Nassun abruptly realizes. "And here we are," Schaffa murmurs. He sounds a little surprised himself.

Beyond this doorway is a tunnel that curves gradually down into the ground and out of sight. Narrow rectangular panels of light edge the steps on either side, illuminating the way. The curling bit of metal is a railing, she sees now, her perception reorienting as she moves to stand beside Schaffa. Something to hold on to, as one walks down into the depths.

In a distant part of the grass forest that they just traversed, there is a high-pitched grating noise that Nassun immediately identifies as animal. Chitinous, maybe. A closer, louder version of the screeches they heard the night before. Nassun flinches and looks at Schaffa.

"Some sort of grasshopper, I believe," he says. His jaw is tight as he gazes back at the pass they just traversed, though nothing moves there—yet. "Or cicadas, perhaps. Inside now. I've seen something like this mechanism before; it should close after we pass through."

He gestures for her to go first so that he can guard the rear. Nassun takes a deep breath and reminds herself that this is what is necessary to make a world that will hurt no one else. Then she trots down the stairs.

The light panels ignite five or six steps ahead as she progresses, and fade three steps behind. Once they're a few feet down, just as Schaffa predicted, the white material that covered the stairwell reappears, cutting off further screeches from the forest.

Then there is nothing but the light, and the stairs, and the long-forgotten city somewhere below.

*   *   *

2699: Two Fulcrum blackjackets summoned to Deejna comm (Uher Quartent, Western Coastals, near Kiash Traps) when Mount Imher showed eruption signs. Blackjackets informed comm officials that eruption was imminent, and that it would likely touch off the whole Kiash cluster, including Madness (local name for the supervolcano that triggered the Madness Season; Imher sits on the same hot spot). Upon determining that Imher was beyond their ability to quell, the blackjackets—one three-ringer, the other supposedly seven although did not wear rings for some reason—made the attempt anyway, due to insufficient time to send for higher-ringed Imperial Orogenes. They successfully stilled the eruption long enough for a nine-ring senior Imperial Orogene to arrive and push it back into dormancy. (Three-ringer and seven-ringer found holding hands, charred, frozen.)

—*Project notes of Yaetr Innovator Dibars*

Syl Anagist: Three

FASCINATING. ALL OF THIS GROWS easier to remember with the telling...or perhaps I am still human, after all.

*   *   *

At first our field excursion is simply the act of walking through the city. We have spent the brief years since our initial decanting immersed in sesuna, the sense of energy in all its forms. A walk outside forces us to pay attention to our other, lesser senses, and this is initially overwhelming. We flinch at the springiness of pressed-fiber sidewalks under our shoes, so unlike the hard lacquerwood of our quarters. We sneeze trying to breathe air thick with smells of bruised vegetation and chemical by-product and thousands of exhaled breaths. Their first sneeze frightens Dushwha into tears. We clap hands over our ears to try, and fail, to screen out many voices talking and walls groaning and leaves rustling and machinery whining in the distance. Bimniwha tries to yell over it all, and Kelenli must stop and soothe her before she will try speaking normally again. I duck and yelp in fear of the birds that sit in a nearby bush, and I am the calmest of us.

What settles us, at last, is finally having the chance to gaze upon the full beauty of the amethyst plutonic fragment. It is an awesome thing, pulsing with the slow flux of magic as it towers over the city-node's heart. Every node of Syl Anagist has adapted in unique ways to suit its local climate. We have heard of nodes in the desert where buildings are grown from hardened giant succulents; nodes on the ocean built by coral organisms engineered to grow and die on command. (Life is sacred in Syl Anagist, but sometimes death is necessary.) Our node—the node of the amethyst—was once an old-growth forest, so I cannot help thinking that something of ancient trees' majesty is in the great crystal. Surely this makes it more stately and strong than other fragments of the machine! This feeling is completely irrational, but I look at my fellow tuners' faces as we gaze at the amethyst fragment, and I see the same love there.

(We have been told stories of how the world was different, long ago. Once, cities were not just dead themselves, stone and metal jungles that did not grow or change, but they were actually deadly, poisoning soil and making water undrinkable and even changing the weather by their very existence. Syl Anagist is better, but we feel nothing when we think of the city-node itself. It is nothing to us—buildings full of people we cannot truly understand, going about business that should matter but does not. The fragments, though? We hear their voices. We sing their magic song. The amethyst is part of us, and we it.)

"I'm going to show you three things during this trip," Kelenli says, once we've gazed at the amethyst enough to calm down. "These things have been vetted by the conductors, if that matters to you." She makes a show of eying Remwha as she says this, since he was the one who made the biggest stink about having to go on this trip. Remwha affects a bored sigh. They are both excellent actors, before our watching guards.

Then Kelenli leads us forward again. It's such a contrast, her behavior and ours. She walks easily with head high, ignoring everything that isn't important, radiating confidence and calm. Behind her, we start-and-stop-and-scurry, all timid clumsiness, distracted by everything. People stare, but I don't think it's actually our whiteness that they find so strange. I think we just look like fools.

I have always been proud, and their amusement stings, so I straighten and try to walk as Kelenli does, even though this means ignoring many of the wonders and potential threats around me. Gaewha notices, too, and tries to emulate both of us. Remwha sees what we are doing and looks annoyed, sending a little ripple through the ambient: *We will never be anything but strange to them.*

I answer in an angry basso push-wave throb. *This is not about them.*

He sighs but begins emulating me, too. The others follow suit.

We have traveled to the southernmost quartent of the city-node, where the air is redolent with faint sulfur smells. Kelenli explains that the smell is because of the waste reclamation plants, which grow thicker here where sewers bring the city's gray water near the surface. The plants make the water clean again and spread thick, healthy foliage over the streets to cool them, as they were designed to do—but not even the best genegineers can stop plants that live on waste from smelling a bit like what they eat.

"Do you mean to show us the waste infrastructure?" Remwha asks Kelenli. "I feel more contextual already."

Kelenli snorts. "Not exactly."

She turns a corner, and then there is a dead building before us. We all stop and stare. Ivy wends up this building's walls, which are made of some sort of red clay pressed into bricks, and around some of its pillars, which are marble. Aside from the ivy, though, *nothing* of the building is alive. It's squat and low and shaped like a rectangular box. We can sess no hydrostatic pressure supporting its walls; it must use force and chemical fastenings to stay upright. The windows are just glass and metal, and I can see no nematocysts growing over their surfaces. How do they keep safe anything inside? The doors are dead wood, polished dark red-brown and carved with ivy motifs; pretty, surprisingly. The steps are a dull tawny-white sand suspension. (Centuries before, people called this *concrete*.) The whole thing is stunningly obsolete—yet intact, and functional, and thus fascinating for its uniqueness.

"It's so . . . symmetrical," says Bimniwha, curling her lip a little.

"Yes," says Kelenli. She's stopped before this building to let us take it in. "Once, though, people thought this sort of thing was beautiful. Let's go." She starts forward.

Remwha stares after her. "What, inside? Is that thing structurally sound?"

"Yes. And yes, we're going inside." Kelenli pauses and looks back at him, perhaps surprised to realize that at least some of his reticence wasn't an act. Through the ambient, I feel her touch him, reassure him. Remwha is more of an ass when he is afraid

146

or angry, so her comfort helps; the spiky jitter of his nerves begins to ease. She still has to play the game, however, for our many observers. "Though I suppose you could stay outside, if you wanted."

She glances at her two guards, the brown man and woman who stay near her. They have not kept back from our group, unlike the other guards of whom we catch glimpses now and again, skirting our periphery.

Woman Guard scowls back at her. "You know better."

"It was a thought." Kelenli shrugs then, and gestures with her head toward the building, speaking to Remwha now. "Sounds like you don't actually have a choice. But I promise you, the building won't collapse on your head."

We move to follow. Remwha walks a little slower, but eventually he comes along, too.

A holo-sign writes itself in the air before us as we cross the threshold. We have not been taught to read, and the letters of this sign look strange in any case, but then a booming voice sounds over the building's audio system: "Welcome to the story of enervation!" I have no idea what this means. Inside, the building smells . . . wrong. Dry and dusty, the air stale as if there's nothing taking in its carbon dioxide. There are other people here, we see, gathered in the building's big open foyer or making their way up its symmetrical twin curving stairs, peering in fascination at the panels of carved wooden decoration which line each stair. They don't look at us, distracted by the greater strangeness of our environs.

But then, Remwha says, "What is that?"

His unease, prickling along our network, makes us all look at him. He stands frowning, tilting his head from one side to the other.

"What is—" I start to ask, but then I hear? sess? it too.

"I'll show you," says Kelenli.

She leads us deeper into the boxy building. We walk past display crystals, each holding preserved within itself a piece of incomprehensible—but obviously old—equipment. I make out a book, a coil of wire, and a bust of a person's head. Placards near each item explain its importance, I think, but I cannot fathom any explanation sufficient to make sense of it all.

Then Kelenli leads us onto a wide balcony with an old-fashioned ornate-wood railing. (This is especially horrifying. We are to rely on a rail made from a dead tree, unconnected to the city alarm grid or anything, for safety. Why not just grow a vine that would catch us if we fell? Ancient times were horrible.) And there we stand above a huge open chamber, gazing down at something that belongs in this dead place as much as we do. Which is to say, not at all.

My first thought is that it is another plutonic engine—a whole one, not just a fragment of a larger piece. Yes, there is the tall, imposing central crystal; there is the socket from which it grows. This engine has even been activated; much of its structure hovers, humming just a little, a few feet above the floor. But this is the only part of the engine that makes sense to me. All around the central crystal float longer, inward-curving structures; the whole of the design is somehow floral, a stylized chrysanthemum. The central crystal glows a pale gold, and the supporting crystals fade from green bases to white at the tips. Lovely, if altogether strange.

Yet when I look at this engine with more than my eyes, and touch it with nerves attuned to the perturbations of the earth, I gasp. Evil Death, the lattice of magics created by the structure is magnificent! Dozens of silvery, threadlike lines supporting one another; energies across spectra and forms all interlinked and state-changing in what seems to be a chaotic, yet utterly controlled, order. The central crystal flickers now and again, phasing through potentialities as I watch. And it's so small! I have never seen an engine so well constructed. Not even the Plutonic Engine is this powerful or precise, for its size. If it had been built as efficiently as this tiny engine, the conductors would never have needed to create us.

And yet this structure makes no sense. There isn't enough magic being fed into the mini-engine to produce all the energy I detect here. And I shake my head, but now I can hear what Remwha heard: a soft, insistent ringing. Multiple tones, blending and haunting and making the little hairs on the back of my neck rise . . . I look at Remwha, who nods, his expression tight.

This engine's magics have no purpose that I can see, other than to look and sound and be beautiful. And somehow—I shiver, understanding instinctively but resisting because this contradicts everything I have learned from the laws of both physics and arcanity—*somehow* this structure is generating more energy than it consumes.

I frown at Kelenli, who's watching me. "This should not exist," I say. Words only. I don't know how else to articulate what I'm feeling. Shock. Disbelief? Fear, for some reason. The Plutonic Engine is the most advanced creation of geomagestry ever built. That is what the conductors have told us, over and over again for all the years since we were decanted...and yet. This tiny, bizarre engine, sitting half-forgotten in a dusty museum, is *more* advanced. And it seems to have been built for no purpose other than beauty.

Why does this realization frighten me?

"But it does exist," Kelenli says. She leans back against the railing, looking lazily amused—but through the soft shimmering harmony of the structure on display, I sess her ping on the ambient.

Think, she says without words. She watches me in particular. Her thinker.

I glance around at the others. As I do, I notice Kelenli's guards again. They've taken up positions on either end of the balcony, so that they can see the corridor we came down as well as the display room. They both look bored. Kelenli brought us here. Got the conductors to agree to bringing us here. Means for us to see something in this ancient engine that her guards do not. What?

I step forward, putting my hands on the dead railing, and peer intently at the thing as if that will help. What to conclude? It has the same fundamental structure as other plutonic engines. Only its *purpose* is different—no, no. That's too simple an assessment. What's different here is...philosophical. Attitudinal. The Plutonic Engine is a tool. This thing? Is...*art*.

And then I understand. No one of Syl Anagist built this.

I look at Kelenli. I must use words, but the conductors who

hear the guards' report should not be able to guess anything from it. "*Who?*"

She smiles, and my whole body tingles all over with the rush of something I cannot name. I am her thinker, and she is pleased with me, and I have never been happier.

"You," she replies, to my utter confusion. Then she pushes away from the railing. "I have much more to show you. Come."

* * *

All things change during a Season.

—*Tablet One, "On Survival," verse two*

7

you're planning ahead

YKKA IS MORE INCLINED TO adopt Maxixe and his people than you were expecting. She's not happy that Maxixe has an advanced case of ash lung—as Lerna confirms after they've all had sponge baths and he's given them a preliminary examination. Nor does she like that four of his people have other serious medical issues, ranging from fistulas to the complete lack of teeth, or that Lerna says they're all going to be touch and go on surviving refeeding. But, as she informs those of you on her impromptu council, loudly so that anyone listening will hear, she can put up with a lot from people who bring in extra supplies, knowledge of the area, and precision orogeny that can help safeguard the group against attack. And, she adds, Maxixe doesn't have to live forever. Long enough to help the comm will be enough for her.

She doesn't add, *Not like Alabaster*, which is kind—or at least conspicuously not-cruel—of her. It's surprising that she respects your grief, and maybe it's also a sign that she is beginning to forgive you. It'll be good to have a friend again. Friends. Again.

That's not enough, of course. Nassun is alive and you've more or less recovered from your post-Gate coma, so now it becomes a struggle, daily, to remember why you're staying with Castrima. It helps, sometimes, to go through the reasons for staying. For Nassun's future, that's one, so that you can have somewhere to shelter her once you've found her again. Because you can't do it alone is the second reason—and you can't rightly let Tonkee come with you anymore, however willing she might be. Not with your orogeny compromised; the long journey back south would be a death sentence for both of you. Hoa isn't going to be able to help you get dressed, or cook food, or do any of the other things one needs two good hands for. And Reason Number Three, the most important of the set: You don't know where to go anymore. Hoa has confirmed that Nassun is on the move, and has been traveling away from the site of the sapphire since you opened the Obelisk Gate. It was too late to find her before you ever woke up.

But there is hope. In the small hours of one morning after Hoa has taken the stone burden of your left breast from you, he says quietly, "I think I know where she's going. If I'm right, she'll stop soon." He sounds uncertain. No, not uncertain. Troubled.

You sit on a rocky outcrop some ways from the encampment, recovering from the…excision. It wasn't as uncomfortable as you thought it would be. You pulled off your clothing layers to bare the stoned breast. He put a hand on it and it came away from your body, cleanly, into his palm. You asked why he didn't do that for your arm and he said, "I do what's most comfortable for you." Then he lifted your breast to his lips and you decided to become fascinated by the flat, slightly roughened cautery of stone over the space where your breast was. It aches a little, but you're not sure whether this is the pain of amputation or something more existential.

(Three bites, it takes him, to eat the breast that Nassun liked best. You're perversely proud to feed someone else with it.)

As you awkwardly pull undershirts and shirts back on with one arm—stuffing one side of your bra with the lightest undershirt so it won't slip off—you probe after that hint of unease that you heard in Hoa's voice earlier. "You know something."

Hoa doesn't answer at first. You think you're going to have to remind him that this is a partnership, that you're committed to catching the Moon and ending this endless Season, that you *care* about him but he can't keep hiding things from you like this—and then he finally says, "I believe Nassun seeks to open the Obelisk Gate herself."

Your reaction is visceral and immediate. Pure fear. It probably isn't what you should feel. Logic would dictate disbelief that a ten-year-old girl can manage a feat that you barely accomplished. But somehow, maybe because you remember the feel of your little girl thrumming with angry blue power, and you knew in that instant that she understood the obelisks better than you ever will, you have no trouble believing Hoa's core premise—that your little girl is bigger than you thought.

"It will kill her," you blurt.

"Very likely, yes."

Oh, Earth. "But you can track her again? You lost her after Castrima."

"Yes, now that she is attuned to an obelisk."

Again, though, that odd hesitation is in his voice. Why?

Why would it bother him that— Oh. Oh, rusty burning Earth. Your voice shakes as you understand. "Which means that *any* stone eater can 'perceive' her now. Is that what you're saying?" Castrima all over again. Ruby Hair and Butter Marble and Ugly Dress, may you never see those parasites again. Fortunately, Hoa killed most of them. "Your kind get interested in us then, right? When we start using obelisks, or when we're close to being able to."

"Yes." Inflectionless, that one soft word, but you know him by now.

"Earthfires. One of you *is* after her."

You didn't think stone eaters were capable of sighing, but sure enough the sound emerges from Hoa's chest. "The one you call Gray Man."

Cold runs through you. But yes. You'd guessed already, really. There have been, what, three orogenes in the world lately who mastered connecting to the obelisks? Alabaster and you and now Nassun. Uche, maybe, briefly—and maybe there was even a stone eater lurking about Tirimo back then. Rusting bastard must be terribly disappointed that Uche died by filicide rather than stoning.

Your jaw tightens as your mouth tastes of bile. "He's manipulating her." To activate the Gate and transform herself into stone, so that she can be *eaten*. "That's what he tried to do at Castrima, force Alabaster, or me, or—rust it, or Ykka, any of us, to try to do something beyond our ability so we might turn ourselves into—" You put a hand on the stone marker of your breast.

"There have always been those who use despair and desperation as weapons." This is delivered softly, as if in shame.

Suddenly you're furious with yourself, and your impotence. Knowing that you're the real target of your own anger doesn't stop you from taking it out on him. "Seems to me *all* of you do that!"

Hoa has positioned himself to gaze out at the dull red horizon, a statue paying homage to nostalgia in pensive shadowed lines. He does not turn, but you hear hurt in his voice. "I haven't lied to you."

"No, you've just withheld the truth so much it's the same fucking thing!" You rub your eyes. Had to take the goggles off to put your shirt back on, and now you've got ash in them. "You know what, just—I don't want to hear anything else right now. I need to rest." You get to your feet. "Take me back."

His hand is abruptly extended in your direction. "One more thing, Essun."

"I told you—"

"Please. You need to know this." He waits until you settle into a fuming silence. Then he says, "Jija is dead."

You freeze.

*   *   *

In this moment I remind myself of why I continue to tell this story through your eyes rather than my own: because, outwardly, you're too good at hiding yourself. Your face has gone blank, your gaze hooded. But I know you. *I know you.* Here is what's inside you.

*   *   *

You surprise yourself by being surprised. Surprised, that is, and not angry, or thwarted, or sad. Just…surprised. But that is because your first thought, after relief that *Nassun's safe now*, is…

Isn't she?

And then you surprise yourself by being afraid. You aren't sure of what, but it's a stark, sour thing in your mouth. "How?" you ask.

Hoa says, "Nassun."

The fear increases. "She couldn't have lost control of her orogeny, she hasn't done that since she was five—"

"It was not orogeny. And it was intentional."

There, at last: the foreshock of a Rifting-level shake, inside you. It takes you a moment to say aloud, "She *killed* him? On purpose?"

"Yes."

You fall silent then, dazed, troubled. Hoa's hand is still extended toward you. An offer of answers. You aren't sure you want to know, but... but you take his hand anyway. Perhaps it's for comfort. You don't imagine that his hand folds about your own and squeezes, just a little, in a way that makes you feel better. Still he waits. You're very, very glad for his consideration.

"Is he... Where is," you begin, when you feel ready. You're not ready. "Is there a way I can go there?"

"There?"

You're pretty sure he knows where you mean. He's just making sure *you* know what you're asking for.

You swallow hard and try to reason it out. "They were in the Antarctics. Jija didn't keep her on the road forever. She had somewhere safe, time to get stronger." A lot stronger. "I can hold my breath underground, if you... Take me to where she w—" But no. That's not really where you want to go. Stop dancing around it. "Take me to where *Jija* is. To... to where he died."

Hoa doesn't move for perhaps half a minute. You've noticed this about him. He takes varying amounts of time to respond to conversational cues. Sometimes his words nearly overlap yours when he replies, and sometimes you think he hasn't heard you before he finally gets around to replying. You don't think he's thinking during that time, or anything. You think it just doesn't mean anything to him—one second or ten, now or later. He heard you. He'll get around to it eventually.

In token of which, at last, he blurs a bit, though you see the slowness of the end of the gesture as he puts his other hand over yours as well, sandwiching you between his hard palms. The pressure of both hands increases until the grip is quite firm. Not uncomfortable, but still. "Close your eyes."

He's never suggested this before. "Why?"

He takes you down. It's further down than you've ever been before, and it isn't instantaneous this time. You gasp inadvertently—somehow—and thus discover that you don't need to hold your breath after all. As the dark gets darker, it brightens with flashes of red, and then for just a moment you blur through molten reds and oranges and catch the most fleeting glimpse of a wavering open space where something in the distance is bursting apart in a shower of semiliquid glowing chunks—and then there is black around you again, and then you stand on open ground beneath a thinly clouded sky.

"That's why," Hoa says.

"Rusty flaking *fuck*!" You try to yank your hand free and fail. "Shit, Hoa!"

Hoa's hands stop pressing so hard on yours, so that you can slip free. You stagger a few feet away and then clap hands over yourself, checking for injury. You're fine—not burned to death, not crushed by the pressure as you should have been, not suffocated, not even shaken up. Much.

You straighten and rub your face. "Okay. I'm really going to have to remember that stone eaters don't say anything without reason. Never wanted to actually *see* the Fire-Under-Earth."

But you're here now, standing atop a hill that is itself on some kind of plateau. The sky is your place-marker. It's later in the morning here than it was where you were—a little after dawn, instead of predawn. The sun is actually visible, though thin through the scrim of ash clouds overhead. (You surprise yourself by feeling an ache of longing at the sight.) But the fact that you can see it means that you're much farther from the Rifting than you were a few moments ago. You glance to the west, and the faint shimmer of a dark blue obelisk in the distance confirms your guess. This is where, a month or so ago when you opened the Obelisk Gate, you felt Nassun.

(That way. She's gone that way. But that way lies thousands of square miles of the Stillness.)

You turn to find that you're standing amid a small cluster of wooden buildings positioned at the top of the hill, including one storeshack on stilts, a few lean-tos, and what look like dormitories or classroom buildings. All of it is surrounded, however, by a neat, precisely level fence of columnar basalt. That an orogene has made this, harnessing the slow explosion of the great volcano beneath your feet, is as plain to you as the sun in the sky. But equally obvious is the fact that the compound is empty. There's no one in sight, and the reverberations of footprints on the ground are farther away, beyond the fence.

Curious, you walk to a break in the basalt fence, where a pathway that is half dirt and half cobbles wends down. At the foot of the hill is a village, occupying the rest of the plateau. The village could be any comm anywhere. You make out houses in varying shapes, most with still-growing housegreens, several standing storecaches, what looks like a bathhouse, a kiln shed. The people moving among the buildings don't glance up to notice you, and why would they? It's a lovely day, here where the sun still mostly shines. They've got fields to tend and—are those little rowboats tied to one of the watchtowers?—trips to the nearby sea to organize. This compound, whatever it is, is unimportant to them.

You turn away from the village, and that's when you spot the crucible.

It's near the edge of the compound, elevated a little above the rest of it, though visible from where you are. When you climb the path to look into the crucible bowl, which is marked out in cobbles and brick, it's old habit to thrust your senses into the ground to find the nearest marked stone. Not far, only maybe five or six feet down. You search its surface and find the faint pressure indentations of a chisel, maybe a hammer. FOUR. It's too easy; in your day the stones were marked with paint and numbers, which made them less distinctive. Still, the stone is small enough that, yes, anyone below a four-ringer would have trouble finding and identifying it. They've got the details of the training wrong, but the basics are spot-on.

"This can't be the Antarctic Fulcrum," you say, crouching to finger one of the stones of the ring. Just pebbles instead of the beautiful tile mosaic you remember, but again, they've got the idea.

Hoa's still standing where you emerged from the ground, hands still positioned to press down on yours, perhaps for the return trip. He doesn't answer, but then you're mostly talking to yourself.

"I always heard that Antarctic was small," you continue, "but this is nothing. This is a camp." There's no Ring Garden. No Main building. Also, you've heard that the Arctic and Antarctic Fulcrums were lovely, despite their size and remote location. That makes sense; the Fulcrum's beauty was all that official, state-sanctioned orogene-kind ever had to show for itself. This sorry collection of shacks doesn't fit the ideology. Also—"It's on a volcano. And too close to those stills down the hill." That village isn't Yumenes, surrounded on all sides by node maintainers and with the added protection of the most powerful senior orogenes. One overwrought grit's tantrum could turn this whole region into a crater.

"It isn't the Antarctic Fulcrum," Hoa says. His voice is usually soft, but he's turned away now, and that makes him softer. "That's farther to the west, and it has been purged. No orogenes live there anymore."

Of course it's been purged. You set your jaw against sorrow. "So this is somebody's idea of homage. A survivor?" Inadvertently you find another marker underground—a small round pebble, maybe fifty feet down. NINE is written on it, in ink. You have no trouble reading it. Shaking your head, you rise and turn to explore the compound further.

Then you stop, tensing, as a man limps out of one of the dormitory-looking buildings. He stops, too, staring at you in surprise. "Who the rust are you?" he asks, in a noticeable Antarctic drawl.

Your awareness plummets into the earth—and then you wrench it back up. Stupid, because remember? Orogeny will kill you? Also, the man isn't even armed. He's fairly young, probably only in his twenties despite an already-receding hairline. The limp is an easy thing, and one of his shoes is built higher than the other—ah. The village handyman, probably, come to do some basic caretaking on buildings that might again be needed someday.

"Uh, hi," you stammer. Then you fall silent, not sure what to say from there.

"Hi." The man sees Hoa and flinches, then stares with the open shock of someone who's only heard of stone eaters in lorist tales, and maybe didn't quite believe them. Only belatedly does he seem to remember you, frowning a little at the ash on your hair and clothing, but it's clear you're not as impressive a sight. "Tell me that's a statue," he says to you. Then he laughs a little, nervously. "Except it wasn't here when I came up the hill. Uh, hi, I guess?"

Hoa doesn't bother replying, though you see his eyes have shifted to watch the man instead of you. You steel yourself and step forward. "Sorry to alarm you," you say. "You from this comm?"

The man finally focuses on you. "Uh, yeah. And you're not." Instead of showing unease, however, he blinks. "You another Guardian?"

Your skin prickles all over. For an instant you want to shout *no*, and then sense reasserts itself. You smile. They always smile. "Another?"

The young man's looking you up and down now, maybe suspicious. You don't care, as long as he answers your questions and doesn't attack you. "Yeah," he says, after a moment. "We found the two dead ones after the children left on that training trip." His lip curls, just a little. You're not sure whether he doesn't believe the children have gone off training, whether he's really upset about "the two dead ones," or whether that's just the usual lip-curl that people wear when they talk about roggas, since it's obvious that's what the children in question must be. If Guardians were here. "Headwoman did say there might be other Guardians along someday. The three we had all popped up out of nowhere, after all, at different times down the years. You're just a late one, I guess."

"Ah." It is surprisingly easy to pretend to be a Guardian. Just keep smiling, and never offer information. "And when did the others leave on their...training trip?"

"About a month ago." The young man shifts, getting comfortable, and turns to gaze after the sapphire obelisk in the distance. "Schaffa said they were going far enough away that we wouldn't feel any aftershakes of what the kids did. Guess that's pretty far."

Schaffa. The smile freezes on your face. You can't help hissing it. "*Schaffa.*"

The young man frowns at you. Definitely suspicious now. "Yeah. Schaffa."

It can't be. He's dead. "Tall, black hair, icewhite eyes, strange accent?"

The young man relaxes somewhat. "Oh. You know him, then?"

"Yes, very well." So easy to smile. Harder to wrestle down the urge to scream, to grab Hoa, to demand that he plunge you both into the earth now, now, now, so you can go and rescue your daughter. Hardest of all not to fall to the ground and curl into a ball, trying to clench the hand you no longer have but that *hurts*; Evil Earth, it aches like it's broken all over again, phantom pain so real your eyes prickle with pain tears.

Imperial Orogenes do not lose control. You haven't been a blackjacket for going on twenty years, and you lose control all the rusting time—but nevertheless the old discipline helps you pull yourself together. Nassun, your baby, is in the hands of a monster. You need to understand how this happened.

"*Very* well," you repeat. No one will think repetition strange, from a Guardian. "Can you tell me about one of his charges? Midlatter girl, brown and willowy, curly hair, gray eyes—"

"Nassun, right. Jija's girl." The young man relaxes completely now, not noticing that you've tensed that much more. "Evil Earth, I hope Schaffa kills her while they're on that trip."

The threat is not to you, but your awareness dips again anyway, before you drag it back. Ykka's right: You really do need to stop defaulting to *kill everything*. At least your smile hasn't faltered. "Oh?"

"Yeah. I think she's the one who did it... Rust, could've been any of 'em, though. That girl's just the one who gave me the shivers the most." His jaw tightens as he finally notices the sharp edges of your smile. But that, too, isn't something that anyone familiar with Guardians would question. He just looks away.

"'Did it'?" you ask.

"Oh. Guess you wouldn't know. Come on, I'll show you."

He turns and limps toward the northern end of the compound. You follow, after a moment's exchanged glance with

Hoa. There's another slight rise here, culminating in a flat area that's clearly been used before for stargazing or just staring at the horizon; you can see much of the surrounding countryside, which still shows shocking amounts of green beneath a relatively recent and still-thin layer of whitening ash.

But here, though, is something strange: a pile of rubble. You think at first it's a glass recycling pile; Jija used to keep one of those near the house back in Tirimo, and neighbors would dump their broken glasses and such there for him to use in glassknife hilts. Some of this looks like higher-quality stuff than just glass; maybe someone's tossed in some unworked semiprecious stone. All jumbled colors, tan and gray and a bit of blue, but rather a lot of red. But there's a pattern to it, something that makes you pause and tilt your head and try to take in the whole of what you're seeing. When you do, you notice that the colors and arrangement of stones at the nearer edge of the pile vaguely resemble a mosaic. Boots, if someone had sculpted boots out of pebbles and then knocked them over. Then those would be pants, except there's the off-white of bone among them and—

No.

Fire. Under. Earth.

No. Your Nassun didn't do this, she couldn't have, she—

She did.

The young man sighs, reading your face. You've forgotten to smile, but even a Guardian would be sobered by this. "Took us a while to realize what we were seeing, too," he says. "Maybe this is something you understand." He glances at you hopefully.

You just shake your head, and the man sighs.

"Well. It was just before they all left. One morning we hear something like thunder. Go outside and the obelisk—big blue one that had been lurking around for a few weeks, you know how they are—is gone. Then later that day there's the same loud *ch-kow*—" He claps his hands as he imitates the sound. You manage not to jump. "And it's back. And then Schaffa suddenly tells the headwoman he's got to take the kids away. No explanation for the obelisk stuff. No mention that Nida and Umber—those are the other two, the Guardians who used to run this place with Schaffa—are dead. Umber's head is staved in. Nida..." He shakes his head. The look on his face is pure revulsion. "The *back* of her head is...But Schaffa doesn't say anything. Just takes the kids away. Lot of us are starting to hope he never brings them back."

Schaffa. That's the part you should focus on. That's what matters, not what was but what is...but you can't take your eyes off Jija. *Burning rust, Jija. Jija.*

*   *   *

I wish I were still flesh, for you. I wish that I were still a tuner, so that I could speak to you through temperatures and pressures and reverberations of the earth. Words are too much, too indelicate, for this conversation. You were fond of Jija, after all, to the degree that your secrets allowed. You thought he loved you—and he did, to the degree that your secrets allowed. It's just that love and hate aren't mutually exclusive, as I first learned so very long ago.

I'm sorry.

*   *   *

You make yourself say, "Schaffa won't be coming back." Because you need to find him and kill him—but even through your fear and horror, reason asserts itself. This strange imitation Fulcrum, which is not the true Fulcrum that he should have brought Nassun to. These children, gathered and not slaughtered. Nassun, openly controlling an obelisk well enough to do *this*...and yet Schaffa has not killed her. Something's going on here that you're not getting.

"Tell me more about this man," you say, lifting your chin toward the pile of jumbled jewels. Your ex-husband.

The young man shrugs in an audible stirring of cloth. "Oh, right, uh. So, his name was Jija Resistant Jekity." Because the young man is sighing down at the pile of rubble, you don't think he sees you twitch at the wrongness of the comm name. "New to the comm, a knapper. We got too many men, but we needed a knapper bad, so when he turned up, we basically would've taken him in as long as he wasn't old or sick or *obviously* crazy. You know?" He shrugs. "The girl seemed all right when they first got here. Wouldn't know her for one of them, she was so proper and polite. Somebody raised her right." You smile again. Perfect tight-jawed Guardian smile. "We only knew what she was because Jija had come here, see. Heard the rumors about how roggas could become...un-roggas, I guess. We get a lot of visitors who ask about that."

You frown and nearly look away from Jija. Un-roggas?

"Not that it ever happened." The young man sighs and adjusts his cane for comfort. "And not that we'd have taken in a kid who used to be one of them, right? What if that kid grew up and had kids who were wrong, too? Got to breed the taint out somehow. Anyway, the girl minded her father well enough until a few weeks ago. Neighbors said they heard him shouting at her one night, and then she moved up here to the compound with the others. You could see how the change sort of...*untied* Jija. He started talking to himself about how she wasn't his daughter anymore. Cursing out loud, now and again. Hitting things— walls and such—when he thought you weren't looking.

"And the girl, she pulled away. Can't say I blame her; everybody was on eggshells around him for that while. Always the quiet ones, right? So I saw her hanging around Schaffa more. Like a duckling, always right there in his shadow. Whenever he'd hold still, she'd take his hand. And he—" The young man eyes you warily. "Don't usually see you lot being affectionate. But he seemed to think the world of her. I hear he nearly killed Jija when the man came at her, actually."

The hand that you don't have twinges again, but it is more tentative this time and not the throb of before. Because... he wouldn't have had to break Nassun's hand, would he? No, no, no. You did that to her yourself. And Uche was another broken hand, inflicted by Jija. Schaffa *protected* her from Jija. Schaffa was affectionate with her, as you struggled to be. And now everything inside you shudders at the thought that follows, and it takes the willpower that has destroyed cities to keep this shudder internal, but...

But...

How much more welcome would a Guardian's conditional, predictable love have been to Nassun, after her parents' unconditional love had betrayed her again and again?

You close your eyes for a moment, because you don't think Guardians cry.

With an effort, you say, "What is this place?"

He looks at you in surprise, then glances at Hoa, a ways

behind you. "This is the comm of Jekity, Guardian. Though Schaffa and the others—" He gestures around you, at the compound. "They called this part of the comm 'Found Moon.'"

Of course they did. And of course Schaffa already knew the secrets of the world that you've paid in flesh and blood to learn.

In your silence, the young man regards you thoughtfully. "I can introduce you to the headwoman. I know she'll be glad to have Guardians around again. Good help against raiders."

You're looking at Jija again. You see one piece of jewel in the perfect likeness of a pinky finger. You know that pinky finger. You kissed that pinky finger—

It's too much, you can't do this, you've got to get a grip, get out of here before you break down any further. "I—I n-need—" Deep breath for calm. "I need some time to consider the situation. Would you go and let your headwoman know I'll come pay my respects shortly?"

The young man side-gazes you for a moment, but you know now that it's not a bad thing if you seem a little off. He's used to Guardian-style offness. Perhaps because of this, he nods and shuffles back awkwardly. "Can I ask you a question?"

No. "Yes?"

He bites his lip. "What's going on? It feels like...Nothing that's happening is normal lately. I mean, it's a Season, but even that feels wrong. Guardians not taking roggas to the Fulcrum. Roggas doing things nobody's ever heard of them doing." He chin-points toward the pile of Jija. "Whatever the rust went on up north. Even those things in the sky, the obelisks...It's all... People are talking. Saying maybe the world's not going to go back to normal. Ever."

You're staring at Jija, but you're thinking of Alabaster. Don't know why.

"One person's normal is another person's Shattering." Your face aches from smiling. There is an art to smiling in a way that others will believe, and you're terrible at it. "Would've been nice if we could've all had normal, of course, but not enough people wanted to share. So now we all burn."

He stares at you for a long, vaguely horrified moment. Then he mumbles something and finally goes away, skirting wide around Hoa. Good riddance.

You crouch beside Jija. He is beautiful like this, all jewels and colors. He is monstrous like this. Beneath the colors you perceive the crazed every-which-wayness of the magic threads in him. It's wholly different from what happened to your arm and your breast. He has been smashed apart and rearranged at random, on an infinitesimal level.

"What have I done?" you ask. "What have I made her?"

Hoa's toes have appeared in your peripheral vision. "Strong," he suggests.

You shake your head. Nassun was that on her own.

"*Alive.*"

You close your eyes again. It's the only thing that should matter, that you've brought three babies into the world and this one, this precious last one, is still breathing. And yet.

*I made her me. Earth eat us both, I made her into **me**.*

And maybe that's why Nassun is still alive. But it's also, you realize as you stare at what she's done to Jija, and as you realize you can't even get revenge on him for Uche because *your daughter has done that for you* . . . why you are terrified of her.

170

And there it is—the thing you haven't faced in all this time, the kirkhusa with ash and blood on its muzzle. Jija owed you a debt of pain for your son, but you owe Nassun, in turn. You *didn't* save her from Jija. You *haven't* been there when she's needed you, here at the literal end of the world. How dare you presume to protect her? Gray Man and Schaffa; she has found her own, better, protectors. She has found the strength to protect herself.

You are so very proud of her. And you don't dare go anywhere near her, ever again.

Hoa's heavy, hard hand presses down on your good shoulder. "It isn't wise for us to stay here."

You shake your head. Let the people of this comm come. Let them realize you aren't a Guardian. Let one of them finally notice how alike you and Nassun look. Let them bring their crossbows and slingshots and—

Hoa's hand curves to grip your shoulder, vise-tight. You know it's coming and still you don't bother to brace yourself as he drags you into the earth, back north. You keep your eyes open on purpose this time, and the sight doesn't bother you. The fires within the earth are nothing to what you're feeling right now, failed mother that you are.

The two of you emerge from the ground in a quiet part of the encampment, though it's near a small stand of trees that a lot of people, by the stink, have apparently been using for a pisser. When Hoa lets you go, you start to walk away and then stop again. Your thoughts have gone blank. "I don't know what to do."

Silence from Hoa. Stone eaters don't bother with unnecessary movement or words, and Hoa has already made his intentions clear. You imagine Nassun talking with Gray Man, and you laugh softly, because he seems more animate and talkative than most of his kind. Good. He's a good stone eater, for her.

"I don't know where to go," you say. You've been sleeping in Lerna's tent lately, but that isn't what you mean. Inside you, there's a clump of emptiness. A raw hole. "I don't have anything left now."

Hoa says, "You have comm and kin. You'll have a home, once you reach Rennanis. You have your life."

Do you really have these things? *The dead have no wishes*, says stonelore. You think of Tirimo, where you didn't want to wait for death to come for you, and so you killed the comm. Death is always with you. Death *is* you.

Hoa says to your slumped back, "I can't die."

You frown, jarred out of melancholy by this apparent non sequitur. Then you understand: He's saying you won't ever lose him. He will not crumble away like Alabaster. You can't ever be surprised by the pain of Hoa's loss the way you were with Corundum or Innon or Alabaster or Uche, or now Jija. You can't hurt Hoa in any way that matters.

"It's safe to love you," you murmur, in startled realization.

"Yes."

Surprisingly, this eases the knot of silence in your chest. Not much, but...but it helps.

"How do you do it?" you ask. It's hard to imagine. Not being able to die even when you want to, even as everything you know and care about falters and fails. Having to go on, no matter what. No matter how tired you are.

"Move forward," Hoa says.

"What?"

"*Move. Forward.*"

And then he is gone, into the earth. Nearby, somewhere, if you need him. Right now, though, he's right: you don't.

Can't think. You're thirsty, and hungry and tired besides. It stinks in this part of camp. The stump of your arm hurts. Your heart hurts more.

You take a step, though, toward the camp. And then another. And another.

Forward.

*　　*　　*

2490: Antarctics near eastern coast; unnamed farming comm twenty miles from Jekity City. Initially unknown event caused everyone in the comm to turn to glass. (?? Is this right? Glass, not ice? Find tertiary sources.) Later, headman's second husband found alive in Jekity City; discovered to be rogga. Under intensive questioning by comm militia, he admitted to somehow doing the deed. Claimed that it was the only way to stop the Jekity volcano from erupting, though no eruption signs were observed. Reports indicate the man's hands were also stone. Questioning interrupted by a stone eater, who killed seventeen militia members and took rogga into earth; both vanished.

—*Project notes of Yaetr Innovator Dibars*

8

Nassun underground

THE WHITE STAIR WINDS DOWNWARD for quite some while. The tunnel walls are close and claustrophobic, but the air somehow isn't stale. Just being free of the ashfall is novelty enough, but Nassun notices that there's not much dust, either. That's weird, isn't it? All of this is weird.

"Why isn't there dust?" Nassun asks as they walk. She speaks in hushed tones at first, but gradually she relaxes—a little. It's still a deadciv ruin, after all, and she's heard lots of lorist tales about how dangerous such places can be. "Why do the lights still work? That door we came through back there, why did it still work?"

"I haven't a clue, little one." Schaffa now precedes her down the steps, on the theory that anything dangerous should encounter him first. Nassun can't see his face, and must gauge his mood by his broad shoulders. (It bothers her that she does this, watching him constantly for shifts of mood or warnings of tension. It is another thing she learned from Jija. She cannot seem to shed it with Schaffa, or anyone else.) He's tired, she can see, but otherwise well. Satisfied, perhaps, that they have made it here. Wary, of what they might find—but that makes two of them. "With deadciv ruins, sometimes the answer is simply 'because.'"

"Do you...remember anything, Schaffa?"

A shrug, not as nonchalant as it should be. "Some. Flashes. The why, rather than the what."

"Then, why? Why do Guardians come here, during a Season? Why don't they just stay wherever they are, and help the comms they join the way you helped Jekity?"

The stairs are ever so slightly too wide for Nassun's stride, even when she keeps to the more narrow inner bend. Periodically she has to stop and put both feet on one step in order to rest, then trot to catch up. He is drumbeat-steady, proceeding without her—but abruptly, just as she asks these questions, they reach a landing within the stairwell. To Nassun's great relief, Schaffa stops at last, signaling that they can sit down and rest. She's still soaked with sweat from the frantic scrabble through the grass forest, though it has begun to dry now that she's moving slower. The first drink of water from her canteen is sweet, and the floor feels comfortingly cool, though hard. She's abruptly sleepy. Well, it *is* night outside, up on the surface where grasshoppers or cicadas now cavort.

Schaffa rummages in his pack and hands her a slab of dried meat. She sighs and begins the laborious process of gnawing on it. He smiles at her grumpiness, and perhaps to soothe her, he finally answers her question.

"We leave during Seasons because we have nothing to offer to a comm, little one. I cannot have children, for one thing, which makes me a less than ideal community adoptee. However much I might contribute toward the survival of any comm, its investment in me will return only short-term gains." He shrugs. "And without orogenes to tend, over time, we Guardians become…difficult to live with."

Because the things in their heads make them want magic all the time, she realizes. And although orogenes make enough of the silver to spare, stills don't. What happens when a Guardian takes silver from a still? Maybe that's why Guardians leave—so no one will find out.

"How do you know you can't have children?" she presses. This is maybe too personal a question, but he has never minded her asking those. "Did you ever try?"

He's taking a drink from his canteen. When he lowers it, he looks bemused. "It would be clearer to say that I *should* not," he says. "Guardians carry the trait of orogeny."

"Oh." Schaffa's mother or father must have been an orogene! Or maybe his grandparents? Anyway, the orogeny didn't come out in him the way it has in Nassun. His mother—she decides arbitrarily that it was his mother, for no particular reason—never needed to train him, or teach him to lie, or break his hand. "Lucky," she murmurs.

He's in the middle of raising the canteen again when he pauses. Something flows over his face. She's learned to read this look of his in particular, despite the fact that it's such a rare one. Sometimes he's forgotten things he wishes he could remember, but right now, he is remembering what he wishes he could forget.

"Not so lucky." He touches the nape of his neck. The bright, nerve-etched network of searing light within him is still active—hurting him, driving at him, trying to break him. At the center of that web is the shard of corestone that someone put into him. For the first time, Nassun wonders *how* it was put into him. She thinks about the long, ugly scar down the back of his neck, which she thinks he keeps his hair long to cover. She shivers a little with the implications of that scar.

"I don't—" Nassun tries to drag her thoughts away from the image of Schaffa screaming while someone *cuts* him. "I don't understand Guardians. The other kind of Guardian, I mean. I don't . . . They're awful." And she cannot even begin to imagine Schaffa being like them.

He doesn't reply for a while, as they chew through their meal. Then, softly, he says, "The details are lost to me, and the names, and most of the faces. But the feelings remain, Nassun. I remember that I *loved* the orogenes to whom I was Guardian—or at least, I believed that I loved them. I wanted them to be safe, even if that meant inflicting small cruelties to hold the greater at bay. Anything, I felt, was better than genocide."

Nassun frowns. "What's genocide?"

He smiles again, but it is sad. "If every orogene is hunted down and slain, and if the neck of every orogene infant born thereafter is wrung, and if every one like me who carries the trait is killed or effectively sterilized, and if even the notion that orogenes are human is denied . . . that would be genocide. Killing a people, down to the very *idea* of them as a people."

"Oh." Nassun feels queasy again, inexplicably. "But that's . . ."

Schaffa inclines his head, acknowledging her unspoken *But that's what's been happening.* "This is the task of the Guardians,

177

little one. We prevent orogeny from disappearing—because in truth, the people of the world would not survive without it. Orogenes are essential. And yet because you are essential, you cannot be permitted to have a *choice* in the matter. You must be tools—and tools cannot be people. Guardians keep the tool... and to the degree possible, while still retaining the tool's usefulness, kill the person."

Nassun stares back at him, understanding shifting within her like an out-of-nowhere niner. It is the way of the world, but it isn't. The things that happen to orogenes don't just happen. They've been *made* to happen, by the Guardians, after years and years of work on their part. Maybe they whispered ideas into the ears of every warlord or Leader, in the time before Sanze. Maybe they were even there during the Shattering—inserting themselves into ragged, frightened pockets of survivors to tell them who to blame for their misery, and how to find them, and what to do with the culprits found.

Everybody thinks orogenes are so scary and powerful, and they are. Nassun is pretty sure she could wipe out the Antarctics if she really wanted, though she would probably need the sapphire to do it without dying. But despite all her power, she's still just a little girl. She has to eat and sleep like every other little girl, among people if she hopes to *keep* eating and sleeping. People need other people to live. And if she has to fight to live, against every person in every comm? Against every song and every story and history and the Guardians and the militia and Imperial law and stonelore itself? Against a father who could not reconcile *daughter* with *rogga*? Against her own despair when she contemplates the gargantuan task of simply trying to be happy?

What can orogeny do against something like that? Keep her breathing, maybe. But breathing doesn't always mean living, and maybe... maybe genocide doesn't always leave bodies.

And now she is more certain than ever that Steel was right.

She looks up at Schaffa. "Till the world burns." It's what he said to her, when she told him what she meant to do with the Obelisk Gate.

Schaffa blinks, then smiles the tender, awful smile of a man who has always known that love and cruelty are two faces of the same coin. He pulls her close and kisses her forehead, and she hugs him tight, so very glad to have one parent, at last, who loves her as he should.

"Till the world burns, little one," he murmurs against her hair. "Of course."

*　　*　　*

In the morning, they resume walking down the winding stair.

The first sign of change is the appearance of another railing on the other side of the stairwell. The railing itself is made of strange stuff, bright gleaming metal not marred at all by verdigris or tarnish. Now, though, there are twin railings, and the stairwell widens enough that two people can walk abreast. Then the winding stairwell begins to unwind—still descending at the same angle, but less and less curved, until finally it extends straight ahead, into darkness.

After an hour or so of walking, the tunnel suddenly opens out, walls and roof vanishing. Now they descend along a trail of lighted, linked stairs that are completely unsupported, somehow, in open air. The stairs should not be possible, held up as they are by nothing but the railing and, apparently, each other—but there is no judder or creak as Nassun and Schaffa walk down. Whatever the stuff that comprises the steps is, it's much stronger than ordinary stone.

And now they're descending into a massive cavern. It's impossible to see how large it is in the darkness, although shafts of illumination slant down from occasional circles of cool white light that dot the cavern's ceiling at irregular intervals. The light illuminates...nothing. The cavern's floor is a vast expanse of empty space filled with irregular, lumpen piles of sand. But now that they are within what Nassun once thought was an empty magma chamber, she can sess things more clearly, and all at once she realizes just how wrong she was.

"This isn't a magma chamber," she tells Schaffa in an awed tone. "It wasn't a cavern at all when this city was built."

"What?"

She shakes her head. "It wasn't *enclosed*. It must have been...I don't know? Whatever's left when a volcano blows up completely."

"A crater?"

She nods quickly, excited with the realization. "It was open to the sky then. People built the city in the crater. But then there was another eruption, right in the middle of the city." She points ahead of them, into the dark; the stairwell is going right toward what she sesses is the epicenter of this ancient destruction.

But that can't be right. Another eruption, depending on the type of lava, should simply have destroyed the city and filled the old crater. Instead, somehow, all the lava went *up and over* the city, spreading out like a canopy and solidifying over it to form this cavern. Leaving the city within the crater more or less intact.

"Impossible," Schaffa says, frowning. "Not even the most viscous lava would behave that way. But…" His expression clouds. Again he is trying to sift through memories truncated and trimmed, or perhaps simply dimmed by age. On impulse Nassun grabs his hand, to encourage him. He glances at her, smiles absently, and resumes frowning. "But I think…an orogene *could* do such a thing. It would take one of rare power, however, and probably the aid of an obelisk. A ten-ringer. At least."

Nassun frowns in confusion at this. The gist of what he's said fits, though: Someone *did* this. Nassun looks up at the ceiling of the cavern and realizes belatedly that what she thought were odd stalactites are actually—she gasps—the leftover impressions of buildings that are no longer there! Yes, there is a narrowing point that must have been a spire; here a curving arch; there a geometric strangeness of spokes and curves that looks oddly organic, like the under-ribs of a mushroom cap. But while these imprints fossil all over the ceiling of the cavern, the solidified lava itself stops a few hundred feet above the ground. Belatedly, Nassun realizes that the "tunnel" from which they emerged is also the remains of a building. Looking back, she sees that the outside of the tunnel looks like one of the cuttlebones that her father once used for fine knapping work—more solid, and made from the same strange white material as the slab up on the surface. That must have been the top of the building. But a few feet below where the canopy ends, the building does, too, to be replaced by this strange white stair. That must have been done sometime after the disaster—but how? And by whom? And why?

Trying to understand what she's seeing, Nassun looks

more closely at the cavern's floor. The sand is mostly pale, though there are mottling patches of darker gray and brown laced throughout. In a few places, twisted lengths of metal or immense broken fragments of something larger—other buildings, maybe—poke through the sand like bones from a half-unearthed grave.

But this is wrong, too, Nassun realizes. There isn't enough material here to be the remnants of a city. She hasn't seen many deadciv ruins, or cities for that matter, but she's read about them and heard stories. She's pretty sure that cities are supposed to be full of stone buildings and wooden storecaches and maybe metal gates and cobbled streets. *This* city is nothing, relatively speaking. Just metal and sand.

Nassun puts down her hands, which she's raised without thinking while her fleshless senses flicker and search. Inadvertently she glances down, which makes the distance between the stair she stands on and that sandy cavern floor yawn and seem to stretch. This makes her step back closer to Schaffa, who puts a reassuring hand on her shoulder.

"This city," Schaffa says. She glances at him in surprise; he looks thoughtful. "There is a word in my mind, but I don't know what it is. A name? Something that holds meaning in another language?" He shakes his head. "But if this is the city I think it is, I have heard tales of its grandeur. Once, they say, this city held billions of people."

That seems impossible. "In one city? How big was Yumenes?"

"A few million." He smiles at her openmouthed gape, then sobers somewhat. "And now there can't be many more people than that, altogether, across the whole of the Stillness. When we lost the Equatorials, we lost the bulk of humanity. Still. Once, the world was even bigger."

It can't be. The volcanic crater is only so vast. And yet... Delicately, Nassun sesses below the sand and debris, searching for evidence of the impossible. The sand is much deeper than she thought. Far beneath its surface, though, she finds pressed pathways in long, straight lines. Roads? Foundations, too, though they are in oblong and round and other odd shapes: hourglass loops and fat S-curves and bowl-shaped dips. Not a single square. She puzzles over the odd composition of these foundations, and then abruptly realizes that it all has the sess of something mineralized, alkaline. Oh, it's petrifying! Which means that originally—Nassun gasps.

"It's wood," she blurts aloud. A building foundation of wood? No, it's something *like* wood, but also a bit like the polymer stuff that her father used to make, and a little like the strange not-stone of the stair they're standing on. All the roads she can sess are something similar. "*Dust.* Everything down there, Schaffa. It's not sand, it's dust! It's *plants*, lots of them, dead so long ago that it's all just dried up and crumbled away. And..." Her gaze is drawn back up to the lava canopy overheard. What must it have been like? The whole cavern lit up in red. The air too hot to breathe. The buildings lasted longer, long enough for the lava to start to cool around them, but every person in this city would have roasted within the first few hours of being buried under a bubble of fire.

That's what's in the sand, too, then: countless people, cooked into char and crumbled away.

"Intriguing," Schaffa says. He leans on the railing, heedless of the distance to the ground as he gazes out over the cavern. Nassun's belly clenches in fear for him. "A city built of plants." Then his gaze sharpens. "But nothing's growing here now."

Yes. That's the other thing Nassun has noticed. She's traveled enough now, and seen enough other caves to know that this place should be teeming with life, like lichens and bats and blind white insects. She shunts her perception into the realm of the silver, searching for the delicate lines that should be everywhere amid so much living detritus. She finds them, lots of them, but...Something is strange. The lines flow together and focus, tiny threads becoming thicker channels—much like the way magic flows within an orogene. She's never seen this happen in plants or animals or soil before. These more concentrated flows come together and continue forward—the direction in which the stairway is going. She follows them well past the stairway she can see, thickening, brightening...and then somewhere ahead, they abruptly stop.

"Something bad is here," Nassun says, her skin prickling. Abruptly she stops sessing. She does not want to sess what's ahead, for some reason.

"Nassun?"

"Something is *eating* this place." She blurts the words, then wonders why she's said them. But now that she's said it, she feels like it was the right thing to say. "That's why nothing grows. Something is taking all the magic away. Without that, everything's dead."

Schaffa regards her for a long moment. One of his hands, Nassun sees, is on the hilt of his black glass poniard, where it's strapped against his thigh. She wants to laugh at this. What's ahead isn't something he can stab. She doesn't laugh because it's cruel, and because she's suddenly so scared that if she starts laughing, she might not stop.

"We don't have to go forward," Schaffa suggests. It is gentle, and badly needed reassurance that he will not lose respect for her if she abandons her mission out of fear.

It bothers Nassun, though. She has her pride. "N-no. Let's keep going." She swallows hard. "Please."

"Very well, then."

They proceed. Someone or something has dug a channel through the dust, beneath and around the impossible stair. As they continue to descend, they pass mountains of the stuff. Presently, though, Nassun sees another tunnel looming ahead. This one is set against the floor of the cavern—at last—and its mouth is immense. Concentric arches, each carved from marble in different shades, loom high overhead as the stairway finally reaches the ground and flattens into the surrounding stones. The tunnel narrows further in; there's only darkness beyond. The floor of the entryway is something that looks like lacquer, tiled in gradient shades of blue and black and dark red. It is rich and lovely color, a relief to the eyes after so much white and gray, and yet it, too, is impossibly strange. Somehow, none of the city's dust has blown or subsided into this entryway.

Dozens of people could pass through that archway. Hundreds in a minute. Now, however, only one stands here, watching them from under a band of rose marble that contrasts sharply against his paler, colorless lines. Steel.

He doesn't move as Nassun walks over to him. (Schaffa comes over, too, but he is slower, tense.) Steel's gray gaze is fixed on an object beside him that is not familiar to Nassun but which would be to her mother: a hexagonal plinth rising from the floor, like a smoky quartz crystal shaft that has been sheared off halfway. Its topmost surface is at a slight angle. Steel's hand is held toward it in a gesture of presentation. *For you.*

So Nassun focuses on the plinth. She reaches toward it and jerks back as something lights up around its rim before her fingers can touch the slanted surface. Bright red marks float in the air above the crystal, etching symbols into empty space. She cannot fathom their meaning, but the color unnerves her. She looks up at Steel, who has not moved and looks as if he's been in the same position since this place was built. "What does it say?"

"That the transport vehicle I told you about is currently nonfunctional," says the voice from within Steel's chest. "You'll need to power and reboot the system before we can use this station."

"'R-re . . . boot?'" She tries to figure out what putting on boots has to do with ancient ruins, then decides to run with the part she understands. "How do I give it power?"

Abruptly, Steel is in a different position, facing the archway that leads deeper into the station. "Go inside and provide power at the root. I'll stay here and key in the start-up sequence once there's enough power."

"What? I don't—"

His gray-on-gray eyes shift over to her. "You'll see what to do inside."

Nassun chews on the inside of her cheek, looking into the archway. It's really dark in there.

Schaffa's hand touches her shoulder. "I'll go with you, of course."

Of course. Nassun swallows and nods, grateful. Then she and Schaffa walk into the dark.

It doesn't stay dark for long. Like on the white stair, small panels of light begin glowing along the sides of the tunnel as they progress. The lights are dim, and yellowy in a way that suggests age, weathering, or... well, or *weariness*. That's the word that pops into Nassun's head for some reason. The light is enough to glimmer off the edges of the tiles beneath their feet. There are doors and alcoves along the tunnel walls, and at one point Nassun spots a strange contraption jutting out about ten feet up. It looks like... a wagon bed? Without wheels or a yoke, and as if that wagon bed was made of the same smooth material as the stair, and as if that wagon bed ran along some kind of track set into the wall. It seems obviously made to transport people; maybe it's how people who couldn't or wouldn't walk got around? Now it is still and dark, locked to the wall forever where its last driver left it.

They notice the peculiar bluish light illuminating the tunnel up ahead, but that still isn't adequate warning enough to prepare them for when the path suddenly curves left, and they find themselves in a new cavern. This much smaller cavern isn't full of dust, or at least not much of it. What it does contain, instead, is a titanic column of solid blue-black volcanic glass.

The column is huge, and irregular, and impossible. Nassun just stares, openmouthed, at this *thing* that fills nearly the whole cavern, ground to ceiling and beyond. That it is the solidified, rapidly cooled product of what must have been a titanic explosion is immediately obvious. That it is somehow the source of the lava canopy which flowed into the adjoining cavern is equally indisputable.

"I see," Schaffa says. Even he sounds overwhelmed, his voice softened by awe. "Look." He points down. This is what finally provides Nassun the focal point to establish perspective, and size, and distance. The thing is huge, because now she can see tiers that descend toward its base, ringing it in concentric octagons. Three of them. On the outermost tier are buildings, she thinks. They're badly damaged, half fallen in, just shells, but she sesses at once why they still exist where the ones in the cavern beyond have crumbled. The heat that must have filled this cavern has metamorphized something in the buildings' construction, hardening and preserving them. Some sort of concussion has done damage, too: All the buildings are torn open on the same side, facing the great glass column. Looking from what she guesses is a three-story building to the glass column, she guesstimates that the column is not as far away as it looks; it's just much bigger than she initially guessed. The size of...oh.

"An obelisk," she whispers. And then she can sess and guess what happened, as clearly as if she were there.

Long ago, an obelisk sat here, at the bottom of this cavern, one of its points jammed into the ground like some kind of bizarre plant. At some point, the obelisk lifted free of the pit, to float and shimmer like its fellows above the strange immensity of the city—and then something went very, very wrong. The obelisk...fell. Where it struck the earth, Nassun imagines she can hear the echo of the concussion; it did not merely fall, it *drove* its way in, punching through and churning down and down and down, powered by all the force of concentrated silver within its core. Nassun can't track its path for more than a mile or so down, but there's no reason to think it didn't just keep going. To where, she cannot guess.

And in its wake, channeled straight up from the most molten part of the earth, came a literal fountain of earthfire to bury this city.

There's still nothing around that looks like a way to supply power to the station. Nassun notices, though, that the cavern's illumination comes from enormous pylons of blue light near the base of the glass column. These make up the lower- and inner-most tier of the chamber. *Something* is making that light.

Schaffa, too, has come to the same conclusion. "The tunnel ends here," he says, gesturing toward the blue pylons and the column's base. "There's nowhere else to go but to the foot of this monstrosity. But are you certain you want to follow in the footsteps of whoever did this?"

Nassun bites her bottom lip. She does not. Here is the wrongness that she sessed from the stair, though she cannot tell its source yet. Still... "Steel wants me to see whatever is down there."

"Are you certain you want to do what he wishes, Nassun?"

She isn't. Steel cannot be trusted. But she's already committed herself to the path of destroying the world; whatever Steel wants cannot be worse than this. So when Nassun nods, Schaffa simply inclines his head in acquiescence, and offers her his hand so that they can walk down the road to the pylons together.

Walking past the tiers feels like moving through a grave-yard, and Nassun feels compelled to a respectful silence for that reason. Between the buildings, she can make out carbonized walkways, melted-glass troughs that must have once held plants, strange posts and structures whose purpose she isn't sure she'd be able to fathom even if they weren't half-melted. She decides that this post is for tying horses, and that frame is where the tanners racked drying hides. Remapping the familiar onto the strange doesn't work very well, of course, because nothing about this city is normal. If the people who lived here rode mounts, they were not horses. If they made pottery or tools, those were not shaped from clay or obsidian, and the crafters who made such things were not merely knappers. These are people who built, and then lost control of, an obelisk. There is no telling what wonders and horrors filled their streets.

In her anxiety, Nassun reaches up to touch the sapphire, mostly just to reassure herself that she can do so through tons of cooled lava and petrifying decayed city. It is as easy to connect to here as it was up there, which is a relief. It tugs at her gently—or as gently as any obelisk does—and for a moment she lets herself be drawn into its flowing, watery light. It does not frighten her to be so drawn in; to the degree that one can trust an inanimate object, Nassun trusts the sapphire obelisk. It is the thing that told her about Corepoint, after all, and now she senses another message in the shimmering interstices of its tight-packed lines—

"Up ahead," she blurts, startling herself.

Schaffa stops and looks at her. "What?"

Nassun has to shake her head, drawing her mind back into itself and out of all that blue. "The . . . the place to put in power. Is up ahead, like Steel said. Past the track."

"Track?" Schaffa turns, gazing down the sloping walkway. Up ahead is the second tier—a smooth, featureless plane of more of that not-stone white stuff. The people who built the obelisks seem to have used that stuff in all their oldest and most enduring ruins.

"The sapphire...knows this place," she tries to explain. It's a fumbling sort of explanation, as hard as trying to describe orogeny to a still. "Not this place specifically, but somewhere like it..." She reaches for it again, asking for more without words, and is nearly overwhelmed with a blue flicker of images, sensations, *beliefs*. Her perspective changes. She stands at the center of three tiers, no longer in a cavern but facing a blue horizon across which pleasant clouds churn and race and vanish and are reborn. The tiers around her teem with activity—though it all blurs together, and what she can discern of the few instants of stillness makes no sense. Strange vehicles like the car she saw in the tunnel run along the sides of buildings, following tracks of differently colored light. The buildings are *covered* in green, vines and grassy rooftops and flowers curling over lintels and walls. People, hundreds of them, go in and out of these, and walk up and down the paths in unbroken blurs of motion. She cannot see their faces, but she catches glimpses of black hair like Schaffa's, earrings of artfully curled vine motifs, a dress swirling about ankles, fingers flicking while adorned with sheaths of colored lacquer.

And everywhere, *everywhere*, is the silver that lies beneath heat and motion, the stuff of the obelisks. It spiders and flows, converging not just into trickles but rivers, and when she looks down she sees that she stands in a pool of liquid silver, soaking in through her feet—

Nassun staggers a little as she comes back this time, and Schaffa's hand lands firmly on her shoulder to steady her. "Nassun."

"I'm all right," she says. She isn't sure of that, but she says it anyway because she doesn't want him to worry. And because it is easier to say this than *I think I was an obelisk for a minute.*

Schaffa moves around to crouch in front of her, gripping her shoulders. The concern in his expression almost, almost, eclipses the weary lines, the hint of distraction, and the other signs of struggle that are building beneath the surface of him. His pain is worse, here underground. He hasn't said that it is, and Nassun doesn't know why it's getting worse, but she can tell.

But. "Don't trust the obelisks, little one," he says. This does not seem nearly as strange or wrong a thing for him to say as it should. On impulse Nassun hugs Schaffa; he holds her tight, rubbing comfort into her back. "We allowed a few to progress," he murmurs in her ear. Nassun blinks, remembering poor, mad, murderous Nida, who said the same thing once. "Back in the Fulcrum. I was permitted to remember that much because it's important. The few who reached ninth- or tenth-ring status... they were always able to sense the obelisks, and the obelisks could sense them in turn. They would have drawn you to them one way or another. They're missing something, incomplete somehow, and that's what they need an orogene to provide.

"But the obelisks killed them, my Nassun." He presses his face into her hair. She's filthy and hasn't truly washed since Jekity, but his words strip away such mundane thoughts. "The obelisks...I *remember.* They will change you, remake you, if they can. That's what that rusting stone eater wants."

His arms tighten for an instant, with a hint of his old strength, and it is the most beautiful feeling in the world. She knows in this moment that he will never falter, never not be there when she needs him, never devolve into a mere fallible human being. And she loves him more than life for his strength.

"Yes, Schaffa," she promises. "I'll be careful. I won't let them win."

Him, she thinks, and she knows he thinks it too. She won't let *Steel* win. At least not without getting what she wants first.

So they are resolved. When Nassun pulls back, Schaffa nods before getting to his feet. They go forward again.

The innermost tier sits in the glass column's blue, gloomy shadow. The pylons are bigger than they looked from afar— perhaps twice as tall as Schaffa, three or four times as wide, and humming faintly now that Nassun and Schaffa are close enough to hear. They're arranged in a ring around what must have once been the resting place of an obelisk, like a buffer protecting the outer two tiers. Like a fence, separating the bustling life of the city from…this.

This: At first Nassun thinks it is a thicket of thorns. The thornvines curl and tangle along the ground and up the inner surface of the pylons, filling all the available space between them and the glass column itself. Then she sees that they aren't thornvines: no leaves. No thorns. Just these curling, gnarling, ropelike twists of something that looks woody but smells a little like fungus.

"How odd," Schaffa says. "Something alive at last?"

"M-maybe they aren't alive?" They do look dead, though they stand out by being still recognizably plants and not crumbled bits of decay on the ground. Nassun does not like it here, amid these ugly vines and in the shadow of the glass column. Is that what the pylons are for, to cut off sight of the vines' grotesquerie from the rest of the city? "And maybe they grew here after... the rest."

Then she blinks, noticing something new about the vine nearest her. It's different from the others around it. Those are obviously dead, withered and blackened and broken off in places. This one, however, looks as though it might be alive. It is ropy and knotted in places, with a wood-like surface that looks old and rough, but whole. Debris litters the floor beneath it—grayish lumps and dust, scraps of dry-rotted cloth, and even a moldering length of frayed rope.

There is a thing Nassun has resisted doing since entering the cavern of the glass column; some things she doesn't quite want to know. Now, however, she closes her eyes and reaches inside the vine with her sense of the silver.

At first it's hard. The cells of the thing—because it *is* alive, more like a fungus than a plant, but there is also something artificial and mechanical about the way it has been made to function—press together so tightly that she doesn't expect to see any silver between them. More dense than the stuff in people's bodies. The arrangement of its substance is almost crystalline, in fact, cells lined up in neat little matrices, which she's never seen in a living thing before.

And now that Nassun has seen down into the interstices of the vine's substance, she can see that it doesn't have any silver in it. What it has instead are... She isn't sure how to describe it. Negative spaces? Where silver should be, but isn't. Spaces that *can be filled* with silver. And as she gingerly explores them, fascinated, she begins to notice the way they pull at her perception, more and more, until—with a gasp, Nassun jerks her perception free.

You'll see what to do, Steel has said. *It should be obvious.*

Schaffa, who has crouched to peer at the bit of rope, pauses and glances at her, frowning. "What is it?"

She stares back at him, but she doesn't have the words to say what needs to be done. The words do not exist. She knows, however, what she needs to do. Nassun takes a step closer to the living vine.

"Nassun," Schaffa says, his voice tight and warning with sudden alarm.

"I have to, Schaffa," she says. She's already lifting her hands. This is where all the silver of the outer cavern has been going, she realizes now; these vines have been eating it up. Why? She knows why, in the deepest and most ancient design of her flesh. "I have to, um, power the system."

Then, before Schaffa can stop her, Nassun wraps both hands around the vine.

It does not hurt. That's the trap of it. The sensation that spreads throughout her body is pleasant, in fact. Relaxing. If she could not perceive the silver, or the way the vine instantly starts dragging every bit of silver out of the spaces between her cells, she would think it was doing something good for her. As it is, it will kill her in moments.

She has access to more silver than just her own, though. Lazily, through the languor, Nassun reaches for the sapphire— and the sapphire responds instantly, easily.

Amplifiers, Alabaster called them, long before Nassun was ever born. *Batteries* is how you think of them, and how you once explained them to Ykka.

What Nassun understands the obelisks to be is simply *engines*. She's seen engines at work—the simple pump-and-turbine things that regulated geo and hydro back in Tirimo, and occasionally more complex things like grain elevators. What she understands about engines would fill less than a thimble, but this much is clear even to a ten-year-old: To work, engines need fuel.

So she flows with the blue, and the sapphire's power flows through her. The vine in her hands seems to gasp at the sudden influx, though this is just her imagination, she's sure. Then it hums in her hands, and she sees how the empty, yawning spaces of its matrices fill and flow with glimmering silver light, and something immediately shunts that light away to somewhere else—

A loud clack echoes through the cavern. This is followed by other, fainter clacks, ramping up to a rhythm, and then a rising, low hum. The cavern brightens suddenly as the blue pylons turn white and blaze brighter, as do the tired yellow lights that they followed down the mosaic tunnel. Nassun flinches even in the depths of the sapphire, and in half a breath Schaffa has grabbed her away from the vine. His hands shake as he holds her close, but he doesn't say anything, his relief palpable as he lets Nassun flop against him. She's suddenly so drained that only his grip holds her up.

And in the meantime, something is coming along the track.

It is a ghostly thing, iridescent beetle green, graceful and sleek and nearly silent as it emerges from somewhere behind the glass column. Nothing of it makes sense to Nassun's eyes. The bulk of it is roughly teardrop-shaped, though its narrower, pointy end is asymmetrical, the tip curving high off the ground in a way that makes her think of a crow's beak. It's huge, easily the size of a house, and yet it floats a few inches above the track, unsupported. The substance of it is impossible to guess, though it seems to have...skin? Yes; up close, Nassun can see that the surface of the thing has the same finely wrinkled texture as thick, well-worked leather. Here and there on that skin she glimpses odd, irregular lumps, each perhaps the size of a fist; they seem to have no visible purpose.

It blurs and flickers, though, the thing. From solidity to translucence and back, just like an obelisk.

"Very good," says Steel, who is suddenly in front of them and to one side of the thing.

Nassun is too drained to flinch, though she's recovering. Schaffa's hands tighten on her shoulders in reflex, then relax. Steel ignores them both. One of the stone eater's hands is upraised toward the strange floating thing, like a proud artist displaying his latest creation. He says, "You gave the system rather more power than absolutely necessary. The overflow has gone into lighting, as you can see, and other systems such as environmental controls. Pointless, but I suppose it does no harm. They'll run down again in a few months, without any source to provide additional power."

Schaffa's voice is very soft and cold. "This could have killed her."

Steel is still smiling. Nassun finally begins to suspect that this is Steel's attempt to mock a Guardian's frequent smiles. "Yes, if she hadn't used the obelisk." There is nothing of apology in his tone. "Death is what usually happens when someone charges the system. Orogenes capable of channeling magic can survive it, however—as can Guardians, who usually can draw upon an outside source."

Magic? Nassun thinks in fleeting confusion.

But Schaffa stiffens. Nassun is confused by his fury at first, and then she realizes: Ordinary Guardians, the uncontaminated kind, draw silver from the earth and put it into the vines. Guardians like Umber and Nida can probably do the same, though they would try only if it served Father Earth's interests. But Schaffa, despite his corestone, cannot rely on the Earth's silver, and cannot draw more of it at will. If Nassun was in danger from the vine, that was because of Schaffa's inadequacy.

Or so Steel means to suggest. Nassun stares at him incredulously, then turns back to Schaffa. She's getting some of her strength back already. "I knew I could do it," she says. Schaffa is still glaring at Steel. Nassun balls up her fists in his shirt and tugs to make him look at her. He blinks and does so, in surprise. "I knew! And I wouldn't have *let* you do the vines, Schaffa. It's because of me that—"

She falters then, her throat closing with impending tears. Some of this is just nerves and exhaustion. Much of it, though, is the sense of guilt that has been lurking and growing within her for months, only now spilling out because she's too tired to keep it in. *It's her fault* that Schaffa has lost everything: Found Moon, the children he cared for, the companionship of his fellow Guardians, the reliable power that should have come from his corestone, even peaceful sleep at night. She's why he's down here in the dust of a dead city, and why they're about to entrust themselves to machinery older than Sanze and maybe the whole *Stillness*, to go to an impossible place and do an impossible thing.

Schaffa sees all this instantly, with the skill of a longtime caretaker of children. The frown clears from his face, and he shakes his head and crouches to face her. "No," he says. "Nothing is your fault, my Nassun. No matter what it has cost me, and no matter what it may cost yet, always remember that I— that I—"

His expression falters. For a fleeting instant, that horrible, blurry confusion is there, threatening to wipe away even this moment in which he means to declare his strength to her. Nassun catches her breath and focuses on him in the silver and bares her teeth as she sees that the corestone in him is alive again, working viciously along his nerves and spidering over his brain, even now trying to force him to heel.

No, she thinks in a sudden fury. She grips his shoulders and shakes him. It takes her whole body to do this because he's such a big man, but it makes him blink and focus through the blur. "You're Schaffa," she says. "You are! And...and you *chose.*" Because that's important. That's the thing the world doesn't want people like them to do. "You're not my Guardian anymore, you're—" She dares to say it aloud at last. "You're my new father. Okay? And th-that means we're family, and...and we have to work together. That's what family does, right? You let me protect *you* sometimes."

Schaffa stares at her, then he sighs and leans forward to kiss her forehead. He stays there after the kiss, nose pressed into her hair; Nassun makes a mighty effort and does not burst into tears. When he speaks at last, the horrible blurriness has faded, as have even some of the pain-lines around his eyes. "Very well, Nassun. *Sometimes*, you may protect me."

That settled, she sniffs, wipes her nose on a sleeve, and then turns to face Steel. He hasn't changed position, so she pulls away from Schaffa and goes over to him, stopping right in front of him. His eyes shift to follow her, lazily slow. "Don't do that again."

She half expects him to say, in his too-knowing voice, *Do what?* Instead he says, "It's a mistake to bring him with us."

Cold washes through Nassun, followed by hot. Is it a threat, or a warning? She doesn't like it, either way. Her jaw feels so tight that she almost bites her tongue trying to speak. "I don't care."

Silence in reply. Is this capitulation? Agreement? Refusal to argue? Nassun doesn't know. She wants to yell at him: *Say you won't hurt Schaffa again!* Even though it feels wrong to yell at any adult. Yet she has also spent the past year and a half learning that adults are people, and sometimes they are wrong, and sometimes somebody *should* yell at them.

But Nassun is tired, so instead she retreats to Schaffa, taking his hand tightly and glaring back at Steel, daring him to say anything else. He doesn't, though. Good.

The huge green thing sort of ripples then, and they all turn to face it. Something is—Nassun shudders, both revolted and fascinated. Something is *growing* from the weird nodules all over the thing's surface. Each is several feet long, narrow, featherlike, attenuating near the tips. In a moment there are dozens of them, curling and waving gently in an unfelt breeze.

Cilia, Nassun thinks suddenly, remembering a picture in an old biomestry creche book. Of course. Why wouldn't people who made buildings out of plants also make carriages that look like germs?

Some of the feathers are flickering faster than others, clustering together for a moment at a point along the thing's side. Then the feathers all peel back, flattening against the mother-of-pearl surface, to reveal a soft rectangle of a door. Beyond, Nassun can see gentle light and surprisingly comfortable-looking chairs, in rows. They will ride in style to the other side of the world.

Nassun looks up at Schaffa. He nods back at her with jaw tight. She does not look at Steel, who hasn't moved and makes no attempt to join them.

Then they climb aboard, and the feathers weave the door shut behind them. As they sit down, the great vehicle utters a low, resonant tone, and begins to move.

*　　*　　*

Wealth has no value when the ash falls.

—*Tablet Three, "Structures," verse ten*

Syl Anagist: Two

I**T'S A MAGNIFICENT HOUSE, COMPACT** but elegantly designed and full of beautiful furnishings. We stare at its arches and bookcases and wooden bannisters. There are only a few plants growing from the cellulose walls, so the air is dry and a little stale. It feels like the museum. We cluster together in the big room at the front of the house, afraid to move, afraid to touch anything.

"Do you live here?" one of the others asks Kelenli.

"Occasionally," she says. Her face is expressionless, but there is something in her voice that troubles me. "Follow me."

She leads us through the house. A den of stunning comfort: every surface soft and sittable, even the floor. What strikes me is that nothing is white. The walls are green and in some places painted a deep, rich burgundy. In the next room, the beds are covered in blue and gold fabric in contrasting textures. Nothing is hard and nothing is bare and I have never *thought* before that the chamber I live in is a prison cell, but now for the first time, I do.

I have thought many new things this day, especially during our journey to this house. We walked the whole way, our feet aching with the unaccustomed use, and the whole way, people stared. Some whispered. One reached out to stroke my hair in passing, then giggled when I belatedly twitched away. At one point a man followed us. He was older, with short gray hair almost the same texture as ours, and he began to say angry things. Some of the words I did not know ("Niesbred" and "forktongue," for example). Some I knew, but did not understand. ("Mistakes" and "We should have wiped you out," which makes no sense because we were very carefully and intentionally made.) He accused us of lying, though none of us spoke to him, and of only pretending to be gone (somewhere). He said that his parents and his parents' parents taught him the true horror, the true enemy, monsters like us were the enemy of all good people, and he was going to make sure we didn't hurt anyone else.

Then he came closer, big fists balled up. As we stumbled along gawping, so confused that we did not even realize we were in danger, some of our unobtrusive guards abruptly became more obtrusive and pulled the man into a building alcove, where they held him while he shouted and struggled to get at us. Kelenli kept walking forward the whole time, her head high, not looking at the man. We followed, knowing nothing else to do, and after a while the man fell behind us, his words lost to the sounds of the city.

Later, Gaewha, shaking a little, asked Kelenli what was wrong with the angry man. Kelenli laughed softly and said, "He's Sylanagistine." Gaewha subsided into confusion. We all sent her quick pulses of reassurance that we are equally mystified; the problem was not her.

This is normal life in Syl Anagist, we understand, as we walk through it. Normal people on the normal streets. Normal touches that make us cringe or stiffen or back up quickly. Normal houses with normal furnishings. Normal gazes that avert or frown or ogle. With every glimpse of normalcy, the city teaches us just how abnormal we are. I have never minded before that we were merely constructs, genegineered by master biomagests and developed in capsids of nutrient slush, decanted fully grown so that we would need no nurturing. I have been...proud, until now, of what I am. I have been content. But now I see the way these normal people look at us, and my heart aches. I don't understand why.

Perhaps all the walking has damaged me.

Now Kelenli leads us through the fancy house. We pass through a doorway, however, and find an enormous sprawling garden behind the house. Down the steps and around the dirt path, there are flower beds everywhere, their fragrance summoning us closer. These aren't like the precisely cultivated, genegineered flower beds of the compound, with their color-coordinated winking flowers; what grows here is wild, and perhaps inferior, their stems haphazardly short or long and their petals frequently less than perfect. And yet...I like them. The carpet of lichens that covers the path invites closer study, so we confer in rapid pulse-waves as we crouch and try to understand why it feels so springy and pleasant beneath our feet. A pair of scissors dangling from a stake invites curiosity. I resist the urge to claim some of the pretty purple flowers for myself, though Gaewha tries the scissors and then clutches some flowers in her hand, tightly, fiercely. We have never been allowed possessions of our own.

I watch Kelenli surreptitiously, compulsively, while she watches us play. The strength of my interest confuses and frightens me a little, though I seem unable to resist it. We've always known that the conductors failed to make us emotionless, but we...well. *I* thought us above such *intensity* of feeling. That's what I get for being arrogant. Now here we are, lost in sensation and reaction. Gaewha huddles in a corner with the scissors, ready to defend her flowers to the death. Dushwha spins in circles, laughing deliriously; I'm not sure exactly at what. Bimniwha has cornered one of our guards and is peppering him with questions about what we saw during the walk here; the guard has a hunted look and seems to be hoping for rescue. Salewha and Remwha are in an intense discussion as they crouch beside a little pond, trying to figure out whether the creatures moving in the water are fish or frogs. Their conversation is entirely auditory, no earthtalk at all.

And I, fool that I am, watch Kelenli. I want to understand what she means us to learn, either from that art-thing at the museum or our afternoon garden idyll. Her face and sessapinae reveal nothing, but that's all right. I also want to simply look at her face and bask in that deep, powerful orogenic presence of hers. It's nonsensical. Probably disturbing to her, though she ignores me if so. I want her to look at me. I want to speak to her. I want to *be* her.

I decide that what I'm feeling is love. Even if it isn't, the idea is novel enough to fascinate me, so I decide to follow where its impulses lead.

After a time, Kelenli rises and walks away from where we wander the garden. At the center of the garden is a small structure, like a tiny house but made of stone bricks rather than the cellulose greenstrate of most buildings. One determined ivy grows over its nearer wall. When she opens the door of this house, I am the only one who notices. By the time she's stepped inside, all the others have stopped whatever they were doing and stood to watch her, too. She pauses, amused—I think—by our sudden silence and anxiety. Then she sighs and jerks her head in a silent *Come on*. We scramble to follow.

Inside—we cram carefully in after Kelenli; it's a tight fit—the little house has a wooden floor and some furnishings. It's nearly as bare as our cells back at the compound, but there are some important differences. Kelenli sits down on one of the chairs and we realize: This is hers. *Hers.* It is her...cell? No. There are peculiarities all around the space, things that offer intriguing hints as to Kelenli's personality and past. Books on a shelf in the corner mean that someone has taught her to read. A brush on the edge of the sink suggests that she does her own hair, impatiently to judge by the amount of hair caught in its bristles. Maybe the big house is where she is supposed to be, and maybe she actually sleeps there sometimes. This little garden house, however, is...her home.

"I grew up with Conductor Gallat," Kelenli says softly. (We've sat down on the floor and chairs and bed around her, rapt for her wisdom.) "Raised alongside him, the experiment to his control—just as I'm your control. He's ordinary, except for a drop of undesirable ancestry."

I blink my icewhite eyes, and think of Gallat's, and suddenly I understand many new things. She smiles when my mouth drops open in an O. Her smile doesn't last long, however.

"They—Gallat's parents, who I thought were my parents—didn't tell me at first what I was. I went to school, played games, did all the things a normal Sylanagistine girl does while growing up. But they didn't treat me the same. For a long time I thought it was something I'd done." Her gaze drifts away, weighty with old bitterness. "I wondered why I was so horrible that even my parents couldn't seem to love me."

Remwha crouches to rub a hand along the wooden slats of the floor. I don't know why he does anything. Salewha is still outside, since Kelenli's little house is too cramped for her tastes; she has gone to stare at a tiny, fast-moving bird that flits among the flowers. She listens through us, though, through the house's open door. We all need to hear what Kelenli says, with voice and vibration and the steady, heavy weight of her gaze.

"Why did they deceive you?" Gaewha asks.

"The experiment was to see if I could be human." Kelenli smiles to herself. She's sitting forward in her chair, elbows braced on her knees, looking at her hands. "See if, raised among decent, natural folk, I might turn out at least decent, if not natural. And so my every achievement was counted a Sylanagistine success, while my every failure or display of poor behavior was seen as proof of genetic degeneracy."

Gaewha and I look at each other. "Why would you be indecent?" she asks, utterly mystified.

Kelenli blinks out of her reverie and stares at us for a moment, and in that time we feel the gulf between us. She thinks of herself as one of us, which she is. She thinks of herself as a person, too, though. Those two concepts are incompatible.

"Evil Death," she says softly, wonderingly, echoing our thoughts. "You really don't know anything, do you?"

Our guards have taken up positions at the top of the steps leading into the garden, nowhere in earshot. This space is as private as anything we have had today. It is almost surely bugged, but Kelenli does not seem to care, and we don't, either. She draws up her feet and wraps her arms around her knees, curiously vulnerable for someone whose presence within the strata is as deep and dense as a mountain. I reach up to touch her ankle, greatly daring, and she blinks and smiles at me, reaching down to cover my fingers with her hand. I will not understand my feelings for centuries afterward.

The contact seems to strengthen Kelenli. Her smile fades and she says, "Then I'll tell you."

Remwha is still studying her wooden floor. He rubs the grain of it with his fingers and manages to send along its dust molecules: *Should you?* I am chagrined because it's something I should have considered.

She shakes her head, smiling. No, she shouldn't.

But she does anyway, through the earth so we will know it's true.

*   *   *

Remember what I have told you: The Stillness in these days is three lands, not one. Their names, if this matters, are Maecar, Kakhiarar, and Cilir. Syl Anagist started out as part of Kakhiarar, then all of it, then all of Maecar, too. All became Syl Anagist.

Cilir, to the south, was once a small and nothing land occupied by many small and nothing peoples. One of these groups was the Thniess. It was hard to say their name with the proper pronunciation, so Sylanagistines called them Niess. The two words did not mean the same thing, but the latter is what caught on.

The Sylanagistines took their land. The Niess fought, but then responded like any living thing under threat—with diaspora, sending whatever was left of themselves flying forth to take root and perhaps survive where it could. The descendants of these Niess became part of *every* land, *every* people, blending in among the rest and adapting to local customs. They managed to keep hold of who they were, though, continuing to speak their own language even as they grew fluent in other tongues. They maintained some of their old ways, too—like splitting their tongues with salt acid, for reasons known only to them. And while they lost much of the distinctive look that came of isolation within their small land, many retained enough of it that to this day, icewhite eyes and ashblow hair carry a certain stigma.

Yes, you see now.

But the thing that made the Niess truly different was their magic. Magic is everywhere in the world. Everyone sees it, feels it, flows with it. In Syl Anagist, magic is cultivated in every flower bed and tree line and grapevine-draped wall. Each household or business must produce its share, which is then funneled away in genegineered vines and pumps to become the power source for a global civilization. It is illegal to kill in Syl Anagist because life is a valuable resource.

The Niess did not believe this. Magic could not be owned, they insisted, any more than life could be—and thus they wasted both, by building (among many other things) plutonic engines that did nothing. They were just ... pretty. Or thought-provoking, or crafted for the sheer joy of crafting. And yet this "art" ran more efficiently and powerfully than anything the Sylanagistine had ever managed.

How did it begin? You must understand that fear is at the root of such things. Niespeople looked different, behaved differently, *were* different—but every group is different from others. Differences alone are never enough to cause problems. Syl Anagist's assimilation of the world had been over for a century before I was ever made; all cities were Syl Anagist. All languages had become Sylanagistine. But there are none so frightened, or so strange in their fear, as conquerors. They conjure phantoms endlessly, terrified that their victims will someday do back what was done to them—even if, in truth, their victims couldn't care less about such pettiness and have moved on. Conquerors live in dread of the day when they are shown to be, not superior, but simply lucky.

So when Niess magic proved more efficient than Sylanagistine, even though the Niess did not use it as a weapon...

This is what Kelenli told us. Perhaps it began with whispers that white Niess irises gave them poor eyesight and perverse inclinations, and that split Niess tongues could not speak truth. That sort of sneering happens, cultural bullying, but things got worse. It became easy for scholars to build reputations and careers around the notion that Niess sessapinae were fundamentally different, somehow—more sensitive, more active, less controlled, less civilized—and that this was the source of their magical peculiarity. This was what made them not the same kind of human as everyone else. Eventually: not *as* human as everyone else. Finally: not human at all.

Once the Niess were gone, of course, it became clear that the fabled Niess sessapinae did not exist. Sylanagistine scholars and biomagestres had plenty of prisoners to study, but try as they might, no discernible variance from ordinary people could be found. This was intolerable; more than intolerable. After all, if the Niess were just ordinary human beings, then on what basis had military appropriations, pedagogical reinterpretation, and entire disciplines of study been formed? Even the grand dream itself, Geoarcanity, had grown out of the notion that Sylanagistine magestric theory—including its scornful dismissal of Niess efficiency as a fluke of physiology—was superior and infallible.

If the Niess were merely human, the world built on their inhumanity would fall apart.

So...they made us.

We, the carefully engineered and denatured remnants of the Niess, have sessapinae far more complex than those of ordinary people. Kelenli was made first, but she wasn't different enough. Remember, we must be not just tools, but myths. Thus we later creations have been given exaggerated Niess features—broad faces, small mouths, skin nearly devoid of color, hair that laughs at fine combs, and we're all so short. They've stripped our limbic systems of neurochemicals and our lives of experience and language and knowledge. And only now, when we have been made over in the image of their own fear, are they satisfied. They tell themselves that in us, they've captured the quintessence and power of who the Niess really were, and they congratulate themselves on having made their old enemies useful at last.

But we are not the Niess. We aren't even the glorious symbols of intellectual achievement that I believed we were. Syl Anagist is built on delusions, and we are the product of lies. *They have no idea what we really are.*

It's up to us, then, to determine our own fate and future.

*   *   *

When Kelenli's lesson is done, a few hours have passed. We sit at her feet, stunned, changed and changing by her words.

It's getting late. She gets up. "I'm going to get us some food and blankets," she says. "You'll stay here tonight. We'll visit the third and final component of your tuning mission tomorrow."

We have never slept anywhere but our cells. It's exciting. Gaewha sends little pulses of delight through the ambient, while Remwha is a steady buzz of pleasure. Dushwha and Bimniwha spike now and again with anxiety; will we be all right, doing this thing that human beings have done throughout history— sleeping in a different place? The two of them curl together for security, though this actually increases their anxiety for a time. We are not often allowed to touch. They stroke one another, though, and this gradually calms them both.

Kelenli is amused by their fear. "You'll be all right, though I suppose you'll figure that out for yourselves in the morning," she says. Then she heads for the door to go. I am standing at the door, looking through its window at the newly risen Moon. She touches me because I'm in her way. I don't move at once, though. Because of the direction that the window in my cell faces, I don't get to see the Moon often. I want to savor its beauty while I can.

"Why have you brought us here?" I ask Kelenli, while still staring at it. "Why tell us these things?"

She doesn't answer at once. I think she's looking at the

Moon, too. Then she says, in a thoughtful reverberation of the earth, *I've studied what I could of the Niess and their culture. There isn't much left, and I have to sift the truth from all the lies. But there was a . . . a practice among them. A vocation. People whose job it was to see that the truth got told.*

I frown in confusion. "So . . . what? You've decided to carry on the traditions of a dead people?" Words. I'm stubborn.

She shrugs. "Why not?"

I shake my head. I'm tired, and overwhelmed, and perhaps a little angry. This day has upended my sense of self. I've spent my whole life knowing I was a tool, yes; not a person, but at least a symbol of power and brilliance and pride. Now I know I'm really just a symbol of paranoia and greed and hate. It's a lot to deal with.

"Let the Niess go," I snap. "They're dead. I don't see the sense in trying to remember them."

I want her to get angry, but she merely shrugs. "That's your choice to make—once you know enough to make an informed choice."

"Maybe I didn't want to be informed." I lean against the glass of the door, which is cool and does not sting my fingers.

"You wanted to be strong enough to hold the onyx."

I blurt a soft laugh, too tired to remember I should pretend to feel nothing. Hopefully our observers won't notice. I shift to earthtalk, and speak in an acid, pressurized boil of bitterness and contempt and humiliation and heartbreak. *What does it matter?* is what it means. *Geoarcanity is a lie.*

She shakes apart my self-pity with gentle, inexorable slipstrike laughter. "Ah, my thinker. I didn't expect melodrama from you."

"What is melo—" I shake my head and fall silent, tired of not knowing things. Yes, I'm sulking.

Kelenli sighs and touches my shoulder. I flinch, unused to the warmth of another person's hand, but she keeps it in place and this quiets me.

"Think," she repeats. "Does the Plutonic Engine work? Do your sessapinae? You aren't what they made you to be; does that negate what you *are*?"

"I— That question doesn't make sense." But now I'm just being stubborn. I understand her point. I'm not what they made me; I'm something different. I am powerful in ways they did not expect. They made me but they do not *control* me, not fully. This is why I have emotions though they tried to take them away. This is why we have earthtalk . . . and perhaps other gifts that our conductors don't know about.

She pats my shoulder, pleased that I seem to be working through what she's told me. A spot on the floor of her house calls to me; I will sleep so well tonight. But I fight my exhaustion, and remain focused on her, because I need her more than sleep, for now.

"You see yourself as one of these . . . truth-tellers?" I ask.

"Lorist. The last Niess lorist, if I have the right to claim such a thing." Her smile abruptly fades, and for the first time I realize what a wealth of weariness and hard lines and sorrow her smiles cover. "Lorists were warriors, storytellers, nobility. They told their truths in books and song and through their art engines. I just . . . talk. But I feel like I've earned the right to claim some part of their mantle." *Not all fighters use knives, after all.*

In earthtalk there can be nothing but truth—and sometimes

more truth than one wants to convey. I sense...something, in her sorrow. Grim endurance. A flutter of fear like the lick of salt acid. Determination to protect...something. It's gone, a fading vibration, before I can identify more.

She takes a deep breath and smiles again. So few of them are real, her smiles.

"To master the onyx," she continues, "you need to understand the Niess. What the conductors don't realize is that it responds best to a certain emotional resonance. Everything I'm telling you should help."

Then, finally, she pushes me gently aside so that she can go. The question must be asked now. "So what happened," I say slowly, "to the Niess?"

She stops, and chuckles, and for once it is genuine. "You'll find out tomorrow," she says. "We're going to see them."

I'm confused. "To their graves?"

"Life is sacred in Syl Anagist," she says over her shoulder. She's passed through the door; now she keeps going without stopping or turning back. "Don't you know that?" And then she is gone.

It is an answer that I feel I should understand—but in my own way, I am still innocent. Kelenli is kind. She lets me keep that innocence for the rest of the night.

*   *   *

To: Alma Innovator Dibars
From: Yaetr Innovator Dibars

Alma, the committee can't pull my funding. Look, this is just the dates of the incidents I've gathered. Just look at the last ten!

2729
2714–2719: Choking
2699
2613
2583
2562
2530
2501
2490
2470
2400
2322–2329: Acid

Is Seventh even interested in the fact that our popular conception of the frequency of Season-level events is completely wrong? These things aren't happening every two hundred or three hundred years. It's more like every thirty or forty! If not for roggas, we'd be a thousand times dead. And with these dates and the others I've compiled, I'm trying to put together a predictive model for the more intensive Seasons. There's a cycle here, a rhythm. Don't we need to know in advance if the next Season is going to be longer or worse somehow? How can we prepare for the future if we won't acknowledge the past?

9

the desert, briefly, and you

DESERTS ARE WORSE THAN MOST places, during Seasons. Tonkee lets Ykka know that water will be easy; Castrima's Innovators have already assembled a number of contraptions they're calling dew-catchers. The sun won't be an issue either, thanks to the ash clouds that you never thought you'd have cause to thank. It will be chilly, in fact, though less so by day. You might even get a bit of snow.

No, the danger of deserts during a Season is simply that nearly all animals and insects there hibernate, deep under the sand where it's still warm. There are those who claim to have figured out a surefire method of digging up sleeping lizards and such, but those are usually scams; the few comms that edge the desert guard such secrets jealously. The surface plants will have already shriveled away or been eaten by creatures preparing for hibernation, leaving nothing aboveground but sand and ash. Stonelore's advice on entering deserts during Seasons is simply: don't. Unless you mean to starve.

The comm spends two days camped at the edge of the Merz,

preparing, though the truth is—as Ykka has confided in you, while you sat with her sharing your last mellow—there's really no amount of preparation that will make the journey any easier. People are going to die. You won't be one of them; it's a curious feeling knowing that Hoa can whisk you away to Corepoint if there's any real danger. It's cheating, maybe. Except it's not. Except you're going to help as much as you can—and because you won't die, you're going to watch a lot of other people suffer. That's the least you can do, now that you've committed to the cause of Castrima. Bear witness, and fight like earthfires to keep death from claiming more than its share.

In the meantime, the folks on cookfire duty pull double shifts roasting insects, drying tubers, baking the last of the grain stores into cakes, salting meat. After they were fed enough to have some strength, Maxixe's surviving people turned out to be especially helpful with foraging, since several are locals and remember where there might be abandoned farms or debris from the Rifting shake that hasn't been too picked over. Speed will be of the essence; survival means winning the race between the Merz's width and Castrima's supplies. Because of this, Tonkee—who is increasingly becoming a spokesperson for the Innovators, much to her own disgruntlement—oversees a quick and dirty breakdown and rebuilding of the storage wagons to a new lighter, more shock-resistant design that should pull more easily over desert sand. The Resistants and Breeders redistribute the remaining supplies to make sure the loss of any one wagon, if it must be abandoned, won't cause some kind of critical shortage.

The night before the desert, you're hunkered down beside one of the cookfires, still-awkwardly navigating how to feed yourself with one arm, when someone sits down beside you. It startles you a little, and you jerk enough to knock your cornbread off the plate. The hand that reaches into your view to retrieve it is broad and bronze and nicked with combat scars, and there's a bit of yellow watered silk—filthy and ragged now, but still recognizable as such—looped around the wrist. Danel.

"Thanks," you say, hoping she won't use the opportunity to strike up a conversation.

"They say you were Fulcrum once," she says, handing the cornbread back to you. No such luck, then.

It really shouldn't surprise you that the people of Castrima have been gossiping. You decide not to care, using the cornbread to sop up another mouthful of stew. It's especially good today, thickened with corn flour and rich with the tender, salty meat that's been plentiful since the stone forest. Everybody needs as much fat on them as they can pack away, to prepare for the desert. You don't think about the meat.

"I was," you say, in what you hope sounds like a tone of warning.

"How many rings?"

You grimace in distaste, consider trying to explain the "unofficial" rings that Alabaster gave you, consider how far you've come beyond even those, consider being humble...and then finally you settle for accuracy. "Ten." Essun Tenring, the Fulcrum would call you now, if the seniors would bother to acknowledge your current name, and if the Fulcrum still existed. For what it's worth.

Danel whistles appreciatively. So strange to encounter someone who knows and cares about such things. "They say," she continues, "that you can do things with the obelisks. That's how you beat us, at Castrima; I had no idea you'd be able to rile up the bugs that way. Or trap so many of the stone eaters."

You pretend not to care and concentrate on the cornbread. It's just a little sweet; the cookfire squad is trying to use up the sugar, to make room for edibles with more nutritional value. It's delicious.

"They say," Danel continues, watching you sidelong, "that a ten-ring rogga broke the world, up in the Equatorials."

Okay, no. "Orogene."

"What?"

"*Orogene*." It's petty, maybe. Because of Ykka's insistence on making *rogga* a use-caste name, all the stills are tossing the word around like it doesn't mean anything. It's not petty. It means something. "Not 'rogga.' *You* don't get to say 'rogga.' You haven't earned that."

Silence for a few breaths. "All right," Danel says then, with no hint of either apology or humoring you. She just accepts the new rule. She also doesn't insinuate again that you're the person who caused the Rifting. "Point stands, though. You can do things most orogenes can't. Yeah?"

"Yeah." You blow a stray ash flake off the baked potato.

"They say," Danel says, planting her hands on her knees and leaning forward, "that you know how to end this Season. That you're going to be leaving soon to go somewhere and actually try. And that you'll need people to go with you, when you do."

What. You frown at your potato. "Are you volunteering?"

"Maybe."

You stare at her. "You *just* got accepted into the Strongbacks."

Danel regards you for a moment longer, expression unreadably still. You don't realize she's wavering, trying to decide whether to reveal something about herself to you, until she sighs and does it. "I'm Lorist caste, actually. Danel Lorist Rennanis, once. Danel Strongback Castrima's never gonna sound right."

You must look skeptical as you try to visualize her with black lips. She rolls her eyes and looks away. "Rennanis didn't *need* lorists, the headman said. It needed soldiers. And everybody knows lorists are good in a fight, so—"

"What?"

She sighs. "Equatorial lorists, I mean. Those of us who come out of the old Lorist families train in hand-to-hand, the arts of war, and so forth. It makes us more useful during Seasons, and in the task of defending knowledge."

You had no idea. But— "Defending *knowledge*?"

A muscle flexes in Danel's jaw. "Soldiers might get a comm through a Season, but storytellers are what kept Sanze going through seven of them."

"Oh. Right."

She makes a palpable effort to not shake her head at Midlatter provincialism. "Anyway. Better to be a general than cannon fodder, since that was the only choice I was given. But I've tried not to forget who I really am . . ." Abruptly her expression grows troubled. "You know, I can't remember the exact wording of Tablet Three anymore? Or the Tale of Emperor Mutshatee. Just two years without stories, and I'm losing them. Never thought it would happen so fast."

You're not sure what to say to that. She looks so grim that you almost want to reassure her. *Oh, it'll be all right now that you're no longer occupying your mind with the wholesale slaughter of the Somidlats,* or something like that. You don't think you could pull that off without sounding a little snide, though.

Danel's jaw tightens in a determined sort of way anyway as she looks sharply at you. "I know when I see new stories being written, though."

"I . . . I don't know anything about that."

She shrugs. "The hero of the story never does."

Hero? You laugh a little, and it's got an edge. Can't help thinking of Allia, and Tirimo, and Meov, and Rennanis, and Castrima. Heroes don't summon swarms of nightmare bugs to eat their enemies. Heroes aren't monsters to their daughters.

"I *won't* forget what I am," Danel continues. She's braced one hand on her knee and is leaning forward, insistent. Somewhere in the last few days, she's gotten her hands on a knife, and used it to shave the sides of her scalp. It gives her a naturally lean, hungry look. "If I'm possibly the last Equatorial lorist left, then it's my duty to go with you. To write the tale of what happens— and if I survive, to make sure the world hears it."

This is ridiculous. You stare at her. "You don't even know where we're going."

"Figured we'd settle the issue of *whether* I'm going first, but we can skip to the details if you want."

"I don't trust you," you say, mostly in exasperation.

"I don't trust you, either. But we don't have to like each other to work together." Her own plate is empty; she picks it up and waves to one of the kids on cleanup duty to come take it. "It's not like I have a reason to kill you, anyway. This time."

And it's worse that Danel has said this—that she remembers

siccing a shirtless Guardian on you and is unapologetic about it. Yes, it was war and, yes, you later slaughtered her army, but . . . "People like you don't need a reason!"

"I don't think you have any real idea who or what 'people like me' are." She's not angry; her statement was matter-of-fact. "But if you need more reasons, here's another: Rennanis is shit. Sure, there's food, water, and shelter; your headwoman's right to lead you there if it's true that the city is empty now. Better than commlessness, or rebuilding somewhere with no storecaches. But shit otherwise. I'd rather stay on the move."

"Bullshit," you say, frowning. "No comm is that bad."

Danel just lets out a single bitter snort. It makes you uneasy.

"Just think about it," she says finally, and gets up to leave.

*   *   *

"I agree that Danel should come with us," Lerna says, later that night when you tell him about the conversation. "She's a good fighter. Knows the road. And she's right: she has no reason to betray us."

You're half-asleep, because of the sex. It's an anticlimactic thing now that it's finally happened. What you feel for Lerna will never be intense, or guilt-free. You'll always feel too old for him. But, well. He asked you to show him the truncated breast and you did, thinking that would mark the end of his interest in you. The sandy patch is crusty and rough amid the smoother brown of your torso—like a scab, though the wrong color and texture. His hands were gentle as he examined the spot and pronounced it sound enough to need no further bandaging. You told him that it didn't hurt. You didn't say that you were afraid you couldn't feel *anything* anymore. That you were changing, hardening in more ways than one, becoming nothing but the weapon everyone keeps trying to make of you. You didn't say, *Maybe you're better off with unrequited love.*

But even though you didn't say any of these things, after the examination he looked at you and replied, "You're still beautiful." You apparently needed to hear that a lot more than you realized. And now here you are.

So you process his words slowly because he's made you feel relaxed and boneless and human again, and it's a good ten seconds before you blurt, "'Us'?"

He just looks at you.

"Shit," you say, and drape an arm over your eyes.

The next day, Castrima enters the desert.

* * *

There comes a time of greater hardship for you.

All Seasons are hardship, *Death is the fifth, and master of all,* but this time is different. This is personal. This is a thousand people trying to cross a desert that is deadly even when acid rain isn't sheeting from the sky. This is a group force-march along a highroad that is shaky and full of holes big enough to drop a house through. Highroads are built to withstand shakes, but there's a limit, and the Rifting definitely surpassed it. Ykka decided to take the risk because even a damaged highroad is faster to travel than the desert sand, but this takes a toll. Every orogene in the comm has to stay on alert, because anything worse than a microshake while you're up here could spell disaster. One day Penty, too exhausted to pay attention to her own instincts, steps on a patch of cracked asphalt that's completely unstable. One of the other rogga kids snatches her away just as a big piece simply falls through the substructure of the road. Others are less careful, and less lucky.

The acid rain was unexpected. Stonelore does not discuss the ways in which Seasons can impact weather, because such things are unpredictable at the best of times. What happens here is not entirely surprising, however. Northward, at the equator, the Rifting pumps heat and particulates into the air. Moisture-laden tropical winds coming off the sea hit this cloud-seeding, energy-infusing wall, which whips them into storm. You remember being worried about snow. No. It's endless, miserable rain.

(The rain is not so very acid, as these things go. In the Season of Turning Soil—long before Sanze, you would not know of it—there was rain that stripped animals' fur and peeled the skins off oranges. This is nothing compared to that, and diluted as it is by water. Like vinegar. You'll live.)

Ykka sets a brutal pace while you're on the highroad. On the first day everyone makes camp well after nightfall, and Lerna does not come to the tent after you wearily put it up. He's busy tending half a dozen people who are going lame from slips or twisted ankles, and two elders who are having breathing problems, and the pregnant woman. The latter three are doing all right, he tells you when he finally crawls into your bedroll, near dawn; Ontrag the potter lives on spite, and the pregnant woman has both her household and half the Breeders taking care of her. What's troubling are the injuries. "I have to tell Ykka," he says as you push a slab of rain-soaked cachebread and sour sausage into his mouth, then cover him up and make him lie still. He chews and swallows almost without noticing. "We can't keep going at this pace. We'll start losing people if we don't—"

"She knows," you tell him. You've spoken as gently as you can, but it still silences him. He stares until you lie back down beside him—awkwardly, with only one arm, but successfully. Eventually exhaustion overwhelms anguish, and he sleeps.

You walk with Ykka one day. She's setting the pace like a good comm leader should, pushing no one harder than herself. At the lone midday rest stop, she takes off one boot and you see that her feet are streaked with blood from blisters. You look at her, frowning, and it's eloquent enough that she sighs. "Never got around to requisitioning better boots," she says. "These are too loose. Always figured I'd have more time."

"If your feet rot off," you begin, but she rolls her eyes and points toward the supply pile in the middle of the camp.

You glance at it in confusion, start to resume your scolding, and then pause. Think. Look at the supply pile again. If every wagon carries a crate of the salted cachebread and another of sausage, and if those casks are pickled vegetables, and those are the grains and beans . . .

The pile is so small. So little, for a thousand people who have weeks yet to go through the Merz.

You shut up about the boots. Though she gets some extra socks from someone; that helps.

It shocks you that you're doing as well as you are. You're not *healthy*, not exactly. Your menstrual cycle has stopped, and it's probably not menopause yet. When you undress to basin-wash, which is sort of pointless in the constant rain but habit is habit, you notice that your ribs show starkly beneath loose skin. That's only partly because of all the walking, though; some of it is because you keep forgetting to eat. You feel tired at the end

226

of the day, but it's a distant, detached sort of thing. When you touch Lerna—not for sex, you don't have the energy, but cuddling for warmth saves calories, and he needs the comfort—it feels good, but in an equally detached way. You feel as though you're floating above yourself, watching him sigh, listening to someone else yawn. Like it's happening to someone else.

This is what happened to Alabaster, you remember. A detachment from the flesh, as it became no longer flesh. You resolve to do a better job of eating at every opportunity.

Three weeks into the desert, as expected, the highroad veers off to the west. From there on, Castrima must descend to the ground and contend with desert terrain up close and personal. It's easier, in some ways, because at least the ground isn't likely to crumble away beneath your feet. On the other hand, sand is harder to walk on than asphalt. Everyone slows down. Maxixe earns his keep by drawing enough of the moisture out of the topmost layer of sand and ash and icing it a few inches down, to firm it up beneath everyone's feet. It exhausts him to do this on a constant basis, though, so he saves it for the worst patches. He tries to teach Temell how to do the same trick, but Temell's an ordinary feral; he can't manage the necessary precision. (You could have done it once. You don't let yourself think about this.)

Scouts sent forth to try to find a better path all come back and report the same thing: rusting sand-ash-mud everywhere. There is no better path.

Three people got left behind on the highroad, unable to walk any further because of sprains or breaks. You don't know them. In theory, they'll catch up once they've recovered, but you can't see how they'll recover with no food or shelter. Here on the ground it's worse: a half-dozen broken ankles, one broken leg, one wrenched back among the Strongbacks pulling the wagons, all in the first day. After a while, Lerna stops going to them unless they ask for his help. Most don't ask. There's nothing he can do, and everyone knows it.

On a chilly day, Ontrag the potter just sits down and says she doesn't feel like going any further. Ykka actually argues with her, which you weren't expecting. Ontrag has passed on her skill of pottery to two younger comm members. She's redundant, long past childbearing; it should be an easy headwoman's choice, by the rules of Old Sanze and the tenets of stonelore. But in the end, Ontrag herself has to tell Ykka to shut up and walk away.

It's a warning sign. "I can't do this anymore," you hear Ykka say later, when Ontrag has fallen out of sight behind you. She plods forward, her pace steady and ground-eating as usual, but her head is down, hanks of wet ashblow hair obscuring her face. "I can't. It isn't right. It shouldn't be like this. It shouldn't just be—there's more to being Castrima than being rusting *useful*, for Earth's sake, she used to *teach* me in creche, she knows *stories*, I rusting *can't*."

Hjarka Leadership Castrima, who was taught from an early age to kill the few so the many might live, only touches her shoulder and says, "You'll do what you have to do."

Ykka doesn't say anything for the next few miles, but maybe that's just because there's nothing to say.

The vegetables run out first. Then the meat. The cachebread Ykka tries to ration for as long as she can, but the plain fact is that people can't travel at this speed on nothing. She has to give everyone at least a wafer a day. That's not enough, but it's better than nothing—until there is nothing. And you keep walking anyway.

In the absence of all else, people run on hope. On the other side of the desert, Danel tells everyone around a campfire one night, there's another Imperial Road you can pick up. Easy traveling all the way to Rennanis. It's a river delta region, too, with good soil, once the breadbasket of the Equatorials. Lots of now-abandoned farms outside of any comm. Danel's army had good foraging there on its way south. If you can get through the desert, there will be food.

If you can get through the desert.

You know the end to this. Don't you? How could you be here listening to this tale if you didn't? But sometimes it is the *how* of a thing, not just the endgame, that matters most.

So this is the endgame: Of the nearly eleven hundred souls who went into the desert, a little over eight hundred and fifty reach the Imperial Road.

For a few days after that, the comm effectively dissolves. Desperate people, no longer willing to wait for orderly foraging by the Hunters, stagger off to dig through sour soil for half-rotted tubers and bitter grubs and barely chewable woody roots. The land around here is scraggly, treeless, half-desert and half-fertile, long depopulated by the Rennies. Before she loses too many people, Ykka orders camp made on an old farm with several barns that have managed to survive the Season thus far. The walls, apart from basic framing, haven't fared as well, but then they haven't collapsed, either. It's the roofs she wanted, since the rain still falls here on the desert's edge, though it's lighter and intermittent. Nice to sleep dry, at last.

Three days, Ykka gives it. During that time, people creep back in ones and twos, some bringing food to share with others too weak to forage. The Hunters who bother to return bring fish from one of the river branches that's relatively nearby. One of them finds the thing that saves you, the thing that feels like life after all the death behind you: a farmer's private housecache of cornmeal, sealed in clay urns and kept hidden under the floorboards of the ruined house. You have nothing to mix it with, no milk or eggs or dried meat, just the acid water, but food is that which nourishes, stonelore says. The comm feasts on fried corn mush that night. One urn has cracked and teems with mealybugs, but no one cares. Extra protein.

A lot of people don't come back. It's a Season. All things change.

At the end of three days, Ykka declares that anyone still in the camp is Castrima; anyone who hasn't returned is now ashed out and commless. Easier than speculating on how they might have died, or who might have killed them. What's left of the group strikes camp. You head north.

*   *   *

Was this too fast? Perhaps tragedies should not be summarized so bluntly. I meant to be merciful, not cruel. That you had to live it is the cruelty... but distance, detachment, heals. Sometimes.

I could have taken you from the desert. You did not have to suffer as they did. And yet... they have become part of you, the people of this comm. Your friends. Your fellows. You needed to see them through. Suffering is your healing, at least for now.

Lest you think me inhuman, a stone, I did what I could to help. Some of the beasts that hibernate beneath the sand of the desert are capable of preying on humans; did you know that? A few woke as you passed, but I kept them away. One of the wagons' wooden axles partially dissolved in the rain and began to sag, though none of you noticed. I transmuted the wood— petrified it, if you prefer to think that way—so that it would last. I am the one who moved the moth-eaten rug in that abandoned farmhouse, so that your Hunter found the cornmeal. Ontrag, who had not told Ykka about the growing pain in her side and chest, or her shortness of breath, did not live long after the comm left her behind. I went back to her on the night that she died, and tuned away what little pain she felt. (You've heard the song. Antimony sang it for Alabaster once. I'll sing it for you, if...) She was not alone, at the end.

Does any of this comfort you? I hope so. I'm still human, I told you. Your opinion matters to me.

Castrima survives; that is also what matters. You survive. For now, at least.

And at last, some while later, you reach the southernmost edge of Rennanis's territory.

*   *   *

Honor in safety, survival under threat. Necessity is the only law.

—*Tablet Three, "Structures," verse four*

10

Nassun, through the fire

ALL OF THIS HAPPENS IN the earth. It is mine to know, and to share with you. It is hers to suffer. I'm sorry.

Inside the pearlescent vehicle, the walls are inlaid with elegant vining designs wrought of what looks like gold. Nassun isn't sure if the metal is purely decorative or has some sort of purpose. The hard, smooth seats, which are pastel colors and shaped something like the shells of mussels that she ate sometimes at Found Moon, have amazingly soft cushions. They are locked to the floor, Nassun finds, and yet it is possible to turn them from side to side or lean back. She cannot fathom what the chairs are made of.

To her greater shock, a voice speaks in the air a moment after they settle in. The voice is female, polite, detached, and somehow reassuring. The language is...incomprehensible, and not remotely familiar. However, the pronunciation of the syllables is no different from that of Sanze-mat, and something about the rhythm of the sentences, their order, fits the expectations of Nassun's ear. She suspects that part of the first sentence is a greeting. She thinks a word that keeps being repeated, amid a passage that has the air of a command, might be a softening word, like *please*. The rest, however, is wholly foreign.

The voice speaks only briefly, and then falls silent. Nassun glances at Schaffa and is surprised to see him frowning, eyes narrowed in concentration—though some of that is also tension in his jaw, and a hint of extra pallor around his lips. The silver is hurting him more, and it must be bad this time. Still, he looks up at her in something like wonder. "I *remember* this language," he says.

"Those weird words? What did she say?"

"That this..." He grimaces. "Thing. It's called a vehimal. The announcement says it will depart from this city and begin the transit to Corepoint in two minutes, to arrive in six hours. There was something about other vehicles, other routes, return trips to various...nodes? I don't remember what that means. And she hopes we will enjoy the ride." He smiles thinly.

"Oh." Pleased, Nassun kicks a little in her chair. Six hours to travel all the way to the other side of the planet? But she shouldn't be amazed by that, maybe, since these are the people who built the obelisks.

There seems to be nothing to do but get comfortable. Cautiously, Nassun unslings her runny-sack and lets it hang from the back of her chair. This causes her to notice that something like lichen grows all over the floor, though it cannot be natural or accidental; the blooms of it spread out in pretty, regular patterns. She stretches down a foot and finds that it is soft, like carpet.

Schaffa is more restless, pacing around the comfortable

confines of the…vehimal…and touching its golden veins now and again. It's slow, methodical pacing, but even that is unusual for him, so Nassun is restless, too. "I have been here," he murmurs.

"What?" She heard him. She's just confused.

"In this vehimal. Perhaps in that very seat. I have been here, I feel it. And that language—I don't remember ever having heard it, and yet." He bares his teeth suddenly, and thrusts his fingers into his hair. "Familiarity, but no, no…context! No meaning! Something about this journey is wrong. Something is wrong *and I don't remember what.*"

Schaffa has been damaged for as long as Nassun has known him, but this is the first time he has *seemed* damaged to her. He's speaking faster, words tumbling over one another. There is an oddness to the way his eyes dart around the vehimal interior that makes Nassun suspect he's seeing things that aren't there.

Trying to conceal her anxiety, she reaches out and pats the shell-chair beside her. "These are soft enough to sleep in, Schaffa."

It's too obvious a suggestion, but he turns to gaze at her, and for a moment the haunted tension of his expression softens. "Always so concerned for me, my little one." But it stops the restlessness as she'd hoped, and he comes over to sit.

Just as he does—Nassun starts—the woman's voice speaks again. It's asking a question. Schaffa frowns and then translates, slowly, "She—I think this is *the vehimal's* voice. It speaks to us now, specifically. Not just an announcement."

Nassun shifts, suddenly less comfortable inside the thing. "It talks. It's alive?"

"I'm not certain the distinction between living creature and lifeless object matters to the people who built this place. Yet—" He hesitates, then raises his voice to haltingly speak strange words to the air. The voice answers again, repeating something Nassun heard before. She's not sure where some of the words begin or end, but the syllables are the same. "It says that we are approaching the ... transition point. And it asks if we would like to ... experience?" He shakes his head, irritable. "To see something. Finding the words in our own tongue is more difficult than understanding what's being said."

Nassun twitches with nerves. She draws her feet up into her chair, irrationally afraid of hurting the creature-thing's insides. She isn't sure what she means to ask. "Will it hurt, to see?" *Hurt the vehimal,* she means, but she cannot help also thinking, *Hurt us.*

The voice speaks again before Schaffa has time to translate Nassun's question. "No," it says.

Nassun jumps in pure shock, her orogeny twitching in a way that would have earned her a shout from Essun. "Did you say no?" she blurts, looking around at the vehimal's walls. Maybe it was a coincidence.

"Biomagestric storage surpluses permit—" The voice slips back into the old language, but Nassun is certain she did not imagine hearing those oddly pronounced words of Sanze-mat. "—processing," it concludes. Its voice is soothing, but it seems to come from the very walls, and it troubles Nassun that she has nothing to look at, no face to orient on while she's listening to it. How is it even speaking with no mouth, no throat? She imagines the cilia on the outside of the vehicle somehow rubbing together like insects' legs, and her skin crawls.

It continues, "Translation—" Something. "—linguistic drift." That sounded like Sanze-mat, but she doesn't know what it means. It continues for a few more words, incomprehensible again.

Nassun looks at Schaffa, who's also frowning in alarm. "How do I answer what it was asking before?" she whispers. "How do I tell it that I want to see whatever it's talking about?"

In answer, though Nassun had not meant to ask this question directly of the vehimal, the featureless wall in front of them suddenly darkens into round black spots, as if the surface has suddenly sprouted ugly mold. These spread and merge rapidly until half of the wall is nothing but blackness. As if they're looking through a window into the bowels of the city, but outside the vehimal there's nothing to see but black.

Then light appears on the bottom edge of this window—which really is a window, she realizes; the entire front end of the vehimal has somehow become transparent. The light, in rectangular panels like the ones that lined the stairway from the surface, brightens and marches forward into the darkness ahead, and by its illumination Nassun is able to see walls arching around them. Another tunnel, this one only large enough for the vehimal, and curving through dark rocky walls that are surprisingly rough-hewn given the obelisk-builders' penchant for seamless smoothness. The vehimal is moving steadily along this tunnel, though not quickly. Propelled by its cilia? By some other means Nassun cannot fathom? She finds herself simultaneously fascinated and a little bored, if that is possible. It seems impossible that something which goes so slow can get them to the other side of the world in six hours. If all of those hours will be like this, riding a smooth white track through a rocky black tunnel, with nothing to occupy them except Schaffa's restlessness and a disembodied voice, it will feel much longer.

And then the curve of the tunnel straightens out, and up ahead Nassun sees the hole for the first time.

The hole isn't large. There's something about it that is immediately, viscerally impressive nevertheless. It sits at the center of a vaulted cavern, surrounded by more panel lights, which have been set into the ground. As the vehimal approaches, these turn from white to bright red in a way that Nassun decides is another signal of warning. Down the hole is a yawning blackness. Instinctively she sesses, trying to grasp its dimensions—but she cannot. The circumference of the hole, yes; it's only about twenty feet across. Perfectly circular. The depth, though...she frowns, uncurls from her chair, concentrates. The sapphire tickles at her mind, inviting use of its power, but she resists this; there are too many things in this place that respond to the silver, to *magic*, in ways she doesn't understand. And anyway, she's an orogene. Sessing the depth of a hole should be easy...but this hole stretches deep, deep, beyond her range.

And the vehimal's track runs right up to the hole, and over its edge.

Which is as it should be, should it not? The goal is to reach Corepoint. Still, Nassun cannot help a surge of alarm that is powerful enough to edge along panic. "Schaffa!" He immediately reaches for her hand. She grips it tightly with no fear of hurting him. His strength, which has only ever been used to protect her, never in threat, is desperately needed reassurance right now.

"I have done this before," he says, but he sounds uncertain. "I have survived it."

But you don't remember how, she thinks, feeling a kind of terror that she doesn't know the word for.

(That word is *premonition.*)

Then the edge is there, and the vehimal tips forward. Nassun gasps and clutches at the armrests of her chair—but bizarrely, there is no vertigo. The vehimal does not speed up; its movement pauses for a moment, in fact, and Nassun catches a fleeting glimpse of a few of the thing's cilia blurring at the edges of the view, as they somehow adjust the trajectory of the vehimal from *forward* to *down.* Something else has adjusted with this change, so that Nassun and Schaffa do not fall forward out of their seats; Nassun finds that her back and butt are just as firmly tucked into the chair now as before, even though this is impossible.

And meanwhile, a faint hum within the vehimal, which until now has been too low to be much more than subliminal, abruptly begins to grow louder. Unseen mechanisms reverberate faster in an unmistakable cycling-up pattern. As the vehimal completes its tilt, the view fills with darkness again, but this time Nassun knows it is the yawning black of the pit. There's nothing ahead anymore. Only down.

"Launch," says the voice within the vehimal.

Nassun gasps and clutches Schaffa's hand harder as she is pressed back into her seat then by motion. It isn't as much momentum as she *should* be feeling, however, because her every sense tells her that they have just shot forward at a tremendous rate, going much, much faster than even a running horse.

Into the dark.

At first the darkness is absolute, though broken periodically by a ring of light that blurs past as they hurtle through the tunnel. Their speed continues to increase; presently these rings pass so quickly that they are just flashes. It takes three before Nassun is able to discern what she's seeing and sessing, and then only once she watches a ring as they pass it: *windows*. There are windows set into the walls of the tunnel, illuminated by the light. There's living space down here, at least for the first few miles. Then the rings stop, and the tunnel is nothing but dark for a while.

Nassun sesses impending change an instant before the tunnel suddenly brightens. They can see a new, ruddy light that intersperses the rock walls of the tunnel. Ah, yes; they've gone far enough down that some of the rock has melted and glows bright red. This new light paints the vehimal's interior bloody and makes the gold filigree along its walls seem to catch fire. The forward view is indistinct at first, just red amid gray and brown and black, but Nassun understands instinctively what she's seeing. They have entered the mantle, and her fear finally begins to ebb amid fascination.

"The asthenosphere," she murmurs. Schaffa frowns at her, but naming what she sees has eased her fear. Names have power. She bites her lip, then finally lets go of Schaffa's hand to rise and approach the forward view. Up close it's easier to tell that what she's seeing is just an illusion of sorts—tiny diamonds of color rising on the vehimal's inner skin, like a blush, to form a mosaic of moving images. How does it work? She can't begin to fathom it.

Fascinated, she reaches up. The vehimal's inner skin gives off no heat, though she knows they are already at a level underground where human flesh should burn up in an instant. When she touches the image on the forward view, it ripples ever so slightly around her finger, like waves in water. Putting her whole hand on a roil of brown-red color, she cannot help smiling. Just a few feet away, on the other side of the vehimal's skin, is the burning earth. She's *touching* the burning earth, thinly removed. She puts her other hand up, presses her cheek against the smooth plates. Here in this strange deadciv contraption, she is part of the earth, perhaps more so than any orogene before her has ever been. It is *her*, it is *in* her, she is in *it*.

When Nassun glances back over her shoulder at Schaffa, he's smiling, despite the lines of pain around his eyes. It's different from his usual smile. "What?" she asks.

"The Leadership families of Yumenes believed that orogenes once ruled the world," he says. "That their duty was to keep your kind from ever regaining that much power. That you would be monstrous rulers of the world, doing back to ordinary folk what had been done to you, if you ever got the chance. I don't think they were right about any of it—and yet." He gestures, as she stands there illuminated by the fire of the earth. "*Look* at you, little one. If you are the monster they imagined you to be . . . you are also glorious."

Nassun loves him so much.

It's why she gives up the illusion of power and goes back to sit beside him. But when she gets close, she sees just how much strain he's under. "Your head hurts a lot."

His smile fades. "It's bearable."

Troubled, she puts her hands on his shoulders. Dozens of nights of easing his pain have made it easy—but this time when she sends silver into him, the white-hot burn of lines between his cells does not fade. In fact, they blaze *brighter*, so sharply that Schaffa tenses and pulls away from her, rising to begin pacing again. He has plastered a smile on his face, more of a rictus as he prowls restlessly back and forth, but Nassun can tell that the smile-endorphins are doing nothing.

Why did the lines get brighter? Nassun tries to understand this by examining herself. Nothing of her silver is different; it flows in its usual clearly delineated lines. She turns her silver gaze on Schaffa—and then, belatedly, notices something stunning.

The vehimal is *made* of silver, and not just fine lines of it. It is surrounded by silver, permeated with it. What she perceives is a wave of the stuff, rippling in ribbons around herself and Schaffa, starting at the nose of the vehicle and enclosing them behind. This sheath of magic, she understands suddenly, is what's pushing away the heat and pushing back on the pressure and tilting the lines of force within the vehimal so that gravity pulls toward its floor and not toward the center of the earth. The walls are only a framework; something about their structure makes it easier for the silver to flow and connect and form lattices. The gold filigree helps to stabilize the churn of energies at the front of the vehicle—or so Nassun guesses, since she cannot understand all the ways in which these *magic* mechanisms work together. It's just too complex. It is like riding inside an obelisk. It's like being carried by the wind. She had no idea the silver could be so amazing.

But there is something beyond the miracle of the vehimal's walls. Something outside the vehimal.

At first Nassun isn't sure what she's perceiving. More lights? No. She's looking at it all wrong.

It's the silver, same as what flows between her own cells. It's *a single thread* of silver—and yet it is titanic, curling away between a whorl of soft, hot rock and a high-pressure bubble of searing water. A single thread of silver... and it is longer than the tunnel they have traversed so far. She can't find either of its ends. It's wider than the vehimal's circumference and then some. Yet otherwise it's just as clear and focused as any one of the lines within Nassun herself. The same, just... immense.

And Nassun *understands* then, she *understands*, so suddenly and devastatingly that her eyes snap open and she stumbles backward with the force of the realization, bumping into another chair and nearly falling before she grabs it to hold herself upright. Schaffa makes a low, frustrated sound and turns in an attempt to respond to her alarm—but the silver within his body is so bright that when it flares, he doubles over, clutching at his head and groaning. He is in too much pain to fulfill his duty as a Guardian, or to act on his concern for her, because the silver in his body has grown to be as bright as that immense thread out in the magma.

Magic, Steel called the silver. The stuff underneath orogeny, which is made by things that live or once lived. This silver deep within Father Earth wends between the mountainous fragments of his substance in exactly the same way that they twine among the cells of a living, breathing thing. And that is because *a planet* is a living, breathing thing; she knows this now with the certainty of instinct. All the stories about Father Earth being alive are real.

But if the mantle is Father Earth's body, why is his silver getting brighter?

No. Oh no.

"Schaffa," Nassun whispers. He grunts; he has sagged to one knee, gasping shallowly as he clutches at his head. She wants to go to him, comfort him, help him, but she stands where she is, her breath coming too fast from rising panic at what she suddenly knows is coming. She wants to deny it, though. "Schaffa, p-please, that thing in your head, the piece of iron, you called it a corestone, Schaffa—" Her voice is fluttery. She can't catch her breath. Fear has nearly closed her throat. No. No. She did not understand, but now she does and she has no idea how to stop it. "*Schaffa, where does it come from, that corestone thing in your head?*"

The vehimal's voice speaks again with that greeting language, and then it continues, obscene in its detached pleasantry. "—a marvel, only available—" Something. "—route. This vehimal—" Something. "—heart, illuminated—" Something. "—for your pleasure."

Schaffa does not reply. But Nassun can sess the answer to her question now. She can *feel* it as the paltry thin silver that runs through her own body resonates—but that is a faint resonance, from *her* silver, generated by her own flesh. The silver in Schaffa, in all Guardians, is generated by the corestone that sits lodged in their sessapinae. She's studied this stone sometimes, to the degree that she is able while Schaffa sleeps and she feeds him magic. It's iron, but like no other iron she's ever sessed. Oddly dense. Oddly energetic, though some of that is the magic that it channels into him from . . . somewhere. Oddly alive.

And when the whole right side of the vehimal dissolves to let its passengers glimpse the rarely seen wonder that is the world's unfettered heart, it already blazes before her: a silver sun underground, so bright that she must squint, so heavy that perceiving it hurts her sessapinae, so powerful with magic that it makes the lingering connection of the sapphire feel tremulous and weak. It is the Earth's core, the source of the corestones, and before her it is a world in itself, swallowing the viewscreen and growing further still as they hurtle closer.

It does not look like rock, Nassun thinks faintly, beneath the panic. Maybe that's just the waver of molten metal and magic all round the vehimal, but the immensity before her seems to shimmer when she tries to focus on it. There's some solidity to it; as they draw closer, Nassun can detect anomalies dotting the surface of the bright sphere, made tiny by contrast—even as she realizes they are obelisks. Several dozen of them, jammed into the heart of the world like needles in a pincushion. But these are nothing. Nothing.

And Nassun is nothing. Nothing before this.

It's a mistake to bring him, Steel had said, of Schaffa.

Panic snaps. Nassun runs to Schaffa as he falls to the floor, thrashing. He does not scream, though his mouth is open and his icewhite eyes have gone wide and his every limb, when she wrestles him onto his back, is muscle-stiff. One flailing arm hits her collarbone, flinging her back, and there is a flash of terrible pain, but Nassun barely spares a thought for it before she scrambles back to him. She grabs his arm with both of her own and tries to hold on because he is reaching for his head and his hands are forming claws and his nails are *raking* at his scalp and face—"*Schaffa, no!*" she cries. But he cannot hear her.

And then the vehimal goes dark inside.

It's still moving, though slower. They've actually passed into the semisolid stuff of the core, the vehimal's route skimming its surface—because of course the people who built the obelisks would revel in their ability to casually pierce the planet for entertainment. She can feel the blaze of that silver, churning sun all around her. Behind her, however, the wall-window goes suddenly dim. There's something just outside the vehimal, pressing against its sheath of magic.

Slowly, with Schaffa writhing in silent agony in her lap, Nassun turns to face the core of the Earth.

And here, within the sanctum of its heart, the Evil Earth notices her back.

When the Earth speaks, it does not do so in words, exactly. This is a thing you know already, but that Nassun only learns in this moment. She sesses the meanings, hears the vibrations with the bones of her ears, shudders them out through her skin, feels them pull tears from her eyes. It is like drowning in energy and sensation and emotion. It *hurts*. Remember: The Earth wants to kill her.

But remember, too: Nassun wants it just as dead.

So it says, in microshakes that will eventually stir a tsunami somewhere in the southern hemisphere, *Hello, little enemy.*

(This is an approximation, you realize. This is all her young mind can bear.)

And as Schaffa chokes and goes into convulsions, Nassun clutches at his pain-wracked form and stares at the wall of rusty darkness. She isn't afraid anymore; fury has steeled her. She is so very much her mother's daughter.

"You let him go," she snarls. "*You let him go right now.*"

The core of the world is metal, molten and yet crushed into solidity. There is some malleability to it. The surface of the red darkness begins to ripple and change as Nassun watches. Something appears that for an instant she cannot parse. A pattern, familiar. A *face*. It is just a suggestion of a person, eyes and a mouth, shadow of a nose—but then for just an instant the eyes are distinct in shape, the lips lined and detailed, a mole appearing beneath the eyes, *which open*.

No one she knows. Just a face...where there should be none. And as Nassun stares at this, dawning horror slowly pushing aside her anger, she sees another face—and another, more of them appearing all at once to fill the view. Each is pushed aside as another rises from underneath. Dozens. Hundreds. This one jowled and tired-looking, that one puffy as if from crying, that one openmouthed and screaming in silence, like Schaffa. Some look at her pleadingly, mouthing words she wouldn't be able to understand even if she could hear.

All of them ripple, though, with the amusement of a greater presence. *He is mine.* Not a voice. When the Earth speaks, it is not in words. Nevertheless.

Nassun presses her lips together and reaches into the silver of Schaffa and ruthlessly cuts as many of the tendrils etched into his body as she can, right around the corestone. It doesn't work like it usually does when she uses the silver for surgery. The silver lines in Schaffa reestablish themselves almost instantly, and throb that much harder when they do. Schaffa shudders each time. She's hurting him. She's making it worse.

There's no other choice. She wraps her own threads around his corestone to perform the surgery he would not permit her to do a few months before. If it shortens his life, at least he will not suffer for what is left of it.

But another ripple of amusement makes the vehimal shudder, and a flare of silver blazes through Schaffa that shrugs off her paltry threads. The surgery fails. The corestone is seated as firmly as ever amid the lobes of his sessapinae, like the parasitic thing it is.

Nassun shakes her head and looks around for something, anything else, that might help. She is distracted momentarily by the boil and shift of faces in the surface of the rusty dark. Who are these people? Why are they here, churning amid the Earth's heart?

Obligation, the Earth returns, in wavelets of heat and crushing pressure. Nassun bares her teeth, struggling against the weight of its contempt. *What was stolen, or lent, must be recompensed.*

And Nassun cannot help but understand this too, here within the Earth's embrace, with its meaning thrumming through her bones. The silver—magic—comes from life. Those who made the obelisks sought to harness magic, and they succeeded; oh, how they succeeded. They used it to build wonders beyond imagining. But then they wanted more magic than just what their own lives, or the accumulated aeons of life and death on the Earth's surface, could provide. And when they saw how much magic brimmed just beneath that surface, ripe for the taking...

It may never have occurred to them that so much magic, so much *life*, might be an indicator of...awareness. The Earth does not speak in words, after all—and perhaps, Nassun realizes, having seen entirely too much of the world to still have much of a child's innocence, perhaps these builders of the great obelisk network were not used to respecting lives different from their own. Not so very different, really, from the people who run the Fulcrums, or raiders, or her father. So where they should have seen a living being, they saw only another thing to exploit. Where they should have asked, or left alone, they raped.

For some crimes, there is no fitting justice—only reparation. So for every iota of life siphoned from beneath the Earth's skin, the Earth has dragged a million human remnants into its heart. Bodies rot in soil, after all—and soil sits upon tectonic plates, plates eventually subduct into the fire under the Earth's crust, which convect endlessly through the mantle . . . and there within itself, the Earth eats everything they were. This is only fair, it reasons—coldly, with an anger that still shudders up from the depths to crack the world's skin and touch off Season after Season. It is only right. The Earth did not start this cycle of hostilities, it did not steal the Moon, it did not burrow into anyone else's skin and snatch bits of its still-living flesh to keep as trophies and tools, it did not plot to enslave humans in an unending nightmare. It did not start this war, but it will rusting well *have. Its. Due.*

And oh. Does Nassun not understand this? Her hands tighten in Schaffa's shirt, trembling as her hatred wavers. Can she not empathize?

For the world has taken so much from her. She had a brother once. And a father, and a mother whom she also understands but wishes she did not. And a home, and dreams. The people of the Stillness have long since robbed her of childhood and any hope of a real future, and because of this she is so angry that she cannot think beyond THIS MUST STOP and I WILL STOP IT—

—so does she not resonate with the Evil Earth's wrath, herself?

She does.

Earth eat her, she does.

Schaffa has gone still in her lap. There is wetness beneath one of her legs; he's urinated on himself. His eyes are still open, and he breathes in shallow gasps. His taut muscles still twitch now and again. Everyone breaks, if torture goes on long enough. The mind bears the unbearable by going elsewhere. Nassun is ten years old, going on a hundred, but she has seen enough of the world's evil to know this. Her Schaffa. Has gone away. And might never, ever, come back.

The vehimal speeds onward.

The view begins to grow bright again as it emerges from the core. Interior lights resume their pleasant glow. Nassun's fingers curl loosely in Schaffa's clothes now. She gazes back at the turning mass of the core until the stuff of the sidewall turns opaque again. The forward view lingers, but it, too, begins to darken. They have entered another tunnel, this one wider than the first, with solid black walls somehow holding back the churning heat of the outer core and mantle. Now Nassun senses that the vehimal is tilted up, away from the core. Headed back toward the surface, but this time on the other side of the planet.

Nassun whispers, to herself since Schaffa has gone away, "This has to stop. I will stop it." She closes her eyes and the lashes stick together, wet. "I promise."

She does not know to whom she makes this promise. It doesn't matter, really.

Not long after, the vehimal reaches Corepoint.

Syl Anagist: One

THEY TAKE KELENLI AWAY IN the morning.

It is unexpected, at least by us. It also isn't really about us, we realize fairly quickly. Conductor Gallat arrives first, although I see several other high-ranking conductors talking in the house above the garden. He does not look displeased as he calls Kelenli outside and speaks to her in a quiet but intent voice. We all get up, vibrating guilt though we have done nothing wrong, just spent a night lying on a hard floor and listening to the strange sound of others' breath and occasional movement. I watch Kelenli, fearing for her, wanting to protect her, though this is inchoate; I don't know what the danger is. She stands straight and tall, like one of them, as she speaks to Gallat. I sess her tension, like a fault line poised to slip.

They are outside of the little garden house, fifteen feet away, but I hear Gallat's voice rise for a moment. "How much longer do you mean to keep up this foolishness? Sleeping in the shed?"

Kelenli says, calmly, "Is there a problem?"

Gallat is the highest ranked of the conductors. He is also the cruelest. We don't think he means it. It's just that he does not seem to understand that cruelty is possible, with us. We are the machine's tuners; we ourselves must be attuned for the good of the project. That this process sometimes causes pain or fear or decommissioning to the briar patch is... incidental.

We have wondered if Gallat has feelings himself. He does, I see when he draws back now, expression all a-ripple with hurt, as if Kelenli's words have struck him some sort of blow. "I've been good to you," he says. His voice wavers.

"And I'm grateful." Kelenli hasn't shifted the inflection of her voice at all, or a muscle of her face. She looks and sounds, for the first time, like one of us. And as we so often do, she and he are having a conversation that has nothing to do with the words coming from their mouths. I check; there's nothing in the ambient, save the fading vibrations of their voices. And yet.

Gallat stares at her. Then the hurt and anger fade from his expression, replaced by weariness. He turns away and snaps, "I need you back at the lab today. There are fluctuations in the subgrid again."

Kelenli's face finally moves, her brows drawing down. "I was told I had three days."

"Geoarcanity takes precedence over your leisure plans, Kelenli." He glances toward the little house where I and the others cluster, and catches me staring at him. I don't look away, mostly because I'm so fascinated by his anguish that I don't think to. He looks fleetingly embarrassed, then irritated. He says to her, with his usual air of impatience, "Biomagestry can only do distance scans outside of the compound, but they say they're actually detecting some interesting flow clarification in the tuners' network. Whatever you've been doing with them obviously isn't a complete waste of time. I'll take them, then, to wherever you were planning to go today. Then you can go back to the compound."

She glances around at us. At me. *My thinker.*

"It should be an easy enough trip," she says to him, while looking at me. "They need to see the local engine fragment."

"The amethyst?" Gallat stares at her. "They live in its shadow. They see it constantly. How does that help?"

"They haven't seen the socket. They need to fully understand its growth process—more than theoretically." All at once she turns away from me, and from him, and begins walking toward the big house. "Just show them that, and then you can drop them off at the compound and be done with them."

I understand precisely why Kelenli has spoken in this dismissive tone, and why she hasn't bothered to say farewell before leaving. It's no more than any of us do, when we must watch or sess another of our network punished; we pretend not to care. (*Tetlewha. Your song is toneless, but not silent. From where do you sing?*) That shortens the punishment for all, and prevents the conductors from focusing on another, in their anger. Understanding this, and feeling nothing as she walks away, are two very different things, however.

Conductor Gallat is in a terrible mood after this. He orders us to get our things so we can go. We have nothing, though some of us need to eliminate waste before we leave, and all of us need food and water. He lets the ones who need it use Kelenli's small toilet or a pile of leaves out back (I am one of these; it is very strange to squat, but also a profoundly enriching experience), then tells us to ignore our hunger and thirst and come on, so we do. He walks us very fast, even though our legs are shorter than his and still aching from the day before. We are relieved to see the vehimal he's summoned, when it comes, so that we can sit and be carried back toward the center of town.

The other conductors ride along with us and Gallat. They keep speaking to him and ignoring us; he answers in terse, one-word replies. They ask him mostly about Kelenli—whether she is always so intransigent, whether he believes this is an unforeseen genegineering defect, why he even bothers to allow her input on the project when she is, for all intents and purposes, just an obsolete prototype.

"Because she's been right in every suggestion she's made thus far," he snaps, after the third such question. "Which is the very reason we developed the tuners, after all. The Plutonic Engine would need another seventy years of priming before even a test-firing could be attempted, without them. When a machine's sensors are capable of telling you exactly what's wrong and exactly how to make the whole thing work more efficiently, it's stupid not to pay heed."

That seems to mollify them, so they leave him alone and resume talking—though to each other, not to him. I am sitting near Conductor Gallat. I notice how the other conductors' disdain actually increases his tension, making anger radiate off his skin like the residual heat of sunlight from a rock, long after night has fallen. There have always been odd dynamics to the conductors' relationships; we've puzzled them out as best we could, while not really understanding. Now, however, thanks to Kelenli's explanation, I remember that Gallat has *undesirable ancestry.* We were made this way, but he was simply born with pale skin and icewhite eyes—traits common among the Niess. He isn't Niess; the Niess are gone. There are other races, Sylanagistine races, with pale skin. The eyes suggest, however, that somewhere in his family's history—distant, or he would not have been permitted schooling and medical care and his prestigious current position—someone made children with a Niesperson. Or not; the trait could be a random mutation or happenstance of pigment expression. Apparently no one thinks it is, though.

This is why, though Gallat works harder and spends more hours at the compound than anyone, and is in charge, the other conductors treat him as if he is less than what he is. If he did not pass on the favor in his dealings with us, I would pity him. As it is, I am afraid of him. I always have been afraid of him. But for Kelenli, I decide to be brave.

"Why are you angry with her?" I ask. My voice is soft, and hard to hear over the humming metabolic cycle of the vehimal. Few of the other conductors notice my comment. None of them care. I have timed the asking well.

Gallat starts, then stares at me as if he has never seen me before. "What?"

"Kelenli." I turn my eyes to meet his, although we have learned over time that the conductors do not like this. They find eye contact challenging. But they also dismiss us more easily when we do not look at them, and I don't want to be dismissed in this moment. I want him to *feel* this conversation, even if his weak, primitive sessapinae cannot tell him that my jealousy and resentment have raised the temperature of the city's water table by two degrees.

He glares at me. I gaze impassively back. I sense tension in the network. The others, who of course have noticed what the conductors ignore, are suddenly afraid for me…but I am almost distracted from their concern by the difference I suddenly perceive in us. Gallat is right: We *are* changing, complexifying, our ambient influence strengthening, as a result of the things Kelenli has shown us. Is this an improvement? I'm not certain yet. For now, we are confused where before, we were mostly unified. Remwha and Gaewha are angry at me for taking this risk without seeking consensus first—and this recklessness, I suppose, is my own symptom of change. Bimniwha and Salewha are, irrationally, angry at Kelenli for the strange way she is affecting me. Dushwha is done with all of us and just wants to go home. Beneath her anger, Gaewha is afraid for me but she also pities me, because I think she understands that my recklessness is a symptom of something else. I have decided that I am in love, but love is a painful hotspot roil beneath the surface of me in a place where once there was stability, and I do not like it. Once, after all, I believed I was the finest tool ever created by a great civilization. Now, I have learned that I am a mistake cobbled together by paranoid thieves who were terrified of their own mediocrity. I don't know how to feel, *except* reckless.

None of them are angry at Gallat for being too dangerous to have a simple conversation with, though. There's something very wrong with that.

Finally, Gallat says, "What makes you think I'm angry with Kelenli?" I open my mouth to point out the tension in his body, his vocal stress, the look on his face, and he makes an irritated sound. "Never mind. I know how you process information." He sighs. "And I suppose you're right."

I am definitely right, but I know better than to remind him of what he doesn't want to know. "You want her to live in your house." I was unsure that it was Gallat's house until the morning's conversation. I should have guessed, though; it smelled like him. None of us is good at using senses other than sesuna.

"It's *her* house," he snaps. "She grew up there, same as me."

Kelenli has told me this. Raised alongside Gallat, thinking she was normal, until someone finally told her why her parents did not love her. "She was part of the project."

He nods once, tightly, his mouth twisted in bitterness. "So was I. A human child was a necessary control, and I had...useful characteristics for comparison. I thought of her as my sister until we both reached the age of fifteen. Then they told us."

Such a long time. And yet Kelenli must have suspected that she was different. The silver glimmer of magic flows around us, through us, like water. Everyone can sess it, but we tuners, we live it. It lives in us. She cannot have ever thought herself normal.

Gallat, however, had been completely surprised. Perhaps his view of the world had been as thoroughly upended as mine has been now. Perhaps he floundered—flounders—in the same way, struggling to resolve his feelings with reality. I feel a sudden sympathy for him.

"I never mistreated her." Gallat's voice has gone soft, and I'm not certain he's still speaking to me. He has folded his arms and crossed his legs, closing in on himself as he gazes steadily through one of the vehimal's windows, seeing nothing. "Never treated her like..." Suddenly he blinks and darts a hooded glance at me. I start to nod to show that I understand, but some instinct warns me against doing this. I just look back at him. He relaxes. I don't know why.

He doesn't want you to hear him say "like one of you," Remwha signals, humming with irritation at my obtuseness. *And he doesn't want you to know what it means, if he says it. He reassures himself that he is not like the people who made his own life harder. It's a lie, but he needs it, and he needs us to support that lie. She should not have told us that we were Niess.*

We aren't *Niess,* I gravitic-pulse back. Mostly I'm annoyed that he had to point this out. Gallat's behavior is obvious, now that Remwha has explained.

To them we are. Gaewha sends this as a single microshake whose reverberations she kills, so that we sess only cold silence afterward. We stop arguing because she's right.

Gallat continues, oblivious to our identity crisis, "I've given her as much freedom as I can. Everyone knows what she is, but I've allowed her the same privileges that any normal woman would have. Of course there are restrictions, limitations, but that's reasonable. I can't be seen to be lax, if…" He trails off, into his own thoughts. Muscles along his jaw flex in frustration. "She acts as if she can't understand that. As if *I'm* the problem, not the world. I'm trying to help her!" And then he lets out a heavy breath of frustration.

We have heard enough, however. Later, when we process all this, I will tell the others, *She wants to be a person.*

She wants the impossible, Dushwha will say. *Gallat thinks it better to own her himself, rather than allow Syl Anagist to do the same. But for her to be a person, she must stop being…ownable. By anyone.*

Then Syl Anagist must stop being Syl Anagist, Gaewha will add sadly.

Yes. They will all be right, too, my fellow tuners...but that does not mean Kelenli's desire to be free is wrong. Or that something is impossible just because it is very, very hard.

The vehimal stops in a part of town that, amazingly, looks familiar. I have seen this area only once and yet I recognize the pattern of the streets, and the vineflowers on one greenstrate wall. The quality of the light through the amethyst, as the sun slants toward setting, stirs a feeling of longing and relief in me that I will one day learn is called homesickness.

The other conductors leave and head back to the compound. Gallat beckons to us. He's still angry, and wants this over with. So we follow, and fall slowly behind because our legs are shorter and the muscles burn, until finally he notices that we and our guards are ten feet behind him. He stops to let us catch up, but his jaw is tight and one hand taps a brisk pattern on his folded arms.

"Hurry up," he says. "I want to do start-up trials tonight."

We know better than to complain. Distraction is often useful, however. Gaewha says, "What are we hurrying to see?"

Gallat shakes his head impatiently, but answers. As Gaewha planned, he walks slower so that he can speak to us, which allows us to walk slower as well. We desperately catch our breath. "The socket where this fragment was grown. You've been told the basics. For the time being each fragment serves as the power plant for a node of Syl Anagist—taking in magic, catalyzing it, returning some to the city and storing the surplus. Until the Engine is activated, of course."

Abruptly he stops, distracted by our surroundings. We have

reached the restricted zone around the base of the fragment—
a three-tiered park with some administrative buildings and a
stop on the vehimal line that (we are told) does a weekly run to
Corepoint. It's all very utilitarian, and a little boring.

Still. Above us, filling the sky for nearly as high as the eye can
see, is the amethyst fragment. Despite Gallat's impatience, all of
us stop and stare up at it in awe. We live in its colored shadow,
and were made to respond to its needs and control its output. It
is us; we are it. Yet rarely do we get to see it like this, directly.
The windows in our cells all point away from it. (Connectivity,
harmony, lines of sight and waveform efficiency; the conductors
want to risk no accidental activation.) It is a magnificent thing,
I think, both in its physical state and its magical superposition.
It glows in the latter state, crystalline lattice nearly completely
charged with the stored magic power that we will soon use to
ignite Geoarcanity. When we have shunted the world's power
systems over from the limited storage-and-generation of the
obelisks to the unlimited streams within the earth, and when
Corepoint has gone fully online to regulate it, and when the
world has finally achieved the dream of Syl Anagist's greatest
leaders and thinkers—

—well. Then I, and the others, will no longer be needed. We
hear so many things about what will happen once the world
has been freed from scarcity and want. People living forever.
Travel to other worlds, far beyond our star. The conductors have
assured us that we won't be killed. We will be celebrated, in fact,
as the pinnacle of magestry, and as living representations of
what humanity can achieve. Is that not a thing to look forward
to, our veneration? Should we not be proud?

But for the first time, I think of what life I might want for myself, if I could have a choice. I think of the house that Gallat lives in: huge, beautiful, cold. I think of Kelenli's house in the garden, which is small and surrounded by small growing magics. I think of living with Kelenli. Sitting at her feet every night, speaking with her as much as I want, in every language that I know, without fear. I think of her smiling without bitterness and this thought gives me incredible pleasure. Then I feel shame, as if I have no right to imagine these things.

"Waste of time," Gallat mutters, staring at the obelisk. I flinch, but he does not notice. "Well. Here it is. I've no idea why Kelenli wanted you to see it, but now you see it."

We admire it as bidden. "Can we . . . go closer?" Gaewha asks. Several of us groan through the earth; our legs hurt and we are hungry. But she replies with frustration. *While we're here, we might as well get the most out of it.*

As if in agreement, Gallat sighs and starts forward, walking down the sloping road toward the base of the amethyst, where it has been firmly lodged in its socket since the first growth-medium infusion. I have seen the top of the amethyst fragment, lost amid scuds of cloud and sometimes framed by the white light of the Moon, but this part of it is new to me. About its base are the transformer pylons, I know from what I have been taught, which siphon off some of the magic from the generative furnace at the amethyst's core. This magic—a tiny fraction of the incredible amount that the Plutonic Engine is capable of producing—is redistributed via countless conduits to houses and buildings and machinery and vehimal feeding stations throughout the city-node. It is the same in every city-node of

Syl Anagist, all over the world—two hundred and fifty-six fragments in total.

My attention is suddenly caught by an odd sensation—the strangest thing I have ever sessed. Something diffuse...something nearby generates a force that...I shake my head and stop walking. "What is that?" I ask, before I consider whether it is wise to speak again, with Gallat in this mood.

He stops, glowers at me, then apparently understands the confusion in my face. "Oh, I suppose you're close enough to detect it here. That's just sinkline feedback."

"And what is a *sinkline?*" asks Remwha, now that I have broken the ice. This causes Gallat to glare at him in fractionally increased annoyance. We all tense.

"Evil Death," Gallat sighs at last. "Fine, easier to show than to explain. Come on."

He speeds up again, and this time none of us dares complain even though we are pushing our aching legs on low blood sugar and some dehydration. Following Gallat, we reach the bottommost tier, cross the vehimal track, and pass between two of the huge, humming pylons.

And there...we are destroyed.

Beyond the pylons, Conductor Gallat explains to us in a tone of unconcealed impatience, is the start-up and translation system for the fragment. He slips into a detailed technical explanation that we absorb but do not really hear. Our network, the nigh-constant system of connections through which we six communicate and assess each other's health and rumble warnings or reassure with songs of comfort, has gone utterly silent and still. This is shock. This is horror.

The gist of Gallat's explanation is this: The fragments could not have begun the generation of magic on their own, decades ago when they were first grown. Nonliving, inorganic things like crystal are inert to magic. Therefore, in order to help the fragments initiate the generative cycle, raw magic must be used as a catalyst. Every engine needs a starter. Enter the sinklines: They look like vines, thick and gnarled, twisting and curling to form a lifelike thicket around the fragment's base. And ensnared in these vines—

We're going to see them, Kelenli told me, when I asked her where the Niess were.

They are still alive, I know at once. Though they sprawl motionless amid the thicket of vines (lying atop the vines, twisted among them, wrapped up in them, speared by them where the vines grow through flesh), it is impossible not to sess the delicate threads of silver darting between the cells of this one's hand, or dancing along the hairs of that one's back. Some of them we can see breathing, though the motion is so very slow. Many wear tattered rags for clothes, dry-rotted with years; a few are naked. Their hair and nails have not grown, and their bodies have not produced waste that we can see. Nor can they feel pain, I sense instinctively; this, at least, is a kindness. That is because the sinklines take all the magic of life from them save the bare trickle needed to keep them alive. Keeping them alive keeps them generating more.

It is the briar patch. Back when we were newly decanted, still learning how to use the language that had been written into our brains during the growth phase, one of the conductors told us a story about where we would be sent if we became unable to work for some reason. That was when there were fourteen of us. We would be retired, she said, to a place where we could still serve the project indirectly. "It's peaceful there," the conductor said. I remember it clearly. She smiled as she said it. "You'll see."

The briar patch's victims have been here for years. Decades. There are hundreds of them in view, and thousands more out of sight if the sinkline thicket extends all the way around the amethyst's base. Millions, when multiplied by two hundred and fifty-six. We cannot see Tetlewha, or the others, but we know that they, too, are here somewhere. Still alive, and yet not.

Gallat finishes up as we stare in silence. "So after system priming, once the generative cycle is established, there's only an occasional need to reprime." He sighs, bored with his own voice. We stare in silence. "Sinklines store magic against any possible need. On Launch Day, each sink reservoir should have approximately thirty-seven lammotyrs stored, which is three times..."

He stops. Sighs. Pinches the bridge of his nose. "There's no point to this. She's playing you, fool." It is as if he does not see what we're seeing. As if these stored, componentized lives mean nothing to him. "Enough. It's time we got all of you back to the compound."

So we go home.

And we begin, at last, to plan.

*   *   *

Thresh them in
Line them neat
Make them part of the winter wheat!
Tamp them down

263

Shut them up
Just a hop, a skip, and a jump!
Seal those tongues
Shut those eyes
Never you stop until they cry!
Nothing you hear
Not one you'll see
This is the way to our victory!

 —*Pre-Sanze children's rhyme popular in Yumenes, Haltolee,*
   Nianon, and Ewech Quartents, origin unknown. Many
    variants exist. This appears to be the baseline text.

11

you're almost home

THE GUARDS AT THE NODE station actually seem to think they can fight when you and the other Castrimans walk out of the ashfall. You suppose that the lot of you *do* look like a larger-than-usual raider band, given your ashy, acid-worn clothing and skeletal looks. Ykka doesn't even have time to get Danel to try to talk them down before they start firing crossbows. They're terrible shots, which is lucky for you; the law of averages is on their side, which isn't. Three Castrimans go down beneath the bolts before you realize Ykka hasn't got a clue how to use a torus as a shield—but after you've remembered that you can't do it, either, without Consequences. So you shout at Maxixe and he does it with diamond precision, shredding the incoming bolts into wood-flecked snow, not so differently from the way you started things off in Tirimo that last day.

He's not as skilled now as you were then. Part of the torus remains around him; he just stretches and reshapes its forward edge to form a barrier between Castrima and the big scoria gates of the node station. Fortunately there's no one in front of him (after you shouted at people to get out of the way). Then with a final flick of redirected kinetics he smashes the gates apart and ices the crossbow wielders before letting the torus spin away. Then while Castrima's Strongbacks charge in and take care of things, you go over to find Maxixe sprawled in the wagon bed, panting.

"Sloppy," you say, catching one of his hands and pulling it to you, since you can't exactly chafe it between your own. You can feel the cold of his skin through four layers of clothing. "Should've anchored that torus ten feet away, at least."

He grumbles, eyes drifting shut. His stamina's gone completely to rust, but that's probably because starvation and orogeny don't mix well. "Haven't needed to do anything fancier than just freeze people, for a couple of years now." Then he glowers at you. "*You* didn't bother, I see."

You smile wearily. "That's because I knew you had it." Then you scrape away a patch of ice from the wagon bed so you can have somewhere to sit until the fighting's done.

When it's over, you pat Maxixe—who's fallen asleep—and then get up to go find Ykka. She's just inside the gates with Esni and a couple of other Strongbacks, all of them looking at the tiny paddock in wonder. There's a *goat* in there, eying everyone with indifference as it chews on some hay. You haven't seen a goat since Tirimo.

First things first, though. "Make sure they don't kill the doctor, or doctors," you say to Ykka and Esni. "They're probably barricaded in with the node maintainer. Lerna won't know how to take care of the maintainer; it takes special skills." You pause. "If you're still committed to this plan."

Ykka nods and glances at Esni, who nods and glances at another woman, who eyeballs a young man, who then runs into the node facility. "What are the chances the doctor will kill the maintainer?" Esni asks. "For mercy?"

You resist the urge to say, *Mercy is for people.* That way of thinking needs to die, even if you're thinking it in bitterness. "Slim. Explain through the door that you're not planning to kill anyone who surrenders, if you think that will help." Esni sends another runner to do this.

"Of course I'm still committed to the plan," Ykka says. She's rubbing her face, leaving streaks in the ash. Beneath the ash there's just more ash, deeper ingrained. You're forgetting what her natural coloring looks like, and you can't tell if she's wearing eye makeup anymore. "I mean, most of us can handle shakes in a controlled way, even the kids by now, but..." She looks up at the sky. "Well. There's *that.*" You follow her gaze, but you know what you'll see already. You've been trying not to see it. Everyone has been.

The Rifting.

On this side of the Merz, the sky doesn't exist. Further south, the ash that the Rifting pumps forth has had time to rise into the atmosphere and thin out somewhat, forming the rippling clouds that have dominated the sky as you've known it for the past two years. Here, though. Here you try to look up, but before you even get to the sky, what grabs your eyes is something like a slow-boiling wall of black and red across the entire visible northern horizon. In a volcano, what you're seeing would be called an eruption column, but the Rifting is not just some solitary vent. It is a thousand volcanoes put end-to-end, an unbroken line of earthfire and chaos from one coast of the Stillness to the other. Tonkee's been trying to get everyone to call what you're seeing by its proper term: *Pyrocumulonimbus*, a massive stormwall cloud of ash and fire and lightning. You've already heard people using a different term, however—simply, *the Wall*. You think that's going to stick. You suspect, in fact, that if anybody's still alive in a generation or two to name this Season, they'll call it something like the Season of the Wall.

You can hear it, faint but omnipresent. A rumble in the earth. A low, ceaseless snarl against your middle ear. The Rifting isn't just a shake; it is the still-ongoing, dynamic divergence of two tectonic plates along a newly created fault line. The aftershakes from the initial Rifting won't stop for years. Your sessapinae have been all a-jangle for days now, warning you to brace or run, twitching with the need to *do something* about the seismic threat. You know better, but here's the problem: Every orogene in Castrima is sessing what you're sessing. Feeling the same twitchy urge to react. And unless they happen to be Fulcrum-precise highringers able to yoke other highringers before activating an ancient network of deadciv artifacts, *doing something* will kill them.

So Ykka is now coming to terms with a truth you've understood since you woke up with a stone arm: To survive in Rennanis, Castrima will need the node maintainers. It will need to take care of them. And when those node maintainers die, Castrima will need to find some way to replace them. No one's talking about that last part yet. First things first.

After a while, Ykka sighs and glances at the open doorway of the building. "Sounds like the fighting's done."

"Sounds like," you say. Silence stretches. A muscle in her jaw tightens. You add, "I'll go with you."

She glances at you. "You don't have to." You've told her about your first time seeing a node maintainer. She heard the still-fresh horror in your voice.

But no. Alabaster showed you the way, and you no longer shirk the duty he's bestowed upon you. You'll turn the maintainer's head, let Ykka see the scarring in the back, explain about the lesioning process. You'll need to show her how the wire minimizes bedsores. Because if she's going to make this choice, then she needs to know exactly what price she—and Castrima—must pay.

You will do this—make her see these things, make yourself face it again, because this is the *whole* truth of what orogenes are. The Stillness fears your kind for good reason, true. Yet it should also revere your kind for good reason, and it has chosen to do only one of these things. Ykka, of all people, needs to hear everything.

Her jaw tightens, but she nods. Esni watches you both, curious, but then she shrugs and turns away as you and Ykka walk into the node facility, together.

*   *   *

The node has a fully stocked storeroom, which you guess is meant to be an auxiliary storage site for the comm itself. It's more than even hungry, commless Castrima can eat, and it includes things everyone's been increasingly desperate for, like dried red and yellow fruit and canned greens. Ykka stops people from turning the occasion into an impromptu feast—you've still got to make the stores last for Earth knows how long—but that doesn't prevent the bulk of the comm from getting into a nearly festive mood as everyone bunkers for the night with full bellies for the first time in months.

Ykka posts guards at the entrance to the node maintainer's chamber—"Nobody but us needs to see that shit," she declares, and by this you suspect that she doesn't want any of the comm's stills getting ideas—and on the storeroom. She puts a triple guard on the goat. There's an Innovator girl from a farming comm who's been assigned to figure out how to milk the creature; she manages. The pregnant woman, who lost one of her household mates in the desert, gets first dibs on the milk. This might be pointless. Starvation and pregnancy don't mesh, either, and she says the baby hasn't moved in days. Probably best that she lose it now, if she's going to, here where Lerna's got antibiotics and sterile instruments available and can at least save the mother's life. Still, you see her take the little pot of milk when it's given to her, and drink it down even though she grimaces at the taste. Her jaw is set and hard. There's a chance. That's what matters.

Ykka also sets up monitors at the node station's shower room. They're not guards, exactly, but they're necessary, because a lot of people in Castrima are from rough little Midlatter comms and they don't know how indoor plumbing works. Also, some people have been just standing under the hot spray for an hour or more, weeping as the ash and leftover desert sand comes off their acid-dried skins. Now, after ten minutes, the monitors gently nudge people out and over to benches along the sides of the room, where they can keep crying while others get their turn.

You take a shower and feel nothing, except clean. When you claim a corner of the station's mess hall—which has been emptied of furnishings so that several hundred people can sleep ash-free for the night—you sit there atop your bedroll, leaning against the scoria wall, letting your thoughts drift. It's impossible not to notice the mountain lurking within the stone just behind you. You don't call him out because the other people of Castrima are leery of Hoa. He's the only stone eater still around, and they remember that stone eaters are not neutral, harmless parties. You do reach back and pat the wall with your one hand, however. The mountain stirs a little, and you feel something—a hard nudge—against the small of your back. Message received and returned. It's surprising how good this private moment of contact makes you feel.

You need to feel again, you think, as you watch a dozen small tableaus play out before you. Two women argue over which of them gets to eat the last piece of dried fruit in their comm share. Two men, just beyond them, furtively exchange whispers while one passes over a small soft sponge—the kind Equatorials like to use for wiping after defecation. Everyone likes their little luxuries, when fortune provides. Temell, the man who now teaches the comm's orogene children, lies buried in them as he snores on his bedroll. One boy is nestled in a curl at his belly; meanwhile, Penty's sock-clad foot rests on the back of his neck. Across the room, Tonkee stands with Hjarka—or rather, Hjarka's holding her hands and trying to coax her into some kind of slow dance, while Tonkee stands still and tries to just roll her eyes and not smile.

You're not sure where Ykka is. Probably spending the night

in one of the sheds or tents outside, knowing her, but you hope she lets one of her lovers stay with her this time. She's got a rotating stable of young women and men, some of them time-sharing with other partners and some singles who don't seem to mind Ykka using them for occasional stress relief. Ykka needs that now. Castrima needs to take care of its headwoman.

Castrima needs, and you need, and just as you think this, Lerna comes out of nowhere and settles beside you.

"Had to end Chetha," he says quietly. Chetha, you know, is one of the three Strongbacks shot by the Rennies—ironically, a former Rennie herself, conscripted into the army along with Danel. "The other two will make it, probably, but the bolt per-forated Chetha's bowel. It would've been slow and awful. Plenty of painkillers here, though." He sighs and rubs his eyes. "You've seen that…thing…in the wire chair."

You nod, hesitate, then reach for his hand. He's not particu-larly affectionate, you've been relieved to discover, but he does need little gestures sometimes. A reminder that he is not alone, and that all is not hopeless. To this end you say, "If I succeed in shutting down the Rifting, you may not need to keep the node maintainers." You're not sure that's true, but you hope it is.

He clasps your hand lightly. It's been fascinating to realize that he never initiates contact between you. He waits for you to offer, and then he meets your gestures with as much or as little intensity as you've brought to the effort. Respecting your boundaries, which are sharp-edged and hair-triggered. You never knew he was so observant, all these years—but then, you should've guessed. He figured out you were an orogene just by watching you, years ago. Innon would've liked him, you decide.

As if he has heard your thoughts, Lerna then looks over at you, and his gaze is troubled.

"I've been thinking about not telling you something," he says. "Or rather, not pointing out something you've probably chosen not to notice."

"What an opening."

He smiles a little, then sighs and looks down at your clasped hands, the smile fading. The moment attenuates; the tension grows in you, because this is so unlike him. Finally, though, he sighs. "How long has it been since you last menstruated?"

"How—" You stop talking.

Shit.

Shit.

In your silence, Lerna sighs and leans his head back against the wall.

You try to make excuses in your own head. Starvation. Extraordinary physical effort. You're forty-four years old—you think. Can't remember what month it is. The chances are slimmer than Castrima's were of surviving the desert. But... your menses have run strong and regular for your entire life, stopping only on three prior occasions. Three *significant* occasions. That's why the Fulcrum decided to breed you. Half-decent orogeny, and good Midlatter hips.

You knew. Lerna's right. On some level, you noticed. And then chose not to notice, because—

Lerna has been silent beside you for some while, watching the comm unwind, his hand limp in yours. Very softly he says, "Am I correct in understanding that you need to finish your business at Corepoint within a time frame?"

His tone is too formal. You sigh, shutting your eyes. "Yes."

"Soon?"

Hoa has told you that *perigee*—when the Moon is closest—will be in a few days. After that, it will pass the Earth and pick up velocity, slingshotting back into the distant stars or wherever it's been all this time. If you don't catch it now, you won't.

"Yes," you say. You're tired. You…hurt. "Very soon."

It is a thing you haven't discussed, and probably should have for the sake of your relationship. It is a thing you never needed to discuss, because there was nothing to be said. Lerna says, "Using all the obelisks once did that to your arm."

You glance at the stump unnecessarily. "Yes." You know where he's going with the conversation, so you decide to skip to the end. "You're the one who asked what I was going to do about the Season."

He sighs. "I was angry."

"But not wrong."

His hand twitches a little on your own. "What if I asked you not to do it?"

You don't laugh. If you did, it would be bitter, and he doesn't deserve that. Instead, you sigh and shift to lie down, pushing him until he does the same thing. He's a little shorter than you, so you're the big spoon. This of course puts your face in his gray hair, but he's availed himself of the shower, too, so you don't mind. He smells good. Healthy.

"You wouldn't ask," you say against his scalp.

"But what if I did?" It's weary and heatless. He doesn't mean it.

You kiss the back of his neck. "I'd say, 'Okay,' and then there would be three of us, and we'd all stay together until we die of ash lung."

He takes your hand again. You didn't initiate it this time, but it doesn't bother you. "Promise," he says.

He doesn't wait for your answer before falling asleep.

*　　*　　*

Four days later, you reach Rennanis.

The good news is that you're no longer plagued by ashfall. The Rifting's too close, and the Wall is busy carrying the lighter particulates upward; you'll never have to worry about that again. What you have instead are periodic gusts laden with incendiary material—lapilli, tiny bits of volcanic material that are too big to inhale easily but are still burning as they come down. Danel says the Rennies called it sparkfall, and that it's mostly harmless, though you should keep spare canteens of water situated at strategic points throughout the caravan in case any of the sparks should catch and smolder.

More dramatic than the sparkfall, however, is the way lightning dances over the city's skyline, this close to the Wall. The Innovators are excited about this. Tonkee says there are all sorts of uses for reliable lightning. (This would have made you stare at her, if it hadn't come from Tonkee.) None of it strikes the ground, though—only the taller buildings, which have all been fitted with lightning rods by the city's previous denizens. It's harmless. You'll just have to get used to it.

Rennanis isn't what you were expecting, quite. Oh, it's a huge city: Equatorial styling all over the place, still-functioning hydro and filtered well water running smoothly, tall black obsidian walls etched over with dire images of what happens to the city's enemies. Its buildings aren't nearly as beautiful or impressive as those of Yumenes, but then Yumenes was the greatest of the Equatorial cities, and Rennanis barely merited the title. "Only half a million people," you remember someone sneering, a lifetime ago. But two lives ago, you were born in a humble Nomidlats village, and to what remains of Damaya, Rennanis is still a sight to behold.

There are less than a thousand of you to occupy a city that once held hundreds of thousands. Ykka orders everyone to take over a small complex of buildings near one of the city's greenlands. (It has sixteen.) The former inhabitants have conveniently labeled the city's buildings with a color code based on their structural soundness, since the city didn't survive the Rifting entirely unscathed. Buildings marked with a green X are known to be safe. A yellow X means damage that could spell a collapse, especially if another major shake hits the city. Red-marked buildings are noticeably damaged and dangerous, though you see signs that they were inhabited, too, perhaps by those willing to take any shelter rather than be ashed out. There are more than enough green-X buildings for Castrima, so every household gets its pick of apartments that are furnished, sound, and still have working hydro and geo.

There are several wild flocks of chickens running about, and more goats, which have actually been breeding. The greenlands' crops are all dead, however, having gone months unwatered and untended between you killing the Rennies and Castrima's arrival. Despite this, the seed stocks contain lots of dandelion and other hardy, low-light-tolerant edibles, including Equatorial staples like taro. Meanwhile, the city's storecaches are overflowing with cachebread, cheeses, fat-flecked spicy sausages, grains and fruit, herbs and leaves preserved in oil, more. Some of it's fresher than the rest, brought back by the marauding army. All of it is more than the people of Castrima could eat if they threw a feast every night for the next ten years.

It's amazing. But there are a few catches.

The first is that it's more complicated to run Rennanis's water treatment facility than anyone expected. It's running automatically and thus far hasn't broken down, but no one knows how to work the machinery if it does. Ykka sets the Innovators to the task of figuring that out, or coming up with a workable alternative if the equipment fails. Tonkee is highly annoyed: "I trained for six years at Seventh to learn how to clean shit out of sewer water?" But despite her complaining, she's on it.

The second catch is that Castrima cannot possibly guard the city's walls. The city is simply too big, and there are too few of you. You're protected, for now, by the fact that no one comes north if they can possibly help it. If anyone does come a-conquering, however, nothing will stand between the comm and conquest except its wall.

There's no solution to this problem. Even orogenes can only do so much in the martial sense, here in the shadow of the Rifting where orogeny is dangerous. Danel's army was Rennanis's surplus population, and it's currently feeding a boilbug boom down in the southeastern Midlats—not that you'd want them here, anyway, treating you like the interlopers you are. Ykka orders the Breeders to ramp up to replacement-level production, but even if they recruit every healthy comm member to assist,

Castrima won't have enough people to secure the comm for generations. Nothing to do but at least guard the portion of the city that the comm now occupies, as best you can.

"And if another army comes along," you catch Ykka muttering, "we'll just invite them in and assign them each a room. That ought to settle it."

The third catch—and the biggest one, existentially if not logistically—is this: Castrima must live amid the corpses of its conquered.

The statues are everywhere. Standing in apartment kitchens washing dishes. Lying in beds that have sagged or broken beneath their stone weight. Walking up the parapet steps to take over from other statues on guard duty. Sitting in communal kitchens sipping tea long since dried to dregs. They are beautiful in their way, with wild smoky-quartz manes of hair and smooth jasper skin and clothes of tourmaline or turquoise or garnet or citrine. They wear expressions that are smiles or eye rolls or yawns of boredom—because the shockwave of Obelisk Gate power that transformed them was fast, mercifully. They didn't even have time to be afraid.

The first day, everyone edges around the statues. Tries not to sit in their line of sight. To do anything else would be... disrespectful. And yet. Castrima has survived both a war that these people initiated, and life as that war's refugees. It would be equally disrespectful of Castrima's dead to let guilt eclipse this truth. So after a day or two, people start to simply... *accept* the statues. Can't do anything else, really.

Something about it bothers you, though.

You find yourself wandering one night. There's a yellow-X

building that's not too far from the complex, and it's beautiful, with a facade covered in etched vinework and floral motifs, some glimmering with peeling gold foil. The foil catches the light and flickers a little as you move, its angles of reflection shifting to create the overall illusion of a building covered in living, moving greenery. It's an older building than most of those in Rennanis. You like it, though you're not sure why. You go up to the roof, finding only the usual apartments inhabited by statues along the way. The door here is unlocked and stands open; maybe someone was on the roof when the Rifting struck. You check to make sure there's a lightning rod in place before you step through the door, of course; this is one of the taller buildings of the city, though it's only six or seven stories altogether. (*Only*, sneers Syenite. *Only?* thinks Damaya, in wonder. *Yes, only*, you snap at both, to shut them up.) There's not only a rod, there's an empty water tower, so as long as you don't go leaning on any metal surfaces or linger in the rod's immediate vicinity, you probably won't die. Probably.

And here, poised to face the Rifting cloudwall as if he were built up here, gazing north since the building's floral motifs were new, Hoa awaits.

"There aren't as many statues here as there should be," you say as you stop beside him.

You can't help following Hoa's gaze. From here, you still can't see the Rifting itself; looks like there's a dead rainforest and some hilly ridges between the city and the monster. The Wall is bad enough, however.

And maybe one existential horror is easier to face than another, but you remember using the Obelisk Gate on these people, twisting the magic between their cells and transmuting the infinitesimal parts of them from carbon to silicate. Danel told you how crowded Rennanis was—so much that it had to send out a conquering army to survive. Now, however, the city is not crowded with statues. There are signs that it was, once: statues deep in conversation with partners that seem to be missing; only two people sitting at a table set for six. In one of the bigger green-X buildings there's a statue that is lying naked in bed, mouth open and penis permanently stiff and hips thrusting up, hands positioned in just the right places to grip someone's legs. He's alone, though. Someone's horrible, morbid joke.

"My kind are opportunistic feeders," Hoa says.

Yeah, that's exactly what you were afraid he would say.

"And apparently very damned hungry? There were a lot of people here. Most of them must be missing."

"We, too, put aside surplus resources for later, Essun."

You rub your face with your one remaining hand, trying and failing to *not* visualize a gigantic stone eater larder somewhere, now stuffed full of brightly colored statues. "Evil Earth. Why do you bother with me, then? I'm not as—*easy* a meal as those."

"Lesser members of my kind need to strengthen themselves. I don't." There is a very slight shift in the inflection of Hoa's voice. By this point you know him; that was contempt. He's a proud creature (even he will admit). "They are poorly made, weak, little better than beasts. We were so lonely in those early years, and at first we had no idea what we were doing. The hungry ones are the result of our fumbling."

You waver, because you don't really want to know...but you haven't been a coward for some years now. So you steel yourself and turn to him and then say, "You're making another one now. Aren't you? From—from me. If it's not about food for you, then it's...reproduction." Horrifying reproduction, if it is dependent on the death-by-petrification of a human being. And there must be more to it than just turning people to stone. You think about the kirkhusa at the roadhouse, and Jija, and the woman back in Castrima whom you killed. You think about how you hit her, *smashed* her with magic, for the not-crime of making you relive Uche's murder. But Alabaster was not the same, in the end, as what you did to that woman. She was a shining, brightly colored collection of gemstones. He was an ugly lump of brown rock— and yet the brown rock was finely made, precisely crafted, *careful*, where the woman was a disorderly mess beneath her surface beauty.

Hoa is silent in answer to your question, which is an answer in itself. And then you finally remember. Antimony, in the moments after you closed the Obelisk Gate, but before you teetered into magic-traumatized slumber. Beside her, another stone eater, strange in his whiteness, disturbing in his familiarity. Oh, Evil Earth, you don't want to know, but—"Antimony used that..." Too-small lump of brown stone. "Used *Alabaster*. As raw material to—to, oh rust, to make another stone eater. And she made it look like *him*." You hate Antimony all over again.

"He chose his own shape. We all do."

This slaps your rage out of its spiral. Your stomach clenches, this time in something other than revulsion. "That—then—"

You have to take a deep breath. "Then it's *him*? Alabaster. He's...he's..." You can't make yourself say the word.

Flick and Hoa faces you, expression compassionate, but somehow also warning. "The lattice doesn't always form perfectly, Essun," he says. The tone is gentle. "Even when it does, there is always...loss of data."

You have no idea what this means and yet you're shaking. Why? You know why. Your voice rises. "Hoa, if that's Alabaster, if I can talk to him—"

"No."

"Why the rust not?"

"Because it must be his choice, first." Harder voice here. A reprimand. You flinch. "More importantly, because we are fragile at the beginning, like all new creatures. It takes centuries for us, the *who* of us, to...cool. Even the slightest of pressures—like you, demanding that he fit himself to your needs rather than his own—can damage the final shape of his personality."

You take a step back, which surprises you because you hadn't realized you were getting in his face. And then you sag. Alabaster is alive, but not. Is Stone Eater Alabaster even remotely the same as the flesh-and-blood man you knew? Does that even matter anymore, now that he has transformed so completely? "I've lost him again, then," you murmur.

Hoa doesn't seem to move at first, but there's a brief flit of wind against your side, and abruptly a hard hand nudges the back of your soft one. "He will live for an eternity," Hoa says, as softly as his hollow voice can manage. "For as long as the Earth exists, something of who he was will, too. You're the one still in danger of being lost." He pauses. "But if you choose not to finish what we have begun, I will understand."

You look up and then, for only maybe the second or third time, you think you understand him. He knows you're pregnant. Maybe he knew it before you did, though what that means to him, you cannot guess. He knows what underlies your thoughts about Alabaster, too, and he's saying...that you aren't alone. That you *don't* have nothing. You have Hoa, and Ykka and Tonkee and maybe Hjarka, *friends*, who know you in all your rogga monstrosity and accept you despite it. And you have Lerna—quietly demanding, relentless Lerna, who does not give up and does not tolerate your excuses and does not pretend that love precludes pain. He is the father of another child that will probably be beautiful. All of your children so far have been. Beautiful, and powerful. You close your eyes against regret.

But that brings the sounds of the city to your ears, and you are startled to catch laughter on the wind, loud enough to carry up from the ground level, probably over by one of the communal fires. Which reminds you that you have *Castrima*, too, if you want it. This ridiculous comm of unpleasant people who are impossibly still together, which you have fought for and which has, however grudgingly, fought for you in return. It pulls your mouth into a smile.

"No," you say. "I'll do what needs doing."

Hoa considers you. "You're certain."

Of course you are. Nothing has changed. The world is broken and you can fix it; that's what Alabaster and Lerna both charged you to do. Castrima is *more* reason for you to do it, not less. And it's time you stopped being a coward, too, and went to find Nassun. Even if she hates you. Even if you left her to face a terrible world alone. Even if you are the worst mother in the world...you did your best.

And maybe it means you're choosing one of your children—the one who has the best chance of survival—over the other. But that's no different from what mothers have had to do since the dawn of time: sacrifice the present, in hopes of a better future. If the sacrifice this time has been harder than most... Fine. So be it. This is a mother's job, too, after all, and you're a rusting ten-ringer. You'll see to it.

"So what are we waiting for?" you ask.

"Only you," Hoa replies.

"Right. How much time do we have?"

"Perigee is in two days. I can get you to Corepoint in one."

"Okay." You take a deep breath. "I need to say some goodbyes."

With perfect bland casualness, Hoa says, "I can carry others with us."

Oh.

You want it, don't you? To not be alone at the end. To have Lerna's quiet implacable presence at your back. Tonkee will be furious at not getting a chance to see Corepoint, if you leave her behind. Hjarka will be furious if you take Tonkee without her. Danel wants to chronicle the world's transformation, for obscure Equatorial lorist reasons.

Ykka, though—

"No." You sober and sigh. "I'm being selfish again. Castrima needs Ykka. And they've all suffered enough."

Hoa just looks at you. How the rust does he manage to convey such emotion with a stone face? Even if that emotion is dry skepticism of your self-abnegating bullshit. You laugh—once, and it's rusty. Been a while.

"I think," Hoa says slowly, "that if you love someone, you don't get to choose how they love you back."

So many layers in the strata of that statement.

Okay, though. Right. This isn't just about you, and it never has been. All things change in a Season—and some part of you is tired, finally, of the lonely, vengeful woman narrative. Maybe Nassun isn't the only one you needed a home for. And maybe not even you should try to change the world alone.

"Let's go ask them, then," you say. "And then let's go get my little girl."

*   *   *

To: Yaetr Innovator Dibars
From: Alma Innovator Dibars

I've been asked to inform you that your funding has been cut. You are to return to the University forthwith by the least expensive means possible.

And since I know you, old friend, let me add this. You believe in logic. You think even our esteemed colleagues are immune to prejudice, or politics, in the face of hard facts. This is why you'll never be allowed within a mile of the Funding and Allocations committee, no matter how many masterships you earn.

Our funding comes from Old Sanze. From families
so ancient that they have books in their collections
older than all the Universities—and they won't let us
touch them. How do you think those families got to
be so old, Yaetr? Why has Sanze lasted this long? It's
not because of stonelore.

You cannot go to people like that and ask them to
fund a research project that makes heroes of roggas!
You just can't. They'll faint, and when they wake up,
they'll have you killed. They'll destroy you as surely as
they would any threat to their livelihoods and legacy.
Yes, I know that's not what you think you're doing,
but it is.

And if that isn't enough, here is a fact that might
be logical enough even for you: The Guardians are
starting to ask questions. I don't know why. No one
knows what drives those monsters. But that's why I
voted with the committee majority, even if it means
you hate me from here on. I want you alive, old friend,
not dead in an alley with a glass poniard through your
heart. I'm sorry.

Safe travels homeward.

12

Nassun, not alone

COREPOINT IS SILENT.

Nassun notices this when the vehimal in which she's traversed the planet emerges in its corresponding station, on the other side of the world. This is located in one of the strange, slanting buildings that encircle the massive hole at Corepoint's center. She cries for help, cries for someone, cries, as the vehimal's door opens and she drags Schaffa's limp, unresponsive body through the silent corridors and then the silent streets. He's big and heavy, so although she tries in various ways to use magic to assist with dragging his weight—badly; magic is not meant to be used for something so gross and localized, and her concentration is poor in the moment—she makes it only a block or so away from the compound before she, too, collapses, in exhaustion.

*   *   *

Somerusting day, somerusting year.

Found these books, blank. The stuff they're made of isn't paper. Thicker. Doesn't bend easily. Good thing, maybe, or would be dust by now. Preserve my words for eternity! Ha! Longer than my rusting sanity.

Don't know what to write. Innon would laugh and tell me to write about sex. Right, so: I jerked off today, for the first time since A dragged me to this place. Thought about him in the middle of it and couldn't come. Maybe I'm too old? That's what Syen would say. She's just mad I could still knock her up.

Forgetting how Innon used to smell. Everything smells like the sea here, but it's not like the sea near Meov. Different water? Innon used to smell like the water there. Every time the wind blows I lose a little more of him.

Corepoint. How I hate this place.

* * *

Corepoint isn't a ruin, quite. That is, it isn't ruined, and it isn't uninhabited.

On the surface of the open, endless ocean, the city is an anomaly of buildings—not very tall compared to either the recently lost Yumenes or the longer-lost Syl Anagist. Corepoint is unique, however, among both past and present cultures. The structures of Corepoint are sturdily built, of rustless metal and strange polymers and other materials that can withstand the often hurricane-force salt winds that dominate this side of the world. The few plants that grow here, in the parks that were constructed so long ago, are no longer the lovely, designer, hothouse things favored by Corepoint's builders. Corepoint trees—hybridized and feral descendants of the original landscaping—are huge, woody things, twisted into artful shapes by the wind. They have long since broken free of their orderly beds and containers and now gnarl over the pressed-fiber sidewalks. Unlike the architecture of Syl Anagist, here there are many more sharp angles, meant to minimize the buildings' resistance to the wind.

But there is more to the city than what can be seen.

Corepoint sits at the peak of an enormous underwater shield volcano, and the first few miles of the hole drilled at its center are actually lined with a hollowed-out complex of living quarters, laboratories, and manufactories. These underground facilities, originally meant to house Corepoint's geomagests and genegineers, have long since been turned to a wholly different purpose—because this flip side of Corepoint is Warrant, where Guardians are made and dwell between Seasons.

We will speak more of this later.

Above the surface in Corepoint, though, it's late afternoon, beneath a sky whose clouds are sparse amid a shockingly bright blue sky. (Seasons that start in the Stillness rarely have a severe impact on the weather in this hemisphere, or at least not for several months or years after.) As befits the bright day, there are people in the streets around Nassun as she struggles and weeps, but they do not move to help. They do not move at all, mostly—for they are stone eaters, with rose-marble lips and shining mica eyes and braids woven in pyrite gold or clear quartz. They stand on the steps of buildings that have not known human feet for tens of thousands of years. They sit along window ledges of stone or metal that have begun to deform under the pressure of incredible weight applied over decades. One sits with knees upraised and arms propped across them, leaning against a tree whose roots have grown around her; mosses line the upper surfaces of her arms and hair. She watches Nassun, only her eyes moving, in what might be interest.

They all watch, doing nothing, as this quick-moving, noisy human child sobs into the salt-laden wind until she is exhausted, and then just sits there in a huddle with her fingers still tangled in the cloth of Schaffa's shirt.

* * *

Another day, same (?) year

No writing about Innon or Coru. Off-limits from now on.

Syen. I can still feel her—not sess, feel. There's an obelisk here, I think it's a spinel. When I ~~canneck~~ connect to it, it's like I can feel anything they're connected to. The amethyst is following Syen. Wonder if she knows.

Antimony says Syen made it to the mainland and is ~~wannr~~ wandering. That's why I feel like I'm wandering, I guess? She's all that's left but she ki—fuck.

This place is ridiculous. Anniemony was right that it's a way to trigger the Obelisk Gate without control cab? (Onyx. Too powerful, can't risk it, would trigger alignment too quickly and then who's to make the second traj change?) But the rusters that buildt it put everything into tht stupid hole. A told me some of it. Great project, my ass. It's worse to see, though. This whole rusting city is a crime scene. Tooted around and found great big pipes running along the bottom of the ocean. ~~hu~~ HUGE, ready to pump something from the hole all the way to the continent. Magic, Animony says, did they really need so much????? More than the Gate!

Asked Tinimony to take me into the hole today and she said no. What's in the hole, huh? What's in the hole.

* * *

Near sunset, another stone eater appears. Here amid the elegantly gowned, colorful variety of his people, he stands out even more with his gray coloring and bare chest: Steel. He stands over Nassun for several minutes, perhaps expecting her to lift her gaze and notice him, but she does not. Presently, he says, "The ocean winds can be cold at night."

Silence. Her hands clench and unclench on Schaffa's clothes, not quite spasmodically. She's just tired. She's been holding him since the center of the Earth.

After a while longer, as the sun inches toward the horizon, Steel says, "There's a livable apartment in a building two blocks from here. The food stored in it should still be edible."

Nassun says, "Where?" Her voice is hoarse. She needs water. There's some in her canteen, and in Schaffa's canteen, but she hasn't opened either.

Steel shifts posture, pointing. Nassun lifts her head to follow this and sees a street, unnaturally straight, seemingly paved straight toward the horizon. Wearily she gets up, takes a better grip on Schaffa's clothes, and begins dragging him again.

*　　*　　*

Who's in the hole, what's in the whole, where goes the hole, how holed am I!

SEs brought better food today because I don't eat enough. So special, delivery fressssh from the other sigh of the world. Going to dry the seeds, plant them. Remember to scrrrape up tomato I threw at A.

Book language looks almost like Sanze-mat. Characters similar? Precursor? Some words I almost recognize. Some old Eturpic, some Hladdac, a little early-dynasty Regwo. Wish Shinash was here. He would scream to see me putting my feet up on books older than forever. Always so easy to tease. Miss him.

Miss everyone, even people at the rusting Fulcrum (!) Miss voices that come out of rusting mouths. SYENITE could make me eat, you talking rock. SYENITE gave a shit about me and not just whether I could fix this world I don't give a shit about. SYENITE should be here with me, ~~I would give anything to have her here with me~~

No. She should forget me and ~~In~~ Meov. Find some boring fool she actually wants to sleep with. Have a boring life. She deserves that.

*   *   *

Night falls in the time it takes Nassun to reach the building. Steel repositions, appearing in front of a strange asymmetrical building, wedge-shaped, whose high end faces the wind. The sloping roof of the building, in the lee of the wind, is scraggly with overgrown, twisted vegetation. There's plenty of soil on the roof, more than is likely to have accumulated from the wind over centuries. It looks planned, though overgrown. Yet amid the mess, Nassun can see that someone has hacked out a garden. Recently; the plants are overgrown, too, new growth springing up from dropped fruit and split, untended vines, but given the relative dearth of weeds and the still-neat rows, this garden can't be more than a year or two neglected. The Season is now almost two years old.

Later. The building's door moves on its own, sliding aside as Nassun approaches. It closes on its own, too, once she's gotten Schaffa far enough within. Steel moves inside, pointing upstairs. She drags Schaffa to the foot of the stairs and then drops beside him, shaking, too tired to think or go any farther.

Schaffa's heart is still strong, she thinks, as she uses his chest for a pillow. With her eyes shut, she can almost imagine that he's holding her, rather than the other way around. It is paltry comfort, but enough to let her sleep without dreams.

*   *   *

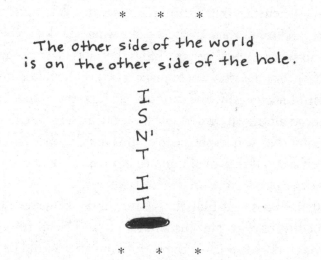

The other side of the world
is on the other side of the hole.

I
S
N'
T
I
T

*   *   *

In the morning, Nassun gets Schaffa up the steps. The apartment is thankfully on only the second floor; the stairwell door opens right into it. Everything inside is strange, to her eye, yet familiar in purpose. There's a couch, though its back is at one end of the long seat, rather than behind it. There are chairs, one fused to some kind of big slanted table. For drawing, maybe. The bed, in the attached room, is the strangest thing: a big wide hemisphere of brightly colored cushion without sheets or pillows. When Nassun tentatively lies down on it, though, she finds that it flattens and conforms to her body in ways that are stunningly comfortable. It's warm, too—actively heating up beneath her until the aches of sleeping in a cold stairwell go away. Fascinated despite herself, Nassun examines the bed and is shocked to realize that it is *full* of magic, and has covered her in same. Threads of silver roam over her body, determining her discomfort by touching her nerves and then repairing her bruises and scrapes; other threads whip the particles of the bed until friction warms them; yet more threads search her skin for infinitesimal dry flakes and flecks of dust, and scrub them away. It's like what she does when she uses the silver to heal or cut things, but automatic, somehow. She can't imagine who would make a bed that could do magic. She can't imagine why. She can't fathom how anyone could have convinced all this silver to do such nice things, but that's what's happening. No wonder the people who built the obelisks needed so much silver, if they used it in lieu of wearing blankets, or taking baths, or letting themselves heal over time.

Schaffa has soiled himself, Nassun finds. It makes her feel ashamed to have to pull his clothes off and clean him, using stretchy cloths she finds in the bathroom, but it would be worse to leave him in his own filth. His eyes are open again, though he does not move while she works. They've opened during the day, and they close at night, but though Nassun talks to Schaffa (pleads for him to wake up, asks him to help her, tells him that she needs him), he does not respond.

She gets him into the bed, leaving a pad of cloths under his bare bottom. She trickles water from their canteens into his mouth, and when that runs out, she cautiously tries to get more from the strange water pump in the kitchen. There are no levers or handles on it, but when she puts her canteen beneath the spigot, water comes out. She's a diligent girl. First she uses the powder in her runny-sack to make a cup of safe from the water, checking for contaminants. The safe dissolves but stays cloudy and white, so she drinks that herself and then brings more water to Schaffa. He drinks readily, which probably means he was really thirsty. She gives him raisins that she first soaks in water, and he chews and swallows, although slowly and without much vigor. She hasn't done a good job of taking care of him.

She will do better, she decides, and heads outside to the garden to pick food for them both.

* * *

Syenite told me the date. Six years. It's been six years? No wonder she's so angry. Told me to go jump in a hole, since it's been so long. She doesn't want to see me again. Such a steelheart. Told her I was sorry. My fault, all of it.

My fault. My Moon. Turned the spare key today. (Lines of sight, lines of force, three by three by three? Cubical arrangement, like a good little crystal lattice.) The key unlocks the Gate. Dangerous to bring so many obelisks to Yumenes, though; Guardians everywhere. Wouldn't have time before they got me. Better to make a spare key out of orogenes, and who can I use? Who is strong enough. Syen isn't, almost but not quite. Innon isn't. Coru is but I can't find him. He's just a baby anyway, not right. Babies. Lots of babies. Node maintainers? Node maintainers!

No. They've suffered enough. Use the Fulcrum seniors instead.

Or the node maintainers.

Why should I do it here? Plugs the hole. Do it there, tho . . . Get Yumenes. Get the Fulcrum. Get a lot of the Guardians.

Stop nagging me, woman. Go tell Innon to fuck you, or something. You're always so cranky when you haven't gotten laid. I'll jump in the hole tomorrow.

* * *

It becomes a routine.

She takes care of Schaffa in the mornings, then goes out in

the afternoon to explore the city and find things they need. There's no need to bathe Schaffa, or to clean up his waste again; astonishingly, the bed takes care of that, too. So Nassun can spend her time with him talking, and asking him to wake up, and telling him that she doesn't know what to do.

Steel vanishes again. She doesn't care.

Other stone eaters periodically show up, however, or at least she feels the impact of their presence. She sleeps on the couch, and one morning wakes to find a blanket covering her. It's just a simple gray thing, but it's warm, and she's grateful. When she starts picking apart one of her sausages to get the fat out of it, intending to make tallow—the candles from her runny-sack are getting low—she finds a stone eater in the stairwell, its finger curled in a beckoning gesture. When she follows it, it stops beside a panel covered in curious symbols. The stone eater is pointing toward one in particular. Nassun touches it and it alights with silver, glowing golden and sending threads questing over her skin. The stone eater says something in a language Nassun does not understand before it vanishes, but when she returns to the apartment, it's warmer, and soft white lights have come on overhead. Touching squares on the wall makes the lights go off.

One afternoon she walks into the apartment to find a stone eater crouched beside a pile of things that look to have come from some comm's storecache: burlap sacks full of root vegetables and mushrooms and dried fruit, a big round of sharp white cheese, hide bags of packed pemmican, satchels of dried rice and beans, and—precious—a small cask of salt. The stone eater vanishes when Nassun approaches the pile, so she cannot even thank it. She has to blow ash off of everything before she puts it away.

Nassun has figured out that the apartment, like the garden, must have been used until recently. The detritus of another person's life is everywhere: pants much too big for her in the drawers, a man's underwear beside them. (One day these are replaced with clothing that fits Nassun. Another stone eater? Or maybe the magic in the apartment is even more sophisticated than she thought.) Books are piled in one of the rooms, many of them native to Corepoint—she's beginning to recognize the peculiar, clean, not-quite-natural look of Corepoint things. A few, however, are normal-looking, with covers of cracking leather and pages still stinky with chemicals and handwritten ink. Some of the books are in a language she can't read. Something Coaster.

One, however, is made of the Corepoint material, but its blank pages have been handwritten over, in Sanze-mat. Nassun opens this one, sits down, and begins to read.

*   *   *

WENT
  IN THE HOLE
  DON'T
  don't bury me
  please DON'T, Syen, I love you, I'm sorry, keep me safe, watch my back and I'll watch yours, there's no one else who's as strong as you, I wish so much that you were here, please DON'T

*   *   *

Corepoint is a city in still life.

Nassun begins losing track of time. The stone eaters occasionally speak to her, but most of them don't know her language, and she doesn't hear enough of theirs to pick it up. She watches them sometimes, and is fascinated to realize that some of them are performing tasks. She watches one malachite-green woman who stands amid the windblown trees, and belatedly realizes the woman is holding a branch up and to one side, to make it grow in a particular way. All of the trees, which look windblown and yet are a little too dramatic, a little too artful in their splaying and bending, have been shaped thus. It must take years.

And near the edge of the city, down by one of the strange spokelike things that jut out into the water from its edge—not piers, really, just straight pieces of metal that make no sense— another stone eater stands every day with one hand upraised. Nassun just happens to be around when the stone eater blurs and there is a splash and suddenly his upraised hand holds by the tail a huge, wriggling fish that is as long as his body. His marble skin is sheened with wet. Nassun has nowhere in particular to be, so she sits down to watch. After a time, an ocean mammal—Nassun has read of these, creatures that look like fish but breathe air—sidles up to the city's edge. It is gray-skinned, tube-shaped; there are sharp teeth along its jaw, but these are small. When it pushes up out of the water, Nassun sees that it is very old, and something about the questing movements of its head makes her realize it has gone blind. There's old scarring on its forehead as well; something has injured the creature's head badly. The creature nudges the stone eater, who of course does not move, and then nips at the fish in its hand, tearing off chunks and swallowing them until the stone eater releases the tail. When it is done, the creature utters a complex, high-pitched sound, like a...chitter? Or a laugh. Then it slides further into the water and swims away.

The stone eater flickers and faces Nassun. Curious, Nassun gets to her feet to go over and speak to him. By the time she's standing, though, he has vanished.

This is what she comes to understand: There is life here, among these people. It isn't life as she knows it, or a life she would choose, but life nevertheless. That gives her comfort, when she no longer has Schaffa to tell her that she is good and safe. That, and the silence, give her time to mourn. She did not understand before now that she needed this.

* * *

I've decided.

It's wrong. Everything's wrong. Some things are so broken that they can't be fixed. You just have to finish them off, sweep away the rubble, and start over. Antimony agrees. Some of the other SEs do, too. Some don't.

Rust those. They killed my life to make me their weapon, so that's what I'm going to be. My choice. My commandment. We'll do it in Yumenes. A commandment is set in stone.

I asked after Syen today. Don't know why I care anymore. Antimony's been keeping tabs, though. (For me?) Syenite is living in some little shithole comm in the Somidlats, I forget the name, playing creche teacher. Playing the happy little still. Married with two new children. How about that. Not sure about the daughter but the boy is pulling on the aquamarine.

Amazing. No wonder the Fulcrum bred you to me. And we did make a beautiful child in spite of everything, didn't we? My boy.

I won't let them find your boy, Syen. I won't let them take him, and burn his brain, and put him in the wire chair. I won't let them find your girl, either, if she's one of us, or even if she's

Guardian-potential. There won't be a Fulcrum left by the time I'm done. What follows won't be good, but it'll be bad for everyone— rich and poor, Equatorials and commless, Sanzeds and Arctics, now they'll all know. Every season is the Season for us. The apocalypse that never ends. They could've chosen a different kind of equality. We could've all been safe and comfortable together, surviving together, but they didn't want that. Now nobody gets to be safe. Maybe that's what it will take for them to finally realize things have to change.

Then I'll shut it down and put the Moon back. (It shouldn't stone me, the first trajectory adjustment. ~~Unless I underestimate~~ Shouldn't.) All I'm rusting good for anyway.

After that . . . it'll be up to you, Syen. Make it better. I know I told you it wasn't possible, that there was no way to make the world better, but I was wrong. I'm breaking it because I was wrong. Start it over, you were right, change it. Make it better for the children you have left. Make a world Corundum could have been happy in. Make a world where people like us, you and me and Innon and our sweet boy, our beautiful boy, could have stayed whole.

Antimony says I might get to see that world. Guess we'll see. Rust it. I'm procrastinating. She's waiting. Back to Yumenes today.

For you, Innon. For you, Coru. For you, Syen.

*   *   *

At night, Nassun can see the Moon.

This was terrifying, on the first night that she looked outside and noticed a strange pale whiteness outlining the streets and trees of the city, and then looked up to see a great white sphere in the sky. It is enormous, to her—bigger than the sun, far larger than the stars, trailed by a faint streak of luminescence that she does not know is the off-gassing of ice that has adhered to the lunar surface over the course of its travels. The *white* of it is the true surprise. She knows very little of the Moon—only what Schaffa told her. It is a satellite, he said, Father Earth's lost child, a thing whose light reflects the sun. She expected it to be yellow, given that. It disturbs her to have been so wrong.

It disturbs her more that there is a *hole* in the thing, at nearly its dead center: a great, yawning darkness like the pinpoint pupil of an eye. It's too small to tell for now, but Nassun thinks that maybe if she stares at it long enough, she will see stars on the other side of the Moon, through this hole.

Somehow it's fitting. Whatever happened ages ago to cause the Moon's loss was surely cataclysmic on multiple levels. If the Earth suffered the Shattering, then the fact that the Moon also bears scars feels normal and right. With a thumb, Nassun rubs the palm of her hand where her mother broke the bones, a lifetime ago.

And yet, when she stands in the roof garden and stares at it for long enough, she begins to find the Moon beautiful. It is an icewhite eye, and she has no reason to think badly of those. Like the silver when it swirls and whorls within something like a snail's shell. It makes her think of Schaffa—that he is watching over her in his way—and this makes her feel less alone.

Over time, Nassun discovers that she can use the obelisks to get a feel for the Moon. The sapphire is on the other side of the world, but there are others here above the ocean, drawn near in response to her summons, and she has been tapping and taming each in turn. The obelisks help her feel (not sess) that the Moon will soon be at its closest point. If she lets it go, it will pass, and begin to rapidly diminish until it vanishes from the sky. Or she can open the Gate, and tug on it, and change everything. The cruelty of the status quo, or the comfort of oblivion. The choice feels clear to her . . . but for one thing.

One night, as Nassun sits gazing up at the great white sphere, she says aloud, "It was on purpose, wasn't it? You not telling me what would happen to Schaffa. So you could get rid of him."

The mountain that has been lingering nearby shifts slightly, to a position behind her. "I did try to warn you."

She turns to look at him. At the look on her face, he utters a soft laugh that sounds self-deprecating. This stops, though, when she says, "If he dies, I'll hate you more than I hate the world."

It is a war of attrition, she's begun to realize, and she's going to lose. In the weeks (?) or months (?) since they came to Corepoint, Schaffa has noticeably deteriorated, his skin developing an ugly pallor, his hair brittle and dull. People aren't meant to lie unmoving, blinking but not thinking, for weeks on end. She had to cut his hair earlier that day. The bed cleans the dirt out of it, but it's gotten oily and lately it keeps getting tangled—and the day before, some of it must have wrapped around his arm when she wrestled him onto his belly, cutting off his circulation in a way she didn't notice. (She keeps a sheet over him, even though the bed is warm and does not need it. It bothers her that he is naked and undignified.) This morning when she finally noticed the problem, the arm was pale and a little gray. She's loosed it, chafed it hoping to bring the color back, but it doesn't look good. She doesn't know what she'll do if something's really wrong with his arm. She might lose all of him like this, slowly but surely, little bits of him dying because she was only almost-nine when this Season began and she's only almost-eleven now and taking care of invalids wasn't something anyone taught her in creche.

"If he lives," Steel replies in his colorless voice, "he will never again experience a moment without agony." He pauses, gray eyes fixed on her face, as Nassun reverberates with his words, with her own denial, with her own growing sick fear that Steel is right.

Nassun gets to her feet. "I n-need to know how to fix him."

"You can't."

She tightens her hands into fists. For the first time in what feels like centuries, part of her reaches for the strata around her. This means the shield volcano beneath Corepoint...but when she "grasps" it orogenically, she finds with some surprise that it is *anchored*, somehow. This distracts her for a moment as she has to alter her perception to shift to the silver—and there she finds solid, scintillating pillars of magic driven into the volcano's foundations, pinning it in place. It's still active, but it will never erupt because of those pillars. It is as stable as bedrock despite the hole at its core burrowing down to the Earth's heart.

She shakes this off as irrelevant, and finally voices the thought that has been gathering in her mind over all the days she has dwelled in this city of stone people. "If...if I turn him into a stone eater, he'll live. And he won't have any pain. Right?" Steel does not reply. In the lengthening silence, Nassun bites her lip. "So you have to tell me how to—to make him like you. I bet I can do it if I use the Gate. I can do anything with that. Except..."

Except. The Obelisk Gate doesn't do small things. Just as Nassun feels, sesses, *knows* that the Gate makes her temporarily omnipotent, she knows, too, that she cannot use it to transform just one man. If she makes Schaffa into a stone eater...every human being on the planet will change in the same manner. Every comm, every commless band, every starving wanderer: Ten thousand still-life cities, instead of just one. All the world will become like Corepoint.

But is that really so terrible a thing? If everyone is a stone eater, there will be no more orogenes and stills. No more children to die, no more fathers to murder them. The Seasons could come and go, and they wouldn't matter. No one would starve to death ever again. To make the whole world as peaceful as Corepoint...would that not be a kindness?

Steel's face, which has been tilted up toward the Moon even as his eyes watch her, now slowly pivots to face her. It's always unnerving to see him move slowly. "Do you know what it feels like to live forever?"

Nassun blinks, thrown. She's been expecting a fight. "What?"

The moonlight has transformed Steel into a thing of starkest shadows, white and ink against the dimness of the garden. "I asked," he says, and his voice is almost pleasant, "if you know what it feels like to live forever. Like me. Like your Schaffa. Do you have any inkling as to how old he is? Do you *care*?"

"I—" About to say that she does, Nassun falters. No. This is not a thing she has ever considered. "I—I don't—"

"I would estimate," Steel continues, "that Guardians typically last three or four thousand years. Can you imagine that length of time? Think of the past two years. Your life since the beginning of the Season. Imagine another year. You can do that, can't you? Every day feels like a year here in Corepoint, or so your kind tell me. Now put all three years together, and imagine them *times one thousand*." The emphasis he puts on this is sharp, precisely enunciated. In spite of herself, Nassun jumps.

But also in spite of herself... she thinks. She feels old, Nassun, at the world-weary age of not-quite-eleven. So much has happened since the day she came home to find her little brother dead on the floor. She is a different person now, hardly Nassun at all; sometimes she is surprised to realize *Nassun* is still her name. How much more different will she be in three years? Ten? Twenty?

Steel pauses until he sees some change in her expression— some evidence, perhaps, that she is listening to him. Then he says, "I have reason to believe, however, that your Schaffa is much, much older than most Guardians. He isn't quite first-generation; those have all long since died. Couldn't take it. He's one of the very early ones, though, still. The languages, you see; that's how you can always tell. They never quite lose those, even after they've forgotten the names they were born with."

Nassun remembers how Schaffa knew the language of the earth-traversing vehicle. It is strange to think of Schaffa having been born back when that tongue was still spoken. It would make him... she can't even imagine. Old Sanze is supposed to be seven Seasons old, eight if one counts the present Season. Almost three thousand years. The Moon's cycle of return and retreat is much older than that, and Schaffa remembers it, so... yes. He's very, very old. She frowns.

"It's rare to find one of them who can really go the distance,"

Steel continues. His tone is casual, conversational; he could be talking about Nassun's old neighbors back in Jekity. "The corestone hurts them so much, you see. They get tired, and then they get sloppy, and then the Earth begins to contaminate them, eating away at their will. They don't usually last long once that starts. The Earth uses them, or their fellow Guardians use them, until they outlive their usefulness and one side or the other kills them. It's a testament to your Schaffa's strength that he lasted so much longer. Or a testament to something else, maybe. What kills the rest, you see, is losing the things that ordinary people need to be happy. Imagine what that's like, Nassun. Watching everyone you know and care about die. Watching your home die, and having to find a new one—again, and again, and again. Imagine never daring to get close to another person. Never having friends, because you'll outlive them. Are you lonely, little Nassun?"

She has forgotten her anger. "Yes," she admits, before she can think not to.

"Imagine being lonely forever." There's a very slight smile on his lips, she sees. It's been there the whole while. "Imagine living here in Corepoint forever, with no one to talk to but me—when I bother to respond. What do you think that will feel like, Nassun?"

"Terrible," she says. Quietly now.

"Yes. So here is my theory: I believe your Schaffa survived by loving his charges. You, and others like you, soothed his loneliness. He truly does love you; never doubt that about him." Nassun swallows back a dull ache. "But he also needs you. You keep him happy. You keep him *human*, where otherwise time would have long since transformed him into something else."

Then Steel moves again. It's inhuman because of its steadiness, Nassun finally realizes. People are quick to do big movements and then slower with fine adjustment. Steel does everything at the same pace. Watching him move is like watching a statue melt. But then he stands with arms outstretched as if to say, *Take a look at me.*

"I am forty thousand years old," Steel says. "Give or take a few millennia."

Nassun stares at him. The words are like the gibberish that the vehimal spoke—almost comprehensible, but not really. Not real.

What *does* that feel like, though?

"You're going to die when you open the Gate," Steel says, after giving Nassun a moment to absorb what he's said. "Or if not then, sometime after. A few decades, a few minutes, it's all the same. And whatever you do, Schaffa will lose you. He'll lose the one thing that has kept him human throughout the Earth's efforts to devour his will. He'll find no one new to love, either—not here. And he won't be able to return to the Stillness unless he's willing to risk the Deep Earth route again. So whether he heals somehow, or you change him into one of my kind, he will have no choice but to go on, alone, endlessly yearning for what he will never again have." Slowly, Steel's arms lower to his sides. "You have no idea what that's like."

And then, suddenly, shockingly, he is right in front of Nassun. No blurring, no warning, just flick and he is *there*, bent at the waist to put his face right in front of hers, so close that she feels the wind of the air he's displaced and smells the whiff of loam and she can even see that the irises of his eyes are striated in layers of gray.

"**BUT I DO,**" he shouts.

Nassun stumbles back and cries out. Between one blink and the next, however, Steel returns to his former position, upright, arms at his sides, a smile on his lips.

"So think carefully," Steel says. His voice is conversational again, as if nothing has happened. "Think with something more than the selfishness of a child, little Nassun. And ask yourself: Even if I could help you save that controlling, sadistic sack of shit that currently passes for your adoptive father figure, why would I? Not even my enemy deserves that fate. No one does."

Nassun's still shaking. She blurts, bravely, "Sch-Schaffa might want to live."

"He might. But *should* he? Should anyone, forever? That is the question."

She feels the absent weight of countless years, and is obliquely ashamed of being a child. But at her core, she is a kind child, and it's impossible for her to have heard Steel's story without feeling something other than her usual anger at him. She looks away twitchily. "I'm . . . sorry."

"So am I." There's a moment's silence. In it, Nassun pulls herself together slowly. By the time she focuses on him again, Steel's smile has vanished.

"I cannot stop you, once you've opened the Gate," he says. "I've manipulated you, yes, but the choice is still ultimately yours. Consider, however. Until the Earth dies, I live, Nassun. That was its punishment for us: We became a part of it, chained fate to fate. The Earth forgets neither those who stabbed it in the back . . . nor those who put the knife in our hand."

Nassun blinks at *our*. But she loses this thought amid misery at the realization that there can be no fixing Schaffa. Until now, some part of her has nursed the irrational hope that Steel, as an adult, had all the answers, including some sort of cure. Now she knows that her hope has been foolish. Childish. She *is* a child. And now the only adult she has ever been able to rely on will die naked and hurt and helpless, without ever being able to say goodbye.

It's too much to bear. She sinks into a crouch, wrapping one arm round her knees and folding the other over her head, so that Steel will not *see* her cry even if he knows that's exactly what's happening.

He lets out a soft laugh at this. Surprisingly, it does not sound cruel.

"You achieve nothing by keeping any of us alive," he says, "except cruelty. Put us broken monsters out of our misery, Nassun. The Earth, Schaffa, me, you…all of us."

Then he vanishes, leaving Nassun alone beneath the white, burgeoning Moon.

Syl Anagist: Zero

A MOMENT IN THE PRESENT, BEFORE I speak again of the past.

Amid the heated, fuming shadows and unbearable pressure of a place that has no name, I open my eyes. I'm no longer alone.

Out of the stone, another of my kind pushes forth. Her face is angular, cool, as patrician and elegant as any statue's should be. She's shed the rest, but kept the pallor of her original coloring; I notice this at last, after tens of thousands of years. All this reminiscing has made me nostalgic.

In token of which, I say aloud, "Gaewha."

She shifts slightly, as close as any of us gets to an expression of...recognition? Surprise? We were siblings once. Friends. Since then, rivals, enemies, strangers, legends. Lately, cautious allies. I find myself contemplating some of what we were, but not all. I've forgotten the all, just as much as she has.

She says, "Was that my name?"

"Close enough."

"Hmm. And you were...?"

"Houwha."

"Ah. Of course."

"You prefer Antimony?"

Another slight movement, the equivalent of a shrug. "I have no preference."

I think, *Nor do I*, but that is a lie. I would never have given my new name to you, I Iua, if not in homage to what I remember of that old name. But I'm woolgathering.

I say, "She is committed to the change."

Gaewha, Antimony, whoever and whatever she is now, replies, "I noticed." She pauses. "Do you regret what you did?"

It's a foolish question. All of us regret that day, in different ways and for different reasons. But I say, "No."

I expect comment in return, but I suppose there's really nothing to be said anymore. She makes minute sounds, settling into the rock. Getting comfortable. She means to wait here with me. I'm glad. Some things are easier when not faced alone.

*   *   *

There are things Alabaster never told you, about himself.

I know these things because I studied him; he is part of you, after all. But not every teacher needs every protégé to know of his every stumble on the journey to mastery. What would be the point? None of us got here overnight. There are stages to the process of being betrayed by your society. One is jolted from a place of complacency by the discovery of difference, by hypocrisy, by inexplicable or incongruous ill treatment. What follows is a time of confusion—unlearning what one thought to be the truth. Immersing oneself in the new truth. And then a decision must be made.

Some accept their fate. Swallow their pride, forget the real truth, embrace the falsehood for all they're worth—because, they decide, they cannot be worth much. If a whole society has dedicated itself to their subjugation, after all, then surely they deserve it? Even if they don't, fighting back is too painful, too impossible. At least this way there is peace, of a sort. Fleetingly.

The alternative is to demand the impossible. It isn't right, they whisper, weep, shout; what has been done to them is not right. They are *not* inferior. They do not deserve it. And so it is the society that must change. There can be peace this way, too, but not before conflict.

No one reaches this place without a false start or two.

When Alabaster was a young man, he loved easily and casually. Oh, he was angry, even then; of course he was. Even children notice when they are not treated fairly. He had chosen to cooperate, however, for the time being.

He met a man, a scholar, during a mission he'd been assigned by the Fulcrum. Alabaster's interest was prurient; the scholar was quite handsome, and charmingly shy in response to Alabaster's flirtations. If the scholar hadn't been busy excavating what turned out to be an ancient lore cache, there would be nothing more to the story. Alabaster would have loved him and left him, perhaps with regret, more likely with no hard feelings.

Instead, the scholar showed Alabaster his findings. There were more, Alabaster told you, than just three tablets of stonelore, originally. Also, the current Tablet Three was rewritten by Sanze. It was actually rewritten *again* by Sanze; it had been rewritten several times prior to that. The original Tablet Three spoke of Syl Anagist, you see, and how the Moon was lost. This knowledge, for many reasons, has been deemed unacceptable again and again down the millennia since. No one really wants to face the fact that the world is the way it is because some arrogant, self-absorbed people tried to put a leash on the rusting planet. And no one was ready to accept that the solution to the whole mess was simply to let orogenes live and thrive and do what they were born to do.

For Alabaster, the lore cache's knowledge was overwhelming. He fled. It was too much for him, the knowledge that all of this had happened before. That he was the scion of a people abused; that those people's forebears were, too, in their turn; that *the world as he knew it could not function without forcing someone into servitude.* At the time he could see no end to the cycle, no way to demand the impossible of society. So he broke, and he ran.

His Guardian found him, of course, three quartents away from where he was supposed to be and with no inkling of where he was going. Instead of breaking his hand—they used different techniques with highringers like Alabaster—Guardian Leshet took him to a tavern and bought him a drink. He wept into his wine and confessed to her that he couldn't take much more of the world as it was. He had tried to submit, tried to embrace the lies, but *it was not right.*

Leshet soothed him and took him back to the Fulcrum, and for one year they allowed Alabaster time to recover. To accept again the rules and role that had been created for him. He was content during this year, I believe; Antimony believes it, in any case, and she is the one who knew him best during this time. He settled, did what was expected of him, sired three children, and even volunteered to be an instructor for the higher-ringed juniors. He never got the chance to act on this, however, because the Guardians had decided already that Alabaster could not go unpunished for running away. When he met and fell in love with an older ten-ringer named Hessionite—

I have told you already that they use different methods on highringers.

I ran away, too, once. In a way.

* * *

It is the day after our return from Kelenli's tuning mission, and I am different. I look through the nematode window at the garden of purple light, and it is no longer beautiful to me. The winking of the white star-flowers lets me know that some genegineer made them, tying them into the city power network so that they can be fed by a bit of magic. How else to get that winking effect? I see the elegant vinework on the surrounding buildings and I know that somewhere, a biomagest is tabulating how many lammotyrs of magic can be harvested from such beauty. Life is sacred in Syl Anagist—sacred, and lucrative, and *useful*.

So I am thinking this, and I am in a foul mood, when one of the junior conductors comes in. Conductor Stahnyn, she is called, and ordinarily I like her. She's young enough to have not yet picked up the worst of the more experienced conductors' habits. And now as I turn to gaze at her with eyes that Kelenli has opened, I notice something new about her. A bluntness to her features, a smallness to her mouth. Yes, it's much more subtle than Conductor Gallat's icewhite eyes, but here is another Sylanagistine whose ancestors clearly didn't understand the whole point of genocide.

"How are you feeling today, Houwha?" she asks, smiling and

glancing at her noteboard as she comes in. "Up to a medical check?"

"I'm feeling up to a walk," I say. "Let's go out to the garden."

Stahnyn starts, blinking at me. "Houwha, you know that's not possible."

They keep such lax security on us, I have noticed. Sensors to monitor our vitals, cameras to monitor our movements, microphones to record our sounds. Some of the sensors monitor our magic usage—and none of them, not one, can measure even a tenth of what we really do. I would be insulted if I had not just been shown how important it is to them that we be lesser. Lesser creatures don't need better monitoring, do they? Creations of Sylanagistine magestry cannot possibly have abilities that surpass it. Unthinkable! Ridiculous! Don't be foolish.

Fine, I *am* insulted. And I no longer have the patience for Stahnyn's polite patronization.

So I find the lines of magic that run to the cameras, and I entangle them with the lines of magic that run to their own storage crystals, and I loop these together. Now the cameras will display only footage that they filmed over the last few hours— which mostly consists of me looking out the window and brooding. I do the same to the audio equipment, taking care to erase that last exchange between me and Stahnyn. I do all of this with barely a flick of my will, because I was designed to affect machines the size of skyscrapers; cameras are nothing. I use more magic reaching for the others to tell a joke.

The others sess what I am doing, however. Bimniwha gets a taste of my mood and immediately alerts the others—because I am the nice one, usually. I'm the one who, until recently, believed in Geoarcanity. Usually Remwha is the resentful one. But right now Remwha is coldly silent, stewing on what we have learned. Gaewha is quiet, too, in despair, trying to fathom how to demand the impossible. Dushwha is hugging themselves for comfort and Salewha is sleeping too much. Bimniwha's alert falls on weary, frustrated, self-absorbed ears, and goes ignored.

Meanwhile, Stahnyn's smile has begun to falter, as she only now realizes I'm serious. She shifts her stance, putting hands on her hips. "Houwha, this isn't funny. I understand you got the chance to leave the other day—"

I have considered the most efficient way to shut her up. "Does Conductor Gallat know that you find him attractive?"

Stahnyn freezes, eyes going wide and round. Brown eyes in her case, but she likes icewhite. I've seen how she looks at Gallat, though I never much cared before. I don't really care now. But I imagine that finding Niess eyes attractive is a taboo thing in Syl Anagist, and neither Gallat nor Stahnyn can afford to be accused of that particular perversion. Gallat would fire Stahnyn at the first whisper of it—even a whisper from me.

I go over to her. She draws back a little, frowning at my forwardness. We do not assert ourselves, we constructs. We tools. My behavior is anomalous in a way that she should report, but that isn't what has her so worried. "No one heard me say that," I tell her, very gently. "No one can see what's happening in this room right now. Relax."

Her bottom lip trembles, just a little, before she speaks. I feel bad, just a little, for having disturbed her so. She says, "You can't get far. Th-there's a vitamin deficiency . . . You and the others were built that way. Without special food—the food we serve you—you'll die in just a few days."

It only now occurs to me that Stahnyn thinks I mean to run away.

It only now occurs to me *to* run away.

What the conductor has just told me isn't an insurmountable hurdle. Easy enough to steal food to take with me, though I would die when it ran out. My life would be short regardless. But the thing that truly troubles me is that I have nowhere to go. All the world is Syl Anagist.

"The garden," I repeat, at last. This will be my grand adventure, my escape. I consider laughing, but the habit of appearing emotionless keeps me from doing so. I don't really want to go anywhere, to be honest. I just want to feel like I have some control over my life, if only for a few moments. "I want to see the garden for five minutes. That's all."

Stahnyn shifts from foot to foot, visibly miserable. "I could lose my position for this, especially if any of the senior conductors see. I could be *imprisoned*."

"Perhaps they will give you a nice window overlooking a garden," I suggest. She winces.

And then, because I have left her no choice, she leads me out of my cell and downstairs, and outside.

The garden of purple flowers looks strange from this angle, I find, and it is an altogether different thing to smell the starflowers up close. They smell strange—oddly sweet, almost sugary, with a hint of fermentation underneath where some of the older flowers have wilted or been crushed. Stahnyn is fidgety, looking around too much, while I stroll slowly, wishing I did not need her beside me. But this is fact: I cannot simply wander the grounds of the compound alone. If guards or attendants or other conductors see us, they will think Stahnyn is on official business, and not question me . . . if she will only be still.

But then I stop abruptly, behind a lilting spider tree. Stahnyn stops as well, frowning and plainly wondering what's happening— and then she, too, sees what I have seen, and freezes.

Up ahead, Kelenli has come out of the compound to stand between two curling bushes, beneath a white rose arch. Conductor Gallat has followed her out. She stands with her arms folded. He's behind her, shouting at her back. We aren't close enough for me to hear what he's saying, though his angry tone is indisputable. Their bodies, however, are a story as clear as strata.

"Oh, no," mutters Stahnyn. "No, no, no. We should—"

"Still," I murmur. I mean to say *be* still, but she quiets anyway, so at least I got the point across.

And then we stand there, watching Gallat and Kelenli fight. I can't hear her voice at all, and it occurs to me that she *cannot* raise her voice to him; it isn't safe. But when he grabs her arm and yanks her around to face him, she automatically claps a hand over her belly. The hand on the belly is a quick thing. Gallat lets go at once, seemingly surprised by her reaction and his own violence, and she moves the hand smoothly back to her side. I don't think he noticed. They resume arguing, and this time Gallat spreads his hands as if offering something. There is pleading in his posture, but I notice how stiff his back is. He begs—but he thinks he shouldn't have to. I can tell that when begging fails, he will resort to other tactics.

I close my eyes, aching as I finally, finally, understand. Kelenli is one of us in every way that matters, and she always has been.

Slowly, though, she unbends. Ducks her head, pretends reluctant capitulation, says something back. It isn't real. The earth reverberates with her anger and fear and unwillingness. Still, some of the stiffness goes out of Gallat's back. He smiles, gestures more broadly. Comes back to her, takes her by the arms, speaks to her gently. I marvel that she has disarmed his anger so effectively. It's as if he doesn't see the way her eyes drift away while he's talking, or how she does not reciprocate when he pulls her closer. She smiles at something he says, but even from fifty feet away I can see that it is a performance. Surely he can see it, too? But I am also beginning to understand that people believe what they want to believe, not what is actually there to be seen and touched and sessed.

So, mollified, he turns to leave—thankfully via a different path out of the garden than the one Stahnyn and I currently lurk upon. His posture has changed completely; he's visibly in a better mood. I should be glad for that, shouldn't I? Gallat heads the project. When he's happy, we are all safer.

Kelenli stands gazing after him until he is gone. Then her head turns and she looks right at me. Stahnyn makes a choked sound beside me, but she is a fool. Of course Kelenli will not report us. Why would she? Her performance was never for Gallat.

Then she, too, leaves the garden, following Gallat.

It was a last lesson. The one I needed most, I think. I tell Stahnyn to take me back to my cell, and she practically moans with relief. When I'm back and I have unwoven the magics of the monitoring equipment, and sent Stahnyn on her way with a

319

gentle reminder not to be a fool, I lie down on my couch to pon-
der this new knowledge. It sits in me, an ember causing everything around it to smolder and smoke.

*　　*　　*

And then, several nights after we return from Kelenli's tuning
mission, the ember catches fire in all of us.

It is the first time that all of us have come together since the
trip. We entwine our presences in a layer of cold coal, which
is perhaps fitting as Remwha sends a hiss through all of us like
sand grinding amid cracks. It's the sound/feel/sess of the sinklines, the briar patch. It's also an echo of the static emptiness
in our network where Tetlewha—and Entiwha, and Arwha,
and all the others—once existed.

This is what awaits us when we have given them Geoarcanity,
he says.

Gaewha replies, *Yes.*

He hisses again. I have never sessed him so angry. He has
spent the days since our trip getting angrier and angrier. But
then, so have the rest of us—and now it's time for us to demand
the impossible. *We should give them nothing,* he declares, and then
I feel his resolve sharpen, turn vicious. *No. We should give back
what they have taken.*

Eerie minor-note pulses of impression and action ripple
through our network: a plan, at last. A way to create the impossible, if we cannot demand it. The right sort of power surge at
just the right moment, after the fragments have been launched
but before the Engine has been spent. All the magic stored
within the fragments—decades' worth, a civilization's worth,
millions of lives' worth—will flood back into the systems of Syl

Anagist. First it will burn out the briar patches and their piti-
ful crop, letting the dead rest at last. Next the magic will blast
through us, the most fragile components of the great machine.
We'll die when that happens, but death is better than what they
intended for us, so we are content.

Once we're dead, the Plutonic Engine's magic will surge unre-
stricted down all the conduits of the city, frying them beyond
repair. Every node of Syl Anagist will shut down—vehimals
dying unless they have backup generators, lights going dark,
machinery stilling, all the infinite conveniences of modern
magestry erased from furnishings and appliances and cosmetics.
Generations of effort spent preparing for Geoarcanity will be
lost. The Engine's crystalline fragments will become so many
oversized rocks, broken and burnt and powerless.

We need not be as cruel as they. We can instruct the fragments to come down away from the most inhabited areas. We
are the monsters they created, and more, but we will be the sort
of monsters we wish to be, in death.

And are we agreed, then?

Yes. Remwha, furious.

Yes. Gaewha, sorrowful.

Yes. Bimniwha, resigned.

Yes. Salewha, righteous.

Yes. Dushwha, weary.

And I, heavy as lead, say, *Yes.*

So we are agreed.

Only to myself do I think, *No,* with Kelenli's face in my
mind's eye. But sometimes, when the world is hard, love must
be harder still.

*　　*　　*

Launch Day.

We are brought nourishment—protein with a side of fresh sweet fruit, and a drink that we are told is a popular delicacy: sef, which turns pretty colors when various vitamin supplements are added to it. A special drink for a special day. It's chalky. I don't like it. Then it is time to travel to Zero Site.

Here is how the Plutonic Engine works, briefly and simply.

First we will awaken the fragments, which have sat in their sockets for decades channeling life-energy through each node of Syl Anagist—and storing some of it for later use, including that which was force-fed to them through the briar patches. They have now reached optimum storage and generation, however, each becoming a self-contained arcane engine of its own. Now when we summon them, the fragments will rise from their sockets. We'll join their power together in a stable network and, after bouncing it off a reflector that will amplify and concentrate the magic still further, pour this into the onyx. The onyx will direct this energy straight into the Earth's core, causing an overflow—which the onyx will then shunt into Syl Anagist's hungry conduits. In effect, the Earth will become a massive plutonic engine too, the dynamo that is its core churning forth far more magic than is put into it. From there, the system will become self-perpetuating. Syl Anagist will feed upon the life of the planet itself, forever.

(Ignorance is an inaccurate term for what this was. True, no one thought of the Earth as alive in those days—but we *should* have guessed. Magic is the by-product of life. That there was magic in the Earth to take . . . We should all have guessed.)

Everything we have done, up to now, has been practice. We could never have activated the full Plutonic Engine here on Earth—too many complications involving the obliqueness of angles, signal speed and resistance, the curvature of the hemisphere. So awkwardly round, planets. Our *target* is the Earth, after all; lines of sight, lines of force and attraction. If we stay on the planet, all we can really affect is the Moon.

Which is why Zero Site has never been on Earth.

Thus in the small hours of the morning we are brought to a singular sort of vehimal, doubtless genegineered from grasshopper stock or something similar. It is diamond-winged but also has great carbon-fiber legs, steaming now with coiled, stored power. As the conductors usher us aboard this vehimal, I see other vehimals being made ready. A large party means to come with us to watch the great project conclude at last. I sit where I am told, and all of us are strapped in because the vehimal's thrust can sometimes overcome geomagestric inertial...Hmm. Suffice it to say, the launch can be somewhat alarming. It is nothing compared to plunging into the heart of a living, churning fragment, but I suppose the humans think it a grand, wild thing. The six of us sit, still and cold with purpose as they chatter around us, while the vehimal leaps up to the Moon.

On the Moon is the moonstone—a massive, iridescent white cabochon embedded in the thin gray soil of the place. It is the largest of the fragments, fully as big as a node of Syl Anagist itself; the whole of the Moon is its socket. Arranged around its edges sits a complex of buildings, each sealed against the airless dark, which are not so very different from the buildings we just left. They're just on the Moon. This is Zero Site, where history will be made.

We are led inside, where permanent Zero Site staff line the halls and stare at us in proud admiration, as one admires precision-made instruments. We are led to cradles that look precisely like the cradles used every day for our practices—although this time, each of us is taken to a separate room of the compound. Adjoining each room is the conductors' observation chamber, connected via a clear crystal window. I'm used to being observed while I work—but not used to being brought into the observation room itself, as happens today for the very first time.

There I stand, short and plainly dressed and palpably uncomfortable amid tall people in rich, complex clothing, while Gallat introduces me as "Houwha, our finest tuner." This statement alone proves that either the conductors really have no clue how we function, or that Gallat is nervous and groping for something to say. Perhaps both. Dushwha laughs a cascading microshake—the Moon's strata are thin and dusty and dead, but not much different from the Earth's—while I stand there and mouth pleasant greetings, as I am expected to do. Maybe that's what Gallat really means: I'm the tuner who is best at pretending that he cares about conductor nonsense.

Something catches my attention, though, as the introductions are made and small talk is exchanged and I concentrate on saying correct things at correct times. I turn and notice a stasis column near the back of the room, humming faintly and flickering with its own plutonic energies, generating the field that keeps something within stable. And floating above its cut-crystal surface—

There is a woman in the room who is taller and more elaborately dressed than everyone else. She follows my gaze and says to Gallat, "Do they know about the test bore?"

Gallat twitches and looks at me, then at the stasis column. "No," he says. He doesn't name the woman or give her a title, but his tone is very respectful. "They've been told only what's necessary."

"I would think context is necessary, even with your kind." Gallat bristles at being lumped in with us, but he says nothing in response to it. The woman looks amused. She bends down to peer into my face, although I'm not *that* much shorter than her. "Would you like to know what that artifact is, little tuner?"

I immediately hate her. "Yes, please," I say.

She takes my hand before Gallat can stop her. It isn't uncomfortable. Her skin is dry. She leads me over near the stasis column, so that I can now get a good look at the thing that floats above it.

At first I think that what I'm seeing is nothing more than a spherical lump of iron, hovering a few inches above the stasis column's surface and underlit by its white glow. It *is* only a lump of iron, its surface crazed with slanting, circuitous lines. A meteor fragment? No. I realize the sphere is moving—spinning slowly on a slightly tilted north-south axis. I look at the warning symbols around the column's rim and see markers for extreme heat and pressure, and a caution against breaching the stasis field. Within, the markers say, it has re-created the object's native environment.

No one would do this for a mere lump of iron. I blink, adjust my perception to the sesunal and magical, and draw back quickly as searing white light blazes at and through me. The iron sphere is *full* of magic—concentrated, crackling, overlapping threads upon threads of it, some of them even extending beyond its surface and outward and…away. I can't follow the ones that whitter away beyond the room; they extend beyond my reach. I can see that they stretch off toward the sky, though, for some reason. And written in the jittering threads that I can see…I frown.

"It's angry," I say. And familiar. Where have I seen something like this, this magic, before?

The woman blinks at me. Gallat groans under his breath. "Houwha—"

"No," the woman says, holding up a hand to quell him. She focuses on me again with a gaze that is intent now, and curious. "What did you say, little tuner?"

I face her. She is obviously important. Perhaps I should be afraid, but I'm not. "That thing is angry," I say. "*Furious*. It doesn't want to be here. You took it from somewhere else, didn't you?"

Others in the room have noticed this exchange. Not all of them are conductors, but all of them look at the woman and me in palpable unease and confusion. I hear Gallat holding his breath.

"Yes," she says to me, finally. "We drilled a test bore at one of the Antarctic nodes. Then we sent in probes that took this from the innermost core. It's a sample of the world's own heart." She smiles, proud. "The richness of magic at the core is precisely what will enable Geoarcanity. That test is why we built Corepoint, and the fragments, and you."

I look at the iron sphere again and marvel that she stands so close to it. *It is angry,* I think again, without really knowing why these words come to me. *It will do what it has to do.*

Who? Will do what?

I shake my head, inexplicably annoyed, and turn to Gallat. "Shouldn't we get started?"

The woman laughs, delighted. Gallat glowers at me, but he relaxes fractionally when it becomes obvious that the woman is amused. Still, he says, "Yes, Houwha. I think we should. If you don't mind—"

(He addresses the woman by some title, and some name. I will forget both with the passage of time. In forty thousand years I will remember only the woman's laugh, and the way she considers Gallat no different from us, and how carelessly she stands near an iron sphere that radiates pure malice—and enough magic to destroy every building in Zero Site.

And I will remember how I, too, dismissed every possible warning of what was to come.)

Gallat takes me back into the cradle room, where I am bidden to climb into my wire chair. My limbs are strapped down, which I've never understood because when I'm in the amethyst, I barely notice my body, let alone move it. The sef has made my lips tingle in a way that suggests a stimulant was added. I didn't need it.

I reach for the others, and find them granite-steady with resolve. Yes.

Images appear on the viewing wall before me, displaying the blue sphere of the Earth, each of the other five tuners' cradles, and a shot of Corepoint with the onyx hovering ready above it. The other tuners look back at me from their images. Gallat comes over and makes a show of checking the contact points of the wire chair, which are meant to send measurements to the Biomagestric division. "You're to hold the onyx, today, Houwha."

From another building of Zero Site, I feel Gaewha's small twitch of surprise. We're very attuned to one another today. I say, "Kelenli holds the onyx."

"Not anymore." Gallat keeps his head down as he speaks, unnecessarily reaching over to check my straps, and I remember him reaching the same way to pull Kelenli back to him, in the garden. Ah, I understand, now. All this while he has been afraid to lose her... to us. Afraid to make her just another tool in the eyes of his superiors. Will they let him keep her, after Geoarcanity? Or does he fear that she, too, will be thrown into the briar patch? He must. Why else make such a significant change to our configuration on the most important day in human history?

As if to confirm my guess, he says, "Biomagestry says you now show more than sufficient compatibility to hold the connection for the required length of time."

He's watching me, hoping I won't protest. I realize suddenly that I *can* do so. With so much scrutiny on Gallat's every decision today, important people will notice if I insist that the new configuration is a bad idea. I can, simply by raising my voice, take Kelenli from Gallat. I can destroy him, as he destroyed Tetlewha.

But that's a foolish, pointless thought, because how can I exercise my power over *him* without hurting *her*? I'm going to hurt her enough as it is, when we turn the Plutonic Engine back on itself. She should survive the initial convulsion of magic; even if she's in contact with any of the devices that flux, she has more than enough skill to shunt the feedback away. Then in the aftermath, she'll be just another survivor, made equal in suffering. No one will know what she really is—or her child, if it ends up like her. Like us. We will have set her free . . . to struggle for survival along with everyone else. But that is better than the illusion of safety in a gilded cage, is it not?

Better than you could ever have given her, I think at Gallat.

"All right," I say. He relaxes minutely.

Gallat leaves my chamber and goes back into the observation room with the other conductors. I am alone. I am never alone; the others are with me. The signal comes that we should begin, as the moment seems to hold its breath. We are ready.

First the network.

Attuned as we are, it is easy, pleasurable, to modulate our silverflows and cancel out resistance. Remwha plays yoke, but he hardly needs to goad any of us to resonate higher or lower or to pull at the same pace; we are aligned. We all want this.

Above us, yet easily within our range, the Earth seems to hum, too. Almost like a thing alive. We have been to Corepoint and back, in our early training; we have traveled through the mantle and seen the massive flows of magic that churn naturally up from the iron-nickel core of the planet. To tap that bottomless font will be the greatest feat of human accomplishment, ever. Once, that thought would have made me proud. Now I share this with the others and a *shiverstone micaflake glimmer* of bitter amusement ripples through all of us. They have never believed us human, but we will prove by our actions today that we are more than tools. Even if we aren't human, we are *people.* They will never be able to deny us this again.

Enough frivolity.

First the network, then the fragments of the Engine must be assembled. We reach for the amethyst because it is nearest on the globe. Though we are a world away from it, we know that it utters a low held note, its storage matrix glowing and brimful with energy as we dive, up, into its torrential flow. Already it has stopped suckling the last dregs from the briar patch at its roots, becoming a closed system in itself; now it feels almost alive. As we coax it from quiescence into resonant activity, it begins to pulse, and then finally to shimmer in patterns that emulate life, like the firing of neurotransmitters or the contractions of peristalsis. *Is it alive?* I wonder this for the first time, a question triggered by Kelenli's lessons. It is a thing of high-state matter, but it coexists simultaneously with a thing of high-state magic made in its image—and taken from the bodies of people who once laughed and raged and sang. Is there anything left of their will in the amethyst?

If so... would the Niess approve of what we, their caricature children, mean to do?

I can spare no more time for such thoughts. The decision has been made.

So we expand this macro-level start-up sequence throughout the network. We sess without sessapinae. We *feel* the change. We know it in our bones—because we are part of this engine, components of humanity's greatest marvel. On Earth, at the heart of every node of Syl Anagist, klaxons echo across the city and warning pylons blaze red warnings that can be seen from far away as one by one, the fragments begin to thrum and shimmer and detach from their sockets. My breath quickens when I, resonant within each, feel the first peeling-away of crystal from rougher stone, the drag as we alight and begin pulsing with the state-change of magic and then begin to rise—

(There is a stutter here, quick and barely noticeable in the heady moment, though glaring through the lens of memory. Some of the fragments hurt us, just a little, when they detach from their sockets. We feel the scrape of metal that should not be there, the scratch of needles against our crystalline skin. We smell a whiff of rust. It's quick pain and quickly forgotten, as with any needle. Only later will we remember, and lament.)

—rise, and hum, and turn. I inhale deeply as the sockets and their surrounding cityscapes fall away below us. Syl Anagist shunts over to backup power systems; those should hold until Geoarcanity. But they are irrelevant, these mundane concerns. I flow, fly, *fall* up into rushing light that is purple or indigo or mauve or gold, the spinel and the topaz and the garnet and the sapphire—so many, so bright! So alive with building power.

(So *alive*, I think again, and this thought sends a shudder through the network, because Gaewha was thinking it, too, and Dushwha, and it is Remwha who takes us to task with a crack like a slipstrike fault: *Fools, we will die if you don't focus!* So I let this thought go.)

And—ah, yes, framed there on-screen, centered in our perception like an eye glaring down at its quarry: the onyx. Positioned, as Kelenli last bade it, above Corepoint.

I am not nervous, I tell myself as I reach for it.

The onyx isn't like the other fragments. Even the moonstone is quiescent by comparison; it is only a mirror, after all. But the onyx is powerful, frightening, the darkest of dark, unknowable. Where the other fragments must be sought and actively engaged, it snatches at my awareness the instant I come near, trying to pull me deeper into its rampant, convecting currents of silver. When I have connected to it before, the onyx has rejected me, as it has done for all the others in turn. The finest magests in Syl Anagist could not fathom why—but now, when I offer myself and the onyx claims me, suddenly I know. *The onyx is alive.* What is just a question in the other fragments has been answered here: It *sesses* me. It learns me, touching me with a presence that is suddenly undeniable.

And in the very moment when I realize this and have enough time to wonder fearfully what these presences think of me, their pathetic descendant made from the fusion of their genes with their destroyers' hate—

—I perceive at last a secret of magestry that even the Niess simply accepted rather than understood. This is magic, after all, not science. There will always be parts of it that no one can fathom. But now I know: Put enough magic into something nonliving, and it becomes alive. Put enough lives into a storage matrix, and they retain a collective will, of sorts. They *remember* horror and atrocity, with whatever is left of them—their souls, if you like.

So the onyx yields to me now because, it senses at last, I too have known pain. My eyes have been opened to my own exploitation and degradation. I am afraid, of course, and angry, and hurt, but the onyx does not scorn these feelings within me. It seeks something else, however, something more, and finally finds what it seeks nestled in a little burning knot behind my heart: determination. I have committed myself to making, of all this wrongness, something right.

That's what the onyx wants. *Justice.* And because I want that too—

I open my eyes in flesh. "I've engaged the control cabochon," I report for the conductors.

"Confirmed," says Gallat, looking at the screen where Biomagestry monitors our neuroarcanic connections. Applause breaks out among our observers, and I feel sudden contempt for them. Their clumsy instruments and their weak, simple sessapinae have finally told them what is as obvious to us as breathing. The Plutonic Engine is up and running.

Now that the fragments have all launched, each one rising to hum and flicker and hover over two hundred and fifty-six city-nodes and seismically energetic points, we begin the ramp-up sequence. Among the fragments, the pale-colored flow buffers ignite first, then we upcycle the deeper jewel tones of the generators. The onyx acknowledges sequence initialization with a single, heavy blat of sound that sends ripples across the Hemispheric Ocean.

My skin is tight, my heart a-thud. Somewhere, in another existence, I have clenched my fists. *We* have done so, across the paltry separation of six different bodies and two hundred and fifty-six arms and legs and one great black pulsing heart. My mouth opens (our mouths open) as the onyx aligns itself perfectly to tap the ceaseless churn of earth-magic where the core lies exposed far, far below. Here is the moment that we were made for.

Now, we are meant to say. This, here, *connect,* and we will lock the raw magical flows of the planet into an endless cycle of service to humankind.

Because this is what the Sylanagistines truly made us for: to affirm a philosophy. Life is sacred in Syl Anagist—as it should be, for the city burns life as the fuel for its glory. The Niess were not the first people chewed up in its maw, just the latest and cruelest extermination of many. But for a society built on exploitation, there is no greater threat than having no one left to oppress. And now, if nothing else is done, Syl Anagist must again find a way to fission its people into subgroupings and create reasons for conflict among them. There's not enough magic to be had just from plants and genengineered fauna; *someone* must suffer, if the rest are to enjoy luxury.

Better the earth, Syl Anagist reasons. Better to enslave a great inanimate object that cannot feel pain and will not object. Better Geoarcanity. But this reasoning is still flawed, because Syl Anagist is ultimately unsustainable. It is parasitic; its hunger for magic grows with every drop it devours. The Earth's core is not limitless. Eventually, if it takes fifty thousand years, that resource will be exhausted, too. Then everything dies.

What we are doing is pointless and Geoarcanity is a lie. And if we help Syl Anagist further down this path, we will have said, *What was done to us was right and natural and unavoidable.*

No.

So. *Now*, we say instead. This, here, connect: pale fragments to dark, all fragments to the onyx, and the onyx...back to Syl Anagist. We detach the moonstone from the circuit entirely. Now all the power stored in the fragments will blast through the city, and when the Plutonic Engine dies, so will Syl Anagist.

It begins and ends long before the conductors' instruments even register a problem. With the others joined to me, our tune gone silent as we settle and wait for the feedback loop to hit us, I find myself content. It will be good not to die alone.

*　　*　　*

But.

But.

Remember. We were not the only ones who chose to fight back that day.

This is a thing I will realize only later, when I visit the ruins of Syl Anagist and look into empty sockets to see iron needles protruding from their walls. This is an enemy I will understand only after I have been humbled and remade at its feet…but I will explain it now, so that you may learn from my suffering.

I spoke to you, not long ago, of a war between the Earth and the life upon its surface. Here is some enemy psychology: The Earth sees no difference between any of us. Orogene, still, Sylanagistine, Niess, future, past—to it, humanity is humanity. And even if others had commanded my birth and development; even if Geoarcanity has been a dream of Syl Anagist since long before even my conductors were born; even if I was just following orders; even if the six of us meant to fight back…the Earth did not care. We were all guilty. All complicit in the crime of attempting to enslave the world itself.

Now, though, having pronounced us all guilty, the Earth handed out sentences. Here, at least, it was somewhat willing to offer credit for intent and good behavior.

This is what I remember, and what I pieced together later, and what I believe. But remember—never forget—that this was only the beginning of the war.

*   *   *

We perceive the disruption first as a ghost in the machine.

A presence alongside us, *inside* us, intense and intrusive and immense. It slaps the onyx from my grasp before I know what's happening, and silences our startled signals of *What?* and *Something is wrong* and *How did that happen?* with a shockwave of earthtalk as stunning to us as the Rifting will one day be to you.

Hello, little enemies.

In the conductors' observation chamber, alarms finally blare. We are frozen in our wire chairs, shouting without words and being answered by something beyond our comprehension, so Biomagestry only notices a problem when suddenly nine percent of the Plutonic Engine—twenty-seven fragments—goes offline. I do not see Conductor Gallat gasp and exchange a horrified look with the other conductors and their esteemed guests; this is speculation, knowing what I know of him. I imagine that at some point he turns to a console to abort the launch. I also do not see, behind them, the iron sphere pulse and swell and shatter, destroying its stasis field and peppering everyone in the chamber with hot, needle-sharp iron shards. I *do* hear the screaming that follows while the iron shards burn their way up veins and arteries, and the ominous silence afterward, but I have my own problems to deal with in this particular moment.

Remwha, he of the quickest wit, slaps us from our shock with the realization that *something else is controlling the Engine.* No time to wonder who or why. Gaewha perceives how and signals frantically: The twenty-seven "offline" fragments are still active. In fact, they have formed a kind of subnetwork—a spare key. This is how the other presence has managed to dislodge the onyx's control. Now all of the fragments, which generate and contain the bulk of the Plutonic Engine's power, are under hostile foreign control.

I am a proud creature at my core; this is intolerable. The onyx was given to *me* to hold—and so I seize it again and shove it back into the connections that comprise the Engine, dislodging the false control at once. Salewha slams down the shockwaves of magic that this violent disruption causes, lest they ricochet throughout the Engine and touch off a resonance that will— well, we don't actually know what such resonance would do, but it would be bad. I hold on throughout the reverberations of this, my teeth bared back in the real world, listening while my siblings cry out or snarl with me or gasp amid the aftershakes of the initial upheaval. Everything is confusion. In the realm of flesh and blood, the lights of our chambers have gone out, leaving only emergency panels to glow around the edges of the room. The warning klaxons are incessant, and elsewhere in Zero Site I can hear equipment snapping and rattling with the overload that we have put into the system. The conductors, screaming in the observation chamber, cannot help us—not that they ever could. I don't know what's happening, not really. I know only that this is a battle, full of moment-to-moment confusion as all battles are, and from here forth nothing is quite clear—

That strange presence that has attacked us pulls hard against the Plutonic Engine, trying to dislodge our control once more. I shout at it in wordless *geyserboil magmacrack* fury. *Get out of here!* I rage. *Leave us alone!*

You started this, it hisses into the strata, trying again. When this fails, however, it snarls in frustration—and then locks, instead, into those twenty-seven fragments that have gone so mysteriously offline. Dushwha senses the hostile entity's intent and tries to grasp some of the twenty-seven, but the fragments slip through their grasp as if coated with oil. This is true enough, figuratively speaking; something has contaminated these fragments, leaving them fouled and nearly impossible to grasp. We might manage it with concerted effort, one by one—but there is no time. And until then, the enemy holds the twenty-seven.

Stalemate. We still hold the onyx. We hold the other two hundred and twenty-nine fragments, which are ready to fire the feedback pulse that will destroy Syl Anagist—and ourselves. We've postponed that, however, because we cannot leave matters like this. Where did this entity, so angry and phenomenally powerful, come from? What will it do with the obelisks that it holds? Long moments pass in pent silence. I cannot speak for the others, but I, at least, begin to think there will be no further attacks. I have always been such a fool.

Into the silence comes the amused, malicious challenge of our enemy, ground forth in magic and iron and stone.

Burn for me, says Father Earth.

*   *   *

I must speculate on some of what follows, even after all these ages spent seeking answers.

I can narrate no more because in the moment everything was nigh-instantaneous, and confusing, and devastating. The Earth changes only gradually, until it doesn't. And when it fights back, it does so decisively.

Here is the context. That first test bore that initiated the Geoarcanity project also alerted the Earth to humanity's efforts to take control of it. Over the decades that followed, it studied its enemy and began to understand what we meant to do. Metal was its instrument and ally; never trust metal for this reason. It sent splinters of itself to the surface to examine the fragments in their sockets—for here, at least, was life stored in crystal, comprehensible to an entity of inorganic matter in a way that mere flesh was not. Only gradually did it learn how to take control of individual human lives, though it required the medium of the corestones to do so. We are such small, hard-to-grasp creatures, otherwise. Such insignificant vermin, apart from our unfortunate tendency to sometimes make ourselves dangerously significant. The obelisks, though, were a more useful tool. Easy to turn back on us, like any carelessly held weapon.

Burndown.

Remember Allia? Imagine that disaster times two hundred and fifty-six. Imagine the Stillness perforated at every nodal point and seismically active site, and the ocean, too—hundreds of hot spots and gas pockets and oil reservoirs breached, and the entire plate-tectonic system destabilized. There is no word for such a catastrophe. It would liquefy the surface of the planet, vaporizing the oceans and sterilizing everything from the mantle up. The world, for us and any possible creature that might ever evolve in the future to hurt the Earth, would end. The Earth itself would be fine, however.

We could stop it. If we wanted to.

I will not say we weren't tempted, when faced with the choice between permitting the destruction of a civilization, or of all life on the planet. Syl Anagist's fate was sealed. Make no mistake: We had meant to seal it. The difference between what the

Earth wanted and what we wanted was merely a matter of scale. But *which* is the way the world ends? We tuners would be dead; the distinction mattered little to me in that moment. It's never wise to ask such a question of people who have nothing to lose.

Except. *I* did have something to lose. In those eternal instants, I thought of Kelenli, and her child.

Thus it was that my will took precedence within the network. If you have any doubt, I'll say it plainly now: *I* am the one who chose the way the world ended.

I am the one who took control of the Plutonic Engine. We could not stop Burndown, but we could insert a delay into the sequence and redirect the worst of its energy. After the Earth's tampering, the power was too volatile to simply pour back into Syl Anagist as we'd originally planned; that would have done the Earth's work for us. That much kinetic force had to be expended somewhere. Nowhere on the planet, if I meant for humanity to survive—but here were the Moon and the moonstone, ready and waiting.

I was in a hurry. There was no time to second-guess. The power could not *reflect* from the moonstone, as it was meant to; that would only increase the power of Burndown. Instead, with a snarl as I grabbed the others and forced them to help me—they were willing, just slow—we shattered the moonstone cabochon.

In the next instant, the power struck the broken stone, failed to reflect, and began to chew its way through the Moon. Even with this to mitigate the blow, the force of impact was devastating in itself. More than enough to slam the Moon out of orbit.

The backlash of misusing the Engine this way should have

simply killed us, but the Earth was still there, the ghost in the machine. As we writhed in our death throes, all of Zero Site crumbling apart around us, it took control again.

I have said that it held us responsible for the attempt on its life, and it did—but somehow, perhaps through its years of study, it understood that we were tools of others, not actors of our own volition. Remember, too, that the Earth does not fully understand us. It looks upon human beings and sees short-lived, fragile creatures, puzzlingly detached in substance and awareness from the planet on which their lives depend, who do not understand the harm they tried to do—perhaps *because* they are so short-lived and fragile and detached. And so it chose for us what seemed, to it, a punishment leavened with meaning: It made us part of it. In my wire chair, I screamed as wave upon wave of alchemy worked over me, changing my flesh into raw, living, solidified magic that looks like stone.

We didn't get the worst of it; that was reserved for those who had offended the Earth the most. It used the corestone fragments to take direct control of these most dangerous vermin—but this did not work as it intended. Human will is harder to anticipate than human flesh. They were never meant to continue.

I will not describe the shock and confusion I felt, in those first hours after my change. I will not ever be able to answer the question of how I returned to Earth from the Moon; I remember only a nightmare of endless falling and burning, which may have been delirium. I will not ask you to imagine how it felt to suddenly find oneself alone, and tuneless, after a lifetime spent singing to others like myself. This was justice. I accept it; I admit my crimes. I have sought to make up for them. But...

Well. What's done is done.

In those last moments before we transformed, we did successfully manage to cancel the Burndown command to the two hundred and twenty-nine. Some fragments were shattered by the stress. Others would die over the subsequent millennia, their matrices disrupted by incomprehensible arcane forces. Most went into standby mode, to continue drifting for millennia over a world that no longer needed their power—until, on occasion, one of the fragile creatures below might send a confused, directionless request for access.

We could not stop the Earth's twenty-seven. We did, however, manage to insert a delay into their command lattices: one hundred years. What the tales get wrong is only the timing, you see? One hundred years after Father Earth's child was stolen from him, twenty-seven obelisks did burn down to the planet's core, leaving fiery wounds all over its skin. It was not the cleansing fire that the Earth sought, but it was still the first and worst Fifth Season—what you call the Shattering. Humankind survives because one hundred years is nothing to the Earth, or even to the expanse of human history, but to those who survived the fall of Syl Anagist, it was just time enough to prepare.

The Moon, bleeding debris from a wound through its heart, vanished over a period of days.

And...

I never saw Kelenli, or her child, again. Too ashamed of the monster I'd become, I never sought them out. She lived, though. Now and again I heard the grind and grumble of her stone voice, and those of her several children as they were born. They were not wholly alone; with the last of their magestric technology, the survivors of Syl Anagist decanted a few more tuners and used them to build shelters, contingencies, systems of warning and protection. Those tuners died in time, however, as their usefulness ended, or as others blamed them for the Earth's wrath. Only Kelenli's children, who did not stand out, whose strength hid in plain sight, continued. Only Kelenli's legacy, in the form of the lorists who went from settlement to settlement warning of the coming holocaust and teaching others how to cooperate, adapt, and remember, remains of the Niess.

It all worked, though. You survive. That was my doing, too, isn't it? I did my best. Helped where I could. And now, my love, we have a second chance.

Time for you to end the world again.

*　　*　　*

2501: Fault line shift along the Minimal-Maximal: massive. Shockwave swept through half the Nomidlats and Arctics, but stopped at outer edge of Equatorial node network. Food prices rose sharply following year, but famine prevented.

—*Project notes of Yaetr Innovator Dibars*

13

Nassun and Essun, on the dark side of the world

IT'S SUNSET WHEN NASSUN DECIDES to change the world.

She has spent the day curled beside Schaffa, using his still-ash-flecked old clothes as a pillow, breathing his scent and wishing for things that cannot be. Finally she gets up and very carefully feeds him the last of the vegetable broth she has made. She gives him a lot of water, too. Even after she has dragged the Moon into a collision course, it will take a few days for the Earth to be smashed apart. She doesn't want Schaffa to suffer too much in that time, since she will no longer be around to help him.

(She is such a good child, at her core. Don't be angry with her. She can only make choices within the limited set of her experiences, and it isn't her fault that so many of those experiences have been terrible. Marvel, instead, at how easily she loves, how thoroughly. Love enough to change the world! She learned how to love like this from *somewhere*.)

As she uses a cloth to dab spilled broth from his lips, she reaches up and begins activation of her network. Here at Corepoint, she can do it without even the onyx, but start-up will take time.

"'A commandment is set in stone,'" she tells Schaffa solemnly. His eyes are open again. He blinks, perhaps in reaction to the sound, though she knows this is meaningless.

The words are a thing she read in the strange handwritten book—the one that told her how to use a smaller network of obelisks as a "spare key" to subvert the onyx's power over the Gate. The man who wrote the book was probably crazy, as evidenced by the fact that he apparently loved Nassun's mother long ago. That is strange and wrong and yet somehow unsurprising. As big as the world is, Nassun is beginning to realize it's also really small. The same stories, cycling around and around. The same endings, again and again. The same mistakes eternally repeated.

"Some things *are* too broken to be fixed, Schaffa." Inexplicably, she thinks of Jija. The ache of this silences her for a moment. "I...I can't make anything better. But I can at least make sure the bad things stop." With that, she gets up to leave.

She does not see Schaffa's face turn, like the Moon sliding into shadow, to watch her go.

* * *

It's dawn when you decide to change the world. You're still asleep in the bedroll that Lerna has brought up to the roof of the yellow-X building. You and he spent the night under the water tower, listening to the ever-present rumble of the Rifting and the snap of occasional lightning strikes. Probably should've had sex there one more time, but you didn't think about it and he didn't suggest, so oh well. That's gotten you into enough trouble, anyway. Had no business relying solely on middle age and starvation for birth control.

He watches as you stand and stretch, and it's a thing you'll never fully understand or be comfortable with—the admiration in his gaze. He makes you feel like a better person than you are. And this is what makes you regret, again, endlessly, that you cannot stay to see his child born. Lerna's steady, relentless goodness is a thing that should be preserved in the world, somehow. Alas.

You haven't earned his admiration. But you intend to.

You head downstairs and stop. Last night, in addition to Lerna, you let Tonkee and Hjarka and Ykka know that it was time—that you would leave after breakfast in the morning. You left the question of whether they could come with you or not open and unstated. If they volunteer, it's one thing, but you're not going to ask. What kind of person would you be to pressure them into that kind of danger? They'll be in enough, just like the rest of humanity, as it is.

You weren't counting on finding all of them in the lobby of the yellow-X building as you come downstairs. *All of them* busy tucking away bedrolls and yawning and frying sausages and complaining loudly about somebody drinking up all the rusting tea. Hoa is there, perfectly positioned to see you come downstairs. There's a rather smug smile on his stone lips, but that doesn't surprise you. Danel and Maxixe do, the former up and doing some kind of martial exercises in a corner while the latter dices another potato for the pan—and yes, he's built a campfire in the building lobby, because that's what commless people do sometimes. Some of the windows are broken; the smoke's going out through them. Hjarka and Tonkee are a surprise, too; they're still asleep, curled together in a pile of furs.

But you really, really weren't expecting Ykka to walk in,

with an air of something like her old brashness and with her eye makeup perfectly applied, once again. She looks around the lobby, taking you in along with the rest, and puts her hands on her hips. "Catch you rusters at a bad time?"

"You can't," you blurt. It's hard to talk. Knot in your throat. Ykka especially; you stare at her. Evil Earth, she's wearing her fur vest again. You thought she'd left that behind in Castrima-under. "You can't come. The comm."

Ykka rolls her dramatically decorated eyes. "Well, fuck you, too. But you're right, I'm not coming. Just here to see you off, along with whoever goes with you. I really should be having you killed, since you're effectively ashing yourselves out, but I suppose we can overlook that little technicality for now."

"What, we can't come back?" Tonkee blurts. She's sitting up finally, though at a distinct lean, and with her hair badly askew. Hjarka, muttering imprecations at being awake, has gotten up and handed her a plate of potato hash from the pile Maxixe has already cooked.

Ykka eyes her. "You? You're traveling to an enormous, perfectly preserved obelisk-builder ruin. I'll never see you again. But sure, I suppose you could come back, if Hjarka manages to drag you to your senses. I need *her*, at least."

Maxixe yawns loudly enough to draw everyone's attention. He's naked, which lets you see that he's looking better at last— still nearly skeletal, but that's half the comm these days. He's coughing less, though, and his hair's starting to grow fuller, although so far it's only at that hilarious bottlebrush stage before ashblow hair develops enough weight to flop decently. It's the first time you've seen his leg-stumps unclothed, and you belatedly realize the scars are far too neat to have been done by some commless raider with a hacksaw. Well, that's his story to tell. You say to him, "Don't be stupid."

Maxixe looks mildly annoyed. "I'm not going, no. But I *could* be."

"No, you rusting couldn't," Ykka snaps. "I already told you, we need a Fulcrum rogga here."

He sighs. "Fine. But no reason I can't at least see you off. Now stop asking questions and come get some food." He reaches for his clothes and starts to pull them on. You obediently go over to the fire to eat something. No morning sickness yet; that's a bit of luck.

As you eat, you watch everyone and find yourself overwhelmed, and also a little frustrated. Of course it's touching that they've come like this to say goodbye. You're glad of it; you can't even pretend otherwise. When have you ever left a place this way—openly, nonviolently, amid laughter? It feels...you don't know how it feels. Good? You don't know what to do with that.

You hope more of them decide to stay behind, though. As it is, Hoa's going to be hauling a rusting caravan through the earth.

But when you eye Danel, you blink in surprise. She's cut her hair again; really doesn't seem to like it long. Fresh shaving on the sides, and...black tint, on her lips. Earth knows where she found it, or maybe she made it herself out of charcoal and fat. But it's suddenly hard to see her as the Strongback general she was. Wasn't. It changes things, somehow, to understand that you go to face a fate that an Equatorial lorist wants to record for posterity. Now it's not just a caravan. It's a rusting quest.

The thought pulls a snort-laugh out of you, and everyone

pauses in what they're doing to stare. "Nothing," you say, waving a hand and setting the empty plate aside. "Just…shit. Come on, then, whoever's coming."

Someone's brought Lerna his pack, which he dons quietly, watching you. Tonkee curses and starts rushing to get herself together, while Hjarka patiently helps. Danel uses a rag to mop sweat from her face.

You go over to Hoa, who has shaped his expression into one of wry amusement, and stand beside him to sigh at the mess. "Can you bring this many?"

"As long as they remain in contact with me or someone who's touching me, yes."

"Sorry. I wasn't expecting this."

"Weren't you?"

You look at him, but then Tonkee—still chewing something and shouldering her pack with her good arm—grabs his upraised hand, though she pauses to blatantly stare at it in fascination. The moment passes.

"So how's this supposed to work?" Ykka paces the room, watching everyone and folding her arms. She's noticeably more restless than usual. "You get there, grab the Moon, shove it into position, and then what? Will we see any sign of the change?"

"The Rifting will go cold," you say. "That won't change much in the short term because there's too much ash in the air already. This Season will have to play itself out, and it's going to be bad no matter what. The Moon might even make things worse." You can sess it pulling on the world already; yeah, you're pretty sure it'll make things worse. Ykka nods, though. She can sess it, too.

But there's a long-term loose end that you haven't been

able to figure out yourself. "If I can do it, though, restore the Moon..." You shrug helplessly and look at Hoa.

"It opens room for negotiation," he says in his hollow voice. Everyone pauses to stare at him. By the flinches, you can tell who's used to stone eaters and who isn't. "And perhaps, a truce."

Ykka grimaces. "'Perhaps'? So we've gone through all this and you can't even be sure it will stop the Seasons? Evil Earth."

"No," you admit. "But it will stop *this* Season." That much you're sure of. That much, alone, is worth it.

Ykka subsides, but she keeps muttering to herself now and again. This is how you know she wants to go, too—but you're very glad she seems to have talked herself out of it. Castrima needs her. You need to know that Castrima will be here after you're gone.

Finally everyone is ready. You take Hoa's right hand with your left. You've got no other arm to spare for Lerna, so he wraps an arm around your waist; when you glance at him he nods, steady, determined. On Hoa's other side are Tonkee and Hjarka and Danel, chain-linked hand to hand.

"This is going to blow, isn't it?" Hjarka asks. She alone looks nervous, of the set. Danel's radiating calm, at peace with herself at last. Tonkee's so excited she can't stop grinning. Lerna's just leaning on you, rock-steady the way he always is.

"Probably!" Tonkee says, bouncing a little.

"This seems like a spectacularly bad idea," Ykka says. She's leaned against a wall of the room, arms folded, watching the group assemble. "Essie's *got* to go, I mean, but the rest of you..." She shakes her head.

"Would you be coming, if you weren't headwoman?" Lerna

asks. It's quiet. He always drops his biggest rocks like that, quietly and out of nowhere.

She scowls and glares at him. Then throws you a look that's wary and maybe a little embarrassed, before she sighs and pushes away from the wall. You saw, though. The lump is back in your throat.

"Hey," you say, before she can flee. "Yeek."

She glares at you. "I *hate* that rusting nickname."

You ignore this. "You told me a while back that you had a stash of seredis. We were supposed to get drunk after I beat the Rennanis army. Remember?"

Ykka blinks, and then a slow smile spreads across her face. "You were in a coma or something. I drank it all myself."

You glare at her, surprised to find yourself honestly annoyed. She laughs in your face. So much for tender farewells.

But... well. It feels good anyway.

"Close your eyes," Hoa says.

"He's not joking," you add, in warning. You keep yours open, though, as the world goes dark and strange. You feel no fear. You are not alone.

*   *   *

It's nighttime. Nassun stands on what she thinks of as Corepoint's town green. It isn't; a city built before the Seasons would have no need of such a thing. It's just a place near the enormous hole that is Corepoint's heart. Around the hole are strangely slanted buildings, like the pylons she saw in Syl Anagist—but these ones are huge, stories high and a block wide apiece. She's learned that when she gets too near these buildings, which don't have any doors or windows that she can see, it sets off warnings

351

composed of bright red words and symbols, several feet high apiece, which blaze in the air over the city. Worse are the low, blatting alarm-sounds that echo through the streets—not loud, but insistent, and they make her teeth feel loose and itchy.

(She's looked into the hole, despite all this. It's enormous compared to the one that was in the underground city—many times that one's circumference, so big that it would take her an hour or more to walk all the way around it. Yet for all its grandeur, despite the evidence it offers of feats of geneering long lost to humankind, Nassun cannot bring herself to be impressed by it. The hole feeds no one, provides no shelter against ash or assault. It doesn't even scare her—though that is meaningless. After her journey through the underground city and the core of the world, after losing Schaffa, nothing will ever frighten her again.)

The spot Nassun has found is a perfectly circular patch of ground just beyond the hole's warning radius. It's odd ground, slightly soft to the touch and springy beneath her feet, not like any material she's ever touched before—but here in Corepoint, that sort of experience isn't rare. There's no actual soil in this circle, aside from a bit of windblown stuff piled up along the edges of the circle; a few seagrasses have taken root here, and there's the desiccated, spindly trunk of a dead sapling that did its best before being blown over, many years before. That's all.

A number of stone eaters have appeared around the circle, she notes as she takes up position at its center. No sign of Steel, but there must be twenty or thirty others on street corners or in the street, sitting on stairs, leaning against walls. A few turned their heads or eyes to watch as she passed, but she ignored and ignores them. Perhaps they have come to witness history. Maybe some are like Steel, hoping for an end to their horrifyingly end-less existence; maybe the ones who've helped her have done so because of that. Maybe they're just bored. Not the most exciting town, Corepoint.

Nothing matters, right now, except the night sky. And in that sky, the Moon is beginning to rise.

It sits low on the horizon, seemingly bigger than it was the night before and made oblong by the distortions of the air. White and strange and round, it hardly seems worth all the pain and struggle that its absence has symbolized for the world. And yet—it pulls on everything within Nassun that is orogene. It pulls on the whole world.

Time for the world, then, to pull back.

Nassun shuts her eyes. They are all around Corepoint now—the spare key, three by three by three, twenty-seven obelisks that she has spent the past few weeks touching and taming and coaxing into orbit nearby. She can still feel the sapphire, but it is far away and not in sight; she can't use it, and it would take months to arrive if she summoned it. These others will do, though. It's strange to see so many of the things in the sky all together, after a lifetime with only one—or no—obelisks in sight at any given time. Stranger to feel them all connected to her, thrumming at slightly different speeds, their wells of power each at slightly different depths. The darker ones are deeper. No telling why, but it is a noticeable difference.

Nassun lifts her hands, splaying her fingers in unconscious imitation of her mother. Very carefully, she begins connecting each of the twenty-seven obelisks—one to one, then those to two apiece, then others. She is compelled by lines of sight, lines of force, strange instincts that demand mathematical relationships she does not understand. Each obelisk supports the forming lattice, rather than disrupting or canceling it out. It's like putting horses in harness, sort of, when you've got one with a naturally quick gait and another that plods along. This is yoking twenty-seven high-strung racehorses... but the principle is the same.

And it is beautiful, the moment when all of the flows stop fighting Nassun and shift into lockstep. She inhales, smiling in spite of herself, feeling pleasure again for the first time since Father Earth destroyed Schaffa. It should be scary, shouldn't it? So much power. It isn't, though. She falls up through torrents of gray or green or mauve or clear white; parts of her that she has never known the words for move and adjust in a dance of twenty-seven parts. Oh, it is so lovely! If only Schaffa could—

Wait.

Something makes the hairs on the back of Nassun's neck prickle. Dangerous to lose concentration now, so she forces herself to methodically touch each obelisk in turn and soothe it back into something like an idle state. They mostly tolerate this, though the opal bucks a little and she has to force it into quiescence. When all are finally stable, though, she cautiously opens her eyes and looks around.

At first the black-and-white moonlit streets are as before: silent and still, despite the crowd of stone eaters that has assembled to watch her work. (In Corepoint, it is easy to feel alone in a crowd.) Then she spies... movement. Something—someone—lurching from one shadow to another.

Startled, Nassun takes a step toward that moving figure. "H-hello?"

The figure staggers toward some kind of small pillar whose purpose Nassun has never understood, though there seems to be one on every other corner of the city. Nearly falling as it grabs the pillar for support, the figure twitches and looks up at the sound of her voice. Icewhite eyes spear at Nassun from the shadows.

Schaffa.

Awake. Moving.

Without thinking, Nassun begins to trot, then run after him. Her heart is in her mouth. She's heard people say things like that and thought nothing of it before—just poetry, just silliness—but now she knows what it means as her mouth goes so dry that she can feel her own pulse through her tongue. Her eyes blur. "Schaffa!"

He's thirty, forty feet away, near one of the pylon buildings that surround Corepoint's hole. Close enough to recognize her—and yet there is nothing in his gaze that seems to know who she is. Quite the contrary; he blinks, and then smiles in a slow, cold way that makes her stumble to a halt in deep, skin-twitching unease.

"Sch-Schaffa?" she says again. Her voice is very thin in the silence.

"*Hello, little enemy,*" Schaffa says, in a voice that reverberates through Corepoint and the mountain below it and the ocean for a thousand miles around.

Then he turns to the pylon building behind him. A high, narrow opening appears at his touch; he stagger-stumbles through. It vanishes behind him in an instant.

Nassun screams and flings herself after him.

*   *   *

You are deep in the lower mantle, halfway through the world, when you sense the activation of part of the Obelisk Gate.

Or so your mind interprets it, at first, until you master your alarm and reach forth to confirm what you're feeling. It's hard. Here in the deep earth, there is so *much* magic; trying to sift through it for whatever is happening on the surface is like trying to hear a distant creek over a hundred thundering waterfalls nearby. It's worse the deeper Hoa takes you, until finally you have to "close your eyes" and stop perceiving magic entirely—because there's something immense nearby that is "blinding" you with its brightness. It is as if there's a sun underground, silver-white and swirling with an unbelievably intense concentration of magic… but you can also feel Hoa skirting wide around this sun, even though that means the overall journey has taken longer than absolutely necessary. You'll have to ask him why later.

You can't see much besides churning red here in the depths. How fast are you going? Without referents, it's impossible to tell. Hoa is an intermittent shadow in the redness beside you, shimmering on the rare occasions when you catch a glimpse of him—but then, you're probably shimmering, too. He isn't pushing through the earth, but becoming part of it and transiting the particles of himself around its particles, becoming a waveform that you can sess like sound or light or heat. Disturbing enough if you don't think about the fact that he's doing it to you, too. You can't feel anything like this, except a hint of pressure from his hand, and the suggestion of tension from Lerna's arm. There's no sound other than an omnipresent rumble, no smell of sulfur or anything else. You don't know if you're breathing, and you don't feel the need for air.

But the distant awakening of multiple obelisks panics you, nearly makes you try to pull away from Hoa so you can concentrate, even though—stupid—that would not just kill you but *annihilate* you, turning you to ash and then vaporizing the ashes and then setting the vapor on fire. "Nassun!" you cry, or try to cry, but words are lost in the deep roar. There is no one to hear your cry.

Except. There is.

Something shifts around you—or, you realize belatedly, you are shifting relative to it. It isn't something you think about until it happens again, and you think you feel Lerna jerk against your side. Then it finally occurs to you to look at the silver wisps of your companions' bodies, which at least you can make out against the dense red material of the earth around you.

There is a human-shaped blaze linked to your hand, heavy as a mountain upon your perception as it forges swiftly upward: Hoa. He is moving oddly, however, periodically shifting to one side or another; that's what you perceived before. Beside Hoa are faint shimmers, delicately etched. One has a palpable interruption in the silverflow of one arm; that has to be Tonkee. You cannot distinguish Hjarka from Danel because you can't see hair or relative size or anything so detailed as teeth. Only knowing that Lerna is closer to you makes him distinct. And beyond Lerna—

Something flashes past, mountain-heavy and magic-bright, human shaped but not human. And not Hoa.

Another flash. Something streaks on a perpendicular trajectory, intercepting and driving it away, but there are more. Hoa lunges aside again, and a new flash misses. But it's close. Lerna seems to twitch beside you. Can he see it, too?

You really hope not, because now you understand what's happening. Hoa is *dodging*. And you can do nothing, nothing, but trust Hoa to keep you safe from the stone eaters who are *trying to rip you away from him.*

No. It's hard to concentrate when you're this afraid—when you've been merged into the high-pressure semisolid rock of the planet's mantle, and when everyone you love will die in slow horror should you fail in your quest, and when you're surrounded by currents of magic that are so much more powerful than anything you've ever seen, and when you're under attack by murderous stone eaters. But. You did not spend your childhood learning to perform under the threat of death for nothing.

Mere threads of magic aren't enough to stop stone eaters. The earth's winding rivers of the stuff are all you have to hand. Reaching for one feels like plunging your awareness into a lava tube, and for an instant you're distracted by wondering whether this is what it will feel like if Hoa lets go—a flash of terrible heat and pain, and then oblivion. You push that aside. A memory comes to you. Meov. Driving a wedge of ice into a cliff face, shearing it off at just the precise time to smash a ship full of Guardians—

You shape your will into a wedge and splint it into the nearest magic torrent, a great crackling, wending coil of a thing. It works, but your aim is wild; magic sprays everywhere, and Hoa must dodge again, this time from your efforts. Fuck! You try again, concentrating this time, letting your thoughts loosen. You're already in the earth, red and hot instead of dark and warm, but how is this any different? You're still in the crucible, just literally instead of a symbolic mosaic. You need to drive your wedge in *here* and aim it *there* as another flash of person-shaped mountain starts to pace you and darts in for the kill—

—just as you shunt a stream of purest, brightest silver directly into its path. It doesn't hit. You're still not good at aiming. You glimpse the stone eater stop short, however, as the magic all but blazes past its nose. Here in the deep red it is impossible to see expressions, but you imagine that the creature is surprised, maybe even alarmed. You hope it is.

"Next one's for you, bastard cannibalson ruster!" you try to shout, but you are no longer in a purely physical space. Sound and air are extraneous. You *imagine* the words, then, and hope the ruster in question gets the gist.

You do not imagine, however, the fact that the flitting, fleeting glimpses of stone eaters stop. Hoa keeps going, but there are no more attacks. Well, then. It's good to be of some use.

He's rising faster now that he is unimpeded. Your sessapinae start to perceive depth as a rational, calculable thing again. The deep red turns deep brown, then cools to deep black. And then—

Air. Light. Solidity. You become *real* again, flesh and blood unadulterated by other matter, upon a road between strange, smooth buildings, tall as obelisks beneath a night sky. The return of sensation is stunning, profound—but nothing compared to the absolute shock you feel when you look up.

Because you have spent the past two years beneath a sky of variable ash, and until now you had no idea that the Moon had come.

It is an icewhite eye against the black, an ill omen writ vast and terrifying upon the tapestry of stars. You can see what it is, even without sessing it—a giant round rock. Deceptively small against the expanse of the sky; you think you'll need the obelisks to sess it completely, but you can see on its surface things that might be craters. You've traveled across craters. The craters on the Moon are big enough to see from here, big enough to take *years* to cross on foot, and that tells you the whole thing is incomprehensibly huge.

"Fuck," says Danel, which makes you drag your eyes from the sky. She's on her hands and knees, as if clinging to the ground and grateful for its solidity. Maybe she's regretting her choice of duty now, or maybe she just didn't understand before this that being a lorist could be fully as awful and dangerous as being a general. "Fuck! Fuck."

"That's it, then." Tonkee. She's staring up at the Moon, too.

You turn to see Lerna's reaction, and—

Lerna. The space beside you, where he held on to you, is empty.

"I didn't expect the attack," Hoa says. You can't turn to him. Can't turn away from the *empty space* where Lerna should be. Hoa's voice is its usual inflectionless, hollow tenor—but is he shaken? Shocked? You don't want him to be shocked. You want him to say something like, *But of course I was able to keep everyone safe, Lerna is just over there, don't worry.*

Instead he says, "I should have guessed. The factions that don't want peace..." He trails off. Falls silent, just like an ordinary person who is at a loss for words.

"Lerna." That last jolt. The one you thought was a near miss.

It isn't what should have happened. You're the one nobly sacrificing yourself for the future of the world. *He* was supposed to survive this.

"What about him?" That's Hjarka, who's standing but bent

over with hands on her knees, as if she's thinking about throwing up. Tonkee's rubbing the small of her back as if this will somehow help, but Hjarka's attention is on you. She's frowning, and you see the moment when she realizes what you're talking about, and her expression melts into shock.

You feel…numb. Not the usual non-feeling that comes of you being halfway to a statue. This is different. This is—

"I didn't even think I loved him," you murmur.

Hjarka winces, but then makes herself straighten and take a deep breath. "All of us knew this might be a one-way trip."

You shake your head in…confusion? "He's…he *was*… so much younger than me." You expected him to outlive you. That's how it was *supposed* to work. You're supposed to die feeling guilty for leaving him behind and killing his unborn child. He's supposed to—

"*Hey.*" Hjarka's voice sharpens. You know that look on her face now, though. It's a Leadership look, or one reminding you that you are the leader here. But that's right, isn't it? You're the one who's running this little expedition. You're the one who didn't make Lerna, or any of them, stay home. You're the one who didn't have the courage to do this by yourself the way you damn well should have, if you really didn't want them hurt. Lerna's death is on you, not Hoa.

You look away from them and involuntarily reach for the stump of your arm. This is irrational. You're expecting battle wounds, scorch marks, something else to show that Lerna was lost. But it's fine. You're fine. You look back at the others; they're all fine, too, because battles with stone eaters aren't things that anyone walks away from with mere flesh wounds.

"It's *prewar*." While you stand there bereft, Tonkee has half turned away from Hjarka, which is a problem because Hjarka's currently leaning on her. Hjarka grumbles and hooks an arm around Tonkee's neck to keep her in place. Tonkee doesn't seem to notice, so wide are her eyes as she looks around. "Evil, eating Earth, look at this place. Completely intact! Not hidden at all, no defensive structuring or camouflage, but then not nearly enough green space to make this place self-sufficient…" She blinks. "They would've needed regular supply shipments to survive. The place *isn't built for survival*. That means it's from before the Enemy!" She blinks. "The people here must have come from the Stillness. Maybe there's some means of transportation around here that we haven't seen yet." She subsides into thought, muttering to herself as she crouches to finger the substance of the ground.

You don't care. But you don't have time to mourn Lerna or hate yourself, not now. Hjarka's right. You have a job to do.

And you've seen the other things in the sky besides the Moon—the dozens of obelisks that hover so close, so low, their energy pent and not a single one of them acknowledging your touch when you reach for them. They aren't yours. But although they've been primed and readied, yoked to one another in a way that you immediately recognize as Bad News, they're not doing anything. Something's put them on hold.

Focus. You clear your throat. "Hoa, where is she?"

When you glance at him, you see he's adopted a new stance: expression blank, body facing slightly south and east. You follow his gaze, and see something that at first awes you: a bank of buildings, six or seven stories high that you can see, wedge-shaped and blank of feature. It's easy to tell that they form a ring, and it's easy to guess what's at the heart of that ring, even though you can't see it because of the angle of the buildings. Alabaster told you, though, didn't he? *The city exists to contain the hole.*

Your throat locks your breath.

"No," Hoa says. Okay. You make yourself breathe. She's not in the hole.

"Where, then?"

Hoa turns to look at you. He does this slowly. His eyes are wide. "Essun...she's gone into Warrant."

*　　　*　　　*

As Corepoint above, so Warrant below.

Nassun runs through obsidian-carved corridors, close and low ceilinged and claustrophobic. It's warm down here—not oppressively so, but the warmth is close and omnipresent. The warmth of the volcano, radiating up through the old stone from its heart. She can sess echoes of what was done to create this place, because it was orogeny, not magic, though a more precise and powerful orogeny than anything she's ever seen. She doesn't care about any of that, though. She needs to find Schaffa.

The corridors are empty, lit above by more of the strange rectangular lights that she saw in the underground city. Nothing else about this place looks like that place. The underground city felt leisurely in its design. There are hints of beauty in the way the station was built that suggest it was developed gradually, piece by piece, with time for contemplation between each phase of construction. Warrant is dark, utilitarian. As Nassun runs down sloping ramps, past conference rooms, classrooms, mess halls, lounges, she sees that all of them are empty. This facility's corridors were beaten and clawed out of the shield volcano over a period of days or weeks—hurriedly, though it isn't clear why. Nassun can tell the hurried nature of the place, somehow, to her own amazement. Fear has soaked into the walls.

But none of that matters. Schaffa is here, somewhere. Schaffa, who's barely moved for weeks and yet is now somehow running, his body driven by something other than his own mind. Nassun tracks the silver of him, amazed that he's managed to get so far in the moments that it took her to try to reopen the door he used and then, when it would not open for her, to use the silver to rip it open. But now he is up ahead and—

—so are others. She stops for a moment, panting, suddenly uneasy. Many of them. Dozens...no. Hundreds. And all are like Schaffa, their silver thinner, stranger, and also bolstered from elsewhere.

Guardians. This, then, is where they go during Seasons...but Schaffa has said they will kill him because he is "contaminated."

They will not. She clenches her fists.

(It does not occur to her that they will kill her, too. Rather, it does, but *They will not* looms larger in the scope of her reality.)

When Nassun runs through a door at the top of a short stair, however, the close corridor suddenly opens out into a narrow but very long high-ceilinged chamber. It's high enough that its ceiling is nearly lost in shadow, and its length stretches farther than her eye can see. And all along the walls of this chamber, in neat rows that stack up to the ceiling, there are dozens—hundreds—of strange, square holes. She is reminded of the chambers in a wasp's nest, except the shape is wrong.

And in every one of them is a body.

Schaffa isn't far ahead. Somewhere in this room, no longer moving forward. Nassun stops too, apprehension finally overwhelming her driving need to find Schaffa. The silence makes her skin prickle. She cannot help fear. The analogy of the wasp's nest has stayed with her, and on some level she fears looking into the cells to find a grub staring back at her, perhaps atop the corpse of some creature (person) it has parasitized.

Inadvertently, she looks into the nearest cell. It's barely wider than the shoulders of the man within, who seems to be asleep. He's youngish, gray-haired, a Midlatter, wearing the burgundy uniform that Nassun has heard of but never seen. He's breathing, although slowly. The woman in the cell beside him is wearing the same uniform, though she's completely different in every other way: an Eastcoaster with completely black skin, hair that has been braided along her scalp in intricate patterns, and wine-dark lips. There is the slightest of smiles on those lips—as if, even in sleep, she cannot lose the habit of it.

Asleep, and more than asleep. Nassun follows the silver in the people in the cells, feeling out their nerves and circulation, and understands then that each is in something like a coma. She thinks maybe normal comas aren't like this, though. None of these people seems to be hurt or sick. And within each Guardian, there is that shard of corestone—quiescent here, instead of angrily flaring like the one in Schaffa. Strangely, the silver threads in each Guardian are reaching out to the ones around them. Networking together. Bolstering each other, maybe? Charging one another to perform some sort of work, the way a network of obelisks does? She cannot guess.

(They were never meant to continue.)

But then, from the center of the vaulted room, perhaps a hundred feet farther in, she hears a sharp mechanical whirr.

She jumps and stumbles away from the cells, darting a quick, frightened look around to see if the noise has awakened any of the cells' occupants. They don't stir. She swallows and calls, softly, "Schaffa?"

Her answer, echoing through the high chamber, is a low, familiar groan.

Nassun stumbles forward, her breath catching. It's him. Down the middle of the strange chamber stand contraptions, arranged in rows. Each consists of a chair attached to a complex arrangement of silver wire in loops and spars; she's never seen anything like it. (You have.) Each contraption seems big enough to hold one person, but they're all empty. And—Nassun leans closer for a better look, then shivers—each rests against a stone pillar that holds an obscenely complicated mechanism. It's impossible not to notice the tiny scalpels, the delicate forcepslike attachments of varying sizes, and other instruments clearly meant for cutting and drilling...

Somewhere nearby, Schaffa groans. Nassun pushes the cutting things out of her thoughts and hurries down the row—

—to stop in front of the room's lone occupied wire chair.

The chair has been adjusted somehow. Schaffa sits in it, but he is facedown, his body suspended by the wires, his chopped-off hair parting around his neck. The mechanism behind the chair has come alive, extending up and over his body in a way that feels predatory to her—but it is already retracting as she approaches. The bloodied instruments disappear into the mechanism; she hears more faint whirring sounds. Cleaning, maybe.

One tiny, tweezer-like attachment remains, however, holding up a prize that still glistens, faintly, with Schaffa's blood. A little metal shard, irregular and dark.

Hello, little enemy.

Schaffa isn't moving. Nassun stares at his body, shaking. She cannot bring herself to shift her perception back to the silver threads, back to *magic*, to see if he is alive. The bloody wound high on the back of his neck has been neatly stitched, right over the other old scar that she has always wondered about. It's still bleeding, but it's clear the wound was inflicted quickly and sealed nearly as fast.

Like a child willing the monster under the bed to not exist, Nassun wills Schaffa's back and sides to move.

They do, as he draws in a breath. "N-Nassun," he croaks.

"Schaffa! Schaffa." She flings herself to her knees and scooches forward to look at his face from underneath the wire contraption, heedless of the blood still dripping down the sides of his neck and face. His eyes, his beautiful white eyes, are half-open—and they are *him* this time! She sees that and bursts into tears herself. "Schaffa? Are you okay? Are you really okay?"

His speech is slow, slurred. Nassun will not think about why. "Nassun. I." Even more slowly, his expression shifts, a seaquake in his brows sending a tsunami of slow realization across the rest. His eyes widen. "There's. No pain."

She touches his face. "The—the thing is out of you, Schaffa. That metal thing."

He shuts his eyes and her belly clenches, but then the furrow vanishes from his brow. He smiles again—and for the first time since Nassun met him, there is nothing of tension or falsehood in it. He isn't smiling to ease his pain or others' fears. His mouth opens. She can see all his teeth, he's *laughing* although weakly, he's weeping, too, with relief and joy, and it is the most beautiful thing she's ever seen. She cups his face, mindful of the wound on the back of his neck, and presses her forehead against his, shaking with his soft laughter. She loves him. She just loves him so much.

And because she is touching him, because she loves him, because she is so attuned to his needs and his pain and making him happy, her perception slips into the silver. She doesn't mean for it to. She just wants to use her eyes to savor the sight of him looking back at her, and her hands to touch his skin, and her ears to hear his voice.

But she is orogene, and she can no longer shut off the sesuna than she can sight or sound or touch. Which is why her smile falters, and her joy vanishes, because the instant she sees how the network of threads within him is already beginning to fade, she can no longer deny that he is dying.

It's slow. He could last a few weeks or months, perhaps as much as a year, with what's left. But where every other living thing churns forth its own silver almost by accident, where it flows and stutters and gums up the works between cells, there is nothing between his cells but a trickle. What's left in him mostly runs along his nervous system, and she can see a glaring, gaping emptiness at what used to be the core of his silver network, in his sessapinae. Without his corestone, as he warned her, he will not last long.

Schaffa's eyes have drifted shut. He's asleep, exhausted by pushing his weakened body through the streets. But he isn't the one who did that, is he? Nassun gets to her feet, shaking, keeping her hands on Schaffa's shoulders. His heavy head presses against her chest. She stares at the little metal shard bitterly, understanding at once why Father Earth did this to him.

It knows she means to bring the Moon down, and that this will create a cataclysm far worse than the Shattering. It wants to live. It knows Nassun loves Schaffa, and that until now she has seen destroying the world as the only way to give him peace. Now, however, it has remade Schaffa, offering him to Nassun as a kind of living ultimatum.

Now he is free, the Earth taunts by this wordless gesture. *Now he can have peace without death. And if you want him to live, little enemy, there is only one way.*

Steel never said it couldn't be done, only that it shouldn't. Maybe Steel is wrong. Maybe, as a stone eater, Schaffa won't be alone and sad forever. Steel is mean and awful, which is why no one wants to be with him. But Schaffa is good and kind. Surely he will find someone else to love.

Especially if all the world is stone eaters, too.

Humanity, she decides, is a small price to pay for Schaffa's future.

* * *

Hoa says that Nassun has gone underground, to Warrant where the Guardians lie, and the panic of this is sour in your mouth as you trot around the hole, looking for a way in. You don't dare ask Hoa to simply transport you to her; Gray Man's allies lurk everywhere now, and they will kill you as surely as they did Lerna. Allies of Hoa are present, too; you have a blurry memory of seeing two streaking mountains crash into one another, one driving the other off. But until this business with the Moon is settled, going into the Earth is too dangerous. All of the stone eaters are here, you sess; a thousand human-sized mountains in and underneath Corepoint, some of them watching you run through the streets looking for your daughter. All of their ancient factions and private battles will come to a head tonight, one way or another.

Hjarka and the others have followed you, though more slowly; they do not feel your panic. At last you spot one pylon building that's been opened—*cut* open, it seems, as if with an enormous knife; three irregular slashes and then someone has made the door fall outward. It's a foot thick. But beyond it is a wide, low-ceilinged corridor going down into darkness.

Someone's climbing out of it, though, as you reach it and stumble to a halt.

"Nassun!" you blurt, because it's her.

The girl framed by the doorway is taller than you remember by several inches. Her hair is longer now, braided back in two plaits that fall behind her shoulders. You barely recognize her. She stops short at the sight of you, a faint wrinkle of confusion between her brows, and you realize she's having trouble recognizing you, too. Then realization comes, and she stares as if you are the last thing in the world she expected to see. Because you are.

"Hi, Mama," Nassun says.

14

I, at the end of days

I AM A WITNESS TO WHAT follows. I will tell this as such.

I watch you and your daughter face each other for the first time in two years, across a gulf of hardship. Only I know what you both have been through. Each of you can judge the other only on presences, actions, and scars, at least for now. You: much thinner than the mother she last saw when she decided to skip creche one day. The desert has weathered you, drying your skin; the acid rain has bleached your locks to a paler brown than they should be, and the gray shows more. The clothes that hang from your body are also bleached by ash and acid, and the empty right sleeve of your shirt has been knotted; it dangles, obviously empty, as you catch your breath. And, also a part of Nassun's first impression of the post-Rifting you: Behind you stands a group of people who all stare at Nassun, some of them with palpable wariness. You, though, show only anguish.

Nassun is as still as a stone eater. She's grown only four inches since the Rifting, but it looks to you like a foot. You can see the advent of adolescence upon her—early, but that is the nature of life in lean times. The body takes advantage of safety and abundance when it can, and the nine months she spent in Jekity were good for her. She's probably going to start menstruating within the next year, if she can find enough food. The biggest changes are immaterial, though. The wariness in her gaze, nothing like the shy diffidence you remember. Her posture: shoulders back, feet braced and square. You told her to stop slouching a million times, and yes, she looks so tall and strong now that she's standing up straight. So beautifully strong.

Her orogeny sits on your awareness like a weight upon the world, rock-steady and precise as a diamond drill. Evil Earth, you think. She sesses just like you.

It's over before it's begun. You sense that as surely as you sess her strength, and both make you desperate. "I've been looking for you," you say. You've raised your hand without thinking about it. Your fingers open and twitch and close and open again in a gesture that is half grasping, half plea.

Her gaze goes hooded. "I was with Daddy."

"I know. I couldn't find you." It's redundant, obvious; you hate yourself for babbling. "Are you . . . all right?"

She looks away, troubled, and it bothers you that her concern so plainly isn't you. "I need to . . . My Guardian needs help."

You go stiff. Nassun has heard from Schaffa of what he was like, before Meov. She knows, intellectually, that the Schaffa you knew and the Schaffa she loves are wholly different people. She's seen a Fulcrum, and the ways in which it warped its inmates. She remembers how you used to go stiff, just the way you are now, at even a glimpse of the color burgundy—and finally, here at the end of the world, she understands why. She knows you better now than ever before in her life.

And yet. To her, Schaffa is the man who protected her from raiders—and from her father. He is the man who soothed her when she was afraid, tucked her into bed at night. She has seen him fight his own brutal nature, and the Earth itself, in order to be the parent she needs. He has helped her learn to love herself for what she is.

Her mother? You. Have done none of these things.

And in that pent moment, as you fight past the memory of Innon falling to pieces and the burning ache of broken bones in a hand you no longer possess, with *Never say no to me* ringing in your head, she intuits the thing that you have, until now, denied:

That it is hopeless. That there can be no relationship, no trust, between you and her, because the two of you are what the Stillness and the Season have made you. That Alabaster was right, and some things really are too broken to fix. Nothing to do but destroy them entirely, for mercy's sake.

Nassun shakes her head once while you stand there twitching. She looks away. Shakes her head again. Her shoulders bow a little, not in a lazy slouch, but weariness. She does not blame you, but neither does she expect anything from you. And right now, you're just in the way.

So she turns to walk away, and that shocks you out of your fugue. "Nassun?"

"He needs help," she says again. Her head is down, her shoulders tight. She doesn't stop walking. You inhale and start after her. "I have to help him."

You know what's happening. You've felt it, feared it, all along. Behind you, you hear Danel stop the others. Maybe she thinks you and your daughter need space. You ignore them and run after Nassun. You grab her shoulder, try to turn her around. "Nassun, what—" She shrugs you off, so hard that you stagger. Your balance has been shot since you lost the arm, and she's stronger than she was. She doesn't notice you almost fall. She keeps going. "Nassun!" She doesn't even look back.

You're desperate to get her attention, to get her to react, something. Anything. You grope and then say, to her back, "I— I—I know about Jija!"

That makes her falter to a halt. Jija's death is still a raw wound within her that Schaffa has cleaned and stitched, but that will not heal for some time. That you know what she has done makes her hunch in shame. That it was necessary, self-defense, frustrates her. That you have reminded her of this, now, tips the shame and frustration into anger.

"I have to *help Schaffa*," she says again. Her shoulders are going up in a way that you recognize from a hundred afternoons in your makeshift crucible, and from when she was two and learned the word *no*. There's no reasoning with her when she gets like this. Words become irrelevant. Actions mean more. But what actions could possibly convey the morass of your feelings right now? You look back at the others helplessly. Hjarka is holding Tonkee back; Tonkee's gaze is fixed on the sky and the assemblage there of more obelisks than you've seen in your whole life. Danel is a little apart from the rest, her hands behind her back, her black lips moving in what you recognize as a lorist mnemonic exercise to help her absorb everything she sees and hears, verbatim. Lerna—

You forgot. Lerna is not here. But if he were here, you suspect, he would be warning you. He was a doctor. Wounds of the family weren't really within his purview...but anyone can see that something here has festered.

You trot after her again. "Nassun. Nassun, rust it, look at me when I'm talking to you!" She ignores you, and it's a slap in the face—the kind that clears your head, though, and not the kind that makes you want to fight. Okay. She won't hear you until she's helped...Schaffa. You push past this thought, though it is like plodding through muck full of bones. Okay. "L-let me help you!"

This actually gets Nassun to slow down, and then stop. Her expression is wary, so wary, when she turns back. "Help me?"

You look beyond her and see then that she was heading for another of the pylon buildings—this one with a broad, railed staircase going up its sloping side. The view of the sky would be excellent at the top...Irrationally you conclude that you have to keep her from going up there. "Yes." You hold out your hand again. *Please.* "Tell me what you need. I'll...Nassun." You're out of words. You're willing her to feel what you feel. "Nassun."

It's not working. She says, in a voice as hard as stone, "I need to use the Obelisk Gate."

You flinch. I told you this already, weeks ago, but apparently you did not *believe.* "What? You can't."

You're thinking: *It will kill you.*

Her jaw tightens. "I will."

She's thinking: *I don't need your permission.*

You shake your head, incredulous. "To do *what?*" But it's too late. She's done. You said you would help but then hesitated.

She is Schaffa's daughter, too, in her heart of hearts; Earthfires, two fathers and *you* of all people to shape her, is it any wonder that she's turned out the way she has? To her, hesitation is the same thing as *no*. She doesn't like it when people say no to her.

So Nassun turns her back on you again and says, "Don't follow me anymore, Mama."

You immediately start after her again, of course. "Nassun—"

She whips back around. She's in the ground, you sess it, and she's in the air, you see the lines of magic, and suddenly the two weave together in a way that you can't even comprehend. The stuff of Corepoint's ground, which is metals and pressed fibers and substances for which you have no name, layered over volcanic rock, heaves beneath your feet. Out of old habit, years spent containing your children's orogenic tantrums, you react even as you stagger, setting a torus into the ground that you can use to cancel her orogeny. It doesn't work, because she isn't just using orogeny.

She sesses it, though, and her eyes narrow. *Your* gray eyes, like ash. And an instant later, a wall of obsidian slams up from the ground in front of you, tearing through the fiber and metal of the city's infrastructure, forming a barrier between you and her that spans the road.

The force of this upheaval flings you to the ground. When the stars clear from your vision and the dust dissipates enough, you stare up at the wall in shock. Your daughter did this. To you.

Someone grabs you and you flinch. It's Tonkee.

"I don't know if it's occurred to you," she says, hauling you to your feet, "but your child seems like she's got *your temper*. So, you know, maybe you shouldn't get too pushy."

"I don't even know what she did," you murmur, dazed, though you nod thanks to Tonkee for helping you up. "That wasn't...I don't..." There was no Fulcrum-esque precision in what Nassun did, even though you taught her Fulcrum fundamentals. You lay your hand against the wall in confusion, and feel the lingering flickers of magic within its substance, dancing from particle to particle as they fade. "She's *blending* magic and orogeny. I've never seen that before."

I have. We called it tuning.

Meanwhile. No longer hampered by you, Nassun has climbed the pylon steps. She stands atop it now, surrounded by turning, bright red warning symbols that dance in the air. A heavy, faintly sulfurous breeze wafts up from Corepoint's great hole, lifting the stray hairs from her twin plaits. She wonders if Father Earth is relieved to have manipulated her into sparing its life.

Schaffa will live if she turns every person in the world into stone eaters. That is all that matters.

"First, the network," she says, lifting her eyes to the sky. The twenty-seven obelisks flicker from solid to magic in unison as she reignites them. She spreads her hands before her.

On the ground below her, you flinch as you sess—feel—are attuned to—the lightning-fast activation of twenty-seven obelisks. They act as one in this instant, thrumming so powerfully together that your teeth itch. You wonder why Tonkee isn't grimacing the way you are, but Tonkee is only a still.

Tonkee's not stupid, though, and this is her life's work. While you stare at your daughter in awe, she narrows her eyes at the obelisks. "Three cubed," she murmurs. You shake your head, mute. She glares at you, irritated by your slowness. "Well, if

I was going to emulate a *big* crystal, I would start by putting smaller crystals into a cubiform lattice configuration."

Then you understand. The big crystal that Nassun means to emulate is the onyx. You need a key to initialize the Gate; that's what Alabaster told you. What Alabaster *didn't* tell you, the useless ass, was that there are many possible kinds of keys. When he tore the Rifting across the Stillness, he used a network composed of all the node maintainers in his vicinity, probably because the onyx itself would have turned him to stone at once. The node maintainers were a lesser substitute for the onyx—a spare key. You didn't know what you were doing that first time, when you yoked the orogenes in Castrima-under into a network, but *he* knew the onyx was too much for you to just grab directly, back then. You didn't have Alabaster's flexibility or creativity. He taught you a safer way.

Nassun, though, is the student Alabaster always wanted. She cannot have ever accessed the Obelisk Gate before—it's been yours, till now—but as you observe in shock, in horror, she reaches beyond her spare-key network, finding other obelisks one by one and binding them. It's slower than it would be with the onyx, but you can tell that it's just as effective. It's working. The apatite, connected and locked. The sardonyx, sending a little pulse from where it hovers out of sight, somewhere over the southern sea. The jade—

Nassun will open the Gate.

You shove Tonkee away. "Get as far from me as you can. All of you."

Tonkee doesn't waste time arguing. Her eyes widen; she turns and runs. You hear her shouting to the others. You hear Danel arguing. And then you can no longer pay heed to them.

Nassun will open the Gate, turn to stone, *and die.*

Only one thing can stop Nassun's network of obelisks: the onyx. You need to reach it first, though, and right now it's all the way on the other side of the planet, halfway between Castrima and Rennanis where you left it. Once, long ago at Castrima-over, it called you to itself. But do you dare wait for it to do that, now, with Nassun grabbing control of every part of the Gate? You need to get to the onyx first. For that, you need magic—much more of it than you can muster just by yourself, here without a single obelisk to your name.

The beryl, the hematite, the iolite—

She's going to die right in front of you if you don't do something.

Frantically you throw your awareness into the earth. Core-point sits on a volcano, maybe you can—

Wait. Something pulls your attention back up to the volcano's mouth. Underground, but closer by. Somewhere underneath this city, you sense a network. Lines of magic woven together, supporting one another, rooted deep to draw up more...It's faint. It's slow. And there is a familiar, ugly buzz at the back of your mind when you touch this network. Buzz upon buzz upon buzz.

Ah, yes. The network you've found is *Guardians,* nearly a thousand of them. Of rusting course. You have never consciously sought the magic of them before, but for the first time you understand what that buzz is—some part of you, even before

Alabaster's training, felt the foreignness of the magic within them. The knowledge sends a sharp, nearly paralyzing lance of fear through you. The network of them is close by, easy to grab, but if you do this, what's to stop all these Guardians from boiling up out of Warrant like angry wasps from a disturbed nest? Don't you have enough problems?

Nassun groans, up on her pylon. To your shock, you can... Evil Earth, you can *see* the magic around her, in her, beginning to flare up like a fire hitting oiled kindling. She burns against your perception, the weight of her growing heavier upon the world by the instant. *The kyanite the orthoclase the scapolite—*

And suddenly your fear is gone, because your baby needs you.

So you set your feet. You reach for that network you found, Guardians or no Guardians. You growl through your teeth and grab everything. The Guardians. The threads that trail from their sessapinae away into the depths, and as much of the magic coming through these as you can pull. The iron shards themselves, tiny depositories of the Evil Earth's will.

You make it all yours, yoke it tight, and then you *take* it.

And somewhere down in Warrant there are Guardians screaming, coming awake and writhing in their cells and grabbing at their heads as you do to every single one of them what Alabaster once did to his Guardian. It is what Nassun yearned to do for Schaffa... only there is no kindness in the way you're doing it. You don't hate them; you just don't care. You snatch the iron from their brains and every bit of silvery light from between their cells—and as you feel them crystallize and die, you finally have enough magic, from your makeshift network, to reach the onyx.

It listens at your touch, far away above the ashscape of the Stillness. You fall into it, diving desperately into the dark, to make your case. *Please*, you beg.

It considers the request. This is not in words or sensation. You simply know its consideration. It examines you in turn— your fear, your anger, your determination to put things right.

Ah—this last has resonance. You know yourself examined again, more closely and with skepticism, since your last request was for something so frivolous. (Merely wiping out a city? You of all people did not need the Gate for that.) What the onyx finds within you, however, is something different this time: Fear for kin. Fear of failure. The fear that accompanies all necessary change. And underneath it all, a driving need to make the world better.

Somewhere far away, a billion dying things shiver as the onyx utters a low, earthshaking blast of sound, and comes online.

Atop her pylon, beneath the pulse of the obelisks, Nassun feels that distant upcycling darkness as a warning. But she is too deep in her summoning; too many obelisks now fill her. She cannot spare any attention from her work.

And as each of the two hundred and sixteen remaining obelisks in turn submits to her, and as she opens her eyes to stare at the Moon that she's going to let fly past untouched, and as she instead prepares to turn all the might of the great Plutonic Engine back upon the world and its people, to transform them as I was once transformed—

—she thinks of Schaffa.

Impossible to delude oneself in a moment like this. Impossible to see only what one wants to see, when the power to

381

change the world ricochets through mind and soul and the spaces between cells; oh, I learned this long before both of you. Impossible not to understand that Nassun has known Schaffa for barely more than a year, and does not truly *know* him, given how much of himself he has lost. Impossible not to realize that she clings to him because she has nothing else—

But through her determination, there is a glimmer of doubt in her mind. It is nothing more than that. Barely even a thought. But it whispers, *Do you really have nothing else?*

Is there not one *person in this world besides Schaffa who cares about you?*

And I watch Nassun hesitate, fingers curling and small face tightening in a frown even as the Obelisk Gate weaves itself into completion. I watch the shiver of energies beyond comprehension as they begin to align within her. I lost the power to manipulate these energies tens of thousands of years ago, but I can still see them. The arcanochemical lattice—what you think of as mere brown stone, and the energetic state that produces it—is forming nicely.

I watch as you see this, too, and understand instantly what it means. I watch you snarl and smash apart the wall between you and your daughter, not even noticing that your fingers have turned to stone as you do it. I watch you run to the foot of the pylon steps and shout at her. "*Nassun!*"

And in response to your sudden, raw, incontrovertible *demand*, the onyx blasts out of nowhere to appear overhead.

The sound of it—a low, bone-shaking blat—is titanic. The blast of air that it displaces is thunderous enough to knock both you and Nassun down. She cries out and slides down a few steps, coming dangerously close to losing her grip on the Gate as the impact jolts her concentration. You cry out as the impact makes you notice your left forearm, which is stone, and collarbone, which is stone, and left foot and ankle.

But you set your teeth. There is no pain in you anymore, save anguish for your daughter. No need within you but one. She has the Gate, but you have the onyx—and as you look up at it, at the Moon glaring through its murky translucence, icewhite iris in a scleral sea of black, you know what you have to do.

With the onyx's help, you reach half a planet away and stab the fulcrum of your intention into the wound of the world. The Rifting shudders as you demand every iota of its heat and kinetic churn, and you shudder beneath the flux of so much power that for a moment you think it's just going to vomit out of you as a column of lava, consuming all.

But the onyx is part of you, too, right now. Indifferent to your convulsions—because you're doing that, flopping along the ground and frothing at the mouth—it takes and taps and balances the power of the Rifting with an ease that humbles you. Automatically it links into the obelisks so conveniently nearby, the network that Nassun assembled in order to try to replicate the onyx's power. But a replica has only power, no will, unlike the onyx. A network has no agenda. The onyx takes the twenty-seven obelisks and immediately begins eating into the rest of Nassun's obelisk network.

Here, though, its will is no longer paramount. Nassun feels it. Fights it. She is just as determined as you. Just as driven by love—you for her, and she for Schaffa.

I love you both. How can I not, after all this? I am still

human, after all, and this is a battle for the fate of the world. Such a terrible and magnificent thing to witness.

It *is* a battle, though, line by line, tendril by tendril of magic. The titanic energies of the Gate, of the Rifting, whip and shiver around you both in a cylindrical aurora borealis of energies and colors, visible light ranging to wavelengths beyond the spectrum. (Those energies *resonate* in you, where the alignment is already complete, and still *oscillate* in Nassun—though her waveform has begun to collapse.) It is the onyx and the Rifting versus the Gate, you against her, and all Corepoint trembles with the sheer force of it all. In the dark halls of Warrant, among the jeweled corpses of the Guardians, walls groan and ceilings crack, spilling dirt and pebbles. Nassun is straining to pull the magic down from what's left of the Gate, to target everyone around you and everyone beyond them—and finally, finally, you understand that she's trying to turn everyone into rusting *stone eaters*. You, meanwhile, have reached up. To catch the Moon, and perhaps earn humanity a second chance. But for either of you to achieve your respective goals, you will need to claim both Gate and onyx, and the additional fuel that the Rifting provides.

It is a stalemate that cannot continue. The Gate cannot maintain its connections forever, and the onyx cannot contain the chaos of the Rifting forever—and two human beings, however powerful and strong-willed, cannot survive so much magic for long.

And then it happens. You cry out as you feel a change, a snapping-into-line: Nassun. The magics of her substance are fully aligned; her crystallization has begun. In desperation and pure instinct you grab some of the energy that seeks to transform her and fling it away, though this only delays the inevitable. In the ocean too near Corepoint, there is a deep judder that even the mountain's stabilizers cannot contain. To the west a mountain shaped like a knife jolts up from the ocean floor; to the east another rises, hissing steam from the newness of its birth. Nassun, snarling in frustration, latches onto these as new sources of power, dragging the heat and violence from them; both crack and crumble away. The stabilizers push the ocean flat, preventing tsunami, but they can do only so much. They were not built for this. Much more and even Corepoint will crumble.

"Nassun!" you shout again, anguished. She cannot hear you. But you see, even from where you are, that the fingers of her left hand have turned as brown and stony as your own. She's aware of it, you know somehow. She made this choice. She is prepared for the inevitability of her own death.

You aren't. Oh, Earth, you just can't watch another of your children die.

So . . . you give up.

I ache with the look on your face, because I know what it costs you to give up Alabaster's dream—and your own. You so wanted to make a better world for Nassun. But more than anything else, you want this last child of yours to *live* . . . and so you make a choice. To keep fighting will kill you both. The only way to win, then, is not to fight anymore.

I'm sorry, Essun. I'm so sorry. Goodbye.

Nassun gasps, her eyes snapping open as she feels your pressure upon the Gate—upon her, while you dragged all of the terrible transforming curls of magic toward yourself—suddenly relax. The onyx pauses in its onslaught, shimmering in tandem with the dozens of obelisks it has claimed; it is full of power that must, *must* be expended. For the moment, however, it holds. The stabilizing magics finally settle the churning ocean around Corepoint. For this one, pent moment, the world waits, still and taut.

She turns.

"Nassun," you say. It's a whisper. You're on the bottom steps of the pylon, trying to reach her, but that won't be happening. Your arm has completely solidified, and your torso is going. Your stone foot slides uselessly on the slick material, then locks as the rest of your leg freezes up. With your good foot, you can still push, but the stone of you is heavy; as crawling goes, you're not doing a very good job of it.

Her brow furrows. You look up at her, and it strikes you. Your little girl. So big, here beneath the onyx and the Moon. So powerful. So beautiful. And you cannot help it: You burst into tears at the sight of her. You *laugh*, though one of your lungs has gone to stone and it's only a soft wheeze instead. So rusting amazing, your little girl. You are proud to lose to her strength.

She inhales, her eyes widening as if she cannot believe what she is seeing: her mother, so fearsome, on the ground. Trying to crawl on stone limbs. Face wet with tears. *Smiling.* You have never, ever smiled at her before.

And then the line of transformation moves over your face, and you are gone.

Still there physically, a brown sandstone lump frozen on the lower steps, with only the barest suggestion of a smile on half-formed lips. Your tears are still there, glistening upon stone. She stares at these.

She stares at these and sucks in a long hollow breath because suddenly there is nothing, *nothing* inside her, she has killed her father and she has killed her mother and Schaffa is dying and there is nothing left, nothing, the world just takes and takes and takes from her and leaves *nothing—*

But she cannot stop staring at your drying tears.

Because the world took and took and took from you, too, after all. She knows this. And yet, for some reason that she does not think she'll ever understand... even as you died, you were reaching for the Moon.

And for her.

She screams. Clutches her head in her hands, one of them now halfway stone. Drops to her knees, crushed beneath the weight of grief as if it is an entire planet.

The onyx, patient but not, aware but indifferent, touches her. She is the only remaining component of the Gate that has a functioning, complementary will. Through this touch she perceives your plan as commands locked and aimed but unfired. Open the Gate, pour the Rifting's power through it, catch the Moon. End the Seasons. Fix the world. This, Nassun sesses-feels-knows, was your last wish.

The onyx says, in its ponderous, wordless way: *Execute Y/N?*

And in the cold stone silence, alone, Nassun chooses.

YES

coda

me, and you

YOU ARE DEAD. BUT NOT you.

The recapture of the Moon is undramatic, from the perspective of the people standing beneath it. At the top of the apartment building where Tonkee and the others have taken shelter, she's used an ancient writing instrument—long gone dry, but resurrected with a bit of spit and blood at the tip—to try to track the Moon's movement between one hour and the next. It doesn't help because she hasn't observed enough variables to do the math correctly, and because she's not some rusting hack astronomest, for Earth's sake. She also isn't sure if she got the first measurement right because of the fiver or sixer shake that occurred right around that moment, just before Hjarka dragged her away from the window. "Obelisk-builder windows don't shatter," she complains afterward.

"My rusting temper *does*," Hjarka retorts, and that ends the argument before it can begin. Tonkee is learning to compromise for the sake of a healthy relationship.

But the Moon has indeed changed, they see as days and then

weeks pass. It does not vanish. It fluxes through shapes and colors in a pattern that does not initially make sense, but it grows no smaller in the sky on successive nights.

The dismantling of the Obelisk Gate is somewhat more dramatic. Having expended its full capability in the achievement of something just as powerful as Geoarcanity, the Gate proceeds as designed through its shutdown protocol. One by one, the dozens of obelisks floating around the world drift toward Corepoint. One by one, the obelisks—wholly dematerialized now, all quantum states sublimated into potential energy, you need not understand it beyond that—drop into the black chasm. This takes several days.

The onyx, however, last and greatest of the obelisks, instead drifts out to sea, its hum deepening as its altitude decreases. It enters the sea gently, on a preplanned course to minimize damage—since unlike its fellow obelisks, it alone has retained material existence. This, as the conductors long ago intended, preserves the onyx against future need. It also puts the last remnants of the Niess to rest, finally, deep in a watery grave.

I suppose we must hope that no intrepid young future orogene ever finds and raises it.

Tonkee is the one to go and find Nassun. It's later in the morning, some hours after your death, under a sun that has risen bright and warm in the ashless blue sky. After pausing for a moment to stare at this sky in wonder and longing and fascination, Tonkee goes back to the edge of the hole, and to the pylon stair. Nassun's still there, sitting on one of the lower steps next to the brown lump of you. Her knees are drawn up, her head bowed, her completely solidified hand—frozen in the splayed gesture that she used while activating the Gate—resting awkwardly on the step beside her.

Tonkee sits down on your other side, gazing at you for a long moment. Nassun starts and looks up as she becomes aware of another presence, but Tonkee only smiles at her, and awkwardly rests a hand on what was once your hair. Nassun swallows hard, scrubs at the dried tear-tracks on her face, and then nods to Tonkee. They sit together, with you, grieving for a time.

Danel is the one who goes with Nassun, later, to fetch Schaffa from the dead darkness of Warren. The other Guardians, who still had corestones, have turned to jewel. Most seem to have simply died where they lay, though some fell out of their cells in their thrashing, and their glittering bodies sprawl awkwardly against the wall or along the floor.

Schaffa alone still lives. He's disoriented, weak. As Danel and Nassun help him back up into the surface light, it becomes clear that his hacked-off hair is already streaked with gray. Danel's worried about the stitched wound on the back of his neck, though it has stopped bleeding and seems to cause Schaffa no pain. That isn't what's going to kill him.

Nevertheless. Once he's capable of standing and the sun has helped to clear his mind somewhat, Schaffa holds Nassun, there beside what remains of you. She doesn't weep. Mostly she's just numb. The others come out, Tonkee and Hjarka joining Danel, and they stand with Schaffa and Nassun while the sun sets and the Moon rises again. Maybe it's a silent memorial service. Maybe they just need time and company to recover from events too vast and strange to comprehend. I don't know.

Elsewhere in Corepoint, in a garden long since gone to

wild meadow, I and Gaewha face Remwha—Steel, Gray Man, whatever—beneath the now-waning Moon.

He's been here since Nassun made her choice. When he finally speaks, I find myself thinking that his voice has become so thin and weary. Once, he made the very stones ripple with the wry, edged humor of his earthtalk. Now he sounds old. Thousands of years of ceaseless existence will do that to a man.

He says: "I only wanted it to end."

Gaewha—Antimony, whatever—says, "That isn't what we were made for."

He turns his head, slowly, to look at her. It is tiring just to watch him do this. Stubborn fool. There is the despair of ages on his face, all because he refuses to admit that there's more than one way to be human.

Gaewha offers a hand. "We were made *to make the world better.*" Her gaze slides to me for support. I sigh inwardly, but offer a hand in truce as well.

Remwha looks at our hands. Somewhere, perhaps among the others of our kind who have gathered to watch this moment, are Bimniwha and Dushwha and Salewha. They forgot who they were long ago, or else they simply prefer to embrace who they are now. Only we three have retained anything of the past. This is both a good and bad thing.

"I'm tired," he admits.

"A nap might help," I suggest. "There is the onyx, after all."

Well! Something of the old Remwha remains. I don't think I deserved that look.

But he takes our hands. Together, the three of us—and the

others, too, all who have come to understand that the world *has to* change, the war *must* end—descend into the boiling depths.

The heart of the world is quieter than usual, we find as we take up positions around it. That is a good sign. It does not rage us away at once, which is a better one. We spell out the terms in placatory fluxes of reverberation: The Earth keeps its life-magic, and the rest of us get to keep ours without interference. We have given it back the Moon, and thrown the obelisks in as a surety of good faith. But in exchange, the Seasons must cease.

There is a period of stillness. I know only later that this is several days. In the moment, it feels like another millennium.

Then a heavy, lurching jolt of gravitation. *Accepted.* And—the best sign of all—it sets loose the numberless presences that it has ingested over the past epoch. They spin away, vanishing into the currents of magic, and I don't know what happens to them beyond that. I won't ever know what happens to souls after death—or at least, I won't know for another seven billion years or so, whenever the Earth finally dies.

An intimidating thing to contemplate. It's been a challenging first forty thousand years.

On the other hand…nowhere to go, but up.

*   *   *

I go back to them, your daughter and your old enemy and your friends, to tell them the news. Somewhat to my surprise, several months have passed in the interim. They've settled into the building that Nassun occupied, living off Alabaster's old garden and the supplies that we brought for him and Nassun. That won't be enough long term, of course, though they've supplemented it admirably with improvised fishing lines and bird-catching traps and dried edible seaweed, which Tonkee seems to have figured out a means of cultivating down at the water's edge. So resourceful, these modern people. But it is becoming increasingly clear that they'll have to go back to the Stillness soon, if they want to keep living.

I find Nassun, who is sitting alone at the pylon again. Your body remains where it fell, but someone has tucked fresh wild-flowers into its one remaining hand. There's another hand beside it, I notice, positioned like an offering near the stump of your arm. It's too small for you, but she meant well. She doesn't speak for a long while after I appear, and I find that this pleases me. Her kind talk so much. It goes on for long enough, though, even I get a little impatient.

I tell her, "You won't see Steel again." In case she was worried about that.

She jerks a little, as if she's forgotten my presence. Then she sighs. "Tell him I'm sorry. I just... couldn't."

"He understands."

She nods. Then: "Schaffa died today."

I had forgotten him. I should not have; he was part of you. Still. I say nothing. She seems to prefer that.

She takes a deep breath. "Will you... The others say you brought them, and Mama. Can you take us back? I know it'll be dangerous."

"There's no longer any danger." When she frowns, I explain all of it to her: the truce, the release of hostages, the cessation of immediate hostilities in the form of no more Seasons. It does not mean complete stability. Plate tectonics will be plate tec-tonics. Season-like disasters will still occur, though with greatly decreased frequency. I conclude: "You can take the vehimal back to the Stillness."

She shudders. I belatedly recall what she suffered there. She also says, "I don't know if I can give it magic. I...I feel like..."

She lifts the stone-capped stump of her left wrist. I understand, then—and yes, she's right. She is aligned perfectly, and will be so for the rest of her life. Orogeny is lost to her, forever. Unless she wants to join you.

I say, "I will power the vehimal. The charge should last six months or so. Leave within that time."

I adjust my position then, to the foot of the stairs. She starts, and looks around to find me holding you. I've picked up her old hand, too, because our children are always part of us. She stands, and for a moment I fear unpleasantness. But the look on her face is not unhappy. Just resigned.

I wait, for a moment or a year, to see if she has any final words for your corpse. She says, instead, "I don't know what will happen to us."

"'Us'?"

She sighs. "Orogenes."

Oh. "The current Season will last for some time, even with the Rifting quelled," I say. "Surviving it will require cooperation among many kinds of people. Cooperation presents opportunities."

She frowns. "Opportunities...for what? You said the Seasons would end after this."

"Yes."

She holds up her hands, or one hand and one stump, to

gesture in frustration. "People killed us and hated us when they *needed* us. Now we don't even have that."

Us. We. She still thinks of herself as orogene, though she will never again be able to do more than listen to the earth. I decide not to point this out. I do say, however, "And you won't need them, either."

She falls silent, perhaps in confusion. To clarify, I add, "With the end of the Seasons and the death of all the Guardians, it will now be possible for orogenes to conquer or eliminate stills, if they so choose. Previously, neither group could have survived without the other's aid."

Nassun gasps. "That's horrible!"

I don't bother to explain that just because something is horrible does not make it any less true.

"There won't be any more Fulcrums," she says. She looks away, troubled, perhaps remembering her destruction of the Antarctic Fulcrum. "I think...They're wrong, but I don't know how else..." She shakes her head.

I watch her flounder in silence for a month, or a moment. I say, "The Fulcrums *are* wrong."

"What?"

"Imprisonment of orogenes was never the only option for ensuring the safety of society." I pause deliberately, and she blinks, perhaps remembering that orogene parents are perfectly capable of raising orogene children without disaster. "Lynching was never the only option. The nodes were never the only option. All of these were choices. Different choices have always been possible."

There is such sorrow in her, your little girl. I hope Nassun learns someday that she is not alone in the world. I hope she learns how to hope again.

She lowers her gaze. "They're not going to choose anything different."

"They will if you make them."

She's wiser than you, and does not balk at the notion of forcing people to be decent to each other. Only the methodology is a problem. "I don't have any orogeny anymore."

"Orogeny," I say, sharply so she will pay attention, "was never the only way to change the world."

She stares. I feel that I have said all I can, so I leave her there to contemplate my words.

I visit the city's station, and charge its vehimal with sufficient magic to return to the Stillness. It will still take a journey of months or more for Nassun and her companions to reach Rennanis from the Antarctics. The Season will likely get worse while they travel, because we have a Moon again. Still ... they are part of you. I hope they survive.

Once they're on their way, I come here, to the heart of the mountain beneath Corepoint. To attend to you.

There is no one true way, when we initiate this process. The Earth—for the sake of good relations I will no longer call it Evil—reordered us instantly, and by now many of us are skilled enough to replicate that reordering without a lengthy gestation. I have found that speed produces mixed results, however. Alabaster, as you would call him, may not fully remember himself for centuries—or ever. You, however, must be different.

I have brought you here, reassembled the raw arcanic substance of your being, and reactivated the lattice that should have preserved the critical essence of who you were. You'll lose some memory. There is always loss, with change. But I have told you this story, primed what remains of you, to retain as much as possible of who you were.

Not to force you into a particular shape, mind you. From here on, you may become whomever you wish. It's just that you need to know where you've come from to know where you're going. Do you understand?

And if you should decide to leave me...I will endure. I've been through worse.

So I wait. Time passes. A year, a decade, a week. The length of time does not matter, though Gaewha eventually loses interest and leaves to attend her own affairs. I wait. I hope...no. I simply wait.

And then one day, deep in the fissure where I have put you, the geode splits and hisses open. You rise from its spent halves, the matter of you slowing and cooling to its natural state.

Beautiful, I think. Locs of roped jasper. Skin of striated ocher marble that suggests laugh lines at eyes and mouth, and stratified layers to your clothing. You watch me, and I watch you back.

You say, in an echo of the voice you once had, "What is it that you want?"

"Only to be with you," I say.

"Why?"

I adjust myself to a posture of humility, with head bowed and one hand over my chest. "Because that is how one survives eternity," I say, "or even a few years. Friends. Family. Moving with them. Moving forward."

Do you remember when I first told you this, back when you despaired of ever repairing the harm you'd done? Perhaps. Your position adjusts, too. Arms folded, expression skeptical. Familiar. I try not to hope and fail utterly.

"Friends, family," you say. "Which am I, to you?"

"Both and more. We are beyond such things."

"Hmm."

I am not anxious. "What do *you* want?"

You consider. I listen to the slow ongoing roar of the volcano, down here in the deep. Then you say, "I want the world to be better."

I have never regretted more my inability to leap into the air and whoop for joy.

Instead, I transit to you, with one hand proffered. "Then let's go make it better."

You look amused. It's you. It's truly you. "Just like that?"

"It might take some time."

"I don't think I'm very patient." But you take my hand.

Don't be patient. Don't ever be. This is the way a new world begins.

"Neither am I," I say. "So let's get to it."

APPENDIX 1

A catalog of Fifth Seasons that have been recorded prior to and since the founding of the Sanzed Equatorial Affiliation, from most recent to oldest

Choking Season: 2714–2719 Imperial. Proximate cause: volcanic eruption. Location: the Antarctics near Deveteris. The eruption of Mount Akok blanketed a five-hundred-mile radius with fine ash clouds that solidified in lungs and mucous membranes. Five years without sunlight, although the northern hemisphere was not affected as much (only two years).

Acid Season: 2322–2329 Imperial. Proximate cause: plus-ten-level shake. Location: unknown; far ocean. A sudden plate shift birthed a chain of volcanoes in the path of a major jet stream. This jet stream became acidified, flowing toward the western coast and eventually around most of the Stillness. Most coastal comms perished in the initial tsunami; the rest failed or were forced to relocate when their fleets and port facilities corroded and the fishing dried up. Atmospheric occlusion by clouds lasted seven years; coastal pH levels remained untenable for many years more.

Appendix 1

Boiling Season: 1842–1845 Imperial. Proximate cause: hot spot eruption beneath a great lake. Location: Somidlats, Lake Tekkaris quartent. The eruption launched millions of gallons of steam and particulates into the air, which triggered acidic rain and atmospheric occlusion over the southern half of the continent for three years. The northern half suffered no negative impacts, however, so archeomests dispute whether this qualifies as a "true" Season.

Breathless Season: 1689–1798 Imperial. Proximate cause: mining accident. Location: Nomidlats, Sathd quartent. An entirely human-caused Season triggered when miners at the edge of the northeastern Nomidlats coalfields set off underground fires. A relatively mild Season featuring occasional sunlight and no ashfall or acidification except in the region; few comms declared Seasonal Law. Approximately fourteen million people in the city of Heldine died in the initial natural-gas eruption and rapidly spreading fire sinkhole before Imperial Orogenes successfully quelled and sealed the edges of the fires to prevent further spread. The remaining mass could only be isolated, where it continued to burn for one hundred and nine years. The smoke of this, spread via prevailing winds, caused respiratory problems and occasional mass suffocations in the region for several decades. A secondary effect of the loss of the Nomidlats coalfields was a catastrophic rise in heating fuel costs and the wider adaption of geothermal and hydroelectric heating, leading to the establishment of the Geneer Licensure.

The Season of Teeth: 1553–1566 Imperial. Proximate cause: oceanic shake triggering a supervolcanic explosion. Location: Arctic Cracks. An aftershock of the oceanic shake breached a previously unknown hot spot near the north pole. This triggered a supervolcanic explosion; witnesses report hearing the sound of the explosion as far as the Antarctics. Ash went upper-atmospheric and spread around the globe rapidly, although the Arctics were most heavily affected. The harm of this Season was exacerbated by poor preparation on the part of many comms, because some nine hundred years had passed since the last Season; popular belief at the time was that the Seasons were merely legend. Reports of cannibalism spread from the north all the way to the Equatorials. At the end of this Season, the Fulcrum was founded in Yumenes, with satellite facilities in the Arctics and Antarctics.

Fungus Season: 602 Imperial. Proximate cause: volcanic eruption. Location: western Equatorials. A series of eruptions during monsoon season increased humidity and obscured sunlight over approximately 20 percent of the continent for six months. While this was a mild Season as such things go, its timing created perfect conditions for a fungal bloom that spread across the Equatorials into the northern and southern Midlats, wiping out then-staple-crop miroq (now extinct). The resulting famine lasted four years (two for the fungus blight to run its course, two more for agriculture and food distribution systems to recover). Nearly all affected comms were able to subsist on their own stores, thus proving the efficacy of Imperial reforms and Season planning, and the Empire was generous in sharing stored seed with those regions that had been miroq-dependent. In its aftermath, many comms of the middle latitudes and coastal regions voluntarily joined the Empire, doubling its range and beginning its Golden Age.

Appendix 1

Madness Season: 3 Before Imperial–7 Imperial. Proximate cause: volcanic eruption. Location: Kiash Traps. The eruption of multiple vents of an ancient supervolcano (the same one responsible for the Twin Season of approximately 10,000 years previous) launched large deposits of the dark-colored mineral augite into the air. The resulting ten years of darkness was not only devastating in the usual Seasonal way, but resulted in a higher than usual incidence of mental illness. The Sanzed Equatorial Affiliation (commonly called the Sanze Empire) was born in this Season as Warlord Verishe of Yumenes conquered multiple ailing comms using psychological warfare techniques. (See *The Art of Madness*, various authors, Sixth University Press.) Verishe named herself Emperor on the day the first sunlight returned.

[Editor's note: Much of the information about Seasons prior to the founding of Sanze is contradictory or unconfirmed. The following are Seasons agreed upon by the Seventh University Archaeomestric Conference of 2532.]

Wandering Season: Approximately 800 Before Imperial. Proximate cause: magnetic pole shift. Location: unverifiable. This Season resulted in the extinction of several important trade crops of the time, and twenty years of famine resulting from pollinators confused by the movement of true north.

Season of Changed Wind: Approximately 1900 Before Imperial. Proximate cause: unknown. Location: unverifiable. For reasons unknown, the direction of the prevailing winds shifted for many years before returning to normal. Consensus agrees that this was a Season, despite the lack of atmospheric occlusion, because only a substantial (and likely far-oceanic) seismic event could have triggered it.

Heavy Metal Season: Approximately 4200 Before Imperial. Proximate cause: volcanic eruption. Location: Somidlats near Eastern Coastals. A volcanic eruption (believed to be Mount Yrga) caused atmospheric occlusion for ten years, exacerbated by widespread mercury contamination throughout the eastern half of the Stillness.

Season of Yellow Seas: Approximately 9200 Before Imperial. Proximate cause: unknown. Location: Eastern and Western Coastals, and coastal regions as far south as the Antarctics. This Season is only known through written accounts found in Equatorial ruins. For unknown reasons, a widespread bacterial bloom toxified nearly all sea life and caused coastal famines for several decades.

Twin Season: Approximately 9800 Before Imperial. Proximate cause: volcanic eruption. Location: Somidlats. Per songs and oral histories dating from the time, the eruption of one volcanic vent caused a three-year occlusion. As this began to clear, it was followed by a second eruption of a different vent, which extended the occlusion by thirty more years.

APPENDIX 2

A Glossary of Terms Commonly Used in All Quartents of the Stillness

Antarctics: The southernmost latitudes of the continent. Also refers to people from antarctic-region comms.

Arctics: The northernmost latitudes of the continent. Also refers to people from arctic-region comms.

Ashblow Hair: A distinctive Sanzed racial trait, deemed in the current guidelines of the Breeder use-caste to be advantageous and therefore given preference in selection. Ashblow hair is notably coarse and thick, generally growing in an upward flare; at length, it falls around the face and shoulders. It is acid-resistant and retains little water after immersion, and has been proven effective as an ash filter in extreme circumstances. In most comms, Breeder guidelines acknowledge texture alone; however, Equatorial Breeders generally also require natural "ash" coloration (slate gray to white, present from birth) for the coveted designation.

Bastard: A person born without a use-caste, which is only possible for boys whose fathers are unknown. Those who distinguish themselves may be permitted to bear their mother's use-caste at comm-naming.

Blow: A volcano. Also called firemountains in some Coastal languages.

Boil: A geyser, hot spring, or steam vent.

Breeder: One of the seven common use-castes. Breeders are individuals selected for their health and desirable conformation. During a Season, they are responsible for the maintenance of healthy bloodlines and the improvement of comm or race by selective measures. Breeders born into the caste who do not meet acceptable community standards may be permitted to bear the use-caste of a close relative at comm-naming.

Cache: Stored food and supplies. Comms maintain guarded, locked storecaches at all times against the possibility of a Fifth Season. Only recognized comm members are entitled to a share of the cache, though adults may use their share to feed unrecognized children and others. Individual households often maintain their own housecaches, equally guarded against non–family members.

Cebaki: A member of the Cebaki race. Cebak was once a nation (unit of a deprecated political system, Before Imperial) in the Somidlats, though it was reorganized into the quartent system when the Old Sanze Empire conquered it centuries ago.

Coaster: A person from a coastal comm. Few coastal comms can afford to hire Imperial Orogenes to raise reefs or otherwise protect against tsunami, so coastal cities must perpetually rebuild and tend to be resource-poor as a result. People from the western coast of the continent tend to be pale, straight-haired, and sometimes have eyes with epicanthic folds. People from the eastern coast tend to be dark, kinky-haired, and sometimes have eyes with epicanthic folds.

Comm: Community. The smallest sociopolitical unit of the Imperial governance system, generally corresponding to one city or town, although very large cities may contain several comms. Accepted members of a comm are those who have been accorded rights of cache-share and protection, and who in turn support the comm through taxes or other contributions.

Commless: Criminals and other undesirables unable to gain acceptance in any comm.

Comm Name: The third name borne by most citizens, indicating their comm allegiance and rights. This name is generally bestowed at puberty as a coming-of-age, indicating that a person has been deemed a valuable member of the community. Immigrants to a comm may request adoption into that comm; upon acceptance, they take on the adoptive comm's name as their own.

Creche: A place where children too young to work are cared for while adults carry out needed tasks for the comm. When circumstances permit, a place of learning.

Equatorials: Latitudes surrounding and including the equator, excepting coastal regions. Also refers to people from equatorial-region comms. Thanks to temperate weather and relative stability at the center of the continental plate, Equatorial comms tend to be prosperous and politically powerful. The Equatorials once formed the core of the Old Sanze Empire.

Fault: A place where breaks in the earth make frequent, severe shakes and blows more likely.

Appendix 2

Fifth Season: An extended winter—lasting at least six months, per Imperial designation—triggered by seismic activity or other large-scale environmental alteration.

Fulcrum: A paramilitary order created by Old Sanze after the Season of Teeth (1560 Imperial). The headquarters of the Fulcrum is in Yumenes, although two satellite Fulcrums are located in the Arctic and Antarctic regions, for maximum continental coverage. Fulcrum-trained orogenes (or "Imperial Orogenes") are legally permitted to practice the otherwise-illegal craft of orogeny, under strict organizational rules and with the close supervision of the Guardian order. The Fulcrum is self-managed and self-sufficient. Imperial Orogenes are marked by their black uniforms, and colloquially known as "blackjackets."

Geneer: From "geoneer." An engineer of earthworks—geothermal energy mechanisms, tunnels, underground infrastructure, and mining.

Geomest: One who studies stone and its place in the natural world; general term for a scientist. Specifically geomests study lithology, chemistry, and geology, which are not considered separate disciplines in the Stillness. A few geomests specialize in orogenesis—the study of orogeny and its effects.

Greenland: An area of fallow ground kept within or just outside the walls of most comms as advised by stonelore. Comm greenlands may be used for agriculture or animal husbandry at all times, or may be kept as parks or fallow ground during non-Seasonal times. Individual households often maintain their own personal housegreen, or garden, as well.

Grits: In the Fulcrum, unringed orogene children who are still in basic training.

Guardian: A member of an order said to predate the Fulcrum. Guardians track, protect, protect against, and guide orogenes in the Stillness.

Imperial Road: One of the great innovations of the Old Sanze Empire, highroads (elevated highways for walking or horse traffic) connect all major comms and most large quartents to one another. Highroads are built by teams of geneers and Imperial Orogenes, with the orogenes determining the most stable path through areas of seismic activity (or quelling the activity, if there is no stable path), and the geneers routing water and other important resources near the roads to facilitate travel during Seasons.

Innovator: One of the seven common use-castes. Innovators are individuals selected for their creativity and applied intelligence, responsible for technical and logistical problem solving during a Season.

Kirkhusa: A mid-sized mammal, sometimes kept as a pet or used to guard homes or livestock. Normally herbivorous; during Seasons, carnivorous.

Knapper: A small-tools crafter, working in stone, glass, bone, or other materials. In large comms, knappers may use mechanical or mass-production techniques. Knappers who work in metal, or incompetent knappers, are colloquially called "rusters."

Lorist: One who studies stonelore and lost history.

Mela: A Midlats plant, related to the melons of Equatorial climates. Mela are vining ground plants that normally produce fruit aboveground. During a Season, the fruit grows underground as tubers. Some species of mela produce flowers that trap insects.

Metallore: Like alchemy and astronomestry, a discredited pseudoscience disavowed by the Seventh University.

Midlats: The "middle" latitudes of the continent—those between the equator and the arctic or antarctic regions. Also refers to people from midlats regions (sometimes called Midlatters). These regions are seen as the backwater of the Stillness, although they produce much of the world's food, materials, and other critical resources. There are two midlat regions: the northern (Nomidlats) and southern (Somidlats).

Newcomm: Colloquial term for comms that have arisen only since the last Season. Comms that have survived at least one Season are generally seen as more desirable places to live, having proven their efficacy and strength.

Nodes: The network of Imperially maintained stations placed throughout the Stillness in order to reduce or quell seismic events. Due to the relative rarity of Fulcrum-trained orogenes, nodes are primarily clustered in the Equatorials.

Orogene: One who possesses orogeny, whether trained or not. Derogatory: rogga.

Orogeny: The ability to manipulate thermal, kinetic, and related forms of energy to address seismic events.

Quartent: The middle level of the Imperial governance system. Four geographically adjacent comms make a quartent. Each quartent has a governor to whom individual comm heads report, and who reports in turn to a regional governor. The largest comm in a quartent is its capital; larger quartent capitals are connected to one another via the Imperial Road system.

Region: The top level of the Imperial governance system. Imperially recognized regions are the Arctics, Nomidlats, Western Coastals, Eastern Coastals, Equatorials, Somidlats, and Antarctics. Each region has a governor to whom all local quartents report. Regional governors are officially appointed by the Emperor, though in actual practice they are generally selected by and/or come from the Yumenescene Leadership.

Resistant: One of the seven common use-castes. Resistants are individuals selected for their ability to survive famine or pestilence. They are responsible for caring for the infirm and dead bodies during Seasons.

Rings: Used to denote rank among Imperial Orogenes. Unranked trainees must pass a series of tests to gain their first ring; ten rings is the highest rank an orogene may achieve. Each ring is made of polished semiprecious stone.

Roadhouse: Stations located at intervals along every Imperial Road and many lesser roads. All roadhouses contain a source of water and are located near arable land, forests, or other useful resources. Many are located in areas of minimal seismic activity.

Runny-sack: A small, easily portable cache of supplies most people keep in their homes in case of shakes or other emergencies.

Safe: A beverage traditionally served at negotiations, first encounters between potentially hostile parties, and other formal meetings. It contains a plant milk that reacts to the presence of all foreign substances.

Sanze: Originally a nation (unit of a deprecated political system, Before Imperial) in the Equatorials; origin of the Sanzed race. At the close of the Madness Season (7 Imperial), the nation of Sanze was abolished and replaced with the Sanzed Equatorial Affiliation, consisting of six predominantly Sanzed comms under the rule of Emperor Verishe Leadership Yumenes. The Affiliation expanded rapidly in the aftermath of the Season, eventually encompassing all regions of the Stillness by 800 Imperial. Around the time of the Season of Teeth, the Affiliation came to be known colloquially as the Old Sanze Empire, or simply Old Sanze. As of the Shilteen Accords of 1850 Imperial, the Affiliation officially ceased to exist, as local control (under the advisement of the Yumenescene Leadership) was deemed more efficient in the event of a Season. In practice, most comms still follow Imperial systems of governance, finance, education, and more, and most regional governors still pay taxes in tribute to Yumenes.

Sanzed: A member of the Sanzed race. Per Yumenescene Breedership standards, Sanzeds are ideally bronze-skinned and ashblow-haired, with mesomorphic or endomorphic builds and an adult height of minimum six feet.

Sanze-mat: The language spoken by the Sanze race, and the official language of the Old Sanze Empire, now the lingua franca of most of the Stillness.

Seasonal Law: Martial law, which may be declared by any comm head, quartent governor, regional governor, or recognized member of the Yumenescene Leadership. During Seasonal Law, quartent and regional governance are suspended and comms operate as sovereign sociopolitical units, though local cooperation with other comms is strongly encouraged per Imperial policy.

Seventh University: A famous college for the study of geomestry and stonelore, currently Imperially funded and located in the Equatorial city of Dibars. Prior versions of the University have been privately or collectively maintained; notably, the Third University at Am-Elat (approximately 3000 Before Imperial) was recognized at the time as a sovereign nation. Smaller regional or quartent colleges pay tribute to the University and receive expertise and resources in exchange.

Sesuna: Awareness of the movements of the earth. The sensory organs that perform this function are the sessapinae, located in the brain stem. Verb form: to sess.

Shake: A seismic movement of the earth.

Shatterland: Ground that has been disturbed by severe and/or very recent seismic activity.

Stillheads: A derogatory term used by orogenes for people lacking orogeny, usually shortened to "stills."

Stone Eaters: A rarely seen sentient humanoid species whose flesh, hair, etc., resembles stone. Little is known about them.

Strongback: One of the seven common use-castes. Strongbacks are individuals selected for their physical prowess, responsible for heavy labor and security in the event of a Season.

Use Name: The second name borne by most citizens, indicating the use-caste to which that person belongs. There are twenty recognized use-castes, although only seven in common use throughout the current and former Old Sanze Empire. A person inherits the use name of their same-sex parent, on the theory that useful traits are more readily passed this way.

Acknowledgments

Whew. That took a bit, didn't it?

The Stone Sky marks more than just the end of another trilogy, for me. For a variety of reasons, the period in which I wrote this book has turned out to be a time of tremendous change in my life. Among other things, I quit my day job and became a full-time writer in July of 2016. Now, I *liked* my day job, where I got to help people make healthy decisions—or at least survive long enough to do so—at one of the most crucial transition points of adult life. I do still help people, I think, as a writer, or at least that's the impression I get from those of you who've sent letters or online messages telling me how much my writing has touched you. But in my day job, the work was more direct, as were its agonies and rewards. I miss it a lot.

Oh, don't get me wrong; this was a good and necessary life transition to make. My writing career has exploded in all the best ways, and after all, I love being a writer, too. But it's my nature to reflect in times of change, and to acknowledge both what was lost as well as what was gained.

Acknowledgments

This change was facilitated by a Patreon (artist crowdfunding) campaign that I began in May of 2016. And on a more somber note...this Patreon funding is also what allowed me to focus wholly on my mother during the final days of her life, in late 2016 and early 2017. I don't often talk about personal things in public, but you can perhaps see how the Broken Earth trilogy is my attempt to wrestle with motherhood, among other things. Mom had a difficult last few years. I think (so many of my novels' underpinnings become clear in retrospect) that on some level I suspected her death was coming; maybe I was trying to prepare myself. Still wasn't ready when it happened...but then, no one ever is.

So I'm grateful to everyone—my family, my friends, my agent, my Patrons, the folks at Orbit, including my new editor, my former coworkers, the staff of the hospice, *everyone*—who helped me through this.

And this is why I've worked so hard to get *The Stone Sky* out on time, despite travel and hospitalizations and stress and all the thousand bureaucratic indignities of life after a parent's death. I definitely haven't been in the best place while working on this book, but I can say this much: Where there is pain in this book, it is real pain; where there is anger, it is real anger; where there is love, it is real love. You've been taking this journey with me, and you're always going to get the best of what I've got. That's what my mother would want.

extras

orbit

meet the author

Photo Credit: Laura Hanifin

N. K. JEMISIN is a Brooklyn author who won the Hugo Award for Best Novel for *The Fifth Season*, which was also a *New York Times* Notable Book of 2015. She previously won the Locus Award for her first novel, *The Hundred Thousand Kingdoms*, and her short fiction and novels have been nominated multiple times for Hugo, World Fantasy, Nebula, and RT Reviewers' Choice awards, and shortlisted for the Crawford and the James Tiptree, Jr. awards. She is a science fiction and fantasy reviewer for the *New York Times*, and you can find her online at nkjemisin.com.

if you enjoyed
THE STONE SKY

look out for

THE HUNDRED THOUSAND KINGDOMS
The Inheritance Trilogy

by

N. K. Jemisin

Yeine Darr is an outcast from the barbarian north. But when her mother dies under mysterious circumstances, she is summoned to the majestic city of Sky. There, to her shock, Yeine is named an heiress to the king. But the throne of the Hundred Thousand Kingdoms is not easily won, and Yeine is thrust into a vicious power struggle with cousins she never knew she had. As she fights for her life, she draws ever closer to the secrets of her mother's death and her family's bloody history.

With the fate of the world hanging in the balance, Yeine will learn how perilous it can be when love and hate—and gods and mortals—are bound inseparably together.

1

Grandfather

I am not as I once was. They have done this to me, broken me open and torn out my heart. I do not know who I am anymore.

I must try to remember.

*   *   *

My people tell stories of the night I was born. They say my mother crossed her legs in the middle of labor and fought with all her strength not to release me into the world. I was born anyhow, of course; nature cannot be denied. Yet it does not surprise me that she tried.

*   *   *

My mother was an heiress of the Arameri. There was a ball for the lesser nobility—the sort of thing that happens once a decade as a backhanded sop to their self-esteem. My father dared ask my mother to dance; she deigned to consent. I have often wondered what he said and did that night to make her fall in love with him so powerfully, for she eventually abdicated her position to be with him. It is the stuff of great tales, yes? Very romantic. In the tales, such a couple lives happily ever after. The tales do not say what happens when the most powerful family in the world is offended in the process.

*   *   *

But I forget myself. Who was I, again? Ah, yes.

My name is Yeine. In my people's way I am Yeine dau she Kinneth tai wer Somem kanna Darre, which means that I am the daughter of Kinneth, and that my tribe within the Darre people is called Somem. Tribes mean little to us these days, though before the Gods' War they were more important.

I am nineteen years old. I also am, or was, the chieftain of my people, called *ennu*. In the Arameri way, which is the way of the Amn race from whom they originated, I am the Baroness Yeine Darr.

One month after my mother died, I received a message from my grandfather Dekarta Arameri, inviting me to visit the family seat. Because one does not refuse an invitation from the Arameri, I set forth. It took the better part of three months to travel from the High North continent to Senm, across the Repentance Sea. Despite Darr's relative poverty, I traveled in style the whole way, first by palanquin and ocean vessel, and finally by chauffeured horse-coach. This was not my choice. The Darre Warriors' Council, which rather desperately hoped that I might restore us to the Arameri's good graces, thought that this extravagance would help. It is well known that Amn respect displays of wealth.

Thus arrayed, I arrived at my destination on the cusp of the winter solstice. And as the driver stopped the coach on a hill outside the city, ostensibly to water the horses but more likely because he was a local and liked to watch foreigners gawk, I got my first glimpse of the Hundred Thousand Kingdoms' heart.

There is a rose that is famous in High North. (This is not a digression.) It is called the altarskirt rose. Not only do its petals unfold in a radiance of pearled white, but frequently it grows an incomplete secondary flower about the base of its stem. In its most prized form, the altarskirt grows a layer of overlarge petals that drape the ground. The two bloom in tandem, seed-bearing head and skirt, glory above and below.

This was the city called Sky. On the ground, sprawling over a small mountain or an oversize hill: a circle of high walls,

mounting tiers of buildings, all resplendent in white, per Arameri decree. Above the city, smaller but brighter, the pearl of its
tiers occasionally obscured by scuds of cloud, was the palace—
also called Sky, and perhaps more deserving of the name. I
knew the column was there, the impossibly thin column that
supported such a massive structure, but from that distance I
couldn't see it. Palace floated above city, linked in spirit, both
so unearthly in their beauty that I held my breath at the sight.

The altarskirt rose is priceless because of the difficulty of producing it. The most famous lines are heavily inbred; it originated as a deformity that some savvy breeder deemed useful.
The primary flower's scent, sweet to us, is apparently repug-
nant to insects; these roses must be pollinated by hand. The
secondary flower saps nutrients crucial for the plant's fertility.
Seeds are rare, and for every one that grows into a perfect altarskirt, ten others become plants that must be destroyed for their
hideousness.

*   *   *

At the gates of Sky (the palace) I was turned away, though not
for the reasons I'd expected. My grandfather was not present,
it seemed. He had left instructions in the event of my arrival.

Sky is the Arameri's home; business is never done there. This
is because, officially, they do not rule the world. The Nobles'
Consortium does, with the benevolent assistance of the Order
of Itempas. The Consortium meets in the Salon, a huge, stately
building—white-walled, of course—that sits among a cluster
of official buildings at the foot of the palace. It is very impressive, and would be more so if it did not sit squarely in Sky's
elegant shadow.

I went inside and announced myself to the Consortium staff,
whereupon they all looked very surprised, though politely so.
One of them—a very junior aide, I gathered—was dispatched

to escort me to the central chamber, where the day's session was well under way.

As a lesser noble, I had always been welcome to attend a Consortium gathering, but there had never seemed any point. Besides the expense and months of travel time required to attend, Darr was simply too small, poor, and ill-favored to have any clout, even without my mother's abdication adding to our collective stain. Most of High North is regarded as a backwater, and only the largest nations there have enough prestige or money to make their voices heard among our noble peers. So I was not surprised to find that the seat reserved for me on the Consortium floor—in a shadowed area, behind a pillar—was currently occupied by an excess delegate from one of the Senm-continent nations. It would be terribly rude, the aide stammered anxiously, to dislodge this man, who was elderly and had bad knees. Perhaps I would not mind standing? Since I had just spent many long hours cramped in a carriage, I was happy to agree.

So the aide positioned me at the side of the Consortium floor, where I actually had a good view of the goings-on. The Consortium chamber was magnificently apportioned, with white marble and rich, dark wood that had probably come from Darr's forests in better days. The nobles—three hundred or so in total—sat in comfortable chairs on the chamber's floor or along elevated tiers above. Aides, pages, and scribes occupied the periphery with me, ready to fetch documents or run errands as needed. At the head of the chamber, the Consortium Overseer stood atop an elaborate podium, pointing to members as they indicated a desire to speak. Apparently there was a dispute over water rights in a desert somewhere; five countries were involved. None of the conversation's participants spoke out of turn; no tempers were lost; there were no snide comments or veiled insults. It was all very orderly and polite, despite the size of the gathering and the fact that most of those present were accustomed to speaking however they pleased among their own people.

One reason for this extraordinary good behavior stood on a plinth behind the Overseer's podium: a life-size statue of the Skyfather in one of His most famous poses, the Appeal to Mortal Reason. Hard to speak out of turn under that stern gaze. But more repressive, I suspected, was the stern gaze of the man who sat behind the Overseer in an elevated box. I could not see him well from where I stood, but he was elderly, richly dressed, and flanked by a younger blond man and a dark-haired woman, as well as a handful of retainers.

It did not take much to guess this man's identity, though he wore no crown, had no visible guards, and neither he nor anyone in his entourage spoke throughout the meeting.

"Hello, Grandfather," I murmured to myself, and smiled at him across the chamber, though I knew he could not see me. The pages and scribes gave me the oddest looks for the rest of the afternoon.

*   *   *

I knelt before my grandfather with my head bowed, hearing titters of laughter.

No, wait.

*   *   *

There were three gods once.

Only three, I mean. Now there are dozens, perhaps hundreds. They breed like rabbits. But once there were only three, most powerful and glorious of all: the god of day, the god of night, and the goddess of twilight and dawn. Or light and darkness and the shades between. Or order, chaos, and balance. None of that is important because one of them died, the other might as well have, and the last is the only one who matters anymore.

The Arameri get their power from this remaining god. He is called the Skyfather, Bright Itempas, and the ancestors of the Arameri were His most devoted priests. He rewarded them by giving them a weapon so mighty that no army could stand against it. They used this weapon—weapons, really—to make themselves rulers of the world.

That's better. Now.

* * *

I knelt before my grandfather with my head bowed and my knife laid on the floor.

We were in Sky, having transferred there following the Consortium session, via the magic of the Vertical Gate. Immediately upon arrival I had been summoned to my grandfather's audience chamber, which felt much like a throne room. The chamber was roughly circular because circles are sacred to Itempas. The vaulted ceiling made the members of the court look taller—unnecessarily, since Amn are a tall people compared to my own. Tall and pale and endlessly poised, like statues of human beings rather than real flesh and blood.

"Most high Lord Arameri," I said. "I am honored to be in your presence."

I had heard titters of laughter when I entered the room. Now they sounded again, muffled by hands and kerchiefs and fans. I was reminded of bird flocks roosting in a forest canopy.

Before me sat Dekarta Arameri, uncrowned king of the world. He was old; perhaps the oldest man I have ever seen, though Amn usually live longer than my people, so this was not surprising. His thin hair had gone completely white, and he was so gaunt and stooped that the elevated stone chair on which he sat—it was never called a throne—seemed to swallow him whole.

"Granddaughter," he said, and the titters stopped. The silence was heavy enough to hold in my hand. He was head of the Arameri family, and his word was law. No one had expected him to acknowledge me as kin, least of all myself.

"Stand," he said. "Let me have a look at you."

I did, reclaiming my knife since no one had taken it. There was more silence. I am not very interesting to look at. It might have been different if I had gotten the traits of my two peoples in a better combination—Amn height with Darre curves, perhaps, or thick straight Darre hair colored Amn-pale. I have Amn eyes: faded green in color, more unnerving than pretty. Otherwise, I am short and flat and brown as forestwood, and my hair is a curled mess. Because I find it unmanageable otherwise, I wear it short. I am sometimes mistaken for a boy.

As the silence wore on, I saw Dekarta frown. There was an odd sort of marking on his forehead, I noticed: a perfect circle of black, as if someone had dipped a coin in ink and pressed it to his flesh. On either side of this was a thick chevron, bracketing the circle.

"You look nothing like her," he said at last. "But I suppose that is just as well. Viraine?"

This last was directed at a man who stood among the courtiers closest to the throne. For an instant I thought he was another elder, then I realized my error: though his hair was stark white, he was only somewhere in his fourth decade. He, too, bore a forehead mark, though his was less elaborate than Dekarta's: just the black circle.

"She's not hopeless," he said, folding his arms. "Nothing to be done about her looks; I doubt even makeup will help. But put her in civilized attire and she can convey…nobility, at least." His eyes narrowed, taking me apart by degrees. My best Darren clothing, a long vest of white civvetfur and calf-length leggings, earned me a sigh. (I had gotten the odd look for this outfit at the Salon, but I hadn't realized it was *that* bad.) He examined my face so long that I wondered if I should show my teeth.

Instead he smiled, showing his. "Her mother has trained her. Look how she shows no fear or resentment, even now."

"She will do, then," said Dekarta.

"Do for what, Grandfather?" I asked. The weight in the room grew heavier, expectant, though he had already named me granddaughter. There was a certain risk involved in my daring to address him the same familiar way, of course—powerful men are touchy over odd things. But my mother had indeed trained me well, and I knew it was worth the risk to establish myself in the court's eyes.

Dekarta Arameri's face did not change; I could not read it. "For my heir, Granddaughter. I intend to name you to that position today."

The silence turned to stone as hard as my grandfather's chair.

I thought he might be joking, but no one laughed. That was what made me believe him at last: the utter shock and horror on the faces of the courtiers as they stared at their lord. Except the one called Viraine. He watched me.

It came to me that some response was expected.

"You already have heirs," I said.

"Not as diplomatic as she could be," Viraine said in a dry tone.

Dekarta ignored this. "It is true, there are two other candidates," he said to me. "My niece and nephew, Scimina and Relad. Your cousins, once removed."

I had heard of them, of course; everyone had. Rumor constantly made one or the other heir, though no one knew for certain which. *Both* was something that had not occurred to me.

"If I may suggest, Grandfather," I said carefully, though it was impossible to be careful in this conversation, "I would make two heirs too many."

It was the eyes that made Dekarta seem so old, I would realize much later. I had no idea what color they had originally been; age had bleached and filmed them to near-white. There were lifetimes in those eyes, none of them happy.

"Indeed," he said. "But just enough for an interesting competition, I think."

"I don't understand, Grandfather."

He lifted his hand in a gesture that would have been graceful, once. Now his hand shook badly. "It is very simple. I have named three heirs. One of you will actually manage to succeed me. The other two will doubtless kill each other or be killed by the victor. As for which lives, and which die—" He shrugged. "That is for you to decide."

My mother had taught me never to show fear, but emotions will not be stilled so easily. I began to sweat. I have been the target of an assassination attempt only once in my life—the benefit of being heir to such a tiny, impoverished nation. No one wanted my job. But now there would be two others who did. Lord Relad and Lady Scimina were wealthy and powerful beyond my wildest dreams. They had spent their whole lives striving against each other toward the goal of ruling the world. And here came I, unknown, with no resources and few friends, into the fray.

"There will be no decision," I said. To my credit, my voice did not shake. "And no contest. They will kill me at once and turn their attention back to each other."

"That is possible," said my grandfather.

I could think of nothing to say that would save me. He was insane; that was obvious. Why else turn rulership of the world into a contest prize? If he died tomorrow, Relad and Scimina would rip the earth asunder between them. The killing might not end for decades. And for all he knew, I was an idiot. If by some impossible chance I managed to gain the throne, I could plunge the Hundred Thousand Kingdoms into a spiral of mismanagement and suffering. He had to know that.

One cannot argue with madness. But sometimes, with luck and the Skyfather's blessing, one can understand it. "Why?"

He nodded as if he had expected my question. "Your mother deprived me of an heir when she left our family. You will pay her debt."

"She is four months in the grave," I snapped. "Do you honestly want revenge against a dead woman?"

"This has nothing to do with revenge, Granddaughter. It is a matter of duty." He made a gesture with his left hand, and another courtier detached himself from the throng. Unlike the first man—indeed, unlike most of the courtiers whose faces I could see—the mark on this man's forehead was a downturned half-moon, like an exaggerated frown. He knelt before the dais that held Dekarta's chair, his waist-length red braid falling over one shoulder to curl on the floor.

"I cannot hope that your mother has taught you duty," Dekarta said to me over this man's back. "She abandoned hers to dally with her sweet-tongued savage. I allowed this—an indulgence I have often regretted. So I will assuage that regret by bringing you back into the fold, Granddaughter. Whether you live or die is irrelevant. You are Arameri, and like all of us, you will serve."

Then he waved to the red-haired man. "Prepare her as best you can."

There was nothing more. The red-haired man rose and came to me, murmuring that I should follow him. I did. Thus ended my first meeting with my grandfather, and thus began my first day as an Arameri. It was not the worst of the days to come.

if you enjoyed
THE STONE SKY

look out for

WAKE OF VULTURES
The Shadow

by

Lila Bowen

Nettie Lonesome dreams of a greater life than toiling as a slave in the sandy desert. But when a stranger attacks her, Nettie wins more than the fight.

Now she's got friends, a good horse, and a better gun. But if she can't kill the thing haunting her nightmares and stealing children across the prairie, she'll lose it all—and never find out what happened to her real family.

Wake of Vultures *is the first novel of the Shadow series featuring the fearless Nettie Lonesome.*

Chapter 1

Nettie Lonesome had two things in the world that were worth a sweet goddamn: her old boots and her one-eyed mule, Blue. Neither item actually belonged to her. But then again, nothing did. Not even the whisper-thin blanket she lay under, pretending to be asleep and wishing the black mare would get out of the water trough before things went south.

The last fourteen years of Nettie's life had passed in a shriveled corner of Durango territory under the leaking roof of this wind-chapped lean-to with Pap and Mam, not quite a slave and nowhere close to something like a daughter. Their faces, white and wobbling as new butter under a smear of prairie dirt, held no kindness. The boots and the mule had belonged to Pap, right up until the day he'd exhausted their use, a sentiment he threatened to apply to her every time she was just a little too slow with the porridge.

"Nettie! Girl, you take care of that wild filly, or I'll put one in her goddamn skull!"

Pap got in a lather when he'd been drinking, which was pretty much always. At least this time his anger was aimed at a critter instead of Nettie. When the witch-hearted black filly had first shown up on the farm, Pap had laid claim and pronounced her a fine chunk of flesh and a sign of the Creator's good graces. If Nettie broke her and sold her for a decent price, she'd be closer to paying back Pap for taking her in as a baby when nobody else had wanted her but the hungry, circling vultures. The value Pap placed on feeding and housing a half-

434

Injun, half-black orphan girl always seemed to go up instead of down, no matter that Nettie did most of the work around the homestead these days. Maybe that was why she'd not been taught her sums: Then she'd know her own damn worth, to the penny.

But the dainty black mare outside wouldn't be roped, much less saddled and gentled, and Nettie had failed to sell her to the cowpokes at the Double TK Ranch next door. Her idol, Monty, was a top hand and always had a kind word. But even he had put a boot on Pap's poorly kept fence, laughed through his mustache, and hollered that a horse that couldn't be caught couldn't be sold. No matter how many times Pap drove the filly away with poorly thrown bottles, stones, and bullets, the critter crept back under cover of night to ruin the water by dancing a jig in the trough, which meant another blistering trip to the creek with a leaky bucket for Nettie.

Splash, splash. Whinny.

Could a horse laugh? Nettie figured this one could.

Pap, however, was a humorless bastard who didn't get a joke that didn't involve bruises.

"Unless you wanna go live in the flats, eatin' bugs, you'd best get on, girl."

Nettie rolled off her worn-out straw tick, hoping there weren't any scorpions or centipedes on the dusty dirt floor. By the moon's scant light she shook out Pap's old boots and shoved her bare feet into into the cracked leather.

Splash, splash.

The shotgun cocked loud enough to be heard across the border, and Nettie dove into Mam's old wool cloak and ran toward the stockyard with her long, thick braids slapping against her back. Mam said nothing, just rocked in her chair by the window, a bottle cradled in her arm like a baby's corpse. Grabbing the rawhide whip from its nail by the warped door, Nettie hurried past Pap on the porch and stumbled across the yard, around two mostly roofless barns, and toward the wet black shape taunting her in the moonlight against a backdrop of stars.

"Get on, mare. Go!"

A monster in a flapping jacket with a waving whip would send any horse with sense wheeling in the opposite direction, but this horse had apparently been dancing in the creek on the day sense was handed out. The mare stood in the water trough and stared at Nettie like she was a damn strange bird, her dark eyes blinking with moonlight and her lips pulled back over long, white teeth.

Nettie slowed. She wasn't one to quirt a horse, but if the mare kept causing a ruckus, Pap would shoot her without a second or even a first thought—and he wasn't so deep in his bottle that he was sure to miss. Getting smacked with rawhide had to be better than getting shot in the head, so Nettie doubled up her shouting and prepared herself for the heartache that would accompany the smack of a whip on unmarred hide. She didn't even own the horse, much less the right to beat it. Nettie had grown up trying to be the opposite of Pap, and hurting something that didn't come with claws and a stinger went against her grain.

"Shoo, fool, or I'll have to whip you," she said, creeping closer. The horse didn't budge, and for the millionth time, Nettie swung the whip around the horse's neck like a rope, all gentle-like. But, as ever, the mare tossed her head at exactly the right moment, and the braided leather snickered against the wooden water trough instead.

"Godamighty, why won't you move on? Ain't nobody wants you, if you won't be rode or bred. Dumb mare."

At that, the horse reared up with a wild scream, spraying water as she pawed the air. Before Nettie could leap back to avoid the splatter, the mare had wheeled and galloped into the night. The starlight showed her streaking across the prairie with a speed Nettie herself would've enjoyed, especially if it meant she could turn her back on Pap's dirt-poor farm and no-good cattle company forever. Doubling over to stare at her scuffed boots while she caught her breath, Nettie felt her hope disappear with hoofbeats in the night.

A low and painfully unfamiliar laugh trembled out of the barn's shadow, and Nettie cocked the whip back so that it was ready to strike.

"Who's that? Jed?"

But it wasn't Jed, the mule-kicked, sometimes stable boy, and she already knew it.

"Looks like that black mare's giving you a spot of trouble, darlin'. If you were smart, you'd set fire to her tail."

A figure peeled away from the barn, jerky-thin and slithery in a too-short coat with buttons that glinted like extra stars. The man's hat was pulled low, his brown hair overshaggy and his lily-white hand on his gun in a manner both unfriendly and relaxed that Nettie found insulting.

"You best run off, mister. Pap don't like strangers on his land, especially when he's only a bottle in. If it's horses you want, we ain't got none worth selling. If you want work and you're dumb and blind, best come back in the morning when he's slept off the mezcal."

"I wouldn't work for that good-for-nothing piss-pot even if I needed work."

The stranger switched sides with his toothpick and looked Nettie up and down like a horse he was thinking about stealing. Her fist tightened on the whip handle, her fingers going cold. She wouldn't defend Pap or his land or his sorry excuses for cattle, but she'd defend the only thing other than Blue that mostly belonged to her. Men had been pawing at her for two years now, and nobody'd yet come close to reaching her soft parts, not even Pap.

"Then you'd best move on, mister."

The feller spit his toothpick out on the ground and took a step forward, all quiet-like because he wore no spurs. And that was Nettie's first clue that he wasn't what he seemed.

"Naw, I'll stay. Pretty little thing like you to keep me company."

That was Nettie's second clue. Nobody called her pretty unless they wanted something. She looked around the yard, but all she saw were sand, chaparral, bone-dry cow patties, and the remains of a fence that Pap hadn't seen fit to fix. Mam was surely asleep, and Pap had gone inside, or maybe around back to piss. It was just the stranger and her. And the whip.

"Bullshit," she spit.

"Put down that whip before you hurt yourself, girl."

"Don't reckon I will."

The stranger stroked his pistol and started to circle her. Nettie shook the whip out behind her as she spun in place to face him and hunched over in a crouch. He stopped circling when the barn yawned behind her, barely a shell of a thing but darker than sin in the corners. And then he took a step forward, his silver pistol out and flashing starlight. Against her will, she took a step back. Inch by inch he drove her into the barn with slow, easy steps. Her feet rattled in the big boots, her fingers numb around the whip she had forgotten how to use.

"What is it you think you're gonna do to me, mister?"

It came out breathless, god damn her tongue.

His mouth turned up like a cat in the sun. "Something nice. Something somebody probably done to you already. Your master or pappy, maybe."

She pushed air out through her nose like a bull. "Ain't got a pappy. Or a master."

"Then I guess nobody'll mind, will they?"

That was pretty much it for Nettie Lonesome. She spun on her heel and ran into the barn, right where he'd been pushing her to go. But she didn't flop down on the hay or toss down the mangy blanket that had dried into folds in the broke-down, three-wheeled rig. No, she snatched the sickle from the wall and spun to face him under the hole in the roof. Starlight fell down on her ink-black braids and glinted off the parts of the curved blade that weren't rusted up.

"I reckon I'd mind," she said.

Nettie wasn't a little thing, at least not height-wise, and she'd figured that seeing a pissed-off woman with a weapon in each hand would be enough to drive off the curious feller and send him back to the whores at the Leaping Lizard, where he apparently belonged. But the stranger just laughed and cracked his knuckles like he was glad for a fight and would take his pleasure with his fists instead of his twig.

"You wanna play first? Go on, girl. Have your fun. You think you're facin' down a coydog, but you found a timber wolf."

As he stepped into the barn, the stranger went into shadow for just a second, and that was when Nettie struck. Her whip whistled for his feet and managed to catch one ankle, yanking hard enough to pluck him off his feet and onto the back of his fancy jacket. A puff of dust went up as he thumped on the ground, but he just crossed his ankles and stared at her and laughed. Which pissed her off more. Dropping the whip handle, Nettie took the sickle in both hands and went for the stranger's legs, hoping that a good slash would keep him from chasing her but not get her sent to the hangman's noose. But her blade whistled over a patch of nothing. The man was gone, her whip with him.

Nettie stepped into the doorway to watch him run away, her heart thumping underneath the tight muslin binding she always wore over her chest. She squinted into the long, flat night, one hand on the hinge of what used to be a barn door, back before the church was willing to pay cash money for Pap's old lumber. But the stranger wasn't hightailing it across the prairie. Which meant...

"Looking for someone, darlin'?"

She spun, sickle in hand, and sliced into something that felt like a ham with the round part of the blade. Hot blood spattered over her, burning like lye.

"Goddammit, girl! What'd you do that for?"

She ripped the sickle out with a sick splash, but the man wasn't standing in the barn, much less falling to the floor. He was hanging upside-down from a cross-beam, cradling his arm. It made no goddamn sense, and Nettie couldn't stand a thing that made no sense, so she struck again while he was poking around his wound.

This time, she caught him in the neck. This time, he fell.

The stranger landed in the dirt and popped right back up into a crouch. The slice in his neck looked like the first carving in an undercooked roast, but the blood was slurry and smelled like rotten meat. And the stranger was sneering at her.

"Girl, you just made the biggest mistake of your short, useless life."

Then he sprang at her.

There was no way he should've been able to jump at her like that with those wounds, and she brought her hands straight up without thinking. Luckily, her fist still held the sickle, and the stranger took it right in the face, the point of the blade jerking into his eyeball with a moist squish. Nettie turned away and lost most of last night's meager dinner in a noisy splatter against the wall of the barn. When she spun back around, she was surprised to find that the fool hadn't fallen or died or done anything helpful to her cause. Without a word, he calmly pulled the blade out of his eye and wiped a dribble of black glop off his cheek.

His smile was a cold, dark thing that sent Nettie's feet toward Pap and the crooked house and anything but the stranger who wouldn't die, wouldn't scream, and wouldn't leave her alone. She'd never felt safe a day in her life, but now she recognized the chill hand of death, reaching for her. Her feet trembled in the too-big boots as she stumbled backward across the bumpy yard, tripping on stones and bits of trash. Turning her back on the demon man seemed intolerably stupid. She just had to get past the round pen, and then she'd be halfway to the house. Pap wouldn't be worth much by now, but he had a gun by his side. Maybe the stranger would give up if he saw a man instead of just a half-breed girl nobody cared about.

Nettie turned to run and tripped on a fallen chunk of fence, going down hard on hands and skinned knees. When she looked up, she saw butternut-brown pants stippled with blood and no-spur boots tapping.

"Pap!" she shouted. "Pap, help!"

She was gulping in a big breath to holler again when the stranger's boot caught her right under the ribs and knocked it all back out. The force of the kick flipped her over onto her back, and she scrabbled away from the stranger and toward the ramshackle round pen of old, gray branches and junk roped together, just barely enough fence to trick a colt into staying put. They'd slaughtered a pig in here, once, and now Nettie knew how he felt.

As soon as her back fetched up against the pen, the stranger crouched in front of her, one eye closed and weeping black and the other brim-full with evil over the bloody slice in his neck. He looked like a dead man, a corpse groom, and Nettie was pretty sure she was in the hell Mam kept threatening her with.

"Ain't nobody coming. Ain't nobody cares about a girl like you. Ain't nobody gonna need to, not after what you done to me."

The stranger leaned down and made like he was going to kiss her with his mouth wide open, and Nettie did the only thing that came to mind. She grabbed up a stout twig from the wall of the pen and stabbed him in the chest as hard as she damn could.

She expected the stick to break against his shirt like the time she'd seen a buggy bash apart against the general store during a twister. But the twig sunk right in like a hot knife in butter. The stranger shuddered and fell on her, his mouth working as gloppy red-black liquid bubbled out. She didn't trust blood anymore, not after the first splat had burned her, and she wasn't much for being found under a corpse, so Nettie shoved him off hard and shot to her feet, blowing air as hard as a galloping horse.

The stranger was rolling around on the ground, plucking at his chest. Thick clouds blotted out the meager starlight, and she had nothing like the view she'd have tomorrow under the white-hot, unrelenting sun. But even a girl who'd never killed a man before knew when something was wrong. She kicked him over with the toe of her boot, tit for tat, and he was light as a tumbleweed when he landed on his back.

The twig jutted up out of a black splotch in his shirt, and the slice in his neck had curled over like gone meat. His bad eye was a swamp of black, but then, everything was black at midnight. His mouth was open, the lips drawing back over too-white teeth, several of which looked like they'd come out of a panther. He wasn't breathing, and Pap wasn't coming, and Nettie's finger reached out as if it had a mind of its own and flicked one big, shiny, curved tooth.

The goddamn thing fell back into the dead man's gaping throat. Nettie jumped away, skitty as the black filly, and her boot toe brushed the dead man's shoulder, and his entire body collapsed in on itself like a puffball, thousands of sparkly motes piling up in the place he'd occupied and spilling out through his empty clothes. Utterly bewildered, she knelt and brushed the pile with trembling fingers. It was sand. Nothing but sand. A soft wind came up just then and blew some of the stranger away, revealing one of those big, curved teeth where his head had been. It didn't make a goddamn lick of sense, but it could've gone far worse.

Still wary, she stood and shook out his clothes, noting that everything was in better than fine condition, except for his white shirt, which had a twig-sized hole in the breast, surrounded by a smear of black. She knew enough of laundering and sewing to make it nice enough, and the black blood on his pants looked, to her eye, manly and tough. Even the stranger's boots were of better quality than any that had ever set foot on Pap's land, snakeskin with fancy chasing. With her own, too-big boots, she smeared the sand back into the hard, dry ground as if the stranger had never existed. All that was left was the four big panther teeth, and she put those in her pocket and tried to forget about them.

After checking the yard for anything livelier than a scorpion, she rolled up the clothes around the boots and hid them in the old rig in the barn. Knowing Pap would pester her if she left signs of a scuffle, she wiped the black glop off the sickle and hung it up, along with the whip, out of Pap's drunken reach. She didn't need any more whip scars on her back than she already had.

Out by the round pen, the sand that had once been a devil of a stranger had all blown away. There was no sign of what had almost happened, just a few more deadwood twigs pulled from the lopsided fence. On good days, Nettie spent a fair bit of time doing the dangerous work of breaking colts or doctoring cattle in here for Pap, then picking up the twigs that got knocked off and roping them back in with whatever twine she could scavenge from the town. Wood wasn't cheap, and there wasn't much of it. But Nettie's hands were twitchy still, and so she picked up the black-splattered stick and wove it back into the fence, wishing she lived in a world where her life was worth more than a mule, more than boots, more than a stranger's cold smile in the barn. She'd had her first victory, but no one would ever believe her, and if they did, she wouldn't be cheered. She'd be hanged.

That stranger—he had been all kinds of wrong. And the way that he'd wanted to touch her—that felt wrong, too. Nettie couldn't recall being touched in kindness, not in all her years with Pap and Mam. Maybe that was why she understood horses. Mustangs were wild things captured by thoughtless men, roped and branded and beaten until their heads hung low, until it took spurs and whips to move them in rage and fear. But Nettie could feel the wildness inside their hearts, beating under skin that quivered under the flat of her palm. She didn't break a horse, she gentled it. And until someone touched her with that same kindness, she would continue to shy away, to bare her teeth and lower her head.

Someone, surely, had been kind to her once, long ago. She could feel it in her bones. But Pap said she'd been tossed out like trash, left on the prairie to die. Which she almost had, tonight. Again.

Pap and Mam were asleep on the porch, snoring loud as thunder. When Nettie crept past them and into the house, she had four shiny teeth in one fist, a wad of cash from the stranger's pocket, and more questions than there were stars.